NIKI UNDERCOVER

NIKI UNDERCOVER

James M. Jackson

First Edition
Trade Paperback Edition: September 2025

Wolf's Echo Press
PO Box 54
Amasa, MI 49903
www.WolfsEchoPress.com

ISBN-13 Trade Paperback: 978-1-943166-44-2
ISBN-13 e-book: 978-1-943166-45-9
ISBN Audiobook   978-1-943166-46-6
Library of Congress Control Number: 2025940476

Printed in the United States of America
1098765432

ONE

Saturday, May 2, 0749 EDT

ASHLEY PRESCOTT'S RACING HEART DOUBLE-CLUTCHED at the sight of a man standing at her apartment door. She caught the fire door to the emergency stairs before it slammed shut, avoiding immediate discovery. She stifled her panting from running up the stairs long enough to backpedal and ease the door shut. Leaning against it, she gulped air. Sweat from the ten-mile run stung her eyes, drenched her body.

Slow down and think.

Innocent neighbor or end of her world?

Information.

She needed information.

She yanked her cellphone from its armband and pressed its sensor with her right index finger. *Fingerprint not recognized.*

Lifting her foot, she dried her finger on her sock. This time, the phone unlocked. She opened the app that controlled three high-resolution cameras she had installed unbeknownst to the apartment manager—or the FBI.

The pinhole camera above her apartment door showed a male Caucasian in a Nationals' ball cap. He cupped ungloved hands to shield his eyes as he peered through the peephole. No visible weapons.

Not a pro assassin . . . unless he has a partner.

The ceiling camera revealed a clear hallway. No suspicious shadows suggested a hidden backup. Wait for him to leave or confront him? She glanced at her watch. She had only a few minutes to shower and change before her meeting. No way would she let this guy torpedo two years of hard work.

Who *are* you?

She switched to the third camera positioned across from her door, hidden below a framed picture of cherry trees in bloom at D.C.'s Tidal Basin, and zoomed in on the threat. His muscular neck poked from a zipped navy-blue jacket. Broad shoulders. Narrow waist.

Come on, asshole. Turn around. She manipulated the lens to scan his lower half. Jeans. No external weapons. Cowboy boots.

Cowboy boots! Shit. Shit. Shit. Under no circumstances should Special Agent Rick-spelled-with-a-silent-P Kaska be here. Unless Gex sent him.

No way, no how would Gex sideline her like that.

Wait!

How did Rick get past the doorman? *If he'd badged his way through—Don't go there.* She'd deal with it when she had to. If he left now, she could still reach her assignment on time and prove to Gex that everything was fine.

Rick stepped back, brow furrowed, eyes squinted, lips drawn into a tight line. He raised his fist and pounded on the metal door.

Even from her hiding place, she heard the racket. *Dammit. If the neighbors saw him—*

She yanked open the fire door and sprinted down the carpeted hall. He pounded on her door again.

"You want all the neighbors to see you?"

He spun around, eyes wide. "Ashley—"

"Shut up, Rick." She unlatched the three locks, flung the door open, and yanked him inside. She hipped the door closed and caught him leering.

"Stop drooling. It's running gear, not your wet dream from Frederick's of Hollywood. Did Gex send you?"

His face crinkled into a smile. "I prefer the Agent Provocateur style myself."

"Is that supposed to be funny?"

He gave her puppy-dog eyes. "Double entendre? They're a British company. They—"

"Don't know. Don't care." She strode into the kitchen, grabbed the metal bottle with her hydration drink.

He stayed right on her heels. "What are you going to do about those phone calls?"

Aha! If Gex *had* sent him, Rick would claim that authority. He was cowboying it. She downed the tangy orange mix in one long draw. Whumped the bottle onto the counter harder than she intended. "Ignore them. Why are you here?" She made a production of checking her watch. "I have just enough time to shower before I catch the Metro to my meet."

He blocked her exit. "You can't possibly think it's okay to go through with it."

The fucking nerve. With his boots he stood only a couple of inches taller than her five-six. She wanted to kick his nuts so hard they'd explode from his nose. Instead, she braced her hands on her hips and glared. "No, Rick. What I can't possibly think is that it's okay to miss today's meeting and torpedo two years of work embedding Niki—meaning me—into Patriots for Freedom. Certainly not because some jerk wakes me up at oh-two-hundred hours and insists it's *imperative* that I drop everything and hop on the private Pendergast jet and meet Robert Pendergast no later than Sunday morning. Bullshit to that. And you—" She shoved his chest with both hands. "—need to get out of my way."

He recovered his balance and widened his stance. "I get it. You're pissed your father crooked his finger for his—what did the guy call you?—Little Spitfire to come home. That's not the issue. The problem—"

"Damn it, Rick. He may have given me half my DNA, but he's never been my father, and he's not sucking me into his drama."

"You, Special Agent Ashley Pendergast Prescott, are missing the damn point. The problem is your father's lackey—this Malachi Cluff guy—didn't call *your* phone. He called *Niki's undercover* phone. No one is supposed to have that number besides your team and your Patriots For Freedom targets. You screwed up. You compromised your cover. If you la-di-da waltz into your meeting today pretending to be Corporal Niki, you're likely to return in a body bag."

Ashley blinked once and said through clenched teeth, "The way I stay alive is I don't *pretend* to be Niki. I *become* Niki. Robert didn't get one single damn piece of information from me. And regarding security breaches, your being here, calling me Ashley in the hallway, is a billion times worse."

Rick's head reeled back as if she had slapped him. "Wrong. If you had answered my calls this morning, I wouldn't have shown up at your door. No one knows I'm here. I grabbed the spare keys from the safe house and used the apartment building's back door." He frowned at the keyring in his hand. "We don't have keys for the extra locks you installed."

"No shit, Sherlock. No woman would let a set of keys lie around where any Tom, Dick, or Harry can make a copy." She adopted a smile, a soothing tone, and a lie. "Look, I agree there's a security breach. And I appreciate your work keeping me safe. I really do. But PFF is not behind that leak. If they discovered their Corporal Niki Foster was an undercover

FBI agent, they wouldn't invoke Robert Pendergast's name to convince me to go to an airport. They'd flat out kill me.

"No, this is Robert Pendergast's doing. The summer I stayed with him, he presented me with a list of my strengths and weaknesses and a long reading list to help me improve."

Her churning gut and angry voice reminded her that despite her promise not to let Robert's single-mindedness get under her skin, he'd done it again. "I was a kid in grammar school, for fuck's sake, and he was already grooming me for his business. No, whatever those calls are about, it's not PFF. My cover with them is secure. I'm safe."

Seeing the objection forming on his face, she steadied her voice and added. "Well, no more at risk than usual. Rick, listen. I am ninety-nine percent sure something huge is about to happen at PFF. We can talk later, but right now, I gotta get ready. Let yourself out. We will discuss *everything* at this afternoon's debriefing because I want to personally rip a new asshole in whoever gave Niki's phone number to Robert." *And since you're all-fired ready to intervene, you're number one on my suspect list.*

She feinted left, slid sideways, and ducked under his outstretched arm. She grabbed Niki's clothes from the spare bedroom and found Rick again blocking her way. "If you don't move, I will fucking break your arm."

He must have realized she was not exaggerating because he backed away.

She locked the bathroom door and cranked the shower to its maximum temperature, knowing she'd be lucky to get it even lukewarm by the time all the people doing laundry on the lower floors took their cut. At least she needn't waste time wiping steam off the mirrors. Gritting her teeth, she stepped under the shower head and let the flow sluice her sweat down the drain.

Moments later, she toweled off, leaving her burr haircut to air dry. She replaced her sports bra with an FBI special that incorporated a GPS tracker. Her weather app claimed the expected high in D.C. was seventy-two. Maryland, the location of the planned meet, was often cooler. Layers would work. She shimmied on a hi-tech base layer and donned camouflage fatigues. She double-knotted the laces on her army-style boots, above which she strapped an ankle holster with a snub-nosed revolver. A patrol cap pulled low completed her visual transformation from Ashley to Niki.

With one deep breath, she became Niki Foster.

She patted her pockets. Niki's wallet. Check. Metro pass. Check. Niki's phone. Yep, and no messages. She dropped the phone into her camo knapsack and felt Niki's Beretta M9. Check.

She breezed from Niki's room to find Rick thumbing through the report on a Chinese assault rifle she had translated from Mandarin and left on the secretary. "I thought I told you to leave."

"And I thought you'd come to your senses. What's this?" He held up the sealed envelope marked **OPEN IN EMERGENCY**.

Enough of this bullshit. "Go ahead. Open it. I dare you."

He dropped it on the table as if it had burned his fingers.

She pointed toward the door. "Your aftershave is polluting my air. Get out before I kick you out. If I ever see you here again, I'll report you for freaking breaking my cover."

His hands shot up in mock surrender. "The Bureau has rules to keep you safe. Despite your preference to be independent, you *are* part of a team. I don't want you hurt, Ash. That's all."

It wasn't like she didn't know the rules; she just didn't always follow them when they didn't make sense. Like now, and she was out of time. She motioned at her outfit. "Do I look like Ash to you? I am Corporal Niki of Patriots For Freedom. Make sure no one sees you leave."

She strode into the kitchen and pulled a die and a quarter from the junk drawer. She rolled the die on the counter. One pip. Main entrance.

"I thought you were in a hurry. What the hell is this?"

"Randomizing my route." She tossed the die into the drawer. "Six exits from this building. The coin . . ." It spun in the air, dinged on the tile, and rolled toward the dishwasher. She stomped on it. "Tails. I walk to the Cleveland Park metro stop. Otherwise, Woodland Park. Didn't they teach you anything at Quantico?"

Rick let out a long sigh. "You do all that random-draw bullshit and ignore a genuine threat? Why can't you hear what I'm saying? Go through with this, and I'm telling you, Gex will make sure it's the last time you get to play weekend warrior."

Two

Saturday, May 2, 0800 EDT

MALACHI CLUFF GLARED AT THE pimply doorman for Ashley Prescott's apartment building. "You're sure she doesn't live here? It's an enormous place. You didn't even check."

"P-r-e-s-c-o-t-t, right?" The kid used a finger to mark his place in an organic chemistry textbook. "Sir, we go from Prescher to Presley. I got nothing to do here but schoolwork and memorize the tenants' names. And before you ask, never been any Prescotts while I've been working here. That's going on two years. Academic years."

Malachi laid the four-by-six photo of Ashley and her three half-brothers on top of the textbook. "Ever seen her?"

"Believe me, I'd remember someone who looks that good."

"She'd be a dozen years older."

"Ah, well . . ." The kid's dating fantasy seemed to evaporate.

"She might have shorter hair, gained some weight."

"Why would she cut off her ponytail?" The kid handed the photo back. "You can check with the day guy if you don't believe me. Be an hour though, he comes on at nine." He returned his attention to his book.

Malachi grabbed the photo and retreated to the sitting area between the entrance and the doorman's table. He tried Ashley's number. Voicemail kicked in and he endured her message again to hear her precise Midwestern diction. "Leave a message if you think I'll call back." Alto, for sure, could cover tenor parts in a pinch. Sexy. All assuming it was her, not some purchased recording.

"This is Malachi Cluff. I'm in your apartment lobby. Please buzz me up or call." Maybe that would get her to respond. He tested the couch cushions. Comfier than the pleather at the airport. He'd wait.

A steady trickle of residents passed by. The doorman greeted each one by their first name. Most ignored him or told "Danny" to have a good day or wished him luck with his finals. A deliveryman brought a box of long-stemmed roses. Danny signed for them and, without consulting the directory, placed a call to alert the recipient.

The longer Malachi sat, the larger the aching hole grew in his stomach. Danny wasn't lazy or lying. Ashley Pendergast Prescott didn't live here. He studied the photo taken at Ashley's mother's funeral. She'd been what, twenty-two? Not long graduated from college. Makeup had covered her grief, and the black pant suit hid her athletic build. Her brothers had aged. She might look nothing like this.

Everything he knew about her was from Robert. It was hard to judge how much was her father bragging and how much was truth. Robert had hoped she would join his business and admitted he'd made a mistake trying again to convince her at her mother's funeral. She'd joined the FBI, been one of the top graduates of her academy class, and had grown into an incredible undercover agent with a knack for ticking off the old-boy network. Robert's face glowed when he related that. According to him, she had more balls than his three sons put together.

Which made Malachi curious. Why did Robert want to see her in St. Paul no later than tomorrow morning? And what did Malachi plan if she didn't return his phone calls? Control what you can; let go of whatever you can't, and plan for everything in between. That's what his SEAL training had taught him.

He laughed at himself. Here he was drawing six figures to sit on a couch, a heck of a lot better deal than freezing his butt off collecting intel in the mountains of Afghanistan. Hearing the words, "Thanks, Danny. No taxi," rocketed him from his memories. The voice that had asked him to leave a message after the beep when Ashley didn't answer her phone. The woman double-timed it past Malachi toward the exit, her head turned away from him. "Metro today."

Dressed in full fatigues—no name, no insignia, she was the right height. But exercise and diet had chiseled away Ashley's curves, leaving a muscular woman, whippet thin.

He extricated himself from the couch and impatiently waited for a guy with two dachshunds tangled around his feet to clear the doorway. Once outside, he spotted her speed-walking down the block, already past shouting range. He hustled in her wake.

Halfway across the Connecticut Avenue bridge crossing the Klinge Valley Trail, she reversed course, walked several steps toward him, reversed again, and continued in her original direction. The SEALs had taught him similar techniques to spot surveillance. Instinctively, he had kept moving at the same pace, closing their gap to shouting distance. He inhaled, preparing to project his voice above the passing traffic noise. A thought froze him. Robert Pendergast had told Malachi she was a highly effective FBI undercover agent. The woman he was following was wearing mossy oak camo fatigues and had performed a surveillance maneuver. Was Ashley on assignment?

How would she react to him yelling her real name? He'd follow and wait.

As Ashley reached the far side of the bridge, a man hopped the green metal fence separating the sidewalk from the park and raced toward her from her blind side. An older woman with a Shih Tzu on a short lead was approaching Ashley on the sidewalk. The dog tore its leash from the woman's grip and bolted toward busy Connecticut Avenue.

Ashley attempted to stomp on the leash, but the dog jerked away. Malachi's stomach knotted as the dog sprinted into the road with Ashley in pursuit. Brakes screeched. Horns blared. Like the all-American second baseman Ashley had been in college, she anticipated the Shih Tzu's path, scooped up the dog one-handed, and reached the relative safety of the double yellow line in the middle of the avenue. Once the traffic in her path stopped, she trotted back to the woman and handed her the dog and leash. After a brief conversation, she gave the woman and dog a quick hug and hustled forward. The guy who had caused the disturbance spoke briefly to the woman, gave the dog a pat, and ran after Ashley.

Malachi realized he was holding his breath and his feet had stopped moving. Unsure what was going on, he followed at double time. The guy got in front of Ashley, made a gesture Malachi interpreted as "just wait." Ashley bore down on the gesticulating man, her arms pistons, fists closed. At the last moment, her interloper stepped aside, and they strode away side-by-side.

The man was marginally taller, but his shorter legs forced him into a faster cadence. Getting slightly ahead, he turned his head sideways. Malachi was too far away to lip-read and, from his angle, couldn't determine whether Ashley responded. The tableau reminded him of a child trying to keep pace with an angry parent. The vibe wasn't something he alone felt; people coming the other way parted like the Red Sea before an approaching Moses.

The two of them reached the next intersection as the light changed to yellow. Ashley slowed, then at the last minute ran across. He, a little slow on the pickup, raced after her, flipping off the driver waiting to make a right who laid on her horn. Ashley clearly didn't want the guy with her, but with a pit bull's determination, he caught up, and they disappeared down the Metro escalator.

Malachi reached the intersection and, using the forced down time, he extracted a credit card from his billfold. Once the signal said he could walk, Malachi sprinted to the station, feet slapping hard on the concrete, jarring his shinbones. He bought a day pass, tapped the turnstile reader. Fifty-fifty chance which direction they went. He followed the larger crowd onto the Glenmont platform. A train was arriving with a push of wind and a squeal of brakes. Following the example of two college-age women, he broke into a run, weaving through others content to take the next train.

At the platform, he spotted Ashley and the guy entering the far door of a car two down from where he was. With a burst of speed, he reached the nearer entrance of the same car and stepped through the closing doors. He brushed by a mountain of a black dude too rude to follow common-courtesy and move into the interior. Malachi grabbed the center pole and set his feet against the expected jerk of the starting train.

Once the ride steadied, he rose on tiptoes and spotted them standing close to the other door. Dropping back down, he checked the metro map posted on the wall. This route would bring her to Union Station, where she could catch Amtrak or MARC and take it to Baltimore/Washington International, the airport where the plane awaited her. Robert had warned him the girl was an independent thinker and did not like being given direction. Was using public transportation rather than accept Robert's offer of a town-car ride to the airport her rebellion against Robert's wishes? He could hope.

If she was traveling to BWI, Malachi didn't want to spook her or tick her off by having her discover he was following her. Yet, dressing like a soldier and stuffing everything she'd want for a trip to St. Paul in her knapsack made little sense. Okay, if she did anything other than get off at Union Station and take a train toward BWI, he'd approach her and make his pitch. Or discover he was a fool because he'd stressed out over the wrong person who *sounded* like Ashley.

The train's automated voice announced the coming stop. Widening his stance to stay balanced, he again rose to his toes to see if Ashley moved toward the door. He kept a vigilant watch, his calves burning from the strain. Once the doors began closing, he relaxed until the next station, where he repeated the process.

Approaching Union Station, he felt the flush of adrenaline flooding his system, his unconscious mind anticipating rapid movement. This time, he narrowed his stance, preparing to follow those in front of him onto the platform. Still, she clung to the strap, and he released a frustrated breath. Which plan two: work his way through the train and approach her or wait until she got off and then connect?

A gaggle of teenagers entered the car at Ashley's door, blocking his view of her. He lasered onto her companion, who was gesticulating in her direction. The incoming crowd flowed around him, thinning to an older woman with an oversized purse who must have waited for the kids before getting on. The automatic voice informed everyone to step back, doors closing. He rolled his neck against the tension.

Over the din, Malachi heard a female voice yell, "Keep your hands to yourself, pervert." Up on tiptoes, looking back toward Ashley, he witnessed her companion knock into the older woman, then grab her. Beyond the kerfuffle, the camouflaged cap exited the door. He pushed off the pole, shouldered aside a kid wearing headphones and smelling strongly of weed, and went to smack the closing door with his hand to force it to re-open.

An iron shackle grabbed his wrist, preventing him from hitting the door. The big black dude jerked him back. "Next station, bro."

Through the door's window, he watched Ashley take a half-dozen steps, stop, and face the train. A crooked smile creased her face. And why not? She had played it perfectly. He should have known she would make that move: it mimicked the same approach she had used at the yellow traffic light to try to ditch the guy.

Malachi excused and pardoned his way down the railcar until he reached the man who had accosted Ashley. Up close, he realized that the man, below average height and all muscle, had narrowed eyes and was audibly grinding his teeth. Precisely groomed, he gave off an air of authority. Like a special forces guy. Or a cop—if cops wore cowboy boots and used too much aftershave.

The door lady's voice announced the next stop. Malachi followed the guy onto the platform and moved to his side. "Excuse me." Malachi used a soft, non-threatening voice. "I thought I recognized an old friend who got on with you. Maybe. Was that Ashley?"

The guy's eyes widened for a millisecond, giving away his lie. "Sorry, bud." He pursed his lips in shared disappointment. "Don't know who you're talking about."

"My bad." Malachi sidled toward the underground's exit, sending a prayer to God that nothing he had done would endanger Ashley. He should have put it together quicker. The doorman didn't know her as Ashley Prescott because she used her undercover name at that address.

In service, sailors died because of bad intel and Robert's had been inaccurate. Malachi's mission still gave him twenty-four hours to bring Ashley to meet his boss. He could hope she was waiting to finish whatever she was doing today before she contacted Malachi, and they'd jet to St. Paul.

If wishes were horses, beggars would ride. He needed new intel fast and knew just who to ask.

THREE

ASHLEY MONITORED RICK'S DEPARTURE ON the camera feed and checked Niki's phone once again. Another call from Malachi. She didn't want him leaving more messages and deleted the voicemail and call logs. Given Rick's unexpected appearance, she wasn't keen on leaving by the main entrance. But breaking her security routine was a slippery slope she did not choose to risk. The moment you stopped being random, you started being predictable. Once the stairway door latched behind Rick, she closed her eyes, mentally adopted her Niki persona, said out loud, "I am Corporal Niki." She triple-locked the door behind her and caught an empty elevator to the lobby. Said hello to Danny, the geeky twenty-year-old doorman. A junior at Georgetown, he unabashedly ogled the T and A passing his desk but could barely make eye contact.

"Hi ya, Niki. Can I get you a cab?"

She smiled, recalling the time she'd embarrassed him with a ten-dollar tip and a kiss for hailing her a ride during a sleet storm. "Thanks, Danny. No taxi." She passed by, waved fingers behind her head at him. Seeing a six-foot-ish, early forties, fit, military cut, pasty-colored guy who resembled the pictures of Malachi Cluff she had found on the internet, she hid her face with her near hand and said over her far shoulder to Danny, "Metro today."

Once through the door, she sprinted through the courtyard to Connecticut Avenue, where she slowed her pace to a fast walk. Rick would go apeshit if he learned Cluff had Niki's address. She wanted to confront Cluff and learn how Robert had gotten Niki's phone number and apartment address. But this shit with Robert was personal, and she would let nothing personal knock her off her stride. Hell, she realized, it already had.

She was thinking as Ashley and supposed to be acting like Niki. "I am Corporal Niki," she muttered under her breath, and kicked her walking speed up another level. Halfway across the bridge, she reversed field, saw

Cluff following. *That's unfortunate.* Niki spun on her heel and continued her original route. If she lost Cluff before she hooked-up with Sergeant Oliver, there was no reason Rick had to know Cluff had spotted and followed her. Without moving her head, she scanned for bogies and caught a flash of movement in the woods beyond the bridge. The Prick, the son of a bitch. The bastard must have cut down the hill from her apartment building, crossed the Klingle Valley Trail, and climbed up to intercept her.

She quickened her pace, moved left to avoid an older woman walking a hairy toy dog. If Ashley was going to have a dog, it needed to be something you could pound on the back without—the dog shot a look at Rick running up behind her and leaped in the opposite direction, pulling the leash from the woman's hand. Niki took two steps and jumped, intending to trap the lead under her boots. The furball shied away from her move, pulling the leash an inch beyond her stomp.

Niki raced after the dog, glanced at the first lane of Connecticut Avenue—clear—and trusted cars in the other lanes would stop before they hit her. She snagged the dog in the third lane, pulling it and the leash tight to her chest. One more step brought her to the center yellow line. Assuring herself the traffic had stopped, she waved her thanks to the drivers and returned to the woman and laid the dog in her arms.

"Bless you, bless you," she said. "You saved Reginald from sure death. Can I give you something?"

"How about a hug?" Niki gathered the woman and dog into a quick embrace. "Make sure to hold on tight to that leash. You never know when jerks, like this guy Rick, will show up out of nowhere." She disengaged and told Rick, "I expect you to apologize to Reginald and his owner." Hopefully, that would slow him down. She took off in a fast walk and heard the woman say, "And thank you for your service."

She waved a hand behind her head to let the woman know she had heard the words. *It's not what you think, but you're welcome, anyway.* The rapid clomping of cowboy boots behind her warned her Rick had not given up. Soon after, he ran in front of her and told her to slow down, motioning with his hands like she was Reginald.

She clenched her hands, narrowed her eyes, felt her teeth grinding as she steamed at him, intending to run him down if he didn't get out of her way.

"Hey, Niki," he said, sweet as a cobra seducing a mouse. At the last moment, he stepped out of her way. Hustling to catch up, he added, "Don't be like that. I thought of another reason you should call today off."

"Right. I'll be at the morgue identifying your body. Can it, Rick. Anything you say can and will be used against you."

"When PFF takes your phone, they'll find those missed calls and check your messages."

"Give me a fucking break. We have no evidence they've *ever* checked that stuff. Collecting my phone is their way to follow army procedure and not allow cell phones on maneuvers. Plus, they believe it provides an alibi for where their members have been while they're on missions. I deleted the messages. And the call log. And I killed voicemail. If Malachi Cluff calls again, he can't leave a message. If he rings while my phone-minder has it, she'll think it's a wrong number. It's not an issue."

"Well, I'll keep watch until the meet. Make sure you stay safe."

"Tiny has that assignment today." And I'd damn sure prefer a six-six, ex-pro linebacker watching my back than a five-six wannabe.

"Two are better than one."

Quit wasting your breath on him. On the bright side, Cluff wasn't coming closer. Maybe Rick was accidentally keeping Cluff at bay. Rick had planted the seed about her cover being blown. Cluff following her was fertilizer for her imagination, tendrils of concern growing. How compromised was she? Would Cluff show up at the gravel pit?

Do your thing and ditch him. Rick, too. But if anything at the meet smells wrong, she promised herself she'd skedaddle. No second thoughts.

Up ahead, the walking man symbol on the crosswalk sign flashed, numbers counting down the seconds. She eased her pace to reach the intersection at zero. "Crud. Won't make it," she said for Rick's benefit. The signal changed to a raised hand. She waited until the declining numbers reached one, then dashed across the street, knapsack thumping on her back. Rick's booted steps followed her. Someone laid on their car horn and Rick yelled, "Get a horse, lady."

She scampered down the concrete stairs to the Metro, staying left to pass, tapped her card, and proceeded to the platform. Following the game plan developed in yesterday's undercover planning meeting, she ambled to the approximate spot for the front entrance to the second car. She ignored Tiny, who wore a Nick Foles Philadelphia jersey. Niki smiled at the inside joke: Nick Foles had been the last quarterback Tiny had sacked before he retired. Washington fans might have something to say about that shirt, except no one was dumb enough to take on a black dude whose arms were thicker than most people's legs.

No sign of either Rick or Cluff. Maybe Rick had given up, and maybe Cluff didn't know how to use the Metro. *Hope for the best; prepare for the worst.* She slipped both arms through her knapsack straps, snugged everything tight around her chest, and flexed her knees to judge the fit. Wearing the pack would annoy some passengers because it occupied extra space, but she wanted flexibility for action.

The first push of fetid air from the arriving train tickled her face. From the corner of her eye, she caught Rick sidling toward her. That sucked, although at least he was respecting her being undercover. No way she'd let him anywhere near her meeting with Sergeant Oliver. With time, she had lots of ways to ditch him. With no time, her only choice was to make sure he stayed on the train when she got off at Union Station.

The train's twin headlights grew brighter, air pressure increased, levitating a scrap of paper from the track. Lights at the edge of the platform blinked for the hearing impaired. She plugged her ears against the squeal, wanted to close her eyes against the sting of the dust, but that could be fatal.

She chose an angled path to the open door. Inside, she grabbed the closest pole, forcing Rick to move past her. Right where she wanted him. Stooping to look through the window, she caught Cluff's sprint, his arms pumping, dodging obstacles, and breathing through his nose. The dude was in shape. He followed Tiny through the car's other door as they were shutting.

Your move, asshole. The train accelerated with a whine. She got a whiff of Rick's sandalwood aftershave and changed her thinking to *assholes.* At least Rick was smart enough not to say anything to her, and when he had used her name, he'd remembered to call her Niki.

Cluff remained where he was. That gave Niki time to mentally rehearse moves to free herself. A buzz of anticipation rippled up her spine as the train approached her exit.

The automated voice announced Union Station, and Rick gave her a little after-you motion. She pretended not to see. He moved closer and said, "Excuse me, ma'am, are you getting off?"

"Nope. Feel free." She held his stare, dropped her hand from the pole, and leaned into it, offering to let him pass. She nudged her feet together, preparing to launch her escape. He inched closer. *Go ahead. Touch me, Rick.* Closer. Waiting. Waiting.

At the Metro's automatic warning that the doors would soon close, she yelled, "Keep your hands to yourself, pervert," and gave Rick a two-handed shove, causing him to stumble into an older woman.

Niki raced through the opening, bouncing off a closing door like it was a pinball bumper. Hearing the hum of the train starting, she stopped and watched the train.

Behind one door, a red-faced Rick stared darts. Behind a second, she spotted Cluff standing next to Tiny.

Double play to end the inning. Now to discover what's up with Sergeant Oliver.

FOUR

Saturday, May 2, 0850 EDT

NIKI MADE A CIRCUIT OF the bustling underground food court at Union Station, checking for additional tails, blocked exits, anything unusual. Not getting a whiff of anything more suspicious than a dried yellow stain under one table, she arrived at the Au Bon Pain with three minutes to spare.

Sergeant Oliver, dressed in camo fatigues but wearing trainers instead of his normal leather boots, sat alone at a table with a to-go cup and an empty plate. He gave her a slight nod, drained his coffee—always the morning blend—licked his finger and tapped it on the plate to capture the last crumbs of what she guessed had been a chocolate croissant. He tongued the crumbs and wiped his hand on his pants. Such class. Standing up, his stomach caught the table, causing it to wobble, which drew stares. *Smooth operator.* The guy wasn't used to the extra twenty pounds he'd put on in the two years since she'd first met him.

Given his subtle exit, she let him clear the area before following his spraddle-legged walk at a distance to the Metro platform for Shady Grove. He stepped into the third car; she chose the fourth. This time she held onto a pole with one hand and pretended to scroll through a news feed on her cellphone.

As the train slowed for the Gallery Place stop, the young bottle-blond PFF used for phone-chaperone duty sidled up to her, popping pink gum. Niki braced herself for the encounter. "Misjudging" the car's sway around a curve, the girl lurched into Niki, sticking her ribs with an elbow.

While disengaging, Niki slipped her phone into her contact's rear pocket. The screeching wheels covered their conversation. "Where's the phone heading today?"

"Shopping at the mall and a movie."

Niki recoiled. The girl had eaten enough garlic to protect her from vampires for a week. If she was chewing gum to cover up the olfactory assault, it wasn't working. Niki asked, "What kind of movie?" and held her breath through the girl's response.

"I'll have the ticket receipt on your phone to let you know what and where. You're getting off at Bethesda Metro today." She moved to the exit and, once the doors opened, loped away on skinny legs.

Bethesda? Niki's heart rate increased. She settled it with a slow exhale. In the best of circumstances, her FBI minders hated the extra work and increased risk to her caused by any changes to the planned scenario. With Rick's objections and Malachi Cluff dogging her, this could hardly rate as best times. Reminding herself of her promise to disengage at the first sign of trouble, Niki caught up to Oliver on the street. "What's with the early exit?"

Through the side of his mouth he said, "We have a guy staying in one of the hotels coming with."

Her gut clenched like he'd punched her, and her body forgot for a moment how to breathe. She maintained her purposeful stride. Once she regained control, she asked, "A squad member?"

"Chink arms dealer named Sam. Colonel Pete wants you to translate. We're supposed to pick him up at the Hyatt Regency and take him to the gravel pit. My ride is parked a few blocks away."

Puzzle pieces clicked into place. For a month, Colonel Pete had hinted PFF would soon acquire new automatic rifles. Two weeks ago, she had met the colonel at the Central Library in Arlington, Virginia and translated three Mandarin documents he'd brought regarding military-grade weapons. The gravel pit in the Maryland countryside was where PFF tested weapons and improved their marksmanship. The ATF agents on the joint ATF/FBI task force had pressed her for more details. Now she'd get them.

The familiar buzz of living on the edge tickled her neck hairs, had her twitching her fingers with nervous energy. She pushed to the deep recesses of her mind her promise to bail if there was any change in today's plans. Translating for the arms dealer would trump any objection Rick raised. The team would get behind this one hundred percent.

Which didn't mean she should let her guard down. Sergeant Oliver was a misogynist with a criminal record for violence. She'd never caught him in a lie, but there was always a first time.

They walked in silence to an underground parking garage, she trailed him by half a step. Oliver heaved open the heavy metal door to the stairwell and marched through. Niki caught the door before it closed and checked to make sure no one could ambush her from a higher landing. Clear.

Oliver's black Suburban, with its tinted windows, was on the next level down.

"Hop in the front passenger seat this time," Oliver said.

Not happening. She would not put herself in a position where someone behind her could hold a gun at her head. The first time they had driven together, she had begun training Oliver to allow her to drive. She'd lied and said she became carsick unless she drove. He didn't buy it and forced her to ride shotgun. Picking a moment while he was concentrating on traffic, she stuck a finger down her throat and puked on his leather seats and console. Since that incident, he mostly let her drive, and when he insisted on driving, he let her sit in the back.

Given a third person, driving was worse than being a front-seat passenger; she had to finagle her way into the rear seat and let the Chinese arms dealer take the front or share the rear with her. "No way Colonel Pete wants me to puke with this guy in the car. I know you're not like this, but a lot of Chinese guys don't want women to drive."

Without waiting for his response, she opened the door behind the driver. Nothing on the seat or in the foot wells or in the far back. She sat and undid the Velcro seam of her knapsack, providing her quick, and now silent, access to her M9.

"Suit yourself." Oliver slid in and turned on the Suburban. In under ten minutes, he steered the car into the Hyatt Regency's circular drive and pulled to the curb past the valet parking sign. Leaving the engine running, he hustled to the passenger side and opened the door opposite her. Keeping her hand near the M9, Niki leaned down to spot the arms dealer.

Oliver not only blocked her view, but his body prevented her from seeing his hands. Her finger itched to move onto the trigger, but Oliver wasn't tense. He'd be rubbing his neck or rolling his shoulders. From behind him, she heard a roller-bag thumping over sidewalk cracks.

Oliver moved aside, revealing a black plain-toed oxford and sharply creased black pant leg. A middle-aged Asian male ducked in, leaving a first impression of chiseled edges. Under a full head of black hair, his brown eyes scanned Niki. A fading scar marred his square jaw. A wide smile creased his face, overlapping tombstone teeth filled his mouth.

"You are my translator? A woman. They not tell me." He spoke English with a British accent. Switching to Mandarin, he added, "My English is terrible."

She rejected her instinct to joke that no one should have to tell him she was a woman. The jest might lose meaning in translation. Instead, she answered using Mandarin, "Your English might be better than my Mandarin."

Her first impression of sharp edges wasn't correct. Strong was more accurate. He sat a couple inches taller than she and was ripped. Pecs and guns to make a marine proud pulled hard against his short-sleeved polo, also black. Instinctively, she wrenched her shoulders back and still failed to match his ramrod posture. If he was carrying, the only place it could be was in a right ankle holster.

Oliver opened the rear lift door, hefted in an oversized metal suitcase, and slammed the door shut, rocking the vehicle. He got behind the wheel, clunked the transmission into gear, and pulled onto the street. If Oliver wouldn't introduce her to her backseat companion, she'd do it herself. She presented a slight head bow. "I am pleased to meet you. My name is Niki."

"You may call me Sam," he said in Mandarin. "I prefer for you to translate. I do not know American expressions."

"Buckle up," Oliver said. "We don't want cops stopping us. And button up. Operational security requires silence until we get there."

Niki translated and added, "He's afraid government agencies can listen to what we say."

Sam's smile widened. "Fearing governments is an excellent way to keep alive."

So is keeping a hand on your M9.

FIVE

Saturday, May 2, Mid-morning EDT

OLIVER STOPPED AT THE RUSTING gate guarding the quarry. Niki unwrapped the false-locked chain snugging the gate to an eight-inch pipe buried into the ground. The temperature had risen during the drive, but the metal chain held the night's chill and stung her fingers. She muscled open the iron gate, which protested with the squeal of hinges exposed to lots of weather and little oil. Oliver eased the SUV through the opening. She closed the gate and arranged the chain to look secure to a casual observer.

They drove around a single-wide trailer business office onto pot-holed asphalt. Niki grabbed the panic strap while the Suburban bumped past parked gravel trucks, chrome shining in the sunlight, and a graveyard of abandoned vehicles in various stages of decay. The road widened into a pit carved from an imposing hill rising a hundred feet.

They parked next to Colonel Pete's newish red Silverado. The Colonel strode to Sam and offered his hand. "We're ready to put your merchandise to one last test." He swept an arm to indicate the shooting range dotted with hand-drawn human-outline targets distanced at what Niki figured were 100, 200, and 400 meters.

Sam shook hands. "To assure we have no misunderstanding, I prefer to speak my language and use your translator," he inclined his head toward Niki.

"That's *one* reason she's here. Let's get started." The colonel marched to the rear of the Silverado, never looking to see if they were following, and lowered the tailgate. Oliver rushed in his wake.

Niki matched Sam's measured pace. He seemed to take everything in. She wondered what Colonel Pete had in mind for her besides translating.

Colonel Pete waited for Sam, then, like a magician cranking up the audience, he flicked aside a tarp spattered with generations of paint drips to reveal a wooden crate the size of a child's coffin. Stamped on its top was, "This side up." With a theatrical flourish, he indicated the scratched crowbar lying on a flag-themed towel next to the crate. "Sergeant Oliver, if you'll do the honors?"

Oliver jammed the bar under the center of the long side of the lid and yanked down. The cover popped up, exposing finishing nails. *Not the original fasteners.* Oliver laid the crowbar on the towel and propped the top against the truck.

Niki leaned in to see what was inside. Oliver handed her a QBZ-95 assault rifle with scope attached and grabbed the next one for himself. Hers had the altered butt stock and trigger guard of the -1 model. Cleaned of its packing grease, it looked new, not some junk that had been used hard. Given the attached scope and a sheen of oil she detected on the gun rails, she guessed someone had recently fired it.

"You have found them satisfactory?" Sam asked in Mandarin, which Niki translated.

"So far. Get the magazines too, Sergeant."

Niki considered explaining to Sam that Colonel Pete didn't mean his clipped response to be disrespectful. He expected excellence and seldom gave praise.

"Last weekend," the colonel said, "Sergeant Oliver and several other experienced soldiers fired hundreds of rounds under a variety of conditions. What I want to know is if they're suitable for smaller, weaker, assets like you, Corporal."

She chomped her tongue and swallowed her anger. While she'd been stuck last Sunday teaching navigation to six PFF recruits who couldn't find their toes without GPS, Sergeant Oliver and a bunch of ex-Army boys had been putting the rifles through their paces. Oliver might be stronger than she, but she was not the weaker asset.

Sam looked to her with eyebrows raised and she remembered to translate. She added, "I'm a better shooter than translator." To Oliver she said. "Sergeant, may I have one that's farther down in the box? They might have prepared the top ones for us to test."

"Last weekend," Colonel Pete said, "we used them all."

Niki translated both her request and the colonel's answer.

Colonel Pete shook his head. "Target shooting is one thing, but I want to learn how well my men shoot tired. I want to evaluate your performance after you run a mile."

Oliver caught her glance at his running shoes and gave her a Cheshire

Cat grin. Nothing fair about this fight, which meant she damn well would not lose. "Can I test fire a few rounds?" Niki asked. "Sight it in?"

"Come on, Corporal," Oliver said. "We don't have all day."

"They're ARs," Colonel Pete said. "Pinpoint accuracy doesn't concern me. I want to observe how you handle them when you're fatigued."

"Understood, sir. But before I fire this thing, I *will* confirm it's okay."

Sam didn't wait for the translation and said in Mandarin, "A warrior must know his weapon."

Interesting that he was backing her up. She broke down the rifle, checked for dirt, excess oil, anything not perfect. Reassembled, she lined up the front notch on the magazine and inserted it to click into the well in the pistol grip. She rocked the rear of the magazine until it snapped into place. The release mechanism wasn't immediately obvious. She found it, pushed it in, and pivoted the magazine forward and out. Tried the sequence again. Faster. Quick. Solid.

"Thank you, sir," she said like he'd given her permission.

Colonel Pete toed a line across the gravel, leaving a deep scratch. "It's a half a mile to the shed you passed. Sam and I will have arranged thirty targets for each of you by the time you finish your run. Sergeant, take her pace. Corporal, it better not be slow. I want you tired when you shoot. Targets on the right are yours, left are his. Three magazines each."

Niki considered asking if they had ear and eye protection, choked it down. Being right but seen as a sissy didn't cut it. She shoved the two extra magazines in her cargo pants pockets and made a quick calculation based on the specs she had translated. The rifle weighed eight pounds loaded. Each magazine carried thirty rounds. That was a lot of weight bouncing around. Oliver was bigger, stronger, younger, but carried a gut. She held the FBI woman's training record for the 1.5-mile run and was sure she had more speed and stamina. Winning the race meant nothing. Only the shooting competition mattered. Given the gear, she figured a nine-minute pace would exhaust Oliver but allow her to still shoot reasonably well. She'd been in awe of biathletes who could cross-country ski fast and then shoot accurately. She placed that picture in her head to maintain focus.

Colonel Pete counted down. At zero, Oliver sprinted ahead. She let him go, confident her nine-minute-a-mile pace would run him to ground. Every hundred steps, she shifted the rifle from one hand to the other. Before they were halfway to the shed, Oliver's technique was falling apart, the shoulder of his gun arm drooping, his other arm flailing, wasting energy to maintain balance. With each step she reeled him in until she eased her stride sufficiently to allow Oliver a slight lead at the turnaround. Mimicking him, she touched the building, pushed off, and placed herself in his shadow. She licked her lips and whistled a loop of the refrain from Queen's "Another one bites the dust."

Oliver swallowed the bait and lurched forward, wasting valuable energy. She let him go, resumed her nine-minute pace, and concentrated on keeping her arms strong and loose. In two hundred meters, she reeled him in, again whistled. He responded with another burst of speed. This time, she caught him in fifty meters, pulled slightly ahead, letting him believe he could stay with her. She played that game, sucking energy from his legs until he groaned like he was delivering a twenty-pound baby. At that, she picked up her pace and didn't look back.

Colonel Pete and Sam, the Mutt-and-Jeff pair now sporting ear protectors and spotting scopes, had placed themselves away from where the brass would soon fly. They had rearranged her targets: at 100 meters away, each of the ten was roughly four meters from the next. Same thing for five of her 200-meter targets; the rest they collected into a single group. The 400-meter targets presented a squad bunched together.

She dropped to the gravel at the colonel's toed line and snapped off the safety. Squinting into the sun, she unloaded her first magazine into the farthest target grouping. Dirt puffs exploded behind the targets. Noise like she hadn't experienced since the last grunge concert she had attended assaulted her ears. The recoils bit her shoulder less than she had expected. Her finger found the magazine release, and she rocked out the empty one, tossed it aside. She rolled over while extracting its replacement from her pocket. Inserting it, she wished she could hear the confirming click, but her ringing ears didn't cooperate.

While hosing down the tight grouping of five targets at the 200-meter mark a boot toe kicked her hip. She jerked her finger from the trigger, re-sighted the targets through the airborne dust and cardboard debris now partially blocking the sun, and emptied the rest of the clip. Twisting onto her side, empty cartridges pressed painfully into her knee. *Shouldn't be there.* A micro-glimpse found Oliver standing above her, his rifle jackhammering his arm. His brass, the bastard.

She exchanged her last full magazine for the empty and resumed her prone position farther away from Oliver. She aimed, squeezed the trigger, verified a white hole punched through the black silhouette. Changed target and repeated. Repeated. Repeated. The metallic taste of blood reminded her to stop biting her tongue as she concentrated. Repeat. Repeat. Pain in the shoulder getting worse. Repeat. Pain. Missed goddammit. Relax. Got it. Repeat. Repeat. Done.

One miss. Fourteen bullets in reserve. Her shoulder ached like six-six Tiny had punched her. She snugged the stock into the pain and used the rifle scope to check all her targets. Single holes punctured all the 100-meter targets. The 200-meter targets all had at least one hole. She couldn't find holes in three of the 400-meter targets. With one shot each she nailed those three. She snapped on the safety and kicked out her foot, hitting Oliver's leg. Rolling away from him and into a standing position, Queen invaded her mind again, this time chanting "We are the champions." She'd crushed the fucker. Run faster. Eliminated the "threat." Finished before him. Her heart swelled at the job well done.

She moved behind Sergeant Oliver to let her body report. Her forearms and wrists ached from running with the rifle. The rifle's recoil must have pushed her shoulder back two inches, but she would not rub anything with Colonel Pete "evaluating her performance." She hoped the ringing in her ears would disappear once Oliver finished shooting. A sharp pain remained in her knee from the cartridges she'd rolled on. Hidden from the colonel and Sam by her leg, she pressed her middle finger hard on the spot and breathed deeply. Never had gunpowder smelled so good.

Oliver finished the three-shot bursts he'd been using and spun around. *If looks could kill, she'd be in a crematorium.* She shifted her attention to Colonel Pete, who looked pleased, and Sam, who observed her with an inscrutable look. She prided herself on her ability to read people. Culture could be part of it, but she suspected Sam was a master of containment. She must become more mindful of him.

Colonel Pete brought them together. "Let's score it up." He glassed the targets and reported the hits for each target: Oliver had drilled all his 100-meter targets with three shots each. Eight of his ten 200-meter targets showed the same trio burst. He'd missed two. At 400 meters, he'd triple-nailed five targets and double-nailed two additional targets. Three targets were still virgins.

Oliver crowed, "I scored seventy-three hits. Totally smashed her measly forty-four."

"Except," Colonel Pete said, "she eliminated all thirty enemy combatants. Five of yours are still standing. If anyone's ass was wiped, it was yours, Sergeant. Proving a weaker asset can be highly effective with this weapon."

"But—"

Colonel Pete pulled a black box from his pocket and pressed its yellow button.

A new cardboard silhouette of a kneeling man rose from behind a rock centered between Niki's and Oliver's 100-meter targets. Without hesitation, Niki raised her rifle, flicked off the safety, and drilled it.

"And, she still had ammunition left to handle contingencies," Colonel Pete said. "We'll take all two hundred of 'em."

Sam did not wait for translation. "Thank you, Colonel." He bowed to Niki and reverted to Mandarin. "And thank you for making my sale. Unfortunately, at the cost of your happiness."

Niki was busy processing Colonel Pete's plan to buy 200 weapons. Because PFF operated platoons independently of each other, she and the Bureau had identified only fifty members, although they knew there were more. This sale provided the first solid intel regarding PFF's true size. Her shooting had impressed Colonel Pete. Sam was pleased with the sale—wait, what was that he tacked on at the end? In Mandarin she asked, "My happiness?"

"The Sergeant has lost face. He will consider you his enemy and try to destroy you."

No loss there. He'd hated her from day one. But interesting that Sam was warning her. That was twice he had taken her side against her superiors.

"What's he saying?" the Colonel asked.

"He thanked you for agreeing to the purchase. He is humbled by your decision and wishes you a long and prosperous life. Well, what he actually said was he wished you longevity like the pine of the south mountain, but that's what it means." She waited to see whether Sam would give her away.

Same unreadable face. "Please ask your Colonel if now would be a good time to show him the truly special weapon."

Six

Saturday, May 2, Late morning EDT

MALACHI WATCHED THE GREVY'S ZEBRAS grazing on grasses in their National Zoo compound. On the other side of a fence, a cheetah paced, frustrated that it could see its quarry but had no way to bring it down. *You and me fella.*

The sign informed him zebra stripes provided camouflage in the dry, hot shrublands of Kenya. In the humid Washington D.C. zoo, their stripes stood out, similar to Ashley's mossy oak clothing on the subway. Where was she going that she required camo?

He checked his phone, knowing he had missed no calls or text messages. Two hours had passed since Ashley had ditched him. Time to try Robert again. Morgan, Robert's assistant, answered the office phone. "Malachi, is she coming?"

"Not yet. May I speak with Robert?"

"First, I have to see him. He wanted me in early, but he's not here. I've left messages on his cell and home phones. Can I help you with something?"

Malachi briefed her on his failure. "Robert may have given me the location where he expected her to be last night, not her actual home address."

"Give me a sec."

The rattle of fingers tapping a keyboard filled the seconds.

"Robert's address book shows a Lincolnia apartment she shares with Special Agent Aaliyah Zylstra. That's Fairfax County in Northern Virginia." She provided the address. "What's the weather?"

"Imagine St. Paul in July with more humidity. Phone number?"

"Nothing in his address book, and online white pages show no listings for either of them. When I hear from Robert, what shall I tell him?"

That I told him it was a lousy idea to send me. "That he better be working on Plan B."

SEVEN

COLONEL PETE RUBBED HIS HANDS. "I hoped we'd see it." He motioned toward the Suburban. "Lead on." Despite his suggestion that Sam lead, the colonel charged ahead of the others and had Sam's suitcase on the ground, waiting for them.

Sam clicked open the locks and removed parts for an Accuracy International Arctic Warfare Magnum from their padding. Niki recalled the specifications from the material Colonel Pete had her translate at their library meeting. Assembled, the sniper rifle was more than four feet long. The sucker weighed fifteen pounds and had a range of up to 1.7 klicks. In the right hands it could kill a mouse a kilometer away and would only use one of the five .338 Lapua Magnum cartridges the magazine carried to accomplish the task.

Sam assembled the rifle, attached a top-mounted scope, and extended the two legs in front to form an inverted V for shooting prone.

"Corporal," Colonel Pete ordered, "prepare several of the targets and bring the spotting scopes." He gestured in their direction. "We'll mosey up to the shed. Sergeant, you get the honors."

Niki erected a half-dozen targets, some in the open, some partially obstructed. Gathering the two spotting scopes, she double-timed it to where the men waited. She plucked tufts of crabgrass and tested the wind. Five miles an hour. Maybe six. A dust devil twisted along the road for several seconds before dispersing. A tricky wind like this was enough to separate real marksmen from wannabes.

Sergeant Oliver was good but nothing special. She *was* special and hoped like hell she'd get a chance to try that baby.

She arranged the spotting scopes in the shade of the shed and translated Sam's offer to demonstrate. Sergeant Oliver didn't bother waiting for her to finish.

"Colonel wants *me* to shoot this. Not him."

She glanced at Sam to see if he reacted to the disdain in Sergeant Oliver's voice. Not a single muscle twitch.

She reminded herself she was Corporal Niki and should speak only when spoken to. She translated Sam's contributions to the discussion concerning windage adjustments given the freshening breeze, temps now in the mid-sixties, and humidity picking up. Oliver was physically twitching to shoot. Colonel Pete asked a few pertinent questions, but she would bet the Taj Mahal that he had never commanded snipers.

Oliver dialed in the agreed adjustments and settled into a prone position. She followed Colonel Pete and Sam to the scopes and held her fingers in her ears while Oliver fired one magazine to zero in the height correction to reflect gravity's effect on a bullet traveling a half mile.

Oliver gave them a thumbs up. "Got it now." He jerked his next trigger pull, and his shot sparked off a rock to the right of the target.

Niki stifled a snort. "Wind musta picked up?"

He made a minor change, had a smoother trigger pull. Nailed a standing target in the crotch.

Colonel Pete told him to shift targets.

Oliver chose a second target she had set at the same height on the hill, meaning he didn't change anything other than rotate. *Smart move.* Oliver pulled the trigger before she covered her ears.

"I don't know if it's the scope or the gun," he growled. "Something's not right here." He settled his eye to the scope and prepared to take another shot.

Sam caught her eye and said in Mandarin, "The weapon is better than the man. You should shoot it."

Oliver yanked his head away from the rifle and produced a theatrical groan. "Come on. I'm shooting."

"Can I try?" Niki slapped a hand to her mouth. She faced Colonel Pete and snapped to attention. "I'm sorry, sir. Sam said it's not the weapon and suggested I try it. My enthusiasm to fire such an awesome piece overwhelmed me. It won't happen again, sir." She held herself ramrod stiff, worried she had totally fucked up.

Colonel Pete's fierce eyes judged them all. She held her breath; Sergeant Oliver's face varied between anger at Sam's observation and pleasure that she was seriously in trouble; and Sam looked like he didn't have a care in the world.

The seconds ticked and Niki recalled another corporal who had acted big for his britches. He'd vanished from their ranks. The Bureau had not determined whether he was even alive.

Colonel Pete relaxed and chuckled. "Apology accepted, soldier. If I had steadier hands, I'd want to play with it. Go ahead, Corporal, given Sam suggested it, take a few shots."

Sergeant Oliver's hand twitched toward the pistol holstered on his garrison belt, stopped himself. "Fine. I'll give it another chance." Shaking with rage, he lowered his head to the eyepiece.

"Sergeant, I said let Corporal Niki try her luck."

Any fool who heard that tone from Colonel Pete knew not to cross him. Oliver didn't move for a half-dozen beats of Niki's pounding heart before he rose, jarring the rifle and brushing against the windage adjustment, changing it by a couple of clicks. "All yours." With a big grin plastered across his red face, he motioned her toward the rifle like a gentleman offering her a dance.

She corrected the windage and settled in. To make herself one with the weapon, she visualized herself fifteen years earlier at the Montana state championships. That day, she had felt calm and comfortable and had crushed the competition. She slowed her breathing, felt her heart steady into a regular lup-dup. When she judged herself ready, she slid her finger on the trigger and met its tension.

"Take the damn shot." Oliver said.

"Sergeant," Colonel Pete said, "be quiet."

Niki shook tension from her hand and repeated the visualizing and breathing exercise until she was ready to place her finger on the trigger. She continued slow, steady breathing, lengthening the pause between exhale and inhale—six seconds, eight seconds, ten seconds. Within that window, she steadily added finger pressure until the gun fired, punching her shoulder, assaulting her ear.

She ignored those physical manifestations of the shot and kept her eye on the scope, which bobbed higher every time she inhaled. A half-second later, a hole appeared in the target: perfect height and only two inches to the left of her intent.

"Even a blind squirrel," Oliver muttered.

Niki shut her mind to him and refocused, steadied her breathing, and waited for a temporary increase in the wind to recede. Her second shot scored an inch closer to the center. *With this weapon, I can do this all day.*

"Switch to the rightmost target, far row," Colonel Pete ordered.

Without waiting for the translation, Sam instructed her in Mandarin how to tweak the scope to reflect the additional 300 meters to the new target. Niki followed his instructions and settled in, focused solely on the target. During her trigger pull sequence, a gust of wind kicked up. She eased her finger from the trigger.

"Well done," Sam said under his breath.

She reset and punched a hole an inch high and three inches to the right of center. *Not a perfect kill, but dead is dead.*

"I've seen enough." The colonel clapped his hands. "Where'd you learn to shoot like that, Corporal?"

Niki blinked herself to the present and mined a piece of her cover story. "Montana gophers know to the inch how far a bullet can travel. On the prairie, there are no close shots."

"Remind me where you learned to speak Chinese."

Niki pushed her nerves aside and recited her backstory. "Two years of community college, sir, but that wasn't where I learned Mandarin. My mother home-schooled me. She insisted I learn Spanish because most of the farm hands were from Mexico or Central America. I added Mandarin later because she said China will be our biggest economic competitor and anyone who knows the language has an enormous advantage in life."

"She taught you?"

Niki tilted her head and gave an exaggerated laugh. "No, sir. I first learned from tapes and then online. I understand better than I speak and speak better than I read."

"Why didn't you get a bachelor's degree? You've got the brains."

She pictured holding her dying mother in her arms and felt the tears on her cheeks. "Mom got cancer. I had to drop out and take care of her. That took all our money." Niki let her posture slump. "Years slip past. You know?"

"And how did you get to D.C.?"

"There's not much call for Mandarin in Montana. I found a translator job in town."

"At ease." He curled his top lip under his teeth and pushed the corner of his mustache into his mouth and chewed on it. "If you wanted to take time off from work on short notice, could you?"

Niki pursed her lips in fake concern. "Maybe a sick day or two."

Colonel Pete ushered Niki away from Sam and Sergeant Oliver. With a lowered voice he asked, "How well does our guest understand English?"

Niki wanted to cozy up to Sam to learn more about Chinese gunrunning, but reminded herself her assignment was to take down PFF. "He speaks British. Better than I do Mandarin."

"That's what I thought. You got a safe place you can store the piece?" He pointed to the sniper rifle still on the ground.

He knows I live in a D.C. apartment with a roommate. Offer to find safe offsite storage? No, act like a corporal and answer the question. "No, sir. Taking a long gun through the lobby of my apartment and up the elevator would not be secure."

"You got any travel plans coming up?"

"Nothing important, sir."

"Good. Keep next weekend open. Inform Sam we'll buy the new rifle, and we'll take four-hundred-thousand rounds to go with those ARs." He raised his voice, "Sergeant, scoot on ahead and start collecting the targets and policing the brass. We'll clean up here and be along shortly."

Oliver reached for the sniper rifle.

"Corporal Niki will bring her weapon."

By the look in Oliver's eye, he wanted to protest but thought better of it. "Yes, sir." He skulked away.

Her weapon. Niki's stomach fluttered in excitement. She had been right; she had needed to be here today. Malachi Cluff and the breach of her security was still an issue, but Rick would eat crow at this afternoon's meeting if he pressed it.

EIGHT

Saturday, May 2, Late afternoon EDT

NIKI SLIPPED IN THE FRONT door of the musty FBI safe house in Northern Virginia, a sixties split-level confiscated from a drug dealer who had traded his freedom for three squares, free health care, and bars protecting his tamper-proof view of the world. Keeping the latch down, she whispered the door shut, then eased to the edge of the steps leading to the lower level and held her breath, hoping to hear them talking, get a feel for the situation.

No go. She avoided the squeak of the third step and leaned her ear against the hollow-core door at the bottom. A click of billiard balls followed by a second click, Rick chuckling. Tiny's, "Nice shot." Good. The boys were playing pool.

She popped the door open and felt the bonhomie race past her replaced by tension thick enough to cut with a spatula. Gex, stony-faced, dressed in a blue pinstripe suit, starched white shirt, red and blue striped tie (no tying him to either the Republicans or Democrats), leaned against the doorframe of the bedroom converted into a conference room. He pushed off the water-stained wall. "Well, Prescott finally decided to grace us with her presence. Kaska, Proulx, leave it." He stepped through the doorway.

Sometimes Niki wondered if Gex even knew their first names were Ashley, Rick and—well, no one called Michael Proulx by his first name; they all called him Tiny.

Niki said, "I have fantastic intel from today's meet. Sorry I'm late. I had a run-in with Sergeant Oliver and had to clean puke from his vehicle with a Q-Tip. That delay messed up the timing for me to retrieve Niki's phone and then . . ." *They don't give a shit.*

Rick laid his cue on the felt and, without glancing at her, scurried like a rat into the conference room. Tiny left the balls scattered on the table but racked both cues. A silent head gesture told her trouble was ahead.

She read sympathy in his face. Her step faltered. If the guy whose primary responsibility on this team was to put her best interests ahead of the assignment's was offering sympathy—she blocked the rest of the thought from forming. Her immediate need was to jettison her Niki persona and revert to Special Agent Ashley Prescott, because that's who had to navigate this meeting. Funny that she could instantaneously switch from Ashley to Niki. She became more alert, her senses sharpened, posture stiffened, voice roughened. Transforming Niki to Ashley was more ragged; it was hard to turn off that heightened awareness.

Tiny enveloped her in a hug, whispering in her ear, "Gex is on the war path. We'll make it work."

She took longer, deeper breaths, and followed the mountain that was Tiny into the conference room, stopping in the doorway to assess the damage. The rattling dehumidifier had lost the battle against the locker room odor. Her route today, relayed by her bra transmitter and color-coded to reflect her travel speed, remained visible on the screen attached to the long wall. She checked the dotted red lines that connected last known points before and after the signal's disruption. Score one for technology: today red only covered the time she was underground on the Metro.

Streaks on the whiteboard pushed into the corner left no clue regarding its recent use. The tea trolley overflowed with the detritus of the day: three Starbucks cups Rick had gone through, an empty water pitcher only Tiny used, and Gex's uncapped thermos—meaning he'd already had sixteen ounces of decaf, each with two spoonsful of fake sugar and four drops of cream. They'd been here a long time.

She sucked her tongue to bring moisture into the desert that was her mouth.

Gex had taken his seat at the head of the table, tapping his fountain pen against his teeth, fiddling with the writing tablet, the top page filled with his Palmer script. Rick slumped into the chair next to him. The water bottle marking Tiny's place implied he had left the other side of Gex for her.

"Anyway," she said. "I have primo intel to share." She ordered her leaden legs forward, pulled out her chair, and noticed they each had a closed manila folder in front of them. She perched on the edge of her seat.

Gex cleared his throat. "Where is Niki's phone?"

Her butt tightened. She forced it to relax. "Shut off. In the Faraday bag compartment of my knapsack. I added Fran's phone to the—"

"Hagen," Gex yelled.

A tech guy she'd seen at FBI headquarters thumped down the stairs and stuck his head into the conference room. Einstein hair, he wore cutoffs and a tee shirt from some obscure band.

"She's got them both electronically secure. Let us know what you find."

"Good thinking," Hagen said to Ashley. "I'm told you have a recorder?"

"Disguised as a spare ammunition magazine. In the zipped inside pocket."

The kid was all smiles carting her knapsack from the room.

Gex, the "Great" behind his back, showed no emotion, a characteristic that had helped propel him to become a top undercover agent working on terror threats post 9/11 and made her boss hard to read. He waited until Hagen closed the door. "Open the file."

A blurry, blown-up, black-and-white photocopy of a Minnesota driver's license stared up at her: a head shot of Malachi Cluff, the guy who had followed her from Niki's apartment. Instinctively, she followed the technique she'd learned from the Hollywood actor the FBI hired to teach them how to hide their reactions. "Create a mental safe spot and go there." Counting down from five, she pictured herself hiking a deserted trail in Glacier National Park, a bald eagle flying low enough she could hear and feel the bird's powerful wingbeats. That brought a smile.

Squinting, she captured the details: Malachi C. Cluff, M, 6'0", 165, gray eyes. She did the math: forty on his birthday next month. Looking directly at Gex, she tinged her voice with curiosity. "Did you question the fucker?"

"You know him?" Gex asked.

She glanced at Rick. Head down, busy arranging papers in that file. Nervous. *What did Rick report?* "Seen him. Waiting for me at Niki's apartment. I ditched him at Union Station. Did you ask who gave him Niki's contact info?"

Gex frowned. "Explain why you did not immediately inform us of the security breach and instead went ahead with the PFF meeting."

Good offense beats poor defense. "I'm curious who sold me out, but it's no biggie. Thing is, PFF is planning a major weapons buy for more people than we know about. And they've got their hands on a sniper rifle. My assignment is critical to finding—"

"Stop the games. The phone calls, Special Agent Prescott. If you had notified us of his call, maybe we *could* have picked him up." Gex leaned both forearms on the table. In a quiet, soothing voice he said, "It can get confusing running simultaneous operations plus your real life." He waved his hands like he was juggling balls. "Niki, Fran, Ashley. I've been there. I'm not concerned *how* you screwed up the phone numbers. What concerns me is your blatant disregard for established procedures designed to protect you and your assignment."

She rocketed to her feet. "I did not give Robert Pendergast or anyone else Niki's number. He paid someone off. Period. End of story."

"Which," Gex said, "I might accept, except this . . ." He tapped the print three times, slowly. "A phone number is one thing. But he knew where to find you, Prescott. That blows your assignment."

She collapsed onto the chair. Magma churned in her stomach, burning up her throat. She choked it down. Gex was against her. Rick would be no help. She gave Tiny a look that begged for his intervention.

Tiny pulled a sheet from his folder. "Actually, I see Cluff showing up at Niki's place as a good thing."

Rick gawped. Gex leaned back in his chair, eyebrows raised. Ashley couldn't breathe.

"Screwing up a phone number, sure. Can you imagine in your wildest dreams you would give outsiders your undercover address as your own? I sure can't. What happens if we take this on face value?"

He read from the sheet of paper. "This message is for Ashley Prescott. I apologize for calling at this hour. My name is Malachi Cluff. Your father has a critical issue. It's imperative that he meet you in person. Today—Saturday—if possible. Sunday morning at the absolute latest. He knows you're in D.C. and sent me on his jet to fetch you. We're at the Signature Flight Support section of the Baltimore/Washington International Airport. It's the area for private planes. We'll reimburse you for a limo. Or call me and I'll arrange a town car. At BWI, ask for the Pendergast pilot. It's mandatory you tell no one."

Tiny cleared his throat. "Then comes an eleven second pause where all we hear is the hiss of an open connection before he continues with, 'Sorry. Had to check my notes. He says you'll want proof this is from him: He wishes you a happy thirty-sixth birthday a day early. His nickname for you was Little Spitfire. Your magic word is flounder. Please call and tell me when you expect to arrive. He says you're an early riser. Could you be at the airport by oh seven hundred?' That's it."

Tiny slipped the sheet into the folder. "What does this tell us? None of us knows what Cluff sounds like, but the fact he showed up at Niki's apartment building gives credence that the phone call was his. Rick confirmed a Gulfstream six-fifty registered to Pendergast Holdings arrived at BWI in the early hours of the morning. An hour ago, it was still there. No future flight plans filed."

Tiny ran his finger down the page. "Cluff has inside information. He knew your father's nickname for you and your magic word."

Ashley said, "That's what convinced me it was from Robert. Flounder is Ariel's best friend in *The Little Mermaid*. We used it only once. In first grade, something delayed my mother, and an elderly neighbor picked me up from school. I don't remember her name. Besides, she'd be in her nineties. Otherwise, just me, Mom—who's been dead for a dozen years—and Robert knew."

Tiny said, "And the caller used military time. Cluff is former Navy SEAL."

Rick spoke to the table. "You forgot to add that Cluff works in her daddy's HR department. Even so, why wouldn't Prescott's father call her regular number?"

Ashley's stomach boiled at this digging into her personal life. "Because I never gave it to him. Look, Robert Pendergast is politically connected. He knows half the cabinet on a first name basis. He could have played the sympathy card to get in touch with his estranged daughter, or hired someone's kid as a quid pro quo, or contributed beaucoup bucks to a PAC or favorite charity. Or, he could have bought an agent or two."

She glanced at Rick to see if he was squirming. Nope. "Or, someone who knows about me, this assignment. Maybe another agency wants the Bureau gone and contacts Robert, offers him a proposition: compromise your daughter's undercover assignment, and we'll turn a blind eye on some shady business deal or award you a billion-dollar contract."

"Prescott—" Gex's tone contained a warning.

"Boss," Tiny said, "if I may?" Gex motioned for him to continue. "Are we looking at this the wrong way? Frankly, Ashley's safe word might be more secure than Niki's telephone number. Assume Robert Pendergast *is* behind the call. Why is it mandatory that Ashley tells no one? That's language kidnappers use. Is he in trouble? Should we contact him? If we ultimately decide we must protect Ashley, we can send her away."

Her hands tapped a frustrated beat on the side of her knees—the rhythm to "America" from *West Side Story*—where the hell did that come from?

Oh, right, this is an argument, two sides of the same story. Tiny's points had allowed her to grow hopeful—until that last. *Ease up, kiddo. He's doing his job, being the voice of caution, making sure I stay safe.* She pressed her fingers into her kneecaps and stopped the percussion.

Rick said, "But if it is a kidnapping, calling could endanger Mr. Pendergast,"

"If Robert was in trouble," Ashley said, "he would tell the kidnappers anything other than Flounder to alert me they were coercing him. That was part of what they taught me."

Tiny gave her a reassuring shoulder tap. "I'm not saying *he* was kidnapped. But getting Ashley onto a private plane is one way to capture a billionaire's daughter for ransom."

NINE

Saturday, May 2, Late afternoon EDT

ASHLEY DECIDED THIS HAD GONE on long enough. "Why in God's name would Robert Pendergast or one of his millionaire sons want to kidnap someone who can barely pay off her credit cards each month?" She faced Gex, laid her hands palms up on the table. "Look, sir, let's leave this minor breach for a moment, and let me brief the team about today's encounter. I think you'll agree I must remain on this assignment."

"That's not the operational procedure," Rick muttered under his breath.

Through clenched teeth she said, "There's a time—"

Gex hand-gestured slashing his throat. "Enough, you two. Prescott, let's hear the big news. But we *will* deal with the phone call, the stalking, and our response."

Ashley gave them a detailed report covering the weapons test, the sniper rifle, and weapons purchases from the Chinese arms dealer going by the name of Sam.

Gex drained his coffee, grimaced. "It is good intel, Prescott. Fortunately, you're alive to give it. Luck is not how I run operations. I want to know how you think we should proceed." He held up a hand to stop Rick's interruption. "Then Kaska, if you believe she's wrong, you can tell us why. I'm sure Proulx will remind us if he thinks we're putting the assignment ahead of Prescott's safety."

"Damn the torpedoes," Ashley made a first-down gesture like a successful wide receiver after bringing in an errant pass. "Full steam ahead. We've invested years in this operation. I'm close. They've trusted me to test the merchandise, and I might have qualified to become their sniper."

Rick said, "And ticked off Sergeant Oliver, who thought the job was his."

Ashley waved her hands to indicate "whatever" and plowed on. "This guy Sam is our lead to where the weapons come from. I don't have to tell anyone how important it is we prevent those guns from reaching the militia. That shipment is in-country. There's no time for a redo. And I think they're planning an assassination. Maybe more than one. If I disappear, they may go to ground, and we lose it all." She faced Tiny. "If PFF knew I was an agent, I'd already be dead. I see no safety issue."

She moderated her tone, becoming the voice of reason. "If Sergeant Oliver becomes a problem, we pick him up. Besides the weapons at PFF gatherings, he always carries a pistol in an ankle holster, which violates his parole. Once we've grabbed the Chinese rifles, if we have to, we can round up the part of the PFF that we've identified. That won't shut them down, though. I prefer we continue our work even after we stop the weapons from reaching them. Learn who's in charge. Who they're targeting. There's too much at stake not to proceed."

She held up a finger to show she had more. "I hope Robert Pendergast coughs up his source so we can destroy the motherfucker who endangered this operation. But we should not take our eye from the prize: PFF and those weapons. Done."

Rick rose, like he was making a presentation. Ashley caught the quirk of a smile cross Tiny's face. "Leaving aside family obligations, it's too risky to allow a blown agent into the field. Because of how PFF operates, we haven't been able to implement our normal safeguards. The Bureau develops procedures for a reason, and Agent Prescott has shown she doesn't value them. At all. Until we know the source of the leak, we must pull her from her assignments. For her safety and ours. Let's put out a story that Niki had an accident and had to go away to recuperate. If this has an innocent explanation, she can recover and continue the assignment. Maybe Ashley'll use the down time to catch up on all her overdue reports. Or attend to her family matters. The only prudent course is to plug the hole, not dig a deeper one."

He rotated his piercing look from her to Tiny to Gex, judging whether his argument had swayed Gex. She stared straight ahead, unwilling to show that he had made a reasoned case for following FBI protocols, which were more to protect management's ass than hers. Her fingers again tapped the "America" beat. She let them burn off her nervous energy.

All eyes turned toward Tiny, who waited to speak until Rick sat. "Rick makes a cogent argument. We must be concerned how the phone number assigned to Niki became known to an unauthorized individual. If this assignment didn't involve national security, I would agree with Rick. However, the automatic weapons sale to domestic terrorists is a ticking clock.

"We risk losing everything if we pull Niki. Whatever Cluff wants, it isn't PFF business. We can defer any final decisions until PFF next contacts Niki. That gives us time, and we should use it to learn how and why the breach occurred. Until we do, we should assign her an agent twenty-four/seven."

Ashley agreed to Tiny's compromise before Rick could get in a negative word.

Gex scratched notes on his pad, each stroke jangling her nerves like fingernails on a blackboard. She hated not being able to read him. He capped his pen and set it down, lining it parallel to the tablet. "Here's how we're playing it. Proulx, you're in charge of determining if Mr. Pendergast directed the unauthorized contact and, if he did, how he got the Niki undercover number and address. Kaska, you get your very own little undercover assignment. You're Niki's cousin, arrived in D.C. for a surprise visit. Stay with her at the UC apartment. Don't let her out of your sight."

The Prick waggled his eyebrows.

Ashley's stomach clenched. "Grow the fuck up, Rick."

Gex looked at each of them. "There a problem I should know about?"

"No, sir," they responded in unison. Rick gloated. Ashley resurrected her mental picture of hiking in Glacier.

"If we're trying to assure her safety," Tiny said, "we should keep her here in this safe house."

Gex rose. "I'll have a team on the two of them tomorrow. I want Niki and her cousin doing normal Sunday tourist stuff. Leave at ten-fifteen, walk around the zoo, grab a bite to eat, wander the national mall. Finish with an early dinner out. Keep Niki's phone on. Use it to check restaurant menus, order museum tickets, whatever."

Tiny asked, "You think someone is tracking the phone?"

"Hagen will tell us, but I doubt it," Gex said. "I was emphasizing that they should do what normal people do. Nothing suspicious like checking for tails. Kaska, I want you out of here after you get a burner phone from Hagen and give us all its number. Pack clothes for a week. Proulx, I'll let the Minnesota office know you'll be calling. I want to talk to Robert Pendergast the moment you find him. Prescott, I'm ordering a sketch artist here to work with you on this Chinese guy. Once Hagen finishes with your phones and you're done with the artist, lock up and use standard practices to return to Niki's pad. When you get there, call Kaska's new burner and let him know."

She responded with, "Yes, sir." To Rick, she said, "The doorman will buzz me to meet you."

Rick gathered the trash into a plastic bag. "Very secure. See you soon, Cuz."

"They don't want strangers skulking around the stairways." She felt a flush of enjoyment watching Rick's face glow pink. As she thought, Rick didn't tell Gex *everything* about this morning.

Gex said, "Assuming tomorrow doesn't kick up anything unusual, we reconvene here at nine Monday morning. Prescott, I expect you at oh-eight-thirty with your report in hand. Let's be perfectly clear . . ." His glare burned through her eyes to the back of her skull. "If either Proulx or I aren't one hundred percent convinced your Niki cover is still secure by the next time PFF contacts you, we're closing shop and rolling up all we can of their operation."

And I will do my damnedest not to let you make that huge fucking mistake.

TEN

Saturday, May 2, Early evening EDT

STILL IN HER NIKI MINDSET, she shouldered open the apartment door and carried the takeout *quatro formaggi* pizza to the kitchen counter and laid it on a trivet. She pushed her sleeves up from covering her hands to protect them from the heat and cracked the box top to let it cool. She wafted the aroma toward her nose, triggering her stomach to grumble. *Patience.*

She poured a glass of Chardonnay and carried it and her knapsack to the master bedroom. "Lights on, dim." The technology performed her request. Removing both UC phones from the Faraday bag compartment, she checked them for messages. Nothing on Niki's. Fran, her other undercover assignment, the rich bitch who could afford this apartment, had a scam robocall that offered to "fix her credit"—a hoot since Fran had a credit rating of 845.

Continuing to delay her call to Rick, she gulped a slug of wine and powered on her personal cellphone. To her surprise, it said she had one message. She tapped in the codes and listened.

"Hey, Ash," Liya, her roommate at her actual apartment in Lincolnia, Virginia said in her sing-song voice. "It's going on eighteen-hundred hours. I got home tonight to discover a studmuffin watching our place. Eyes green as shamrocks. Couldn't decide whether to shoot him or bed him. I didn't do either. Gave him the choice of speaking with the police or telling me what he was doing here. He claims he has an urgent message from your asshole father. He didn't know if you had received his voicemail and wanted to deliver it in person. I said I could relay the message. He refused but gave me his number. He let me snap his picture. I'll IM it to you. Even showed me a Minnesota driver's license and a Pendergast Holdings business card with the name Malachi C. Cluff. Let me know the scoop."

They had bonded at the Academy and kept few secrets from each other. Still, Liya's withholding the phone number was her sneaky way of trying to force Ashley to call her. She already had Cluff's number and didn't want to drag her roommate into this mess. Ashley sipped her wine, opened her messenger app, and stared at an image of Cluff that showed his features more clearly than the social media pics or license had.

No surprise Liya had exaggerated: his eyes were more gray-green than shamrock. A scar cut through his left eyebrow. Crinkles pulled at the edges of his mouth. His lips formed a knowing smile seeming to say, "I know you're snapping my picture, and I have no problem with that." A deep cleft slit his chin. No facial hair hid his Minnesota pallor.

Dinner was waiting, she'd better call Rick before he added one more thing to the list of charges he was undoubtably compiling. She used Niki's phone to call her "cousin." He said he'd be there shortly. On a Saturday night, it would take at least a half hour for him to travel from Gaithersburg, Maryland. Plenty of time to decompress from the day and enjoy the pizza and another glass of wine.

The intercom's buzz interrupted her second bite. "A Mr. Richard Kaska is here to see you."

ELEVEN

Saturday, May 2, Early evening EDT

THE ELEVATOR DOORS OPENED, PROVIDING Niki a long-distance view of Rick as he stood in the lobby staring at a picture of the U.S. capital lit up at night. He'd dressed business casual, provided business casual included cowboy boots with two-inch heels. A nylon computer bag hung from his shoulder, and he held a beat-up leather carryall in his left hand. Her movement from the elevator drew his attention. He raised his hand in recognition. A gigantic smile bloomed on his face. *Probably imagining me standing in my all-together.*

He waited until she was close enough to hear. "Niki, it's been a long time." He dropped his bag between his feet and offered his arms for a hug.

That performance drew the doorman's attention, forcing her to embrace Rick to avoid looking suspicious. Enduring the contact, she realized he had shaved and freshened his sandalwood aftershave. One of Rick's hands crept lower on her back. She whispered through the smile plastered on her face, "If you cop a feel, I promise you won't walk for a week."

His hand froze. "I've missed you so much. I'm starved. You?"

"I *was* hungry."

She motioned him toward the elevator and gave him the silent treatment until she had him in the apartment and secured the three locks on the door. He remained in the hallway, like a puppy waiting for a pet. "What the fuck, Rick? You were to wait for my call."

"I thought if I caught you when you got in, we could grab a bite and talk about what happened today and the ramifications."

"If you had called, I could have disabused you of the idea."

He rolled his eyes. "Would you have picked up?"

She brushed past him. "If Gex wanted us doing something tonight, he would have said so."

"We're supposed to act natural, right? If he didn't want us to, he would have told us." Rick made a big show of checking his aviator watch. "Most single people our age are at a restaurant or bar."

She mimed pressing a finger down on a cash register. "Ching! That's a no sale. Dump your stuff in the living room. Let me show you the rest of the place. The kitchen you've seen. There's a pizza growing cold on the kitchen counter. Scrounge anything you can find in the refrigerator but check the use-by dates."

"You're mad?"

She marched down the hall, past the bedrooms on the right and left, and reached the bathroom. "Lights on full." The room burst into sunlight. "Separate bath and shower. Takes a while for the hot water to get up to this floor. Use the squeegee on the tile and glass after you shower." She pulled a matched set of camo-patterned washcloth and towels and shoved them at him. "Questions?"

He led the way to the spare bedroom. "I don't see a bed."

"Very observant. That's Niki's room. If you want it instead of the convertible couch in the living room, I have a mat and sleeping bag you can throw on the floor. Works great for a sore back."

He flicked on the lights in the main bedroom, "I'd prefer—"

"Careful. A sexual harassment charge would not help advance your career."

His grin broadened. "The couch." He gestured into the larger bedroom. "I don't understand how this fits with Niki's cover. It's mucho opulent."

She surveyed the place as he must see it, having known her only through her Niki assignment. Other than Niki's sparse room, the apartment contained furniture far beyond the budget of typical FBI agents, original art on the wall—although he might not know that. Oriental throw rugs covering the carpeting brought color and style into the bedroom. Froufrou window treatments emphasized the highly decorated approach.

"The spare bedroom helps me mentally prepare to become Niki. Everything else is Fran, my other undercover profile. She's over the top, like her decorating. Likes to party with people with more money than scruples. Occasionally needs to entertain. Fran's name is on the lease. Niki sponges from her and tries to make ends meet."

"They have you running another whole undercover operation? That's crazy."

"That would be. With Niki's work on PFF, I can't get sucked into any other long-term assignments. These days, my twin sister, Fran, is a pretty face used by several offices. Someone who can look dumb and listen to conversations in Mandarin or Spanish. Mostly investigating business types. Rarely drugs."

Rick switched off the bedroom light. His face darkening. "You're lucky. Drug cases can be long and dangerous. I nearly." He stopped and swallowed. "Well, I'm still here. Let's get that food."

She left the light to Niki's room on, planning to settle Rick and return to write the day's report. She scrounged sheets, blankets, and pillows from the linen closet and dropped them on the couch. Hearing the refrigerator's dings, she found him staring at the nearly empty shelves.

He closed the door and checked the cupboards.

"You're looking for?"

"Meat. Bacon bits. Something to dress up the cheese." He waved a slice of pizza at her. "I take it you don't cook."

At the smell of the pizza, her mouth watered. Damned if she was going to eat it now after she'd offered it to Rick. "Niki lives on takeout or goes to sports bars. People buy Fran meals. She has no clue how to do anything domestic. If I want a home-cooked meal, I go home to my apartment. This is a work space, Rick. I'm not here a second longer than I must be."

"I'd kill for a place this big."

"Sorry I didn't think to pick up some beer for you. We'll make a stop tomorrow. I'm gonna leave you to it while I write my report. I assume you can make the bed. The stuff's on the sofa."

"Got the merit badge. Didn't see a TV."

"Gold star. There isn't one."

His look suggested she had two heads.

"If I have spare time, I read. Stream whatever you want. Internet password is Fran1234."

"That's not secure."

"Which fits Fran perfectly. Niki uses a VPN.

He opened and closed the last cupboard door. "I don't see any coffee. What's your plan for tomorrow morning?"

She drained her wine. "I do my long runs on Sunday and treat myself to brunch. I guess the run's screwed."

He swallowed. "Huh. This pizza is surprisingly good. How long is long?"

"Supposed to be a fifteen miler."

He looked like he had swallowed cod liver oil. "Get serious."

"A friend suffered a devastating ankle injury and set his rehab goal to run a marathon. I agreed to join him. We're virtual training buddies, do the same workouts. We've still got five months before the Chicago marathon in October."

"Do I know her?"

"*His* name is Seamus McCree."

"The guy who saved your life on your first UC assignment? Well, doesn't matter. I didn't bring running stuff. Sorry. If I'd known."

How the hell did Rick know her first undercover assignment involved Seamus? And why? Not today's problem. She needed her focus to remain on the PFF assignment. Preparing a compelling report for Gex was a good start. "Pile the dishes in the sink. I'll deal with them tomorrow. Good night, Rick.

He looked like a trained puppy whose owner wouldn't play with the knotted rope and commanded the four-legged one to go place.

She closed the door of Niki's room and leaned against it, letting the room center her as she mentally returned to Niki mode. The room looked spartan to others, but it fit Niki like an old pair of jeans. She could quote chapter and verse from the second amendment rights literature overflowing the top two shelves of the concrete block and board bookcase. She rarely sat in the lounger, preferring the straight-backed chair parked in front of a scarred wooden desk she'd rescued from a street in Georgetown, one leg now resting on a folded piece of cardboard to keep it level. Despite what she told Rick, she mostly slept on the floor in this room. Curled into her sleeping bag, a mat for padding, she'd watch the ambient light play on the moon poster she'd taped to the ceiling and fall into a restful sleep.

Shutting down Niki's PFF work would be downright criminal. Unless they could grab the weapons, it might be a career-killer. She admonished herself to keep that thought in mind as she drafted the report. She sat at the desk and booted up the ancient computer—Niki couldn't afford a new one. While it clicked and groaned to life, she smiled at a poster of her favorite place in the world. This early in May, most of Glacier National Park would still be inaccessible—the best time, before the tourists overran it.

She entered her password and lost herself in her work.

A knock interrupted Niki proofreading her report. She checked the time—wow, quarter of nine. "You forget toothpaste?"

"You decent? I have Tiny on the phone."

A cloak of dread pressed her shoulders. "Enter."

Rick padded in wearing socks patterned in meerkats, holding his phone in front of him. She waved him to the lounge chair and yelled, "Tiny, what's up?"

Down the line came the squeal of Tiny's twins, "Daddy. Daddy. Watch this," followed by a crash.

"Give me a sec," Tiny said.

She pointed to Rick's feet. "What's with the socks?"

"World Wildlife Foundation membership gift. My little rebellion."

Cowboy boots and meerkat socks is more than a little rebellion.

Following a half-minute of silence, Tiny said, "Sorry. When you guys have kids, try to avoid twin boys."

Rick gave her a shit-eating grin, like Tiny had meant she and Rick having twins together. She shut her eyes against that thought. "What's going on, Tiny?"

"I've got a bad feeling," Tiny said. "Your fath—sorry, Robert Pendergast has gone missing. I had agents visit his house twice, the last time a half hour ago. No one home. I found another phone number attached to his name, but I got Junior instead."

It usually took her a few minutes to transition from Niki thinking to return to being Ashley. This time it felt instantaneous.

Tiny continued talking. "He told me his father was due in the office today for an important board meeting and didn't show. Junior had checked Robert's house this afternoon. No Robert and one of his cars was missing."

A fist squeezed Ashley's heart. "You found the car?"

"That wasn't where I was going," Tiny said. "Rick and I were strategizing. What if we use you for bait? You call this Malachi Cluff and tell him you'll go to St. Paul tomorrow morning to meet with Robert, but only if you talk to Robert on the phone. Tonight."

She couldn't put a finger on it, but Tiny sounded worried, and Rick was squirming like a four-year-old. The guys weren't telling her everything they knew. "Why didn't you call Cluff and ask him to put you in touch with Robert?"

"Because you have leverage and I don't. Plus, if something untoward is going on, we don't want to tip our hand about the FBI's involvement."

Two good points. Ashley pinned Rick to the wall with her glare. "Okay, Rick. Earlier you were all for pulling the plug. What changed?"

Tiny said, "I told him that you thought *he* was the one who leaked your phone number."

A sting of anger washed over Ashley. Not for suspecting Rick, but for being transparent to Tiny. "I had you at the top of my list," she admitted.

Rick stopped fidgeting. Hands braced on his knees, he leaned forward and spoke to the floor. "That's some of it. But there's other stuff. I called my dad and asked his advice. I don't know if you are aware he retired from the Bureau a while back."

Over the line, Tiny said, "He was a big wig and still has his finger on the pulse of everything."

Rick picked up, "He said Gex is under consideration for heading Quantico, largely because he's avoided all the controversy in the last decade and has a perfect record running undercover operations."

Tiny said, "Hearing that, Gex's reaction made more sense. Let's say he shuts down your operation. Based on your work, we make a bunch of arrests. That success—I know it's limited—but it highlights his familiarity with domestic terrorism, which is everyone's current hot button issue. On the flip side, if he lets this continue and something goes wrong, he likely loses the promotion. He's got to be super risk averse."

"Tiny and I agree," Rick added like a well-rehearsed tag team, "we need answers before you meet with Gex Monday morning. Otherwise, he pulls the plug." He looked up with leaky eyes. "I don't get it. Why would you even think I gave Niki's phone number away?"

Ashley felt her face get warm. "Because you believe the FBI should never have allowed female special agents and my success stands in your way. You're short and have a continent-sized chip on your shoulder and need to prove yourself to daddy. And you'd step on your mother's neck to crawl one rung higher on the bureaucratic ladder."

"Jesus," Rick said. "If you feel that way, why didn't you tell Gex you wanted someone else to watch your six?"

Lashing out at Rick because he was here was cheap theatrics, and Ashley knew it. "I'm sorry, Rick. That was uncalled for. I'm angry at Gex for threatening to kill the assignment, and I'm pissed at Robert for handing Gex the gun to point at my head. Plus, I had a glass of wine on an empty stomach. If anything happens to me, it torpedoes your career. I figured that would motivate you to keep me safe."

Rick shook his head. "Perfect logic built on flawed data."

Tiny said, "You two can mud-wrestle later. The point is, if we can prove you were not at fault for the phone breach and that it doesn't relate to PFF, Gex has no excuses. For that to happen, we need you to talk to your father—to Robert."

Once again Tiny had her back. "Let's try this," she said. "I'll call Cluff and tell him I'm considering going to St. Paul, but first I want to meet him in a public place and ask some questions. At the meet, I'll convince him to let me talk to Robert. If Cluff refuses, we play the FBI trump card and take him in for a more formal chat. Tiny, I know you're paid to worry about my safety. Despite my infantile outburst concerning Rick, I have every confidence that with his support there's no way I'll be the next Patty Hearst. We can use Ike's Diner. Rick can do a walk-through before I arrive. I'll wire up to allow him to hear everything."

Tiny cleared his throat. "I agree a meet works best, but one agent backing you up isn't enough. Problem is, I'm on kids watch until my wife gets home from her hospital shift."

Not waiting for any other objections, Ashley said, "Pick a time."

TWELVE

HEARING THE DOUBLE TAP OF a car's horn, Colonel Pete punched the green button to activate the oversized door in the converted barn at his farm in the Maryland countryside. A black Lexus LC 500 Inspiration coupe purred past the empty horse stalls into the rear section under the hayloft. Doused its lights.

He slapped the red button, halting the door's rise, and slapped it again, causing the door to close. "Uneventful trip?"

She spun to face him, the tails of her leather double-breasted trench coat hurrying to catch up with her hips. "Give me a kiss and your report."

He air-kissed her offered cheek. "Wine? Brandy?"

"Ten minutes, Peter, or my ride poofs into a pumpkin. What's the status?"

"The weapons are new and excellent. I'll need the money before the Saturday delivery. We have a much better shooter than Sergeant Oliver. Corporal Niki kicked his ass from here to Baltimore. You want this done? She's your man, but she needs a spotter."

Her tattooed eyebrows pulled together. "That I can handle, but I heard there was a problem."

She heard? He hadn't said anything. There were only four of them there, and none of the other three seemed a likely source. Maybe she was fishing. "She's a deadeye with that rifle, but she has no place to store it. Assuming it's a go, I can give it to her at the briefing."

She glanced at her watch, shook her head. "That's not the problem I was referring to. I heard you had some dissention in the ranks."

Did Sergeant Oliver have her ear? When the sniper team they had planned to use from another squad had proved unreliable, he had suggested Sergeant Oliver to replace the original shooter. He'd had to brief her on the sergeant's background. So, not him, and surely not Corporal Niki, so it must be the arms dealer. "You heard from Sam?"

"I heard from the person Sam reports to. What I heard is the corporal is a fine shot and your sergeant—I forget his name—damn near pulled his weapon on her when she showed him up. Patriots for Freedom is not some misogynistic Proud Boys wannabe. We need everyone working together for our common cause. My question is, what do you plan to do about it?"

'Nothing' was clearly not an acceptable answer. "I think it related more to him losing than that she is a woman. I'll speak to him. Make sure we're okay. Do we need to get Corporal Niki together with the spotter to make sure they can work together? There's not much time before Friday morning."

"No need. Sam will be her spotter."

"What the hell? Yeah, he's excellent with windage and all that, but can we trust him? What if this goes sideways? Do we lose the arms sale? Maybe we should delay until we can have our own team do this. What's the harm in waiting when this is just the first of many?"

"Because we're well-prepared for this one and money, not Sam's presence, is the key to the arms deal. I'll get you the money, and they'll deliver the rifles. You've worked with this corporal. Can she do it?"

"Until someone pulls the trigger on a living target, you never know."

She fixed him with the stare of a cobra. "Then make sure if it doesn't happen, there are no witnesses."

THIRTEEN

MALACHI PUSHED OPEN THE DOOR to Ike's Diner and met a wall of heat and humidity smelling of grease and coffee and melted cheese. The diner was an homage to 1950s décor: red and white checks and chrome that shone like the place had opened yesterday. He unzipped his jacket, walked past a rumpled old man hunched over a racing form unfolded on the counter, and waited at the register for someone to offer service. Pride of place above the double doors to the kitchen belonged to a signed picture of President Eisenhower and a framed silver certificate one-dollar bill. The waitress pushed through the doors and placed in front of the geezer a steaming slice of apple pie that made Malachi's mouth water.

Malachi said he'd grab a booth if that was okay. It was. Following Ashley's instructions, he chose one near the rear and, overcoming his caveman fears of being surprised, sat with his back to the front door. To keep his hands visible—another Ashley requirement—he entertained himself reading the jukebox selections. Elvis, of course, Fats Domino, Little Richard, Sinatra, Crosby, and a couple of groups he'd never heard of. Learning what The Clovers "Fool, Fool, Fool" sounded like tempted him to waste a quarter, but he didn't want blasting music to compromise his ability to hear what was happening behind him.

The server placed his order, a glass of milk with ice and a steaming piece of apple pie, on his table. "You look tuckered out, sugar. Sure I can't brew a fresh pot of coffee?"

He smiled up at her. "Thanks, but no thanks."

Five minutes past midnight, the whoosh from passing traffic increased. *Door's open.* Malachi swiveled in his seat. The big black guy who had stopped him from following Ashley off the train walked down the aisle, checking each booth he passed. *Figures.* Malachi waited until the guy reached him, said, "Fancy meeting you here."

He received no acknowledgment, watched the man check both restrooms, and leave. *Anytime now.* Malachi forked in the last bite of the pie and washed it down with milk. Moments later, an air current tickled his neck. Ashley Prescott, sporting a brown wig with a comb holding a knot of hair, set her knapsack on the bench seat opposite him and slid in.

Her jeans and tee shirt under an unbuttoned oxford long-sleeved shirt emphasized how slender she was. Judging by her hands and neck, what there was of her was all muscle. Her complexion was clear and natural with no visible makeup. A single gold stud decorated each ear. Hazel eyes regarded him with interest, not hostility.

He said, "I never would have recognized you."

She graced him with a fleeting smile. "That's the idea."

"Thanks for agreeing to meet me. Your father needs you."

She puffed a dismissive breath. "First things first. Why did Robert Pendergast send some dude who works in his HR department, a former Navy SEAL, to fetch me?"

The server arrived to take Ashley's order, giving Malachi time to consider his response. In one sentence she had made sure he understood she didn't think of Robert as her father and that she had done at least some research on Malachi. She ordered an OJ, unbuttered rye toast, and a packet of marmalade.

He held his answer until they were alone. "Besides my HR duties, Robert sometimes uses me as his messenger. He asked me to convince you to fly home, and we're running out of time." He tapped his phone to emphasize the late hour.

"Which says nothing. Why you? Why not call me himself?"

"I gather he thought you wouldn't answer. Why me? I believe I have earned his trust."

"That's delusional. Robert doesn't trust anyone. Before I go with you, I expect to hear from the horse's mouth what is so important he sends his *trusted* messenger to bring me to him. Robert would expect I'd be skeptical. He wouldn't send you here without giving you a way to contact him. Get him on the line."

Malachi turned his hands palms up, hopefully showing his openness. He held her tractor-beam focus to allow her to read his truth. "Happy to. Thing is, he hasn't answered or responded to my numerous attempts to update him on my progress, including this meeting." He pulled up the recent-calls log on his phone, jabbed the icon to dial, placed the phone on the table, and turned on the speaker.

The phone rang six times before Robert's recorded voice asked for a message. At the beep, Ashley said, "Robert, if you want me in St. Paul, call this number—it's Malachi's cellphone—in the next five minutes." She stabbed the connection closed. "Any other numbers?"

He considered trying the emergency number Robert had given him. Thought it was premature for that. "Not this time of night."

"How did you get my number and address?"

"Robert gave them to me. I apologize if I caused you concern this morning or in any way inhibited your work. After you ditched me, I got your home address from Robert's assistant. Did your roommate contact you?"

"Where did *Robert* get his information?"

"I didn't ask."

She grabbed his phone, scrolled through his recent call log. Deleted the calls he'd made to her and labeled the number she had called him from with Ashley Prescott.

"He gave me your operational cell number? I'm sorry."

Her jaw tightened, and she crossed her arms. "If you're so trusted, he must have told you what he wants. Is he dying? Needs a kidney? Bone marrow?"

Whatever had caused the rift between father and daughter, Robert had done himself no favors by insisting Malachi contact her the way he had. "From the moment of our birth, we are all dying. I don't believe his health had anything to do with it."

"Then why?"

Malachi rotated the empty milk glass on the paper placemat advertising local businesses. "I do not know, and he would not want me to speculate. I don't believe he would have taken this extraordinary step unless he believed it was vital."

Her eye-roll said this was not working. He had to find a different approach but had no idea what it might be. "I know—"

She made a T with her hands. "Here's where we are. By calling me and following me, you jeopardized an undercover operation related to United States security. Ironic, isn't it? You, a man who once swore to defend the Constitution against all enemies, foreign and domestic, who earned the bloody Navy Cross while a SEAL, undermines our national security at the crook of a profiteering billionaire's finger. He wants me to drop everything I've worked for and won't give me a reason? That's a load of crap."

She slammed her empty glass on the tabletop. "I'm not surprised at Robert. That's like blaming ice for being cold. His actions force me to find out whether my colleagues and I are at risk. The only way I can do that is to learn how and from whom he got my information. He tells me that, and, provided you can get me back here Sunday night—that's tonight now—I'll fly with you to St. Paul."

Malachi raised his hands in submission. He had not prepared for the depth of her anger or her pain at whatever had driven a wedge between her and her father. And he had no answers for her. Was this enough of an emergency to justify calling the other number? Yes, if Robert wants to see her today.

She leaned in, lowered her voice. "Sorry. I'm guilty of killing the messenger. You've got my number. If he calls—We've got company. Yours?" Without raising her hand from the table, she pointed behind him.

Malachi turned and felt a ripple of apprehension. He'd concentrated solely on Ashley and hadn't heard the three strapping men enter the diner. Bandannas covered their mouths and noses, do-rags on their heads. One remained in the doorway; the other two waddled down the aisle in drooping pants revealing more underwear than he cared to see.

FOURTEEN

Sunday, May 3, Very early morning EDT

SEEING THE THREE GUYS ENTER the diner, Ashley's first thought was maybe Rick had been right, and this was a setup to snatch her. She slipped her P226 from her knapsack, kept it below the table, and spoke to her chest. "Three bangers from *Mississippi* intent on kidnap or robbery. One at the entry. Two coming toward us."

It could take up to a minute for Tiny and Rick to respond to her use of the word Mississippi to signal she was in imminent danger. She might not have sixty seconds. As Malachi turned to look at the three bogies, she assessed shooting angles.

The rumpled old man and waitress stayed frozen behind the men moving up the aisle. Three more steps and the angle would change enough to render them away from the line of fire, and she could risk showing her weapon.

One. Two. In a single motion, she rose and raised the pistol. "FBI. Special Agent Prescott."

In a move so fast she hardly saw it, Cluff grabbed her pistol and wrist and knocked the gun loose. It clattered on the table and fell to the floor. Cluff released her.

Ashley grabbed a knife from the place setting and hid it behind her. Four to one. No guns visible. Forty-eight seconds, max, until help arrived.

The first guy crashed into Malachi, pushing him onto the bench seat. An elbow to his ribs propelled Malachi toward the window. "Chill," the banger said. "Don't be collateral damage."

Her mind raced. Street thugs don't say *collateral damage*. Or speak more like Princeton than ghetto. Or dress in clothes new enough she might find a price tag. White-collar kidnapping.

The second guy brought a Taser from his pocket. "Ashley Pendergast Prescott, you can come with us easy or come hard. Either way, you're coming."

A setup. Fuck. Teeth aching, Ashley forced her jaw to unclench.

Breathe. Taser guy watched her with hawk eyes. The guy pinning Malachi into the booth was also watching her. Malachi looked like a coiled spring ready to explode. Guy three was shooing the old pie-eater, server, and cook out the door.

Stall. "What do you want?" She tilted her head like she was interested in their answer, getting a better view of the front so she could watch for Rick and Tiny to take care of the third guy.

"You, alive to collect our finder's fee. But lady, it doesn't matter what shape you're in. Daddy just has to recognize you. Slide out nice and easy, and no one gets hurt."

She concentrated on the Taser and noted his knuckles, white from gripping it. He edged away, allowing her room to stand.

Come on Tiny. "You can't seriously think I'm worth a finder's fee." *Stupid thing to say.*

"Lady, three million bucks serious enough for you? Now get moving, or you'll be on the ground shaking like a sack of Mexican jumping beans, and I'll drag you by your hair."

She flashed to her training. Both Taser probes had to engage for the current to flow and take her down. Her clothes were too thin to stop them. He'd nail her before she could grab her knapsack and block him. If she got close enough, one probe might not connect, giving her a chance to disable him. Slim odds. "Whoa." She stretched the word to three syllables. "That's serious bread. Okay, okay. I'm getting up."

She rose, keeping the knife hidden at her side. The guy at the door was more interested in what was going on with her than in guarding the entrance. What were Tiny and Rick waiting for? They should have no problem securing one man, leaving her in a straightforward hostage situation.

The first guy spoke in a soft voice to Malachi. "Easy, dude. Sit still and nothing bad happens. Don't want to hurt you. This is a plain vanilla snatch for bread. Daddy sends the money, and everybody goes home safe. You'll tell him that, right?"

Meaning they knew Malachi. So did she, which meant once they got their money, her life was forfeit. No Tiny. No sirens. No flashing lights. Something had gone wrong.

Mumbling, "Sorry, I'm a little dizzy," she wavered in place and visualized her move. She swung into the aisle, shifting the knife hand to remain hidden. The first guy's eyes widened. *Shit, he saw it.* Before he could give warning, she executed a quick half-step, pivoted, and drove the point of her right elbow into his head. The blow drove him into Malachi. Spinning, she flung the blade at Taser Man.

The Taser fired with a sharp crack followed by static. Its wires sailed past her, snaring the booth's padding. Stopping her spin, she grabbed Malachi's milk glass.

Her attacker lunged, and she rifled the glass into his mouth. His momentum knocked her down, his weight expelling the air from her lungs. Blood and mucus blinded her. She pushed him up to slide from underneath him, but he countered, pinning her neck with a forearm. A thunderous blow to her ribs generated a lightning bolt of pain.

She collapsed to the floor, felt its support, and exploded her hands into his body. Her blow lifted him off her, but her brief relief changed to agony when he dropped heavily onto her bruised ribs.

She jerked a knee up to nail his balls. He deflected the strike with his hip. The force of her knee and his movement loosened his forearm grip on her neck. She ducked her head, protecting her exposed larynx. Pressing one hand against his head, she scraped her other hand's fingers across the floor, praying she'd find the gun, a utensil, the milk glass.

He used his body as a battering ram, crushing her into the floor with each blow.

Niki made a fist, leaving the first and second fingers extended and stiff, and stabbed at his eyes. He ducked and took the blow on his nose.

She raked fingernails across his face and tried again to stab him with her fingers.

A single shot rang out. No voice commands. *Not my team.*

Black painted in the corners of her vision. On the verge of passing out, she arched her back, using the space to collapse and rotate away from the center of his weight. She grabbed his head with both hands and followed the curve of his cheekbone toward his eye. His wrist ground into her neck. He reared back.

Head butt coming.

Thumbs rigid, she raised her hands to cover her forehead and nose. The blow's force bent one thumb back, bringing with it the pain she remembered from dislocating it playing softball. Her other thumb met a pickled onion.

His squeal deafened her.

A second shot rang out.

The dead weight of her attacker collapsed on top of her.

She pushed him off and rose to her knees, wiping blood from her eyes. She struggled to piece together what she was seeing. Her assailant's face covered in blood. One eye missing. His nose bent to one side. Gray brain and white bone showing where hair should be.

The stench of urine filled her nostrils.

Lying beyond him was a second banger and beyond that, Malachi pointed her own gun at her.

He needs me alive to get the money. She knelt next to the guy she had elbowed to check his vitals.

"Dead," Malachi said. "Your elbow nailed the pterion and shattered his skull."

Staring at the man's eyes rolled up into his misshapen head, she spewed sour orange juice on the first person she had ever killed.

"Here." Malachi laid her gun on the table and offered her a napkin. "We need to call the police."

The ringing in her ears resolved into the distant warble of sirens. She grabbed the weapon. "Where's the third guy?"

"I sent a round in his direction, and he split." He handed Niki her knapsack and stepped forward. "Let's get outside so the cops don't accidentally shoot us. Coming?"

Like a terrier that had slipped its lead, her thoughts twisted and spun, not waiting for analysis. Secure the scene. This would piss off Gex. Take Malachi into custody. Where are Tiny and Rick? Guard against number three returning. Did she have rounds in the weapon? The transmitter had failed. No. Rick and Tiny would have interrupted the meet if they'd lost audio. Millions, the would-be kidnapper said.

Damnation. She raced down the aisle, grabbed Malachi's collar. "Not that way. The back exit."

She switched P226 magazines and checked for a chambered round. On the way, she grabbed a napkin and scraped the inside of her mouth. Better. "Wait inside until I make sure it's safe." She pushed open the emergency exit, triggering a shrill alarm.

She scanned the area. No one on the side street. Tiny's minivan parked halfway down the block across the street, driver's door open. Tiny sprawled face up on the pavement. Rick slumped in the passenger seat, head leaning through the open window.

Given the ululations of the approaching sirens, three, maybe four cars, would soon arrive. She reached past Malachi, who had followed her, and yanked the door closed. "Sit on that stoop and don't move. If the police get here before I return, lie face down, spread eagle, and tell them you're doing what Special Agent Prescott ordered. Those are my friends." She motioned toward the minivan. "You do something else and someone likely shoots you: the third gunman, or the cops, or me. Got it?"

He slumped to the ground and rested against the door.

She zig-zagged to Tiny. His weapon lay next to his outstretched hand. She tossed it onto the car seat. Avoiding the slowly spreading pool of blood around his head, she checked his pulse and breathing. Steady. With a head wound, she didn't dare move him.

She scuttled around the van, keeping low, and wrenched open the passenger door, catching Rick's deadweight before it hit the pavement. A blow dart protruded from his neck. *Stop the poison.* She yanked it out and tucked the evidence into his shirt pocket. A dot of blood marked its spot. His shallow breathing worried her. She checked his pulse. Strong. *Good sign.* For his safety, she hauled him onto the parkway, placed him on his side, then removed his weapon from its holster and tossed it into the foot well of the car.

She dialed 9-1-1, gave her credentials and announced two officers down near Ike's Diner, gave the address, told the dispatcher she heard sirens approaching. Seeing the first patrol car a block away, she ignored instructions to stay on the line and stuffed her phone and pistol in her backpack. She palmed her FBI badge holder and ran into the street. Dropping her pack to her feet, she raised her arms in a V, displaying her badge and ID card.

The cruiser screeched to a halt, positioned to shield the officer who ducked out.

She yelled, "I'm FBI. Two special agents are down. I called nine-one-one for ambulances. Understand?"

"Keep your hands where I can see them."

She remained in place, listened to him communicate with dispatch. A second car pulled up, rotated its spotlight, and blinded her. She lowered her gaze and kept her arms raised. "Officers," she yelled. "I have two colleagues requiring assistance. Their weapons are in the van. I've secured mine in my backpack. We have two dead inside Ike's. Third perp escaped. I have a wit sitting by the diner's rear exit. Secure the scene around the minivan. I'm gonna talk to the witness."

Two more patrol cars arrived including a sergeant who took charge. Using standard procedures, the cops determined she was who she said she was. "Malachi," she yelled. "Go prone, we're coming to you."

What a clusterfuck. Tiny and Rick injured. She had handed Gex a twenty-four-carat-gold excuse to end her PFF assignment. They'd stick her on a desk until they cleared her of the killings. Gex would keep his perfect record and take charge at Quantico. She'd be damaged goods, and it was Robert Pendergast's goddamn fault.

Maybe.

Or maybe it was Malachi Cluff's fault.

FIFTEEN

MALACHI FOLLOWED ASHLEY'S ORDER TO lean against the diner's door, which might provide a little protection from the third gunman. From his seated position, he hawked the area, prepared to yell to her if he saw anything. *Thank you for protecting me, Lord. I hope you continue to find me worthy.*

Given the deaths, it was now inconceivable that Ashley could get to St. Paul and meet Robert this morning. Using his cellphone, he dialed the number Robert had sworn him to use only in a one-hundred-percent-absolutely-no-doubt emergency. He regretted not having called it earlier.

The phone buzzed and buzzed, never tripping to voicemail. Only two things could explain Robert's silence: he couldn't answer, or he was unwilling. Unwilling meant he had sent Malachi to bring Ashley to St. Paul for reasons other than those given. The apple pie changed in his stomach to magma, bringing heat and pain.

Malachi replayed his meeting with Robert and came up with no clue and justification to believe that scenario. That meant something bad had happened to Robert, and Malachi was useless, sitting a thousand miles away.

The keen edge of tension in Ashley's voice called him to the present. She and a cop were striding toward him. She'd killed a man and, like him, was in shock. Plus, her comrades were down. Malachi had witnessed seasoned soldiers lose their heads after a land mine blew up best friends. No telling how stable she was.

The cop's hand rested on his gun.

Standing, careful to keep his hands visible and make no sudden moves, he considered asking the police officer for protection from her. Then his head cleared, and he remembered an O-3 shouting at him during training, "Are you a quitter, Cluff?" Not then. Not now.

With a steel grip on his bicep, Ashley steered him to the nearby drugstore. He approved of her tactics: distancing themselves for a private conversation, placing herself where she could watch the minivan while protecting her back.

"Why did you knock the gun from my hand? Everyone might be alive if you hadn't done that."

Settle her down. "Or there could be more dead. Including us. The waitress and the old man were in your line of fire. You couldn't shoot. The guy stationed at the door had an angle on us. I reacted to what I saw."

Her eyes slitted into a hard cop stare. She said nothing.

He pressed on. "I probably saved our lives. You should thank me."

She jabbed his chest with an iron finger. "They knew you."

He had killed the man. Caused his brains to splatter. Broken the sixth commandment. "Do you think I would—" His throat tightened, and he couldn't breathe through his anger. She cocked her head. He croaked, "kill that man if I had been part of it?"

She snorted. "Rats do anything to save themselves. How the hell did they know I'd be there? They sure as shit didn't follow me."

When *he* had tried following her, she had spotted him and ditched him like last week's garbage. His fiery anger vanished in the ice water of her accusation. "They followed me? No one knew I was meeting you." But that wasn't true. "Son of a monkey! I left a message on Robert's phone. Do you think—" He stopped, unsure of anything.

"Robert would kidnap me because I wouldn't talk to him? Bullshit." She gestured at the diner, nearly smacking his face, "That was a snatch for ransom. The guy ordered you to tell your boss. Is that why you executed him?"

The vehemence of her words knocked Malachi onto his heels. Through gritted teeth he said, "I don't know who they were. I swear. You didn't hear me yelling at you two to stop or I'd shoot. He was a former Navy SEAL and was going to kill you." He stopped to grab air. "And, the Lord forgive me, I could not let that happen."

She seemed to grow in front of him, hands now on her hips. "SEAL. You *knew* him?"

"Maybe. I don't know. Their faces were covered, remember?" Malachi pointed to the back of his neck. "He had a bone-frog tattoo. That's SEALs."

Two ambulances came screaming up and stopped behind the cop cars, blocking the street. Lights still flashing, their sirens died with a final whoop.

"Stay here." She jogged toward the EMTs.

Sixteen

Sunday, May 3, Very early morning EDT

ASHLEY TOLD THE EMTS LOADING Rick into the first ambulance that she had tucked a dart into his shirt pocket. They were to inform the docs in hopes they could identify the drug. She helped close the back door, gave the ambulance a stay-safe pat, and stood back as the vehicle roared away. *One hundred percent recovery, Rick. Nothing less is acceptable.*

Outside the second ambulance, she found Tiny sitting on the gurney, declaring he was fine. One EMT supported him while another held a compress to his head.

"Don't listen to him," she said. "They may have darted him, too. He has a history of concussions and requires observation. What happened, Tiny?"

"Don't know. Transmission was fine. We heard you and Cluff. Next thing, I got EMTs crawling up my ass."

"You were leaving your car. You pulled your weapon."

He closed his eyes. "Sorry. Nothing."

"We'll talk after they make sure you're okay." She gave the iron muscles of his shoulder a playful punch.

He grabbed her hand, pulled her in close and whispered, "Get to the bottom of this, Prescott. Rick has his father's friends to protect him. You and me? We're screwed."

Tiny's words made Niki's heart ache. Not only had she torpedoed her career, she'd taken Tiny down with her. Unfair, but in the FBI, tar spattered anything near its brush. Robert had kicked over the tar bucket, but someone had filled the damn thing by leaking her information to him. She would unmask and draw and quarter the bastard even if she had to waterboard Robert.

"You know I won't rest." She gave Tiny a fist bump and marched to Malachi. He was pacing in front of the red neon "Closed" sign of the drugstore, his face and the plate glass oscillating between blue and red. The guy was a cipher. She didn't trust him, but he was her best chance to reach

Robert. That would require—she stopped mid-stride. *Oh crap.* Tiny and Rick had been recording her. She ripped off the shirt button transmitter and pitched a strike through a culvert grate ten yards away.

Reaching Malachi, she said, "Soon as they finish securing the scene, they'll haul us to a precinct to take our statements. Probably fingerprint you. They may arrest you or hold you as a witness, and they'll tie me up for days. Whatever the hell Robert wanted from me can't happen. Or . . ." She paused, waiting for his eyes to meet hers. "Or we leave now, and you take me to Robert."

"Legally—"

"You should stay. Regardless what you decide, I'm leaving. I need to see Robert to learn why this happened. If you're stupid and go with me, I'll back you up when the time comes and you tell them I forced you to leave."

"Robert's not answering his emergency phone. Something's happened to him."

That wasn't exactly turning her down. "You want to find him, right? Any reason to think he's in D.C? Of course not. Where's your car?"

He exhibited all the signs of a man with a quandary, eyes darting right and left, shifting weight from one foot to the other. He opened his mouth as though he would respond but didn't. Then he licked his lips and rubbed his hands together. "There." He pointed to a blue Camry.

She waited for him to take the first step before saying, "We do this, there's no unringing the bell."

SEVENTEEN

Sunday, May 3, Very early morning EDT

ASHLEY SLID INTO THE PASSENGER seat, cradled her knapsack with her hand on the P226. "Drive across the river into Virginia." She positioned the side mirror to allow her to see cars behind them and dialed Gex's cell, praying he had the thing on at—she checked the dash clock—12:29 on a Sunday morning.

"Gex," a sleepy voice croaked.

"Listen, don't talk," she commanded. "Tiny and Rick were doing backup for a meet at Ike's Diner for me with Malachi Cluff, the guy who left the message on Niki's phone. Three guys attempted to kidnap me. Two are dead. One's to the wind. Tiny has a concussion, and a blow gun dart put Rick down. They're both on their way to the hospital. Metro cops have the scene. I have Cluff."

"Prescott! What the—"

"I'll get you a full report, but I'm taking my accumulated vacation starting now." She severed the connection. If she didn't hear Gex give her an order, that was one less order she hadn't followed. To Malachi she said, "Don't talk while I think."

She needed to eliminate anyone's ability to track Malachi. It might take time, but that she could do. She also had to avoid Gex and all the FBI resources he would send after her once he realized she had left the crime scene with the witness. That meant going dark, which meant no phone and no credit cards. She consulted her phone app and directed Malachi to a nearby bank, where she withdrew her daily cash limit. A blue van with Virginia plates cruised by. The same vehicle she'd seen behind them earlier?

Next, she had Malachi drive to a twenty-four-hour Walmart. Their turn into the parking lot gave her a chance to check for that van. Not there. "Thank you for being quiet. I'm giving you my credit card to buy yourself a complete set of new clothes. Shirt, pants, socks, shoes, undies. The works."

"Because?"

"Either someone told those three guys where we'd be, or they followed you. They can make miniature trackers these days."

"In my clothes?"

"Button, heel of your shoe. Anywhere. I can't go in with blood-spattered clothes. Buy me a tee shirt and some sweatpants." She handed him a credit card. "Use the self-checkout."

He returned with a D.C. United tee and gray sweatpants for her. He looked away while she peeled off her clothes and donned the new apparel. The sweatpants fit her waist but were long enough for a giraffe. She rolled up the legs. "I'm going in for some quick shopping. While I'm gone, change your clothes."

She completed a whirlwind buying spree that included a bra, a blond wig with ringlets that would make Dolly Parton jealous, a variety of makeup products, a massive backpack, and a cheap burner phone. A little of her worry disappeared when she saw Malachi standing next to the car, holding his old clothes away from him as if they might catch fire.

"My knapsack is a Faraday cage that prevents our electronics from ratting us out." She sealed their cellphones and wallets in it and closed the flaps, eliminating any electronic leakage. She stored the knapsack in the backpack she had just bought. "We passed a strip mall. Should be a dumpster behind those buildings."

They found a covered trash bin. Seeing no one, she hopped out, her muscles cramped with the sudden activity, and she banged into the bin. *There goes quiet.* It pained her fiscal frugality to part with the GPS tracker embedded in her bra, but the chance of accidentally exposing it any time she retrieved their phones or wallets wasn't worth the risk. She screeched the lid open, making enough noise to wake any sleeping night watchman, held her breath against the stench of food-court waste, and dumped in their old apparel. Even easing the top down, it still screeched.

She got in and Malachi said, "At least your new eau de dumpster covers the smell of blood." He drove around the end of the shopping center, heading toward the road.

"Stop." She pointed to a blue van parked in the shadows at the side of a gas station across the way. "We have company."

With their clothes gone and phones no longer transmitting, either Malachi's rental sported an attached tracker, or their tail now must rely on visual contact. Time for a little old-fashioned evasive action.

"We're gonna shake them," she said. "Let's switch drivers. It'll be easier for me to do it than to tell you what to do."

"Can't do that," he said. "I'm the only driver on the rental agreement."

One look at his face convinced her he was dead serious. What was he, a fucking Boy Scout? "You'll have to break traffic laws to ditch that guy."

"That I can do."

EIGHTEEN

Sunday, May 3, Very early morning EDT

"GOOD JOB." ASHLEY GAVE THE van the finger as it roared past their spot tucked in a dark alley behind a quick-lube operation. "Where did you learn to drive like that?"

"In high school, a bunch of us snuck into the country to drag race."

She laughed at his grin. "I'll bet you did. Do you have a company credit card?"

"Yes. Why?"

"We'll wait five minutes to make sure we don't see them again and drive to a Zipcar location I know."

"Zipcar? Why not head to the plane?"

"Were you a Boy Scout?"

Malachi narrowed his eyes, smile gone. "Yeah. Eagle. Why?"

"They don't give merit badges for undercover survival. Trustworthy is a joke and morally straight is ambiguous. Anyone following you likely knows where the Pendergast plane is waiting. They lose you, they head to BWI. Plus, once the FBI starts looking for us, they'll station someone there, too. They'll access your rental agreement and get your license plate number. Highway scanners are everywhere these days."

"I can't do that. The contract requires me to return this car to the airport."

The whoosh of tires alerted them to a vehicle cruising past the alley, and they both ducked. "SUV," Ashley said. "Not them." She pulled on her new Dolly Parton wig and received a quizzical look from Malachi. "Robert won't quibble over a few hundred bucks if that's what it takes for you to get me to St. Paul. He'll claim the expense for a tax write-off. Besides, at the Zipcar place, we'll leave keys in the rental and the motor running."

"You want someone to steal it? We can't—"

"This costs you and Robert nothing. Your policy covers theft. Somebody'll take it on a joy ride, and if the FBI tracks that license plate—"

"You thought of this off the top of your head?" Malachi offered her a tentative smile, like he still wasn't sure. "That's scary. What are we doing with the Zipcar?"

"Call the crew on the burner phone and have them bring the jet to the Shenandoah Valley Regional Airport near Staunton, Virginia."

"Can't the FBI get the flight plan?"

"With a court order. Look Malachi, if we were SEALs in Afghanistan or wherever you deployed, I wouldn't tell you how to run your operation. This is what I do. To figure out who sent those kidnappers, I need you to tell me *everything* you know. We have miles to go before we sleep. And you have secrets *you may not keep*. Drive."

Sunday, May 3, Early morning EDT

MALACHI FELT VAGUELY GUILTY DRIVING the Volkswagen Golf because Ashley's Zipcar location didn't allow Flex fares, only round trips. When he had signed the airport rental contract, he had every intention of returning the car to the original location. This was different. Ashley justified taking the Zipcar because the contract contained penalties for breaking it, and a lawyer could say that implicitly provided terms for a one-way rental. That kind of thinking greased the road to hell.

While Malachi drove, Ashley focused on the side-view mirror, twice making him exit the highway and immediately re-enter. Those interruptions were a relief from reliving the fight in the diner. Once they reached I-66, she shifted her focus to him, leaning across to check the speedometer.

"Pro tip. People who feel guilty drive at or below the speed limit because they don't want the police to stop them. That behavior draws cops' attention."

"Just because I've already broken the law several times tonight doesn't mean I should continue."

She gave him an appraising look. "When did you last see Robert?"

"Friday evening in his office when he asked me to bring you to him."

"What exactly did he say?"

"We talked for more than an hour. The Pendergast plane was returning to St. Paul late that evening. I was to fly with it to D.C., pick you up. We discussed details, like your address and phone number and your safe word and nickname. I wasn't to contact you until the plane landed. We spent the rest of the time with me arguing he should call you, and him emphasizing your independent streak."

She worried the details into submission. Asked questions multiple ways. Got him to say "yes" to a series of softball questions and hit him with an open-ended one. All techniques the SEALS had taught him to employ. And to resist.

She seemed to switch gears and said, "You've had hours to consider this. Tell me your best guess why he wanted me."

He signaled a lane change and pulled around a pickup truck piled high with bedframes and mattresses, tooted his horn as the truck edged closer to the lane dividing line, waited until he could see both the truck's headlights in his rearview mirror before resuming travel in the right lane. "I don't have one." *At least no* best *guess.*

"What's your plan once we get there?"

"We'll arrive early morning and drive to Robert's house. If he's not there, we'll check his home office to see if he left me a note or new instructions. If not, try—"

"Wait, does he still have a housekeeper? Maybe she knows—"

"She won't. She spends most of Friday and Saturday visiting her parents in Buffalo. Returns in time to cook Robert's Sunday brunch." At her look of obvious confusion, he added, "Buffalo, Minnesota. An hour west. The other place to check is Pendergast Holdings. Maybe he left instructions in my office."

"You don't sound hopeful."

The molten lead burning in his stomach was a testament to that. Either something had happened to Robert or Malachi was an unknowing pawn in a Machiavellian scheme. "I can't think of any good reason Robert wouldn't respond to my messages."

"Bad reasons?"

"Plenty. Since you've confiscated my phone, once we're in the air, I'll try Robert using the sat phone. I'll also engage bodyguards to protect you against another kidnapping. We use an excellent—"

She strained against the seat belt, waved a finger at him. "You actually think I'd let a suspect surround me with a bunch of armed people I don't know? Jesus, Malachi, you sure you were a SEAL? Flying in your plane is a risk I'm willing to take. I'm armed. You're not. Pilots don't enjoy getting shot. I'll call Robert with the sat phone. No reason to allow you to call someone else and use some secret code words."

He choked down his indignation. Waited until he was sure his tone would sound neutral. "You still think I'm involved?"

"If I did, you'd be in a D.C. jail. That doesn't mean I shouldn't be cautious. I still can't understand why someone would kidnap me."

"Ten million dollars."

"Robert would never pay it."

"Pendergast Holdings has a policy that covers that much for any family member." He glanced her way.

She sat slumped in the seat, looking up at the cloth headliner. "Hell, if my friends knew that, *they'd* be tempted. It still doesn't tell us why me and why now."

Nineteen

TUCKING THE ZIPCAR'S KEYS UNDER the floormat, Malachi suffered another spasm of guilt. He vowed to notify the Zipcar company of his violation of the contract. She followed him onto the plane. Given how Ashley carried her backpack in front of her, he assumed she was holding her pistol. The crew met them at the door, and he made the introductions. Ashley was polite enough but didn't offer to shake hands.

Lauren Brock, Malachi's favorite hostess, led them into the cabin scented by recently sprayed air freshener. "Do you want me to make up beds?"

Ashley shook her head. "I have to write a report."

Lauren ushered them past a sitting area with couches on both sides to the middle section of the plane. "We have a wireless printer, and here," she pressed down on the top of the credenza, "is a twenty-four-inch HD monitor. And—"

"I didn't bring my laptop. Can I steal a few sheets of paper?"

"I'll lend you mine. Malachi, you want me to convert the aft stateroom to a berth?"

"Thank you, yes."

Ashley said, "I'd like to see the rest."

Lauren gave her the tour, Ashley acting like a star-struck tourist, not fooling Malachi. She was expertly determining no one was hiding in the bathroom or luggage area.

"Before I make up Malachi's berth, is there anything I can get you prior to take off?"

A brief smile crossed Ashley's face. "Normally, I'd have three or four stiff drinks. But I have a report to write."

Malachi led Ashley to the work area and dropped into a seat. Ashley's pacing reminded him of the cheetah he'd seen at the zoo. "This plane's extremely safe."

"We're flying over the Great Lakes, right?"

"Yeah? And?"

She rolled her neck, producing a crack that made him wince. "What's your biggest fear, Malachi. The absolute worst."

"That I'll go to hell."

She looked at him like he had spoken Swahili.

"I know it's not fashionable. My parents brought me up in The Church of Jesus Christ of Latter-Day Saints. I knew as a toddler that the possibility of hell existed. My parents never hung it over my head with a 'If you're not a good boy you'll go to hell until you repent.' It was deeper than that. If I didn't live a life obedient to the teachings, God would consign me there until my spirit understood and accepted His will."

He raised his voice to project above the jet's engines as the pilots completed their preflight checks. "I've rejected many of The Church's teachings, but that fear remains. And because a thousand years is a long time to suffer, it's a bigger concern than anything that can happen to me on earth."

Lauren arrived from the rear. "You're all set, Malachi. But first, please, both of you buckle up for takeoff."

Ashley pulled the strap tight across her legs. The engines roared and, with a jerk of released brakes, they gained speed, roaring down the runway. She transformed before his eyes, leaning to look out the window, a smile plastering her lips.

Once they were in the air, he said, "You don't look like someone who doesn't like to fly."

"Oh, I love speed. My irrational fear is crashing into water. I was four or five. The TV carried a story of a plane that went down, and everyone drowned. In Montana, water is good for watering livestock or hunting ducks. We figure if we're supposed to be in the stuff, we'd have webbed feet or gills or something. I love seeing it, but I never learned to swim. I'm scared stupid of drowning."

"The FBI lets you in if you can't swim? That's unbelievable."

"I suspect it's required if you want SWAT. They make us jump off a high board and float for like forever. I became proficient enough jumping that I could smack the water with my forearms and keep the top of my head dry, and I broke the world's record for treading water without sticking your face into it."

Malachi would have paid to see that. "You're an athlete, you can learn to swim."

"And you're a smart man. You know that leaving rental cars where they're not supposed to be has nothing to do with the morality that determines heaven and hell."

He had no words to explain his fear of God, and Lauren arriving with a laptop and sat phone saved him from lecturing her on overcoming fear. "You're okay with me leaving you and catching some Zs?"

"Please."

He shut the pocket door behind him, silencing Lauren's instructions concerning her laptop. He kicked off his shoes, extinguished the light, and dropped onto the bed. Not bothering to crawl under the covers, he closed his eyes and willed himself to breathe deeply.

The Grim Reaper, sickle in hand, walked beside him. Ike's Diner shimmered in torchlight. Malachi dragged his heels, but the Reaper's burning grip on his elbow propelled him forward. Malachi struggled to surface from the dream. Now he peered through the glass in the door and saw red light flickering from dozens of fires, painting the diner's interior. His nose pinched to block the sulfurous mist curling under the door.

The Grim Reaper pushed Malachi inside. "Thank you for the work you are about to do." Burning rose in Malachi's throat, choking off oxygen. "Only a thousand years," the Reaper whispered. "Or two."

Malachi's eyes flew open. Heart racing, he sucked in air and blinked away the nightmare. Sleep could wait.

Twenty

Sunday, May 3, Morning CDT

ASHLEY WAS ON FULL ALERT once they landed at the Minneapolis-St. Paul International Airport. She made Malachi perform a series of maneuvers to check for tails on the drive from the parking lot to Robert's house. The light Sunday morning traffic made it easy for the surveillance detection routine to verify no one followed them. She had him drive by the front of the house—no visible lights or other signs of activity—before pulling into the narrow alley that ran behind the houses and provided access to driveways and garages.

Malachi maneuvered his gray Ram 1500 onto the poured concrete slab, pulled far right, and parked facing the original one-car garage, now used for storage. Ashley ran her tongue across her teeth, washing away the syrup film left from the sausage and egg breakfast Lauren had cooked for them on the Pendergast jet. She pushed open the door, saw below her a bed of hostas. "Think you could have given me a little more room?"

"Sorry. I was trying to not block the garage and still leave enough space for Tabitha—Tabitha Maki, the housekeeper?"

While Ashley contorted her way past the hostas without crushing them, Malachi peeked in the two-car garage windows. "The Benz is here, but the Porsche is missing. I was hoping . . ."

She was more than hoping; she was expecting Robert to be waiting at his house. After she had finished her report to Gex, she spent the flight reflecting on recent events. Her conclusion had been that Robert had played her by not answering his phone. Now, she wondered if it was Malachi that had played her. Was this a reprise of the diner where SEALS waited to kidnap her? She drew her pistol and held it at the side of her leg.

Malachi held the wrought-iron gate open for her. Not wanting anyone behind her, she motioned him to proceed and stared at the fieldstone prison Robert called a home until Malachi began moving along the path across the garden that led to the solarium attached to the rear of the house. Once inside the glass enclosure, she was glad to be away from the wind's cutting edge. Good she was only here for the day; otherwise, she'd have to buy another layer or two. Or three.

Malachi pressed the doorbell, yielding only muted strains of Winchester Chimes. He put his ear to the door, gave his head a shake. "Nothing." He flipped up the security keypad cover and entered a six-digit code. A light on the keypad flashed green. "Wasn't secure."

That summer she had lived with Robert, he had emphasized that only six people, including her, had access to the house. She wondered when and why he had given it to Malachi. "How many people have a code?"

"Beats me." He turned the knob and called in, "Robert, it's Malachi and Ashley."

Somewhere inside, a steady beat of water dropping into a deep well broke the tomb's silence. A peg coat rack that held only a Burberry raincoat and a winter parka occupied most of one wall of the hallway leading to the kitchen. Next to it was an antique key holder with four hooks. The near hook held a Mercedes fob. A ring with two door-type keys hung from the farthest hook. A Persian throw rug with warm oranges and browns lay centered on the spotless wood floor. She engaged the door lock and armed the alarm, no reason to give anyone easy entry behind them. Avoiding stepping on the rug, she approached the kitchen entry, the first spot for an ambush.

"Power's been off." She pointed to the blinking microwave and stove clocks. "Looks like one person's dinner dishes in the sink, but nothing from breakfast."

"Too early. Tabitha makes him Sunday brunch."

"There's nothing to suggest he had coffee, and Robert has his first cup before he showers. This is from Friday night or earlier. He didn't rinse the wine glass, and it's dry. The blot of food on the edge of the plate has a hint of fuzz. Let's sweep the house and make sure he isn't here." *Or anyone else.* The refrigerator kicked on, bringing with it the first sign of life. She extracted two pairs of evidence gloves from her pack. "Put these on."

With Malachi leading, they found nothing unexpected in the dining room, living room, or parlor, where a grandfather clock provided the resonant donk, donk, donk that at a distance had sounded like water. Its hands showed a time eight minutes slower than the blinking clocks. The downstairs bathrooms held no surprises, leaving only Robert's home office behind its closed door. During the long summer she had lived in the house, she had never seen the door ajar.

The solid walnut door whispered open on well-oiled hinges. Its movement created a lemony eddy that tickled her nose. The ocean of Robert's polished ebony desk held only a black desk phone and a white cell phone. His chair, updated to an ergonomic monstrosity since she'd last been here, sat away from the desk. No footprints spoiled the parallel vacuum tracks grooved in the deep pile. She knelt, bending to see into the narrow gap between the rug and desk. Her heart raced. Something, maybe, was there. "Wait here," she said. Stepping carefully to avoid crushing any evidence, she tiptoed around the nearest side and peered into the kneehole.

Malachi leaned in the door. "What are you looking for?"

"The lack of footprints means when Junior looked for Robert, the closest he came was standing at the threshold. I thought someone might have left Robert behind the desk and vacuumed after themselves. No body and no notes. What's his cell phone number?"

Malachi told her. She picked up the black phone and dialed the number. The cellphone rang and vibrated, jitterbugging in a circle. "Let's check upstairs."

She followed Malachi up the curved center staircase to the second floor. Assuming Junior had checked Robert's bedroom, she had them first explore the two spare bedrooms to the right of the landing. She peered into the one that had been hers that summer, expecting to see dull tans and grays. "Wow." Deep red walls covered with posters of bands and festivals that she had never heard of gave the room an aura of excitement. A new bedspread sporting an abstract collection of color swatches on a white background decorated the bed she'd used. In its center lay a Nora Roberts' paperback. Piles of books and notebooks covered every horizontal surface. She stepped in to check the closet and bathroom. No bodies—living or dead.

The second bedroom on the first side and the first bedroom they explored on the other side of the landing retained Robert's dull-color pallet. In that one, a set of towels and washcloth lay on the bedspread. Waiting for her? She hesitated to enter Robert's bedroom. She wasn't a little kid sneaking around against the rules. Still, it felt that way.

She observed the rumpled bedsheets on Robert's king-sized bed. The bedside table lamp spilled light on a closed biography of Bill Gates. The light's cord plugged directly into the electrical outlet, so not on a timer. Despite the scene suggesting Robert had recently left his bed, the sheets were cool. A pocket flashlight, which she discovered was dead, lay on the rug next to the bed.

She surveyed the rest of the room. The antique mahogany clothes valet held a plaid blazer and gray dress pants, black belt in place. A pair of polished wingtips waited underneath. Work clothes. Nothing sitting on top of the bureau. Checking the bathroom, she noted the bath towel, warmed by the heated rack, was bone dry. The shower stall was equally dry, although she sensed a whiff of shampoo. Dried toothpaste stained the sink. The wastebasket contained a single strand of dental floss.

Niki flipped on the light to the walk-in closet and eased open the door with her foot. Clothes on wooden hangers were arranged on the color spectrum with no garment touching another. Shoes filled all but two slots of a wooden shoe rack. Inside the wicker clothes hamper, she found dress socks, one pair of silk boxer shorts, and a rumpled dress shirt.

The back of the bathroom door featured an empty hook. "I don't see Robert's pajamas, his bathrobe, or his slippers. You?"

Malachi stepped around her, pushed clothes around. "Dresser?"

They poked through drawers of socks, underwear, and sweaters. No bedclothes. "Weird," she said. "Let's do the attic, then the basement."

The attic stairs creaked under her weight, giving her pause. She muttered, "Come on. This isn't some Alfred Hitchcock film." She twisted the doorknob and pushed the unlocked door inward. Dust motes danced on sunbeams muted by grimy windows. A patina of dust coated everything. Only a ghost could have entered without leaving tracks.

The alarm system's single long beep announced someone had turned off the alarm. She spun around, pointing her pistol back down the stairs. Malachi stood at the bottom looking up at her. Holding a finger to her lips to silence Malachi, she settled her knapsack silently on the landing and eased down the staircase. When she was close enough, she whispered, "Stay here until I know it's safe."

"Probably Tabitha."

"Does she know your truck?"

"Sure."

"Then why hasn't she called your name?"

Twenty-One

Sunday, May 3, Morning CDT

AS SOON AS ASHLEY WAS out of sight, Malachi grabbed the cheap backpack from the attic stairs and brought it into the closest spare bedroom. He extracted his wallet and five cell phones from the foil-lined cloaking compartment of the camouflaged knapsack. His was the only silver one. He left Ashley's phones on the bed and pressed his thumb to his screen. No messages.

More from habit than conviction, Malachi called Robert's private and public office lines and the new emergency-only number and left messages that he and Ashley were at Robert's house. Please call.

Each nonanswer increased Malachi's sick feeling that he had been too trusting. Again. Before this, he would have sworn he knew Robert. Now he increasingly felt like he was the guy's puppet. Would he never learn this lesson?

Robert was a meticulous planner. To lead them astray, he might create the details they had found: Power off and on. Night clothes missing. Porsche gone. Not showing up at work. Not answering his phone. Robert had bought a new cellphone "so Malachi could call him in an emergency." Nothing to say he didn't buy new clothing and cart his PJs and slippers with him to paint a realistic kidnapping scenario.

Malachi could not explain why Robert would want Ashley in St. Paul if he wasn't planning on seeing her. Nor could he explain the kidnap attempt on her. Robert was the only one who knew Malachi was meeting her, assuming Robert had heard Malachi's voicemail.

"Malachi," Ashley called from downstairs. "You were right. It's Tabitha."

"Be down in a minute."

He was experiencing a deep sense that someone was playing him. Was it Robert or Ashley? Or both?

Sunday, May 3, morning CDT

REVERTING TO HER HYPER-ALERT NIKI mode, she flowed down the staircase, keeping close to the wall to avoid the squeaky steps. She paused at the bottom to make sense of the noises coming from the rear of the house. A cupboard closing. Water running in the sink. A bunch of beeps like someone was setting the clocks. No voices.

She eased down the hall, P226 at the ready. The door to the solarium was closed. A multicolored knit hat occupied the end peg and a red wrist coil holding several keys adorned the key holder. Someone who belonged, presumably Tabitha.

Niki lowered her pistol to her side and peered around the corner into the kitchen. A mid-twenties Caucasian, mousy blond hair pulled into a ponytail high on her head, measured coffee grounds. She wore a white sweatshirt patterned with green, blue, red, orange, and black leaves, titled Henri Matisse "*La Gerbe.*" She had poured herself into skinny jeans, didn't wear socks, and had recently polished her white Nike's.

Niki cleared her throat to announce her presence and stepped into the room.

Tabitha dropped the scoop of coffee. The scattering grounds on the table and floor sounded like a spring shower. Her eyes did a quick scan of Niki. "Ashley, right? You startled me. I thought you would look different."

Another fine first impression she was making: a pistol-packing slob wearing a wrinkled D.C. United tee shirt, rolled-up sweatpants, Dolly Parton hairdo, and no makeup.

The woman wiped her hands on the rear of her jeans. "Sorry, where are my manners? I'm Tabitha Maki. Robert told me to expect you. God, what a mess I've made. Where are he and Malachi?"

Niki laid her pistol on a counter. "He told you I'd be here?"

Tabitha pulled a broom and dustpan from next to the refrigerator. "Friday morning before he left for work. Said he hoped you would visit this weekend. Did you find everything okay in your room?"

Niki told herself to dial down into Ashley mode and called upstairs, giving Malachi the all clear. To Tabitha she said, "We arrived this morning. Robert and the Porsche are missing."

Tabitha brushed the coffee grounds on the table into the dustpan and laid it on the floor. "He'll be back. Weather even hints at spring, and he takes his Sunday morning drive with the Porsche's top down and heat blasting." She grinned, showing perfect teeth. "But he never misses brunch. Sometimes he brings fresh bagels."

Malachi arrived and hooked Ashley's backpack on a chair back.

Ashley asked, "Does he ever drive in his pajamas?"

Tabitha stopped chasing coffee with her broom. Her scrunched face implied Ashley was crazy. "When it's cool like this, he wears his bomber jacket—that's what I call his leather jacket." She pointed with the broom handle. "It's not on the pegs. Like I said, he's tootling around." She gathered the last grounds into the dustpan and dumped the mess into the waste can under the sink.

Malachi put the broom away. "Problem is, Robert missed a Saturday board meeting, and I haven't been able to reach him."

"What?" Tabitha's hands flew to her mouth. Her eyes widened, her eyebrows forming two plucked arches. "I need coffee. Join me?"

Ashley waved her refusal. "No caffeine for me."

Tabitha's eyebrows flattened. "Malachi neither. He grew up Mormon and takes decaf. You, too?"

Ashley waved away the question. "Nerves. Humor me for a minute. If Robert left on his own, dressed in his pajamas and bomber jacket, where would he go?"

Tabitha plunked onto a chair. "To Claire's? Um, his lady friend. He sees her every Wednesday night."

A booty call might do it. Tabitha isn't around on weekends to know what was normal. For a brief drive, he throws on his jacket over whatever he's wearing. Except something happened. "You have her number?"

"For emergencies. I guess this qualifies." Tabitha scrolled through her phone contacts and dialed. The conversation soon ended and Tabitha reported, "She has no idea."

Ashley tucked the pistol into the backpack. "Can your coffee wait a minute? I want you to see something in Robert's bedroom."

All three trooped to the second floor. At the bedroom door, Ashley asked Tabitha to tell her if anything looked different than normal. "Don't touch stuff. If you want something opened," she raised her gloved hands, "I'll do it."

Tabitha moved into the room and surveyed the interior before approaching the bed. "He leaves it rumpled like this for me to make, but his folded pajamas should be on the pillow. Plus," She pointed to the clothes valet, "that's what he planned to wear Saturday."

Ashley asked how she knew that.

"He only uses the valet if he expects to wear the same clothes the next day. Otherwise, he hangs up the clothes or tosses them into the hamper. He wore those pants Friday."

Remembering the hamper held only a single pair of socks, a dress shirt, and undershorts, Ashley asked Tabitha when she had last emptied it.

"I dropped everything at the cleaners on my way to school Friday."

"Where's he keep his wallet?"

"Doesn't have one. He has a money clip and a leather case for credit cards, driver's license. Stuff like that. Keeps them in the valet drawer."

Ashley pulled open the drawer. Empty. "Do you know his clothes well enough to tell us what's missing?"

Tabitha rifled through the bureau and moved to the closet, touching each of the empty hangers. "I can check on the dry-cleaning ticket to make sure, but I think the only clothes not here or there are his pajamas, robe, and fleece-lined leather slippers. They have a sole sturdy enough to drive in."

Malachi said, "What I'm hearing is something caused Robert to leave his bed, grab money and credit cards, and—"

Tabitha interrupted. "And a silver pen knife—"

Malachi talked over her. "—threw on his leather jacket, went for a drive, and no one has heard from him since."

Not convincing. "Does the electricity fail frequently?"

Tabita's ponytail swung with her denying headshake. "Occasionally in winter, but not now."

Ashley yawned. Maybe her lack of sleep was affecting her judgment, but the only things she knew for sure were that Robert was missing in circumstances that made little sense, and she was no closer to learning who had given him her undercover contact information. "It's time we call the cops."

Twenty-Two

Sunday, May 3, Mid-morning CDT

THE ST. PAUL OFFICER WHO responded was a grizzled veteran with a bored vibe that suggested he'd seen it all and wasn't buying anything an FBI agent outside her jurisdiction was selling. His body language suggested Ashley had lost him once he realized this involved a rich old guy who had taken off in a car that cost more than he made in a year, including overtime.

Ashley pushed aside her frustration. "At least canvass the neighbors and learn if they saw anything Friday night, probably a few minutes before midnight."

The officer rolled his eyes. "Before midnight?"

"The blinking clocks mean a power interruption. When the power returns, the clocks restart at midnight. They're only a few minutes faster than the grandfather clock. That means the electric came on shortly before twelve."

"Or noon and it doesn't mean that's when he left." The cop hooked his thumbs into his belt. "If he hasn't shown up by Monday, file a missing person report. The unit opens at seven. Call them. They know how to investigate these kinds of things. My experience, older guys show up Sunday night a little hungover with lipstick on their collars."

Sunday, May 3, Mid-morning CDT

WHILE ASHLEY WAS BEATING HER head against the brick wall of the St. Paul cop, Malachi revisited his last conversation with Robert and recalled his boss's personal attorney had interrupted their Friday evening discussion with a phone call. Robert trusted Anton Hack, who, despite his unfortunate surname, had served Robert for more than two decades. He might know something.

Malachi closed the door to Robert's office, found his address book in the top right drawer, and dialed the number using the desk phone. Interrupting Hack's greeting to Robert, Malachi blurted, "Robert's gone missing. This is Malachi Cluff. Ashley Prescott, his daughter, is here and talking to the police. I thought you might know something."

"Possibly. Tell me what happened."

Malachi paced the office, obliterating the vacuum lines in the carpet and explained the situation. He answered Hack's questions, finding the scratching of the lawyer's pen increasingly annoying. Hack's question concerning how Malachi had met Ashley caused him to break into a cold sweat and shiver. He heard the sick crack of Ashley's elbow caving in the man's head; saw the spray of bone and blood and brains when Malachi shot the second one.

"You there, Malachi?"

Malachi blew on his freezing hands. "As Robert requested, I brought her here. He's gone. We're worried. You said you might have some information."

The scritching from Hack's pen filled the silence. "Please ask Ms. Prescott if she'll speak with me."

"She's talking to the police. I'll call you right back on my cell phone, then go find her."

Sunday, May 3, mid-morning CDT

ASHLEY SHOWED THE OFFICER OUT the front door and found Malachi in the kitchen, his face a grim mask. He offered his cellphone. "Robert's personal attorney. Name's Anton Hack. I filled him in."

She accepted the phone. "This is Agent Prescott. Sorry, not on duty. Ashley Prescott. Do you know where Robert is?"

"I do not." His tone sounded warm, a little concerned. "Your father did give me instructions in case he was not there to greet you. Will the officers allow you into the basement?"

"Cop's gone. Told us to call the Missing Persons Unit tomorrow morning."

"You should write this down."

"Hold on a sec." Ashley mouthed the word, "pen." Tabitha handed her one and a pad of paper she pulled from a drawer. "Ready."

"There's a gun safe tucked under the basement stairs. He set the combination to your birthday in a century-year-month-day format. The dial spins right, left, right, left. Inside, you'll find a second safe bolted onto the floor. It uses your mother's birthday, but day-month-century-year. Same right-left procedure. Inside's a legal-sized portfolio, blue leather with your name stamped in gold. You with me so far?"

She nodded, remembered she was on the phone, and asked what was in the portfolio.

"Read the first few pages and call me back. There's a lot to discuss. I can't emphasize strongly enough how much your father trusts you to do the right thing. I know this feels overwhelming, but if he is missing, you don't have much time to make several important decisions. Malachi has my number. Can you give him to me?"

She handed the phone to Malachi and listened to his monosyllabic answers.

Wait! That's Malachi's silver cellphone. She checked her backpack, saw the flap was open. Inside it, her fingers informed her what she feared: the Velcro only partially sealed the secure compartment. *Damn it to hell, Malachi.* The whole point of going rogue was to avoid being stuck in an interview room accomplishing jack shit. The FBI could ping any of the phones and know for sure she was in St. Paul. Local agents could be on their way to force her into their office for questioning.

Spilt milk. Since Malachi had exposed her phones, she could check email and learn whether Gex's explosion regarding the detailed incident report she had sent using the corporate jet's VPN to disguise her location was a grenade or a nuclear bomb.

She found no voicemail or text messages on either her undercover or personal phones. Nervous thumbs required three tries to enter her email password. Nothing in her regular folders. She checked spam. All junk.

A chill raced up her spine. Silence meant Gex was coming for her.

TWENTY-THREE

ASHLEY HOOKED THE BACKPACK OVER her shoulder—she wasn't letting it out of her sight again—and waited for Malachi to finish his conversation with Hack.

"Give me your phone." She held out her hand. "I want to check for spyware." Responding to his squinched face she said, "It's one way someone could have followed you to the diner."

He unlocked the screen and hovered, watching her poke around. She found a commercial app that broadcast notifications of his GPS location, every call he made, every message he sent, everything except for when he farted. No way she could tell who was receiving the information or for how long. She deleted the app.

She found and deleted the same app on Robert's cellphone. Tabitha's was clean. Ashley checked all her phones in case Malachi had messed with them while they were out of her sight. Clean. She stored them in the secure compartment. "Besides the malware I removed, those phones might also have hidden malware that uses the microphone and camera to hear and see everything. Tabitha, stick Robert's on his desk. Malachi, store yours in your truck. Hack wants me to get something from Robert's safe. While I do that, I want you two to check all the nearby hospitals for Robert. And Tabitha, I will take you up on that offer of coffee. Black. No sugar."

Hack had sounded like Robert's lawyer, but she didn't know he was. Unlike using her safe word or Robert's nickname for her, Hack hadn't told her anything only Robert's attorney would know. She didn't have a reason to distrust Malachi, but that didn't mean she shouldn't remain alert to the possibility this was a con.

She examined the latch securing the basement door. Unlike everything else in the house that appeared well-maintained, a hundred years of the house settling had thrown the framing off kilter. The simple deadbolt extended barely far enough into the frame to keep the door shut. If anyone locked her in, she could shoulder the door open. She pulled up on the handle to avoid adding one more grooved arc to those etched into the floor. The door groaned open on binding hinges. A dusty bulb cast yellow light on the steps.

She counted thirteen steps down. Each brought a drop in temperature. By the time she reached the bottom, her heart pounded with the intensity of an Olympic 200-meter sprinter. *This isn't some Stephen King horror novel.*

A dimmer next to the stairs controlled the basement lights. She twisted it and flooded the room with light. A massive workbench with enough tools to deconstruct the cellar spanned the opposite wall. She laughed at her fear. This was not a setup.

The gun safe was taller than she, wider than her outstretched arms, and deeper than she remembered it to be. She put her ear to the lock and entered the combination. Even holding her breath, she couldn't hear or feel the tumblers fall into place. Sweet. She pulled the lever down, hearing and feeling a metallic thunk. The door opened on silent internal hinges. An intense spotlight on the safe's ceiling revealed weapons of all kinds, including Robert's favorite Purdey shotgun. Rifles, cradled in custom-fit racks, lined the rear wall. No automatic rifles, but enough quality hunting weapons to allow her to retire in style.

On shelving under the rifle racks sat original boxes for twenty-four handguns. She stuck her head in and reeled away from the reek of gun oil. Waving her hands, she brought some fresh air into the safe. The boxes were full and, to her delight, two were Sig Sauer P226s, her weapon of choice. She confirmed both appeared to be in perfect condition. Her report to Gex had provided everything he and the Metro police required to investigate the Ike's Diner incident *except for her weapon.* Now she could preserve that evidence and not go unarmed.

She unloaded her FBI service gun and swapped it for one of Robert's Sigs. She replaced the box, lining up the label to alert her if anyone moved it. Not a perfect chain of custody for her gun, but it would do. She used the ammo from her service pistol to load her new weapon.

On half of the safe floor, Robert had stacked boxes of ammo two feet high. Impressive, but nothing compared to the stashes some militia guys kept. Labels on the boxes showed type and caliber. She removed the ammo to the basement floor and exposed the interior safe's lock. Going through the unlocking sequence, she disengaged the latch and swung the lid open, which revealed a blue portfolio embossed in gold letters: Ashley P. Prescott. She grabbed it with one hand, felt its weight, and discovered it was three-inches thick. *What the hell is in here?* Anger blasted through her. She could imagine Robert holing up somewhere laughing his rocks off.

Grabbing the thing with two hands, she yanked it out, revealing four additional thinner portfolios. Containing what? A flashback of her anger at discovering her mother reading her teenage diaries reminded Ashley of her promise to never be that disloyal. Even if it was Robert.

She scooted from the safe into the cool basement air. A shiver ran up her spine. She needed that coffee to warm her and charge her up before she learned what was so all-fired important that Robert had gone to these lengths. She locked the inner safe, concealed it with the ammo.

"Ma'am," Tabitha Maki called with a trembling voice, like someone had a knife to her throat. "I found a note in my room. You have to see it."

Ashley slammed the safe door closed and spun the dial. She grabbed the new P226, dumped the portfolio into her backpack, and raced up the stairs to find Tabitha melted into the chair opposite Ashley's coffee.

Tabitha pointed to a sheet of paper on the kitchen table. "Sit or you'll fall."

Ashley picked up the page by the corners and read.

Socrates,

Sit down. You finding this means something unexpected happened to me this weekend. I had hoped to give Ashley Pendergast Prescott and you an important piece of information after she got here. I've lost my bet with Father Time. Here it is: you're my daughter. She's your sister.

When Ashley arrives, show her this letter. She'll want proof. Her own DNA will provide it.

Robert B. Pendergast

Ashley looked up to find Tabitha scrutinizing her. Looking for physical evidence to support the note's claim? This explained Robert's demand that she come to St. Paul. The line with Father Time sounded like he was dying.

Nothing suggested reasons for him to disappear or why someone followed Malachi in D.C. and attempted to kidnap her.

She mirrored Tabitha's scrutiny, taking in details she had skimmed earlier. Tabitha's face was long, and like Ashley, she had a prominent chin, as if their creators forgot to round the edges. Tabitha's bookish hazel eyes were slightly browner than hers. They could have traded noses, and no one been the wiser.

Ashley figured her own wide mouth came from Robert. Tabitha's looked like Ashley's mother's, especially when she quirked it before asking a question. But some things led Ashley to doubt their sisterhood. Although it had been years since she had hair longer than a burr, Ashley didn't think hers had ever been blond. And their voices sounded nothing alike: Tabitha's voice fit her slender frame and was a register higher than Ashley's. Plus, her mother could not have given birth without Ashley being aware of it.

But Robert had no reason to lie. He knew she would verify his statement that they were sisters. She broke the uneasy silence with something she hoped was neutral. "Socrates?"

Tabitha visibly relaxed. "Robert has nicknames for everyone. I'm always asking questions. What do you think this means?"

Socrates wasn't much better than *Little Spitfire.* "You don't seem super surprised. I thought maybe *you* could tell *me.*"

"Mom told me they had a sperm donor because Dad couldn't have children. I've often wondered if I had half-brothers and sisters. Would I recognize them if I saw them? Robert being my father? That *is* a shocker. It explains some things. This must be a bombshell for you. You look stunned."

Ashley sat down and reread the letter. Robert didn't say half-sister, which is how Tabitha had interpreted it. But he hadn't mentioned her three half-brothers, Junior, Bradlee, and Garrett, either. She sipped the tepid coffee and looked across the table at her mother's mouth. She mirrored the girl's posture as the Bureau had taught her to show empathy, and with gentle questions, she extracted Tabitha's birthday. Hearing the date, Ashley's heart clenched, her lungs refused to breathe.

Tabitha had been born the summer Ashley's mother dumped Ashley with Robert to stay for three months. At their reunion, she found her mother thinner and depressed. Ashley had attributed it to her mom's treatment—supposed treatment?—for ovarian cancer.

"Ma'am," Tabitha broke the silence. "You look like you've seen a ghost. Can I get you water? Brandy?"

Ashley popped from the chair like a cork released from under the ocean and paced the kitchen. "Malachi," she yelled. "We need you."

She showed him the note. "Did you know he wrote this?"

She believed his denial. "Where did you find it, Tabitha?"

"Tucked into a book he left on my bed. It's the one place in the room I don't keep books."

Malachi said, "To make sure you would notice. I wonder if he did something similar for me at work. I tried every hospital in a fifty-mile radius, and I spoke with all three sons. Nothing."

Ashley thanked him for those efforts and agreed he should check his office. "I'm doing what the cops should have done and canvass the neighbors to learn if anybody saw anything. Tabitha, if anyone comes here looking for me, tell them you don't know where I am. It's the honest truth. And then turn on the light by the solarium door."

"You're scaring me."

Ashley reached down and gave Tabitha a hug, felt the girl shiver in the embrace. "They're the good guys from the FBI, but I can't talk to them yet. Okay?"

TWENTY-FOUR

ASHLEY TOSSED HER BACKPACK IN the back seat of Tabitha's ancient Subaru Forester so she didn't have to cart it and that massive binder along, but where she could get it if the Bureau got to Robert's house while she was out. She hung her badge holder on the waistband of her sweats and, starting at the corner house, worked her way down the residences that shared the alley with Robert.

Two saw and heard nothing, four houses didn't answer. She thought she had struck out on the home diagonally across the lane from Robert's. She'd turned to leave and stopped at the sound of an upstairs window rattling open.

"I'm sorry, young lady," an older woman, silver hair in rollers, called through the screen. "I was putting on my face for church."

"There was a recent incident at Robert Pendergast's." She pointed to his house. "Did you see anything unusual this weekend?"

"If you're police, why aren't you in uniform?"

"Undercover FBI." Ashley held up her shield. True enough. If the woman misunderstood and thought she was part of an actual police investigation, well, that was on her. "Probably Friday night."

"I usually sleep pretty good, but that evening I was restless."

Ashley mentally rolled her eyes. A talker who might never get to the point. "Yes?"

"Eleven-fifteen, eleven-thirty maybe? A diesel Xcel Energy bucket truck rumbled into the alley. Noisy. Couldn't tell what they were doing, what with the yellow light twirling around making it hard to see. I became bored and retired. Didn't sleep though."

"Did you lose power?" Ashley shouted.

"I did not. It's been good sleeping weather with my windows open. Anyway, twenty minutes passed before they drove away. Couldn't have been more than two minutes later, Mr. Pendergast's garage door rolled up and down, and he raced off in that throaty little sports car he drives."

Ashley didn't want to put words in the older woman's mouth. She went with the standard open-ended, "Oh?"

"I can't understand why he doesn't fix that door. Squeals like a stuck pig. If it were me, I'd—"

"Friday night, did you see Robert—Mr. Pendergast at all?"

"Maybe talking to the repairmen? I couldn't swear to it. Those blasted yellow lights play heck with my cataracts." She waved a finger at Ashley. "My hearing's topflight. Although you'd have to be profoundly deaf not to hear his garage door. Oh dear. Is the FBI involved because someone kidnapped him? He's a good neighbor, never causes problems, even if he has more money than Noah."

Ashley had never thought of Noah as having *any* money. "You haven't seen or heard Robert since?"

"No. You do realize, I don't sit by the window all day like some nosy parker. I have to finish getting ready or I'll be late to church. I'll say a prayer for him." She rattled the sash shut.

Ashley smiled at the woman's insistence she wasn't a busy body. Thank goodness she was. Ashley tried three more houses: one person heard nothing, two more didn't answer. At Robert's, the back light was not on, so no one was looking for her. *Yet.*

She confirmed the same electric pole serviced Robert's house and the talkative lady's. Whatever caused Robert's power interruption had occurred between the pole and his house. She checked for debris from a downed tree limb big enough to break the connection. Nothing. The cable looked old, but all her wiring knowledge could fit in a pixie's thimble. At the house, the wire snaked down a corner and entered a metal box.

A snipped off lock lay on the ground. Scrapes on the box cover showed someone had recently pried it open. She snapped on a fresh pair of evidence gloves and worked her stubby fingernails under the cover. Ignoring the pain, she applied fingertip pressure and wiggled it open. Inside was a master switch.

Where you could kill the electricity.

Sunday, May 3, Late morning CDT

AFTER RETRIEVING HER BACKPACK, ASHLEY had to punch in the six-digit code she'd seen Malachi use. She found Tabitha at the kitchen table, talking on the phone.

"She's here. I gotta go. Bye Mom. Yep. Love you, too." Tabitha set her cellphone down. "Neighbors any help?"

"Confirmed Robert left around midnight Friday night. What happens if the power goes down? He doesn't have an auxiliary generator or Tesla batteries, does he?"

"The security system sounds a piercing squeal for like fifteen seconds. Wake the dead."

"That fits. The house loses power. The alarm wakes Robert. He grabs his flashlight, but the batteries are dead. The front streetlight provides enough light for him to see. He throws on his robe, steps into his slippers, and what?"

"Wouldn't the streetlamp be off with the outage?"

Smart girl. "Except, the neighbor lady across the alley kept her power. If Robert sees lights outside, but his electric is off, he . . . ?"

"Checks the circuit breakers in the basement?" Tabitha got up and opened the kitchen drawer nearest the hall. "Flashlight's missing."

"Okay, he checks and finds nothing. Or he sees the electric company truck in the alley, throws on his coat to ask what happened. Fair enough, but why wait until the truck leaves before driving away in his jammies? What could they have said or done to cause that reaction? Something triggered him."

"Is that when he wrote the note to me and put it where I'd find it?"

Another question Ashley couldn't answer. "No word from Malachi? I kind of—" The front doorbell's chime sounded its four tones. "Who uses that door?"

"No one." Tabitha's face drained of color. "Do you think the police found something?" Wringing her hands, she hustled to the door.

Ashley heard Tabitha click open the deadbolt. The alarm beeped. With the silence of a cat, she grabbed her backpack and left the kitchen.

"Yes?" Tabitha said.

"FBI to talk with Special Agent Prescott."

"Oh. She's in the kitchen. Did you learn something about Mr. Pendergast?"

So much for I don't know where she is. Ashley snagged Tabitha's wrist band from the key holder and exited through the solarium. She sprinted down the garden path, vaulted the wrought-iron gate. Her feet hit the uneven ground, and the backpack nearly knocked her off-balance.

Reaching Tabitha's car, she used the fob to unlock the doors. She tossed her pack onto the passenger seat, slid inside, and discovered the beast was a stick shift.

She yanked the door shut, jammed in the key, pressed the clutch to the floor, and engaged the ignition. Shifting into reverse, she gave it too much gas, and the engine whined like a jet before takeoff. She cranked the wheel for a tight turn, released the clutch, and jerked backwards, bouncing her into the steering wheel. She crushed the brake pedal to the floor, stopping with the rear bumper inches from the garage.

And stalled the car.

She twisted the key to the start position. Nothing. Two suits punched out the solarium door and raced down the path. Her wrist would break if she added any more pressure to the ignition key. She tapped the lock doors button, hearing the locks engage with a thunk.

"You dummy," she yelled while slamming down the clutch. The engine roared to life, and she jammed the shifter into first gear. The faster agent grabbed her door handle. She popped the clutch and yellow-lined it to the alley, leaving behind a burned-rubber stench, and the agent sprawled on the concrete. Riding the clutch through the turn, she shifted into second gear, increased speed, and gained third.

She stopped at the alley's end without stalling, hung a right, and accelerated.

Ha! Like riding a bicycle.

Twenty-Five

ASHLEY POUNDED HER HEAD ON the Forester's steering wheel, each tap reverberating down to her jaw. What the hell had she been thinking? She *hadn't* been thinking. Pure instinct had propelled her from Robert's house, and here she was in a University of St. Thomas parking lot in a stolen car, having assaulted a federal officer.

And how did you spend your thirty-sixth birthday, Ashley? Well, shortly after midnight, I killed an attempted kidnapper, left the crime scene, and hopped a private jet to confront a billionaire who ghosted. Typed up my incident report on the plane so I got no sleep. Oh, and my father gifted me a brand-new twenty-six-year-old sister. To celebrate, I assaulted an FBI agent and stole my sister's car. And as a bonus, flying from the Eastern to Central time zones gave me a twenty-five-hour day. No cake or candles yet, but I still have fourteen hours left to celebrate.

She opened her mouth wide, straining to break tension's vice grip on her neck. We haven't proven she's my sister, and I don't *actually know* they were FBI agents. They never identified themselves *to me.* I feared it was another kidnap attempt. No one who knew her would believe that, but they couldn't prove otherwise, which meant she could beat the technically correct charge of assaulting a federal agent.

She yanked her personal phone from the Faraday bag and punched in the number for Gex's cell. If she could reach him before he heard from the agents, she might pull this off.

He answered with, "Where—?"

"Someone just tried to kidnap me. Again." She sounded breathless. "I escaped, but—"

"Prescott," Gex shouted. "You okay?"

"Yeah, fine. Tell me about Tiny and Rick. What have you learned?"

"Get your ass to the nearest Bureau location where you'll be safe, and we can take care of what's going on."

"Tell me about the guys. Then I'll fill you in on what I have."

Muffled sounds came down the line. She assumed he was ordering someone to ping her phone.

"Rick's fine." Gex now spoke in that controlled manner he had that concealed his feelings. "According to him, they had the car windows down because of the heat. We think two guys crawled unseen under parked cars to get into position. They popped up, darted Rick and Tiny. Tiny's too big for his own good. Their drug is fast acting and doesn't last long. Because of Tiny's size, it didn't immediately put him down, like it did with Rick, but it slowed him down enough that when he tried to exit the vehicle, someone coshed him on the head. He's got a severe concussion. Given his previous ones from football, doctors are evaluating his condition.

He cleared his throat. "I received your report on Ike's Diner. Crime scene guys confirm it matches the evidence. What it doesn't say is why you left for . . . for wherever you are."

Tell him what he already knows. "St. Paul. I thought personally seeing Robert Pendergast would allow us to learn how he got Niki's contact information and shed light on the motivation for the three men at the diner. But Robert is missing. I can't get the local police to consider him a possible kidnap victim. Can you help with that? I'll be in D.C. tomorrow for our meeting. Gotta go." She disconnected. Gex had never given her a direct order, which meant she wasn't disobeying him—like that would fly.

She must abandon Tabitha's car before they found it, but since they already knew roughly where she was, she checked her undercover phones and email for messages before she changed locations. Niki's phone had two messages. "Rise and shine, corporal. This is Sergeant Oliver. Colonel Pete wants to meet later today. Standard procedures. Call me to set a time."

She queued up the second message. Sam said in English, "I could use a trusted translator for an enterprise I am working on. Your colonel has approved this if it is satisfactory to you. I would pay you well for the inconvenience of having to travel on brief notice. I look earnestly forward to your reply."

She caught the awkward sentence formation and wondered where he had learned English. No matter. This was just one more thing in a long list of one step forward, two steps back starting with Malachi's first phone call. This one-two punch of abysmal timing struck her as some PFF weird loyalty test. Because of the sniping thing? Be a good little corporal and lick some boots. She hit the callback from Oliver's message. To his "hello," she said, "Corporal Niki here, Sergeant. I am so, so sorry. I'm out of town and won't return until midweek. Once I—"

"He expects to see you today. This will piss him off big time because you claimed you had no travel plans."

"I didn't. But because he didn't say anything and since you've given me three- or four-days' notice every time until now, I caught an outrageously cheap flight. Please tell Colonel Pete that I am terribly sorry, but I can't be two places at the same time. I'll try to book an earlier return flight and call you if I can."

"Remember, disobeying a direct order is a serious offense. I'll have to—"

"You're breaking—" She disconnected. Beneath his pissed words, he had sounded pleased. Had she screwed up locking in her role as the sniper? Nothing she could do about that. She could, however, confirm Colonel Pete had approved of Sam contacting her.

PFF's security meant she didn't have Colonel Pete's number. Her highest-level contact was her lieutenant. Given that Oliver would soon report her, time was precious.

And, because that's the way this day was going, she had to leave a voicemail. "Sorry to bother you, sir. This is Corporal Niki. I need to run something up the chain of command to Colonel Pete. Could you please advise him that the Chinese gentleman I met yesterday left me a phone message and offered me employment as a translator? I will do it if that's what the colonel wants, but . . ." She counted to five before continuing, "I do not want to do *anything* to jeopardize our mission. Sorry about the inconvenience, sir, and thank you for your help."

Here she was in Minnesota chasing ghosts, accomplishing nothing—worse than nothing. She should be in D.C., meeting with Colonel Pete and asking him directly about Sam's offer. She wanted nothing more than to stop that weapons transfer, but everything she had tried to get back on track had turned to shit. It was like the universe wanted the militia to get those weapons, assassinate those people, whoever they were.

She thumped the steering wheel and pain raced up her arm to her elbow. "Fuck," she screamed, then looked around to see if anyone had heard her.

The ticking clock in her head told her she had to leave the warmth of the car and move. She electronically secured the phones in her knapsack, locked the Forester's doors, and ambled away to avoid drawing attention.

She needed a toasty restaurant to eat and learn what secrets Robert's blue portfolio contained.

Twenty-Six

Sunday, May 3, Early afternoon CDT

ASHLEY FOUND A STOREFRONT RESTAURANT northeast of the campus and ordered a Monte Cristo biscuit sandwich and water. She unwound the thin leather cord holding the file closed and read the summary memorandum on top. Robert wanted her advice on whether and how to involve the FBI in investigating illegal activity inside Pendergast Holdings, LLC. Plus, he suspected at least one of the other five board members of leaking strategic competitive information concerning a proposed merger. To ferret out the leaker, he had provided each board member with merger plans containing different details.

Amateur hour. Why he thought she was an expert on corporate crime was beyond her. Sure, some of her undercover work had developed intel on individuals involved in money laundering. That didn't mean she understood jack about it.

She flipped to the second page, a handwritten note dated four days ago.

> *Ashley, if you are reading this before talking to me, it means someone at Pendergast Holdings learned of my suspicions and has taken actions to prevent me from discovering the culprit.*

Another "if you're reading this" note from Robert. Damn him. If he thought he was in danger, he should have used a minuscule fraction of his wealth and hired around-the-clock security. This felt like a manipulative drama-queen act, and she wanted to punch him.

Feeling her fist clench, she was reliving her mother's funeral. Robert had caught her alone and made a last push to suck her into the family business. He'd offered her money and power. She'd screamed that if he ever brought this up to her again, she would shove his money up his ass so far he would choke and die. He opened his mouth to reply, and she belted him, at the last moment changing the trajectory of her punch down to his chest.

She refocused on the note, realized her gaze was at the bottom of the page but her brain had read nothing. God, what a wreck. She had believed she'd outgrown his power to upset her. Obviously not.

She uncurled her fist and used her finger to underline the words as she heard his voice in her head.

> *You're the only one I trust. In my absence, I have given you proxy to vote all the Pendergast Holdings shares I control. In addition, I beg you to take the interim-CEO position.*

The handwriting looked like Robert's, but no way would he do something this stupid. She knew zip about the business. She scanned the rest of the note, looking for any clue that Robert had written this under duress, although she couldn't imagine why *anyone* would want her to run Pendergast Holdings. Nothing there. She was to contact Anton Hack, Robert's personal attorney, who she'd already spoken with, who had the legal documents. Blah, blah, blah. Last paragraph:

> *I know this is the last thing you wanted. I am not asking that you do this for me. I am asking for the 40,000 employees who will lose their jobs if Pendergast Holdings fails.*

The bastard *had* written this himself. I this; I that; I the other thing. No one was more conniving, more manipulating, more goddamn cruel than he was, putting 40,000 innocents on her shoulders.

"Do you need another napkin?"

She blinked away her anger, saw the server had delivered her food, and that Ashley had shredded the napkin into a bazillion pieces. "Thanks. It's been one of those days."

Here she was, thirty-six-fucking-years old and acting like a hormonal teenager lashing out. Get your damn act together. You're a trained investigator. Collect and analyze facts. Don't jump to conclusions.

Anton Hack had facts. She wanted them. She called him using the burner phone she had bought in Virginia and had used only to allow Malachi to call the plane's pilot. Hack asked if she had read the material. "For fuck's sake? You couldn't talk him out of this craziness? Was he losing it?" *Way to get your act together, Prescott.*

"I questioned him. His reasons were cogent. His presentation was precise. He knew what he was doing and why. He asked me to apologize to you for the disruption in your life and to assure you that if he could find any other way, he would have respected your desires to avoid Pendergast Holdings."

Which is total bullshit. Remember: facts and analysis. "Who else knows?" Because if someone knew Robert was no longer in the picture, kidnapping her might be a desperate attempt at—she couldn't imagine at what.

"No one that I am aware of," came the measured answer, reminding her she was talking to a lawyer.

"Were you involved in getting my phone number and address?"

"No. Malachi tells me it has caused you considerable distress. I'm sure Robert didn't want that. What I suggest—"

"What happens when I refuse?"

"The whole thing ends up in court. A bunch of lawyers, including me, get rich. Rudderless, Pendergast Holdings may not survive. Please listen. Robert insisted you are the only one of his children he can unequivocally rely on. He's seventy-two and facing major decisions at the company. Money doesn't tempt you to violate your values. We both know you don't owe Robert a blessed thing, but you're missing a major point. He knows you can't run the enterprise by yourself. But unlike your brothers, you have no ego in this and will find the right people to help you.

"Look at how you can benefit by saying yes. As boss, you can give your law enforcement colleagues full access to the firm's records. That may facilitate learning what happened to Robert and to eradicate the illegalities he referenced. You might discover who gave Robert your undercover phone number. The best way to find the answers you seek is to be in charge."

That actually makes some sense.

Hack released a series of percussive breaths, like a steam engine slowing down. "Thing is, you have to decide now because the board meets this afternoon."

Twenty-Seven

Sunday, May 3, Late afternoon CDT

FOUR HOURS AFTER HER SECOND conversation with Anton Hack, Ashley found herself between Malachi and Gerald Nakourma, Pendergast Holding's corporate counsel, peering into the board room through a window at the side of the closed door. Her three half-brothers and a woman she assumed was Gabriella Linz, Pendergast Holding's CFO, sat around the table, Robert's chair at the head remained empty. The doors muffled the conversation, but judging by Junior's flailing arms, he was upset.

The conference room table and side tables sparkled with polish. A herd of cattle gave up their lives to supply all the leather in there. Paintings depicting English fox hunting decorated the walnut-paneled walls. She supposed the whole point of hunting fox with packs of dogs was to impress others that you could afford to waste time and money on such a useless pursuit. Like the polished wood and leather chairs.

Garrett, the youngest and farthest from the empty power seat, was her senior by three years. He appeared to have aged little in the last dozen years. His tanned face was taut, highlighting prominent cheekbones. His Adam's apple protruded above his white polo shirt. Well-developed biceps suggested he used a club membership to advantage. He seemed amused, a wry smile painting his face.

Bradlee, middle son, had gone to fat. He slouched in his seat. She'd bet he wore stretch-waist pants and his loose-fitting shirt hid rolls of stomach fat. Junior, Robert's first son, was recently AARP eligible. He sported a healthy tan, ending abruptly at a cap line just below his prominent widow's peak that hadn't existed a decade ago. The overall effect projected a fleshy sense of primogeniture.

Gabriella Linz, whom she had never met, reminded Ashley of an ocelot. Sleek with silky lines, her claws would tear apart the weak. Or maybe Ashley was projecting.

Gerald Nakourma's knock on the door silenced Junior. Malachi and

Gerald entered, blocking those inside the room from seeing her. Gerald said, "I have important news about Robert."

Junior said, "Finally. We've been twiddling our thumbs waiting for you and his majesty to arrive."

Malachi stiffened. She wondered again what his relationship with Robert was. Gerald seemed nonplussed. In the same calm voice, he said, "Robert is missing. We believe someone has kidnapped him."

The room exploded into shouted questions tumbling over each other. Gerald held up both hands in what looked like submission, but she soon realized was a signal for the board members to settle and listen. She could learn a thing or two from this guy on how to command a room.

Once they quieted, Gerald said, "There has been no communication from whoever is responsible. I spent the last two hours consulting with Anton Hack and reviewing documents his firm drew up at Robert's request."

Junior scowled, made a production over crossing his arms in front, and asked, "To what effect?"

"In his absence, Robert has appointed Ashley Prescott acting CEO."

Ashley expected this announcement to produce an uproar. It had the opposite effect. Incredulity painted Gabriella's face. Had she assumed the CFO was the logical choice to hold the firm's reins temporarily? Junior's tan now had a fire underneath it, and Bradlee looked poleaxed. She'd swear Garrett was trying hard not to smile. Interesting.

Bradlee rallied and raised his hand. "Doesn't appointing an acting CEO require board action?"

"Technically," Gerald said. "Also technically, the current board sits at the pleasure of the majority of the stockholders."

"Which, with Dad's proxy, is us." Junior's arm sweep included his brothers.

Ashley stepped around the lawyer to become visible to those in the room. "Except, your father assigned me his voting proxy."

"He did what?" Junior exploded from his seat.

"Who the hell are you?" Bradlee asked.

Garrett rose and laid a hand on Junior's arm, restraining him from advancing on her. "She's your little sister, Bradlee. Is this one of your undercover disguises, sis?" Garrett grinned.

She filed away for later reflection that Garrett knew she worked undercover. "Robert's proxy and the shares held in the Daughters Trust, which I also control, add to fifty-one percent." She dipped her head toward Gerald. "I'm told that the board may ignore Robert's wishes and appoint someone else acting CEO. But I can call a snap election and replace you all with people who will vote me in."

She strode to the foot of the table. "I suggest you sit, Junior. We have a lot to discuss and little time. Let me be candid. I have no fucking clue how to run a multi-billion-dollar company. That's why Robert hired each of you, and I'm relying on everyone's help."

"I assume, Gerald, you are sure the proxy is legal?" Gabriella's voice rose at the end, changing the statement into a question.

The corporate lawyer stepped into the open space between Ashley and her two brothers. Far enough away to prevent him from towering above her, close enough to suggest he was with her. "I spoke with the notary who witnessed the documents. It is my opinion they will withstand any legal challenges. The Daughters Trust provides that Ms. Prescott may choose to manage it once she attains age thirty-five, which occurred last year. She has followed the procedures detailed in the trust to accept its leadership. I will assist her in any way she wishes, provided it is legal."

Gabriella, a wry smile painting her face, folded her hands. "As should we all."

Ashley sat at the foot of the table and mirrored Gabriella's folded hands position. The wood was solid, cool to her touch, and smelled lemony.

Ashley scanned their expressions. On closer inspection, she decided Gabriella's smile reflected a hint of enjoyment at the surprises. Ashley suspected there was more to that woman than numbers. Junior and Bradlee glared, arms crossed, jaws clenched. Junior's eyes squinted their disgust. The artery at the side of Bradlee's forehead throbbed. She hoped he didn't suffer a stroke. Garrett kept his hands hidden, his face now composed into an unreadable mask. Unlike her ability while undercover to mask her thoughts, his eyes twinkled.

She had expected a fight. With their current acquiescence, her adrenaline lost its purpose and just made her twitchy. Good thing no one could see her knee bouncing under the table. She said, "Perhaps now you should vote and appoint me interim CEO."

Junior shook his head. "We'll do that. But first, let's resolve this divestiture confusion."

Score one for Junior, grabbing the momentum. This must be important to him if he chose to deal with it before addressing whether to give her the CEO position. She pointed to seats for Gerald and Malachi to join them at the table.

Gabriella spoke, her voice calm, factual. "We were discussing how to handle the potential monopoly issue if we make this acquisition. With no divestiture, our sweet corn seed market share jumps from thirty-eight percent to seventy-two. That's why Robert's plan calls for us to first divest—"

Bradlee slammed his fist on his binder. "I still can't find a damn thing in here that says anything about divesting anything."

Junior said, "Hey bro, before we were interrupted—" He looked up and did a double-take seeing Ashley flanked by Gerald and Malachi. "It's—where is the divestiture, Gabriella? Somewhere in with the new material Dad gave us Friday. Didn't you do your homework?"

"Halfway down on page twenty-two," Gabriella recited without opening her binder. "Quote, 'Pendergast Holdings shall spin-off into a separate corporation its subsidiary, American Fertile Seed Company.' End quote. Appendix seventy-six details AFS's estimated assets and liabilities."

Bradlee shoved his binder away in disgust. "Show me."

Garrett pushed his own binder in front of Bradlee and flipped between two pages. "Here and here."

Gabriella gathered Bradlee's binder. "That's strange. Yours is different."

Ashley said, "Because Robert didn't provide you all the same information." She had hoped this news would trigger a reaction to give one of them away, but she read nothing more than confusion in their faces. She raised her voice above the din. "I have a suggestion. Spend a few minutes and compare binders. You'll see I'm telling the truth."

Gabriella said, "Give them to me. I'll verify what Ms. Prescott suggests. While I'm doing that, you three decide on the temporary CEO. Gerald and I abstain." Without waiting for agreement or dissent, she collected the binders.

Gerald said to Gabriella's back. "I'll help shortly, but I need to speak with Ashley for a minute."

Ashley rolled her chair away from the table. "I await your decision. Malachi, where will we be?"

"The others are waiting for you in Robert's office. Yours for now."

Nope, Ashley thought, that is not how I'm playing this.

Twenty-Eight

Sunday, May 3, Late afternoon CDT

MALACHI LED ASHLEY AND GERALD from the conference room. He still struggled with the idea of Robert leaving a person with no business experience to run his enterprise. But she *did* possess a native shrewdness and ability to read and control people he had not expected.

He had warned her that the board, at least her three brothers, would coalesce against her. She had disagreed, anticipating the announcements would expose the fault lines between the brothers and split them from Gabriella and Gerald. She seemed mature and uninterested in power, which most found an aphrodisiac. Yet below her surface, he sensed a caldron of roiling emotions. Her relationship with her father was in shambles, and he guessed the blame wasn't all Robert's. He wished he had a better feel for her moral compass. He rounded a corner and jerked to a stop, feeling a pinch in his lower back.

Cece Kraznik nearly plowed into him. Hands planted on her hips she scowled. "Have they decided?" Her nose wrinkled at Ashley. "Who's she?"

Stepping around Malachi, Ashley presented her hand. "Ashley Prescott."

Cece's brows arched in surprise. "You don't look—never mind. I'm Cece Kraznik, Pendergast Holdings' Director of Public Relations." She pumped Ashley's hand once before focusing on Malachi. "Are they done? Gabriella requested my presence in case the board wanted any press releases."

A hard charger, she wasn't normally that rude. Working on Sunday could do that, he supposed. "I believe Gabriella is in her office." Cece didn't move, and he added, "If you'll excuse us?"

Cece glared at him and stepped aside. What bee was in her bonnet?

Sunday, May 3, Late afternoon CDT

ASHLEY FOUND TABITHA AND ANTON Hack waiting at the glass conference table at one end of Robert's office, a room larger than Ashley's first apartment. While crossing an infield's worth of green carpet, she said. "Everyone sit. We still have much to accomplish. Malachi, please arrange around-the-clock security for Tabitha."

From the looks on their faces, she'd surprised everyone.

"Robert is missing. Someone tried to kidnap me for ransom." She ignored their shocked responses. "People will soon learn Tabitha is Robert's daughter—"

"Which I still can't get my head around," Tabitha said.

"You and I will confirm that with DNA testing. Fact is, Robert included you in the Daughters Trust. I remember thinking it was bad grammar. It should have been apostrophe 's.' Now with two daughters—" She shot a look at Hack. "Just two, right?"

"You and Tabitha, yes."

Ashley pressed the corners of her eyes, willing the pain to focus her attention. She faced Malachi. "Security for Tabitha. Set up a separate account with the company you said Pendergast Holdings uses. Have the Daughters Trust pay. I want minimum two-person teams and make sure they have at least one woman."

Malachi asked, "Starting when?"

"She doesn't leave this building without protection. Tabitha, your bodyguards will smother you like a winter jacket. You go to class, they're in the room. You take a crap, one's outside the stall."

Tabitha's eyes grew deer-in-the-headlights wide. Ashley motioned Tabitha to stand and gave her a long hug, patting her back, feeling the girl's rapid breaths come under control. "I know today has thrown a spanner into the works. We have lots to discuss, but it has to wait." She held her sister at arms length. "Okay?"

Tabitha wiped tears from her cheeks, sobbed a "yes" and sat.

Ashley's mind whirred at warp speed. "Robert's house has only the alarm system, right? I want exterior cameras with monitors for the bodyguards. And motion-sensitive lights installed pronto. Make sure their positioning won't annoy the neighbors. Malachi, can you make that happen?"

"Yes, but—"

"I know, closing the barn door after the horse is gone. Hopefully, we'll get Robert back. In the meantime, we keep Tabitha safe."

Malachi said, "And you?"

"I'm the damn FBI. We keep people safe. We don't worry about it."

Hack shook his head. "Maybe you should."

"Enough." She sliced the air with her hand. "Remember, Tabitha doesn't leave here until she has protection. You three got it?" She waited for three assents. "Thanks. Now, if I could talk with Gerald. Alone. Oh, wait." She dug in her knapsack, removed two twenties and car keys and handed them to Tabitha. "Payment for short-term rental of your car, and your gas gauge is sitting on empty."

She swung into the seat next to Gerald and kept silent until the others shut the door behind themselves. "You wanted me alone. Why?"

He stared at his hands, rubbed them together, cleared his throat. "Your father was—"

"Could we refer to him as Robert, please?" At his questioning look, she added, "He never felt like a father to me."

"Robert believed one of the board members was giving inside information to a competitor."

"He told *you* this?"

"We were working late on the acquisition. He blurted it to me after everyone else had left. At first, I blamed it on his being tired and frustrated that the competition has been anticipating our moves. He explained his reasoning, and I agreed it was possible."

That sounded plausible, but he could have figured it out from Robert giving the board members different binders. "Forgive me if I ask something stupid. How does sabotaging the company benefit the brothers or Gabriella?"

"Industry is consolidating. You either buy them or they buy you. Robert wants his firm to survive. Gabriella's next move is CEO of Pendergast after Robert steps down, which he has given no sign of doing. Or she loses patience and takes the top financial job at a Fortune one hundred conglomerate. If Robert fails to reappear, and she saves Pendergast Holding, one of those two things will happen sooner rather than later."

"They'd make her CEO? Not Junior?"

"Oh, Junior thinks he could do it, but unless Robert left him a controlling interest, Bradlee and Garrett would never allow it."

"But Gabriella didn't know Robert was leaving me his proxy. Junior thought he had it locked up."

"Are you sure? I saw her surprise at Robert naming you CEO, yes, but not the proxy. The brothers have a different calculus. Robert's never been interested in money, only in the company. He works them hard and pays them well. But if someone buys the corporation, they cash in their stock, becoming multi-millionaires without the hassles of work. Sabotaging Robert's merger plans might force the company's sale."

As would getting rid of Robert, which might be the next step if the culprit realized Robert had become wise to them. "What happens to you if the business sells?"

"The acquiring company's legal staff survives. They demote or fire me. My severance agreement pays a year's salary. I'm forty-seven and have three kids in grade school. I hope to retire from here."

"But if someone paid you enough—"

"Yes, of course. And with the sums involved in an acquisition, buying me would be chump change. I can't prove the negative. If you'd prefer to obtain independent counsel, I'd understand."

Her bullshit detector did not register a whiff. He had been nothing but helpful since she and Hack had arrived with copies of the documents from the blue portfolio that had thrust this odious responsibility on her. "Assume we have a mole. Can I pressure the turncoat by moving forward with the acquisition? And make it clear I won't sell?" She snapped her fingers. "Plus, I could sweeten the pot and offer the other firm the CEO and head legal positions for the combined operations. Puts screws on you and Gabriella."

Gerald's eyes blinked in time with tiny head bobs. Internal consultation concluded, his dour expression warmed into a smile. "That is diabolical but won't make you many friends."

"I'm not here for Miss Congeniality. Switching gears, I need one of those proxy assignment thingies."

"If you're worried—"

"Not about my safety. I have an actual job, and I might have to be somewhere else. Give Tabitha power to manage the Daughters Trust and a friend of mine named Seamus McCree voting control of Robert's shares. That way, if everyone else disagrees with something Seamus proposes, they can vote him down. But if he convinces even one, he has a majority. I want that signed, notarized, sealed in blood, whatever it takes to make sure it's totally legal before I leave tonight."

Gerald agreed to work with Mr. Hack and get it done.

"One last thing. How do I get internet access?"

"IT can set you up with a username and password tomorrow. For now, use the guest network. The password is 'visitor,' all small letters."

Ashley saw him to the door and closed it behind him. She grabbed a straight-backed chair from around the glass conference table and banished Robert's ergonomic monstrosity—with more knobs and levers than she had the desire and wits to master—to a corner of the room. She sat at Robert's desk. Finding the portal for PHGuest, she entered the visitor password, then logged into the email account in which she kept personal contact information and found McCree, Seamus.

The Wildlife Biology half of her double major had required a bunch of math. She'd aced her statistics courses, but her finance skills ended at balancing a checkbook and paying her credit cards each month to avoid late fees and interest charges. Seamus was a genius at financial stuff. Some bank even paid him to help with their acquisitions. No reason to use a burner for this; she picked up the desk phone, heard a dial tone, and tapped in the number. It rang into voicemail.

Seamus's genius stopped at his cellphone. Half the time he either forgot to take it with him, let the battery drain, or shut it off. Frustrating to the rest of the world. She left a message including the direct line to Robert's office. She scrolled up one contact to Seamus's son, Patrick. He might know how to reach his father.

The desk phone gave a beep-beep, interrupting her from punching in Patrick's number. She pressed a flashing button and answered with a tentative, "Hello?"

"Sorry," Seamus said. "I don't answer unknown numbers. Too much robojunk. My theory is if someone wants me, they'll leave a message. Which you did. What's up? Oh, and happy birthday. Twenty-one, right? You can legally drink now?"

"Very cute." She related a quick, sanitized version of the situation with Robert missing, her temporary role at Pendergast Holdings, segueing into her request. "I need your expertise to understand the intricacies of corporate finances and tell me what's what."

"Thanks for the vote of confidence, but I was a bank stock analyst when dinosaurs roamed the earth. My sister has a PhD in Agriculture, even testified in Congress on the hazards of GMO monoculture, but I don't know that stuff and that's only one of Pendergast's divisions. And I've never run a company in my life. You need—"

"Bullshit. That's like telling a drowning man you won't throw him a life ring because it can't keep him afloat for a month." She shivered at her drowning metaphor. "Pretty please with sugar on top. I have no clue what I don't know. I'm hopeless. Plus, part of this might relate to financial crimes and that *is* in your wheelhouse. There's plenty of space at Robert's house. You can stay there." Into his silence she added, "Besides, you owe me."

Seamus chuckled. "You *are* desperate. Since it's your birthday, okay. I'm in Chicago visiting my granddaughter. I'll break Megan's little seven-year-old heart and catch the next flight. A Minneapolis hotel close to the office works better. That way I can save time and walk. I'll send you a text, tell you which one."

Excellent. With seven hours left in her birthday, things were starting to go her way.

Twenty-Nine

Sunday, May 3, Early evening CDT

A KNOCK AT THE DOOR awakened Ashley from a snooze she hadn't realized she was taking. Gerald Nakourma held a manila folder. "Sorry to disturb you. Junior requested I draft this contract to cover your interim CEO duties and responsibilities. You should review this before you sign."

"Oh?" Sleeping at the desk had added a neck crick to the aches accumulated the last two days. Nothing pain relievers wouldn't fix.

He apparently interpreted her rubbing her neck as expressing concern. "Actually, you should have external counsel experienced in executive contracts review this."

"Did Mr. Hack do that for Robert?"

"Oh, no, Robert employed a New York firm to negotiate on his behalf. I can get their contact information, but . . ."

Her eyes throbbed with each beat of her heart. She waited until it was clear he would not finish the sentence. "Gerald, I'm exhausted. You're hinting at something, and I'm not smart enough to know what questions to ask. Robert *wanted* me for this. Give me in broad strokes how the contract Junior constructed differs from one Robert might have asked you to compose. Or does that violate some lawyer ethics code?"

He gnawed his bottom lip. "Robert would tell you to call a stockholder meeting to elect a new board of directors, which with your proxy you could choose. It takes time, but serves notice that—"

"Isn't that going nuclear? Is the contract that bad?"

"Until you sign a contract or sit on the board, you don't have *any* position here. They can expel you from the building for trespassing."

This bullshit was one reason she had wanted to avoid Robert, his family, and his corporation. She stifled the urge to bang her head on the desk or just walk out the door. But neither action would bring her answers. "Let's start with the contract. I'd prefer to work in good faith. You didn't answer my question. Is the contract abysmal?"

Gerald looked her straight in the eye and nodded.

"And can you sketch out for me what you guess Robert would want? I know that's speculative. It's just so I can compare them and understand how they want to screw with me."

"Give me half an hour."

Sunday, May 3, Early evening CDT

TO PREVENT HERSELF FROM FALLING asleep again while she waited for Gerald Nakourma to return, Ashley walked the executive corridor. Light leaked through the westward-facing windows from the sun, still high in the sky on this early May evening, fighting its way through gathering thunderheads. With the HVAC system silent, the place reminded her of the night before Christmas with no mice stirring. Or worse, the Rapture had occurred, and she was the one person left.

She entered the last office. Centered on the desk were the merger binders with sticky tabs protruding like porcupine quills. Must be Gabriella's. Stacks of papers covered every horizontal surface. No pictures of family decorated her walls or desk. A series of black and white abstract ink drawings adorned one wall. Plunking herself down in Gabriella's chair, she faced a photograph of the Twin Towers before the 9/11 attacks had brought them to devastating ruin. Understanding Gabriella's choice of art would give her insight into her personality, but Ashley was too tired to pull that together. She tried the drawers. Locked.

Garrett's office was next. Clutter free, you could serve the Queen on the polished surfaces of his bird's-eye maple desk and conference table. Two memos marked up for his assistant to correct sat in his outbox: One contained gobbledygook about a patent application for a chemical she had no guess how to pronounce. The other requested changes to a direct marketing campaign for corn farmers. Boring. His locked desk drawers caused her to wonder what secrets they hid. The nature photographs covering his walls were extraordinary animal action shots. Unsigned. If these were his, the guy had talent.

Bradlee's space was a mess. Layers of files and scraps of paper—some stained with coffee-cup rings—covered his desk and credenza. She guessed Gabriella knew exactly where things were in her piles. It looked like you could mine Bradlee's workspace for archival history. Family photos taken at resorts covered his walls: white sand beaches, drinks with umbrellas, dad, mom, and three kids—two girls and an older boy—outfitted for snorkeling.

Junior's office was next to Robert's. Orderly, but not neat-freak clean. Only in politicians' offices had she seen that many photos of people shaking hands. She stepped closer, recognized a bunch of Republicans, lots of sports figures, and Junior presenting gigantic checks to various charities.

Returning to Robert's office, she downloaded TOR, The Onion Router, to allow her on the internet without giving away her location. She ordered two DNA test kits delivered to Tabitha Maki at Robert's house. Ashley wondered how Tabitha was holding up from the shocks she had suffered earlier in the day. If she were in Tabitha's shoes, she couldn't imagine asking her mother questions over the phone. She'd want that discussion to be in person. At least Tabitha could talk to *her* mom.

Ashley closed her eyes and remembered standing at her mother's grave. She'd squeezed a clump of dirt in her hand, sure it would be a diamond when she dropped it on the coffin. But the loam dribbled through her opened fingers like sand in an hourglass. The patter of it striking the cherry wood reminded her of the start of a high plains' rainstorm. *Oh Mom, I wish we could have talked more.*

Whistling snapped her from her reverie. She dabbed her eyes on the soft cotton of her sweatshirt sleeves, hoping she'd be presentable before Gerald arrived.

He rapped a courtesy knuckle on the door and walked in, animated in a way that he hadn't been before.

Sunday, May 3, Evening CDT

NINETY MINUTES LATER, GERALD SIGNED two copies of a revised interim CEO contract. Unlike the original contract that had required the board to approve any decision she made, under the revised contract she kept all normal CEO powers, including the ability to appoint individuals to fulfill any of her duties. That would cover Seamus stepping into her shoes. The only thing she had agreed to from Junior's proposal was that she would receive no salary. The Bureau would not look favorably on any agent with a second paying job. This, she could claim, wasn't any different from charity work.

Ashley grabbed a pen to also sign.

"Wait until at least three of us have signed," he said. "Are you staying at Robert's? I can give you a lift there or—" He stopped, probably registering her frown. "—to wherever."

He assumed wrong, but she saw no reason to tell him she planned to give Tabitha space. "I still have some internet work before I head to the Mall of America to buy a couple of wardrobe changes. The light rail goes there."

"I'll lock up. The mall's not far. I can drive you."

Bullshit. "Did Junior tell you to make sure I didn't steal anything? Robert's office locks with the push of a button, and the main doors automatically lock. You've been extremely helpful, but unless you're required to babysit me, I'd prefer privacy to get my work done. It's only a half hour."

"You are aware Minneapolis has safety issues? The walk to the light rail can be sketchy off hours, especially for women. At least allow me to arrange a cab. I'll make sure the guard downstairs knows to be on the lookout."

Old-fashioned men were both frustrating and endearing. Better to give him a crumb. "Thank you. Let's say forty minutes to be safe."

"Fine. I'll distribute copies of the contract to the board members' offices and see you tomorrow."

The ding of the elevator sounded clearly in the dead office. She had the place to herself. Her time flew by and with a minute to spare, she reached the lobby. The guard handed her a clipboard with a register on which to sign out. "You missed the excitement."

"Oh?" She printed her name and scrawled her signature two lines below Gerald's and handed him the clipboard.

The guard checked her information. "Cab's for you. One arrived a few minutes before that one showed up. Big argument. Couldn't hear what they were saying, but eventually the first guy drove away. I guess he wasn't happy to lose a fare. Mr. Nakourma said he'd ordered you a cab, so your guy's right. Have a good night."

"That's the plan."

A smartly dressed, white six-footer waved and opened the rear door of the cab. "Miss Prescott?"

She couldn't remember the last time she had a cabbie with an East Coast accent. "You got 'er." She tossed her knapsack onto the seat and followed it in.

The driver grabbed her trailing right arm and plunged a needle into her triceps. "Pleasant dreams."

She attacked, connecting a glancing blow with her fist. He used her arm to lever her into the car. Her aches and pains vanished. She floated above her body, observing the woman below her who could hardly move and couldn't speak. Her vision grew fuzzy, her eyelids drooped and closed. A pressure wave of sound hit her. Some portion of her brain informed her the door had slammed.

Wait, I haven't put on my seat belt.

Her lips wouldn't form the words. She rested her chin on her chest. Everything became calm and quiet and dark, a state of meditation she had never achieved. She knew the sound of one hand clapping.

THIRTY

Sunday, May 3, Late night CDT

A SWARM OF GIANT KILLER bees chased Niki, their buzzing a deep hum. She opened her eyes. An airplane cockpit came into focus and her body spasmed in fear. She closed her eyes, still saw the spinning colors of a crab nebula rotating above a black hole.

She pried her eyelids apart. Not an airplane. Car. Not bees, tires on a dark country road. Twin searchlights drowning in a boundless ocean. A mailbox flashed by her window, the devil's 666 marking her passage into hell.

Hell is a construct or metaphor. Her head ached like she had run full tilt into a catcher blocking the plate. The edges of her vision a rainbow kaleidoscope.

Drugged.

And kidnapped.

She checked the passenger seat. No one. Driver facing forward. Niki curled and clawed at a shoelace, fumbled the knot loose and jerked the lace free. She wrapped an end around fingers of each hand and pulled it taut. Too damn short. She removed the second lace and tied the two together with a square knot. Long enough. Do it before he realized she was awake.

Now!

She popped up and threw the garrote over his head, catching it on his chin. He ducked and reached for it. Before he could get a grip, she yanked it below his chin and leaned away to exert maximum pressure. A bone frog, pulsing red, blue, yellow, stared at her. She closed her eyes to the amphibian and crossed her wrists behind the headrest to cut off his blood flow, deprive his brain of oxygen.

His body twist presaged a swinging hook. The wind of his fist whistling past her nose like a sirocco. Wrong word. Cold wind, not hot. *Bise.* That was it. She pulled harder, tightening the garrote. Her eyes pulsed red, matching her beating heart.

She felt him tense, knew another blow was coming, leaned away. His fist zipped past. She let go of the shoelace, grabbed his wrist with both hands, and threw her body down, yanking him tight against the headrest.

The taxi slewed left with such force she lost her grip and slid against the far door, then it spun, the thrum of tires becoming a screech of brakes and squeal of burning rubber sliding sideways on the road. The vehicle bounced off something massive and shimmied to a silent stop, the blow shattering the rear door window.

Niki leaped from the car. Curling her toes and pigeon-toeing her feet to keep her unlaced shoes on, she stumbled from the car's lights. A couple dozen awkward steps brought her through a ditch and into trees. Ducking branches, she looked behind to see if he was following. Her foot caught a root, and she pitched forward.

Sunday, May 3, Late night CDT

NIKI CAME TO, RAW DRIZZLE spitting into her face. She listened past the patter of rain, heard her own ragged breathing and beneath that a distant low hum. Couldn't hear any critters moving. Closing her eyes against the pain in her skull, she steadied her breathing and reconstructed what had brought her to this place and time: the hallucinations, the taxi, the driver, the arm prick, Pendergast Holdings, bone-frog man. No one had kidnapped Corporal Niki. Ashley Prescott was the victim.

Sensing she couldn't switch off her Niki persona without conscious effort, she silently chanted, "I am Special Agent Ashley Prescott, and this is a crime scene," until she believed it.

She rolled onto her hands and knees and endured a racking, full-body shiver. Once she controlled the spasm, she pushed into a standing position and did a slow three-sixty. Trees everywhere, but a little less dense toward the distant thrum of cars traveling a highway.

If bone-frog man was out there, he was waiting in silence. She couldn't outwait him. If she did nothing, hypothermia might not let her see dawn.

She extended her hands like a zombie, eased one foot forward, then brought her other to it. Each stumble brought a bolt of pain that stole her breath. She reached the edge of the woods and butt-crawled down an embankment she had no memory of climbing. At the bottom was a straight and empty road disappearing in both directions.

White patches on trees across the macadam attracted her like a moth to a lightbulb. There, she found a broken car mirror and pieces of molded plastic. With sudden clarity, she realized she was no longer experiencing the weird light show. Drugs worn off? Had her kidnapper used the same fast-acting drug that had dropped Rick? She blew on her hands to warm them.

Think Ashley. Just because the guy had driven away didn't mean he wasn't still looking for her. With this dark, she wouldn't recognize a bruised yellow cab from any other car until it was too late. Meaning she had to avoid all traffic on this road. Yet she had to find help. She walked toward the traffic sounds using the roadway edge to guide her feet, prepared to dive into the weeds at the first sign of lights.

She found her knapsack in the ditch a half mile from the accident. Pure luck. If she'd chosen to walk the other way or on the opposite side of the road, she'd never have spotted the dark lump. She didn't care whether the kidnapper was dumping evidence or was smart enough to know the police could use her phone to track him; she was grateful for her electronics.

Google, not a diamond, is a girl's best friend. Google Maps pinpointed her location, and Google Search provided the number of Seamus's hotel. The operator dialed the room. To his groggy hello, she said, "It's me. Put on your glasses and write down this location. Please pick me up there. No time for questions. And bring towels. I'm soaked and freezing my ass off."

THIRTY-ONE

Monday, May 4, Morning CDT

MALACHI ARRIVED AT ROBERT PENDERGAST'S house twenty minutes after Ashley Pendergast's summons. One of the third-shift guards he had arranged for her patted him down and forced him to remove and replace everything in his briefcase before ushering him into the dining room. Ashley, Tabitha, and a slim, bearded guy named Seamus McCree were having breakfast.

They all looked sleep-deprived, especially Ashley, whose eyes looked like they had sunk into her head. He plunked onto a chair, and she filled him in on what happened following his departure from the office the previous night. "Few people know I'm in the Twin Cities," she concluded. "You," she swept her arm to include everyone in the room, "the board, Anton Hack, and—"

"Whoever they talked to," Malachi said. "But did anyone other than Gerald Nakourma know you were staying late and taking a cab? I can't imagine—"

She talked right over him. "I'm not counting anyone out. Incapacitating me with a drug is like what happened to Tiny and Rick in D.C. Somebody knows an awful lot about my movements. Besides delivering messages for Robert and being his superego, what is it you do at Pendergast Holdings?"

Malachi felt the burn of not being trusted. Could he offer to take a lie-detector test and prove he was telling the truth? "General human resources work, and I'm its Chief Conscience Officer."

Tabitha, who had been quietly observing the confrontation, straightened with obvious interest. "You mean you act as the company's conscience? How does that work?"

"Three years ago, Robert asked me to advise him on ethical factors he should consider before making decisions. Without Robert's permission, I can't discuss specifics."

Ashley pointed at him, her finger bobbing like a sewing machine needle. "Does he consult you on everything? Did you discuss the ethics of getting me involved with this fucking mess?"

Without proof Robert was in fact dead, Malachi was unprepared to discuss their conversations or let her know that was one of the few times Malachi's arguments had not dented the rock wall of Robert Pendergast's will.

Ashley said, "I can see you won't answer. Seamus wants me to report my kidnapping. For personal reasons, I can't. Instead, I plan to press the police to look for Robert. I won't quit pushing them or anyone else until I smoke out whoever is behind this. What time do the various board members show up for work?"

Malachi checked his watch: six-ten. "Robert arrives before seven. Gabriella usually beats him in. The brothers are at their desks by eight. Gerald takes his kids to school and arrives later."

"Doesn't give us much time. Before I can get Seamus started, I need to secure approval of my contract. Shall we?"

Malachi wondered how this Seamus guy fit in. "Get Gabriella to agree and have her convince any of the brothers. With Gerald already signing, that gives you a majority." He shifted in his chair, uncomfortable at bringing up what might be a sensitive topic. "Undercover, you dress to match the role you're playing, right?" He plowed on, not waiting for her response. "Seamus looks like a high-priced consultant. Nice suit, polished shoes."

Ashley looked from Seamus to herself. "You're saying I should dress corporate. Right, but I can't wait until the stores open at ten for some upscale shopping. We need to leave pronto."

Tabitha said, "My interview clothes might work. They're the only nice stuff I own. What size are you?"

Ashley's fitness and Tabitha's youth produced the same basic sizes. That problem solved, Malachi broached the subject of Ashley's safety.

Ashley waved a dismissive hand. "Robert kept an armory in the basement, including some excellent handguns that will do fine."

Malachi reminded her that Minnesota had tough concealed carry laws.

"I'm still the fucking FBI. Special rules for law enforcement trump state laws. Seamus, while I change, please take care of what we discussed."

She followed Seamus from the room. In the silence, Malachi checked Tabitha's reaction. She was as clueless as he was about what those two had cooked up.

Thirty-Two

Monday, May 4, Morning CDT

ASHLEY, WITH SEAMUS IN TOW, had no problem convincing Gabriella to support the contract. The three of them ambushed Junior at the receptionist's desk. Gabriella thrust the contract at him and urged him to add his signature to hers and Gerald's. Junior turned the page and anger bloomed on his face. To Ashley's surprise, he signed. "Get my brothers to sign this, too," he ordered Gabriella.

Ashley avoided using her middle name unless required and rarely even used her middle initial. With the three board members' signatures in place, she borrowed Junior's pen and signed her full moniker, Ashley Pendergast Prescott, and made the document legal. She hoped the deviation in routine would help her mentally distance the Ashley Prescott she wanted to be—top-notch FBI agent saving the U.S. from terrorists and bringing assholes to justice—from the person wearing borrowed business clothes impersonating a Pendergast Holdings CEO and nominally responsible for 40,000 employees. Lord have mercy on them all.

As her first official act, she introduced Seamus to Junior. "He'll work with Gabriella on the financial implications of everything. I'm sure you'll give him your full cooperation."

Junior's raised eyebrows expressed curiosity, but he chose not to ask questions. They traded a minute of banalities, and Junior headed toward his office, probably to perform an internet search on Seamus McCree.

"Okay, Seamus," Ashley said, "First thing, please review the merger documents and tell me which of the five variations Robert planned to use. Remember, this is more than numbers. It concerns people. Let me know how the transaction affects each board member. You'll work with Seamus on this, Gabriella?" Ashley donned her most innocent smile.

Gabriella thought they could have a high-level analysis complete that morning unless Seamus wanted more information than she had already collected.

"Excellent," Ashley said. "I'll be in Robert's office." She offered her hand to Gabriella. "Thank you so much for your cooperation. I know this isn't easy for you. I keep hoping the next footsteps I hear coming down the hall will be Robert's, ending this nightmare." Ashley appreciated Gabriella's firm handshake.

Walking away, she heard Seamus say, "Let's put this together as though we were presenting to your bankers. It'll keep us focused on the right stuff."

So Seamus-like to bring this around to the financing aspect. She'd have their report on the merger by noon, and Seamus would tell her whether to trust Gabriella. While they worked on that, she planned to catch some shut-eye.

A blond Amazon boiled out of Robert's office and raced toward Ashley. Dressed in a taupe pantsuit, the woman had to be at least six-two and was ripped. She used makeup well, presenting curves on a face that had no body fat to smooth its appearance. She wore her hair pulled into a loose ponytail. If Ashley's hair looked that good, she might grow it long.

Concern etched the woman's sculpted face. "Ms. Prescott," she said. "Good morning, Ma'am. I'm Morgan. Mr. Pendergast's admin. Someone leaked our situation to the press. Shall I contact PR?"

Puerto Rico?

Morgan must have seen the confusion on Ashley's face. "Cece in Public Relations is probably in."

Walking to Robert's office, Ashley needed two steps for each of Morgan's. "What leaked to what press?"

Morgan pulled a steno pad from the desk that guarded the entrance to Robert's door. "A TV station got a message and asked for our comment." She followed Ashley into the office and closed the door behind her. Referring to a series of scribbles that were Sanskrit to Ashley, Morgan read:

Billionaire Missing

Mr. Robert Pendergast, Sr. is MIA. Family doesn't care. Sooner he's gone, sooner they get his money. His daughter shows up from nowhere and takes control of the business. Got to be a story there. I bet she's getting revenge and planning to suck the enterprise dry. She might have killed him for all I know. Police won't listen, but I have faith in an independent press. You ask them what the truth is.

A concerned citizen.

Exactly what she had asked Seamus to do, although she had a thing or two to say about his word choices. "Robert would let PR respond?"

"He would use them to help craft the message," Morgan said. "May I summon Cece?"

Morgan placed the call and confirmed Cece would soon be on her way. Ashley used the time to follow one of the eighty-seven thousand suggestions Seamus had laid on her during their trip to the office: get in Robert's assistant's good graces. That person would know where bodies are buried and have his or her own pipeline into the organization. Ashley composed her face into a smile and asked, "Do you normally work this early?"

"Malachi thought you might require access to Robert's files. Only he—Robert, not Malachi—and I have keys. Do you drink coffee, tea?" She steered Ashley toward the conference table.

Ashley wondered if Morgan was part border collie. "I've sworn off caffeine, thanks. Do you always do what Malachi asks?"

"Usually he speaks for Rob—Mr. Pendergast." Her makeup did not disguise a blooming blush. "I checked with Gabriella—Ms. Linz first."

Seamus kept harping that the little people could make her life easy or hard. Find something, anything, in common and be yourself. This touchy-feely shit was not her style, but she had to learn, right?

"Morgan, please sit. Let's get a few things straight." Ashley sat and leaned back, a gesture she hoped would show her openness. "I also call your boss 'Robert,' and if you use first names for everyone, don't go all formal on me. And, if you haven't cottoned to it already, I have no idea what I'm doing. I'm counting on you to keep me from screwing things up. Deal? Now, which school, which sport, and what was your nickname?"

Morgan's confused smile became a grin. "I looked you up. Four years softball at UCLA. National champs. You look like you could still play. For me, it was Notre Dame, basketball. They called me Streak."

"You were fast?"

"Yeah, but that wasn't it."

"Rabbit for me. After throwing out a batter, I hop high in the air like a jack rabbit." Ashley stood, mimed throwing a ball, and performed a two-footed leap while pumping her fist in victory.

"That's funny. My freshman year, two seniors pranked me. They convinced me they had a secret society of women athletes who had streaked a guy's practice session. Nothing I wanted more than to fit in."

Ashley hooted. Her body had magically relaxed, something the analgesics she'd taken for her aches had not accomplished.

Morgan was grinning. "What can I say? I'd prefer that story not get around."

Ashley crossed her heart.

Morgan placed both hands on the desk, her expression becoming serious. "Cece will be here in a couple. You should know she's sleeping with Bradlee. She's single. He's not. Robert told Bradlee to zip his pants or he'd fire him. Bradlee claimed they were no longer seeing each other, but rumor has them still at it. Also rumored is that she's considering suing the company for treating her unfairly because of the affair."

"Did Robert hear these rumors?"

"Yes, and he planned to resolve it. I don't know how." She rose and smoothed the seat of her pants. "There's one thing else you should know." She walked to the private bathroom beyond Robert's conference area. Ashley followed.

"Robert did not allow anyone to use this. See the keypad?"

Ashley spotted it hidden in the shadows next to a floor-to-ceiling wooden cabinet. "He have drugs locked in there?"

Morgan punched in a four-digit code. The cabinet swung away from the wall, revealing a passageway to a fire door. "It exits to a stairwell. Robert used this if he didn't choose to see someone or wanted to sneak in or out without the other people on the floor knowing. The keypad on the outside uses the same code. What four-digits do you want to use?"

Morgan reset the code to one Ashley provided, and Ashley led them back into the office proper. "Why did you show this to me?"

Morgan shrugged. "I have a feeling you may need it."

A double knock sounded at the door. Dressed like an American flag: blue pantsuit, red blouse, white scarf, a short, curvy woman walked in. Ashley recognized Ms. Kraznik, the one-pump handshake whirlwind she had met yesterday.

Cece marched through the door. "Ah, there you are, Morgan. Oh, and Ashley? Where are the others?"

Ashley ignored her question and pointed Cece toward the conference room table. "Robert is still missing. The board appointed me Interim CEO. Morgan, please read Ms. Kraznik the message and make sure no one disturbs us while we create Pendergast Holdings' response."

Listening, Cece scratched her cheek, bit her lip, wrinkled her brow. No obvious emotion Ashley could read. When Morgan finished, Cece said,

"Type that up and bring me a copy." She pulled pens and papers from her monogrammed calfskin portfolio.

Morgan crooked an eyebrow and slid a sideways glance at Ashley.

"Good idea," Ashley said. "Ms. Kraznik, would you like something to drink while we work?"

"My usual, Morgan."

"Morgan will type the note," Ashley added in a saccharin tone, "Shall I get your 'usual' for you while you consider our response?"

Morgan ducked to hide her grin. Cece colored beet red, which pleased Ashley more than it should have. It was like she had reverted to high school rivalries, and the jocks had scored one over the snooty girls.

"That's not necessary. Call me Cece. Everyone does." Ashley offered a tiny nod of acceptance, allowing Cece to continue. "I'm confused. How did the press find out about this?"

Ashley raised her eyebrows. "Good question. Especially since his housekeeper only filed the missing-persons report this morning. Makes me wonder who's been talking to whom."

Thirty-Three

WHILE THEY DRAFTED THE NEWS release, Cece attempted to learn Ashley's plans. Good luck with that, since she didn't have any. Ashley had more luck probing Cece to understand what made her tick.

Cece grew up a navy brat, having to prove herself every time her father posted to a new base. She'd been the first of her family to graduate from college. Like Ashley, she had married and divorced. In Cece's case, leaving her beached in the Twin Cities, far from the oceans she had grown up on.

"It was during the 2008 financial crisis. I had a good job here. Later, after my brother's enlistment ended, he followed me to the Twin Cities. I helped him open a business."

Cece demonstrated a sharp mind, a biting sense of humor, and grit. Clearly not the stuck-up society girl Ashley had assumed. She thought she could like the PR Director, despite Morgan's warning. She reminded herself to keep an open mind. Morgan might have her own agenda. But if Cece and Bradlee were still screwing around, that was a problem.

Press release complete, she escorted Cece to Morgan's desk. "Morgan, please direct to Cece any further phone calls concerning Robert's absence or Pendergast Holdings' response to the situation. I'm sure she'll do a magnificent job using soothing words while saying nothing." She offered Cece her hand. "I mean that to be a compliment."

They exchanged a two-pump handshake. Firm grip.

Watching Cece walk to the elevator. Ashley was eager to discover how Morgan comported herself. Would she try to find out how things had gone, or provide a catty comment, or move onto something else?

"This was Robert's schedule for today." Morgan handed Ashley a printed calendar marked in six-minute increments: a fine reminder of why Ashley had shunned corporate life. From oh-eight-thirty until noon, there wasn't enough free time even to go to the bathroom. The afternoon was only slightly better.

"Any of these fire-alarm important?"

"Nothing life or death."

"Assume Robert will be here next week and reschedule them. If anyone convinces you they can't wait, make an appointment for them with Seamus. You can shut the door behind you."

Ensconced in Robert's office, Ashley went online and checked messages for all her phones. Both her personal cellphone and Niki's featured Gex pleading multiple times for her to call him before his meeting at 0945 hours with Deputy Director Ambrose. The clock on Robert's desk read 8:40 a.m. Time zone differences meant she had five minutes to catch him.

"What the hell is going on, Prescott?"

Before she let Gex interrogate her, she insisted he update her on Tiny and Rick. Rick was fine and the hospital would release Tiny later that day. She summarized the steps she'd taken, and that there had been a second attempt to grab her.

He surprised her with, "How can I help?"

Gratitude tingled up her spine, replaced by a chill of admiration. Gex was not actually *offering* to help. This was a continuation of his interrogation, a subtle way to understand her plans, her state of mind.

"The local police are skeptical someone kidnapped Robert Pendergast because his car is missing, and no one has made demands. Can you back-channel a way the FBI could offer help?"

"That's a little touchy since they haven't contacted us. I'll see what we can do. Anything else?"

I'm not saying a thing more until you show your cards.

Into the silence, Gex cleared his throat. "There's something you can help me with. Instead of assigning you to desk duty pending the outcome of the shooting investigation, Deputy Director Ambrose wants to suspend you and roll up all your UC assignments."

Like a drag racer, her anger blew from zero to a hundred. "That's nuts. We won't stop the weapons. We won't learn who's running PFF, who funds them. It's—"

"You're preaching to the choir. He thinks you've gone off the rails. I pleaded with him to meet you in person and hear your perspective. See if you can convince him. He's read the reports. Only you can show him how in control you are and make him taste how close we are to real success."

Preaching to the choir was not how she remembered Gex's position. Now that sidelining her was Ambrose's idea, Gex was on *her* side? "But with everything we've already invested—"

"It's risk assessment. He pulls the plug, we round up a bunch of militia. He can spin that to the press to look like a big FBI win. Ambrose wants to be the next director. Sacrificing your career or mine is not his concern. Convince him you are on top of your game, fully in control, not distracted by what's happening to your father or his business. Do it or, at best, you're looking at twenty years of running background checks for security-clearance applicants. More likely, they'll require your removal because you left the scene of a shooting."

She was missing something. His voice oozed with concern for her welfare. Was he cutting his losses, sending her, the sacrificial lamb, to the DD's slaughter? Or did he genuinely believe she could persuade Ambrose to keep her undercover assignments alive? Gex had once been the Bureau's top undercover operator. One reason she had agreed to move to D.C. was to learn from the best. If he were still an UC operator at heart, he'd root for her success.

But he was a suit now, with a mortgage, kids in college, and up for a big promotion. That made him a team player in an organization that stressed team players even if they were holding long knives behind their backs. If he were playing on her ego to get her to D.C., he might not have spent the energy to think through the implications of the most recent twists at Patriots For Freedom.

She tested that theory out. "How do you read the communications I recently received from Sergeant Oliver?"

"I'm worried that showing him up with the sniper rifle is a festering wound that won't heal. Be careful around him. Rick suggested, and I agree, that we take him off the street. Something legal that's temporary and unrelated to PFF. We'll discuss that once you've convinced Ambrose to let us proceed."

That was an appropriate answer, but UC's and former UC's have exceptional abilities to improvise. She already knew how to neutralize Sergeant Oliver. "And the Chinese arms supplier's offer?"

"I want to hear how the militia responds before I brief Ambrose. You handled that well. Played hard to get, showed you were a team player, responded in a timely manner even though you had other issues distracting you. All points we can make to Ambrose. Look . . ."

Ashley pictured Gex removing his cheaters and rubbing his nose while he chose his words.

"We don't have much time. Catch a flight to D.C., and I'll get you on the DD's schedule for eighteen-hundred or eighteen-thirty this evening. You're officially on administrative leave. I am one hundred percent confident you can do it. But it has to be today."

But Gex, I am not nearly that confident in you. He was right that no one could defend the strategic importance of her undercover work better than she could. That gave her an opportunity to put a bug in the DD's ear about the leak. Gex had not mentioned that at all. Maybe because it didn't matter to him if she remained with the FBI. Dammit, it sure mattered *to her.*

"Okay." She stretched the second syllable, like she was struggling for the exact details. "Make it for eighteen-thirty. I can stop by my apartment, change clothes, and freshen up. Leave me the details in an email." She hung up before Gex could request she provide him her flight specifics to arrange for someone to meet her at the airport.

She had plans, and they didn't involve visiting her apartment.

THIRTY-FOUR

AN HOUR INTO THE FLIGHT on the Pendergast jet, Ashley used the facilities and poked Malachi's shoulder before yanking her seatbelt tight.

He awoke with a jerk.

"You've had enough beauty sleep, and I want some answers before we arrive in D.C."

He blinked the grogginess from his eyes. "Look, even if they charge me with murder, I plan to tell them I shot the guy."

"My report makes it clear it was self-defense. They won't charge you. Your first issue was disarming me, and—"

"Maybe in retrospect I should have given you more credit. I'm not changing my story."

"Stick with the truth. They'll pound you six ways from Sunday to understand why an otherwise model citizen left the scene with me."

"I won't lie. I had just killed someone, and I wasn't thinking. You had the gun, were FBI, and told me what to do. I did it." He raised the window shade and leaned toward the window.

They'd find inconsistencies between Malachi's statement and hers. One big one was that, while she had pointed Malachi in the direction she wanted, she had *not told* Malachi to leave the crime scene. That was okay; not finding *any* differences would be a huge red flag that they had coordinated their stories. She switched gears from worrying about what happened at Ike's Diner to the reason they had been there. "How did you first meet Robert?"

He shifted his attention to her, his face hinting a smile. "I got a call one morning telling me the corporate jet was bringing me to Minneapolis. I figured they planned to fire me."

"Excuse me?"

"I told a customer not to spend twelve million dollars buying equipment from us. Ours was overkill. A competitor had a better alternative that solved all his needs and cost four million less."

She reared back in doubt. "Seriously?" She motioned him to continue.

"Thou shalt not bear false witness. The buyer asked if I were in his shoes would I buy the equipment. I told him why I wouldn't."

Ashley rolled that startling piece of information between the hemispheres of her brain. "Are you saying you never lie?"

"Not knowingly."

She gave him a speculative look. "Why did you wait that long to tell him the machine was unsuitable?"

"The buyer was interested only in the specifications, repair history, warranties, power requirements. I answered every question accurately. He never asked if our solution was the best for him. When he did, I explained why it wasn't."

"I can see why you thought they'd fire you. What was your job?"

"Engineering, but often I assisted sales with technical expertise. Anyway, your father—sorry—Robert must approve terminations of anyone above a certain level in the company. He flew me to Minneapolis, listened to my reasoning, and hired me to be his superego."

"Because you won't lie."

He flashed his white teeth. "He wanted someone to tell him the truth, even if he didn't want to hear it."

"But only," Ashley pressed, "if he asks the right question. You *never* lie? You're one hundred percent honest?"

"No."

This was like one of those math logic puzzles she hated. You're stuck on an island of cannibals. Half are truth-tellers; the other half consistently lie. To learn how to escape, you must create the precise question so it doesn't matter which group you ask. Seamus would love those. She had never mastered the double and triple negatives involved.

Oh hell, just ask. "Why no?"

"Sometimes I refuse to answer." He pointed outside. "Doesn't Chicago look attractive in the distance?"

She leaned and caught the Chicago skyline scrolling past. And Lake Michigan below. Her gut leaped into her throat, blocking her from breathing. She pinched her eyes shut and listened to the hum of the engines, every minor deviation in pitch a sure harbinger of engine failure. A newsreel played behind her eyelids: the plane spiraling into the lake, trapping her inside, the fuselage filling with water. *Worse than watching the waves.*

Her hands became super vises on the seat arms. Despite her fear, her glance kept returning to view the terrifying lake below. She forced herself to face him. "Do you know why Robert sent you to fetch me?"

"Other than that he urgently wanted to see you? No."

"How did Robert get my phone number?"

"I don't know."

She shook a finger at him. "You don't know, or you won't say."

"I'd tell you if I knew. Unless Robert asked me not to, but he didn't. I can't tell the police any more than I told you because there isn't any more."

Malachi was an interesting moral puzzle. If she pried off the right pieces of his protective armor, she might wriggle inside it. She wasn't sure whether to believe his no-lie claim, but she would go with that presumption until proved wrong.

She watched his face for any tells and machine-gunned questions at him. "Do you know where Robert is?"

"No."

"Did you tell anyone I was at Pendergast Holdings last night?"

"No."

"Meeting me at the D.C. diner?"

"Only the message I left Robert."

"Any clue how the tracking app got on your phone?"

"No."

She gave him a hard stare, and he added, "I wish you had found it before you made me throw away all my clothes. I don't remember opening any suspicious emails, but it's possible. I leave my phone on my desk all the time at Pendergast Holdings."

Yeah, and if she hadn't removed it, the FBI's computer guys might have learned how someone had installed it. Bad on her. "Did you mention you were coming to D.C. with me today or that you plan to speak with the police?"

"How could I? I didn't know I was flying today until I learned you were taking the plane."

Which didn't exactly answer the question. "The first time, was anyone other than Robert aware you were fetching me? The crew? Your wife? Girlfriend? Boyfriend?"

He chuckled. "No, no, no, and no. The crew knew I expected to bring a passenger."

"This bone-frog tattoo thing. Is it real common for SEALS?"

He frowned. "Some units more than others, why?"

"Because the attempted kidnapper last night also had one on his neck."

"What? Is it safe for you in Washington?"

He sure acted surprised. She assumed the same straight-backed posture he had taken while she questioned him and mimed his inflection. "No."

THIRTY-FIVE

ASHLEY, DISGUISED AS A NONDESCRIPT, middle-aged, worn-down flunky, the sort of person you'd pass by without a second look, arrived thirty minutes early for her eighteen-thirty appointment with Gex and Deputy Director Garland Ambrose. She settled behind an administrative assistant's desk, pulled the keyboard into position, and pretended to type an urgent memo. The jig was up if anyone noticed the dark terminal. At eighteen-fifteen hours, Gex blew by her, knocked on Ambrose's door. Ambrose stuck his head out, did a quick scan, then ushered Gex in and closed the door.

Good. She wanted Gex there while Rick Kaska delivered the material she had sent him. They agreed Rick would arrive five minutes before her meeting was supposed to start.

As the seconds ticked by, her mouth grew dry, and the acid in her stomach burned stronger. Much longer and there'd be a hole in her side. Her watch ticked past eighteen-twenty-five. No Rick. Eighteen-thirty. Where the hell was he? They wouldn't wait for ever. If Gex left on his own, she'd confront Ambrose. If they left together, she'd have to tackle them as a pair.

Eighteen-thirty-four, the elevator door's ding interrupted her typing the billionth iteration of "Mary Had a Little Lamb." Rick rushed by, pausing to hand-comb his hair and straighten his tie before giving a double tap at Ambrose's door.

"Please enter," Ambrose said in a Southern drawl slow enough you could fall asleep between words.

Her research earlier in the day informed her that behind Ambrose's facade of back-slapping bonhomie was one of the sharpest brains in the bureau. A Rhodes Scholar, he slept only four hours a night, educating himself about everything while others snoozed.

Rick opened the door and stepped past the threshold. "Excuse me, sir. I know you're expecting Special Agent Prescott. She asked me to deliver this note."

"Thank you, Agent Kaska. Please, have a seat."

Ashley slipped an ear bud in place and caught the zip of a letter opener slicing the envelope. A whisper of linen paper suggested he had extracted her missive. Guessing Ambrose was reading her note, she strained to catch a sound. She wished she could see into the room to gauge his reaction.

Deputy Director Ambrose:

Someone at the FBI is a security risk. They provided my undercover address and one of my undercover phone numbers to Robert Pendergast, Sr. I understand you believe I have gone "off the rails." Before you pull my badge, I offer you a no-risk opportunity: if I cannot convince you why it is in our national interest to continue my current undercover assignments, I will resign, and you won't have to go through the arduous and open-to-FOIA process necessary to fire me. My only requirement is that our meeting be private because of the previously mentioned security breach.

If you agree, Special Agent Kaska will give you a burner phone on which I will contact you once you are alone.

Special Agent Ashley Prescott

"Read this, Gex," Ambrose said. "You know what this says, Agent Kaska?"

"No sir. A messenger delivered the sealed envelope, this phone, and a note asking me to deliver them both to you. I had trouble with traffic."

"She's your charge, Gex. How do you suggest we handle it?"

Ambrose's voice sounded louder. Rick must have taken the burner phone from his pocket, which allowed its microphone to operate better.

"She's fervent in her beliefs. It's both a great strength and a weakness. With the pressure she's under, I don't know what she might do if you refuse her."

"And you suggest . . . ?"

Ashley smiled, admiring the way Ambrose kept Gex wriggling on the hook.

"She wants to convince you of her position, but this is clearly an insubordinate act." Gex's voice gained strength. "She's on administrative leave, though you wouldn't know it. You should suspend her subject to a complete investigation by the shooter review team. She's reading her emails. Tell her that, and she'll come in to make her statement."

"Do you agree?" Ambrose asked.

Rick cleared his throat. "What do you have to lose by listening to her, sir? Under pressure or not, I trust her. She is the finest undercover agent I know working for the FBI. She believes someone on her team is not trustworthy. I get that. I don't think you're at risk. You can put security in place. Record what she has to say. I'm sure she'll try. If you still need to suspend her, everyone will understand."

Rick had one thing correct. She was recording now.

"Leave the phone," Ambrose said. "I'll discuss my options with legal in the morning. Thank you for your time."

Hearing Ambrose's dismissal, Ashley dropped the ear bud into her lap and ordered her fingers to type the Pledge of Allegiance.

Gex stormed through the doorway, Rick scrambling to catch up. "Don't bother closing the door," Ambrose drawled.

"You in this with her, Kaska? Why didn't you call me rather than schlepping that stuff around like she has a ring through your nose? You looked like a fool calling her the best UC."

"How can he make the right decision if he doesn't know shit about her?"

Gex voice trembled with menace. "Well, now he knows some shit about you."

"He's known me since I was born. Probably watched my mother change my shitty diapers."

Ashley controlled her surprise and switched from typing the Pledge of Allegiance to the witches' song from *Macbeth*. She'd chosen Rick to deliver her note because she figured he'd do it just so he could drink free beers off the story for months. She hadn't factored in Rick's family connections. His father and Ambrose must be friends. She needed to better consider FBI politics in the future.

Gex strode past her, his face a granite block of anger. Rick no longer bothered keeping up with him. She caught him scanning her body. He was incorrigible, but his nonrecognition proved how well she had fashioned her disguise.

Ashley continued typing until the elevator's doors dinged and the whir of the car's descent disturbed the quiet.

Grabbing her knapsack, she strolled to the DD's door and found him behind his desk looking outside, their side-by-side reflections in the window staring back.

"I assume you are Special Agent Prescott. Won't you please come in?"

"Yes, sir."

He settled into his chair. "When I spotted a frumpy, middle-aged, unfamiliar woman working late, I wondered if it was you. Gex walked by you twice. Impressive. Did Agent Kaska know?"

At her denial, he continued. "You went to all this trouble to arrange our meeting. It wouldn't be gentlemanly of me to refuse."

"I'm sorry for the subterfuge, but I don't feel I can trust normal channels." She extracted her badge from her knapsack and laid it on the desk.

THIRTY-SIX

AMBROSE RAISED HIS EYEBROWS, LET them settle. "Sit, please. I read your file today. What made you join the Bureau? We are a hierarchical, rules-bound, male-dominated organization. Why not the CIA with its long tradition of using female assets? You didn't get some romantic idea of following Aloysius Pendergast into the FBI, carrying on the family name, so to speak?"

Was he testing her? Did he know the CIA had unsuccessfully recruited her? She reminded herself to remain calm regardless of what happened.

"First time I heard of Douglas Preston, Lincoln Child, and their fictional FBI agent Aloysius Pendergast was at the academy. My arms instructor made sure everyone knew I was Robert Pendergast's daughter. Called me the little rich bitch who stole a position from a man who deserved it."

"Old school. Did that motivate you to earn top scores for your class and outshoot your instructor?"

"My academy instructor knew his stuff. In retrospect, he not only taught us to shoot, he mentally toughened us. I don't think he believed that line. He knew others did and repeated it so often it lost its bite. I was first in rifle, but only third with a pistol. But target shooting isn't trying to beat an opponent. It's challenging yourself to overcome your limitations. I was a competition shooter before I joined. That day, he had too much caffeine in his system to win."

Ambrose gave her a ghost of a smile. "Why the FBI?"

"I was in high school when al-Qaeda attacked us on nine-eleven, and I knew then that I wanted to protect our country from harm. The CIA tried to recruit me after college to use my language skills to translate intel. I grew up in Big Sky Country. No way did I want a desk job, but before they approached me, I hadn't considered intelligence gathering. Their offer intrigued me, and to spite everyone, I rejected the spooks and applied to the Bureau."

"Spite everyone?"

She'd learned during her stint in Mississippi how important family was to Southerners and decided, for Ambrose, she should refer to Robert as her father. "Specifically, my father. He wanted me to join his business. I made it clear I wouldn't, and he went behind my back and encouraged the CIA to offer me a job."

"Yet it seems your father has gotten his wish to involve you with Pendergast Holdings. Something of a distraction for a special agent doing important undercover work."

She'd wager Ambrose's honey-sweet drawl had lured plenty of people to let their guard down and not realize he was a masterful interrogator. Time to make her pitch. "Yes, sir. I initially rejected my father's request—demand— to meet him this weekend. Once I understood he had suborned someone to provide him with both my undercover phone number *and* address, I thought it important to determine who that person was and what damage they'd done. My father wasn't going to come to me, so I had to go see him. I hoped he would tell me how he got the information, and we could plug that leak. I'm sure you're aware my father is missing—I believe kidnapped and likely killed. You also have my report of the kidnapping attempt on me at the diner."

"We share your concern about the leaker, but your safety concerns me more." If Ambrose were a cat, he'd be purring.

Now to avoid the trap Ambrose had probably set. "The easiest way to keep me safe is to plant false stories of Niki's death. Easy isn't necessarily better. PFF differs from any other domestic terrorist group we've infiltrated. They don't proclaim themselves on social media. No white supremacist bullshit, marching the streets with signs and guns. Obviously," she pointed to herself, "they include females, and I've seen Blacks and Latinos. A captain with a Star of David neck chain. They are a well organized, multi-celled operation, planning to foment anarchy for reasons that are unclear. Now it looks like they're planning assassinations. We have invested a lot in my undercover assignments, but that alone does not justify persisting. The FBI should continue my operations because its future benefits don't merely outweigh, they overwhelm the risks. If I may?"

A sly smile crept onto his face. Was he a cat toying with a mouse before dispatching it or actually interested? His leaning back and linking his hands behind his head meant he would keep listening. For now.

"Nothing any of us can do if someone thinks they can kidnap me for money. That wasn't the militia, anyway. If—"

"You're aware your kidnappers were former servicemen?"

"SEALs, sir. Every veteran I've met in Patriots For Freedom has been Army. No Marines. No Air Force. No Navy." Hearing her words, she realized other PFF cells might contain representatives of those service branches. To cover up that logic flaw, she pressed forward with her case. "If the FBI closes down PFF, we get a few guys on a bunch of diddly-squat charges. Those weapons are already in-country. We lose them, we lose our chance to learn who the most senior PFF members are and to discover their funding sources. Believe me, they're not selling Girl Scout cookies to raise money. Someone has deep pockets.

"We give up the chance to learn who they're targeting for assassination, and we lose the Chinese supplier. Let my assignment run and we secure the weapons, keeping them from *any* terrorists. Make a militia member the scapegoat for the arms sales going sour. That keeps me in PFF's good graces. Plus, if we allow the Chinese buyer to escape, I can work with him. If you sideline me now, you'll lose it all." She was breathing hard and forced herself to sit back in the chair.

"That's it?" His hands shifted from behind his head to rest on his stomach.

Ashley's undercover training had taught her to never oversell. She wasn't sure he *was* sold. But until she heard his objections, she couldn't address them. Sounding for once like a humble Special Agent talking to her boss's boss's boss, she said, "I'm prepared to answer questions."

"Gex wants to suspend you for insubordination. Others want to terminate you for cause. In either event, you still must clear the shooting investigation, which means—"

A dark chasm opened before her. No way had she thought termination was a consideration. "If my assignment didn't have national security implications, I would agree that following department policy makes sense. However, given the—"

"Most would say it *always* makes sense to follow departmental policy. Especially when it involves administrative leave following a shooting." He crossed his arms. "How can you execute your plan if you don't trust your team?"

"Let Metro police handle the deaths at the diner. We know the prosecutor won't charge anyone. Assign agents to investigate the attempted kidnapping of a federal officer. Interview everybody about the leak. That will put everyone on their best behavior." Let him think bygones are bygones. No reason to reveal her plan to ferret out whoever had leaked her information and see them destroyed.

"And the departmental duty to investigate agent-related civilian deaths?"

"Gex and Rick both walked by me twice without recognizing me. I'm sure we can find a way for me to present testimony in a manner that won't compromise operations. I wore a wire that night at Ike's Diner. Have you listened to the audio?"

He smiled and reached a hand toward her.

Yes! It worked! Ashley brought her hand from her lap to shake his.

He collected her badge and dropped it into a drawer. "A short resignation letter will do. Effective . . ." He glanced at the gold watch adorning his left wrist. "Seven o'clock is close enough."

Ashley's stomach spasmed, she choked the burning vomit down her throat. Blinking away tears, she refused to brush them from her eyes, she pulled the blank stationery to her and picked up the gold pen from Ambrose's desk.

As requested by Deputy Director Ambrose in his office on the date and time affixed below, I hereby resign from the Federal Bureau of Investigation effective immediately.

She wondered what she should add, decided anything more would sound like whining or making excuses. She signed and dated the note, laid the pen on the paper, pushed them both to Ambrose, and stood.

He swept them into the same drawer that held her badge—former badge. "Hold on a minute. You've proved yourself resourceful, principled, a woman of her word. I don't want you to stop your work."

Meaning what? If he had something else to say, he could damn well say it without her help. She held his stare.

"The country needs your services. Right now, what's in that drawer is between us. Everyone thinks you are on paid administrative leave until cleared of the shooting. If this works the way you believe it will, I'll return them and life goes on. Fuck up and embarrass us, the world will learn you were impersonating the agent you once were." He flicked a hand in the air. "A paperwork screwup allowed you to get away with it. You won't go to jail, but you'll never work law enforcement again. Do we have a private understanding?"

"You want me to keep doing my job, except without a badge, with no support, and if I don't succeed, you'll have me arrested on a felony impersonating charge. Did I miss anything?"

"Two points, small but not minor. The charges, which won't stick, only happen if you screw up and embarrass the Bureau." He held up a second finger. "If you need support, contact me. I have the burner phone."

"With all due respect, sir, this is total bullshit. But I accept your offer because I know I can succeed. I'll see myself out."

She maintained a steady gait to the elevators, despite her legs feeling like cooked spaghetti. Once inside the elevator, she enunciated into her phone, "Recording stopped by A. Prescott at nineteen-hundred hours six minutes."

THIRTY-SEVEN

ASHLEY WAS EXHAUSTED AND WIRED, a bad combination. Knowing sleep would not come soon, after returning to Minneapolis on the Pendergast private jet, she Ubered to the Pendergast Offices, signed in at the security guard station, and rode the elevator to the executive floor.

Since she hadn't thought to get a key from Morgan, she walked past the entrance to the hallway by the fire escape and used the secret entrance into Robert's private bathroom. A line of light appeared under the office door. Could be cleaning people at ten o'clock on a Monday night. Or something more nefarious. She pulled the pistol from her shoulder harness and hid it behind her. Cracked open the door. Seamus sat at Robert's desk, scribbling notes on a yellow legal pad. She tiptoed up to him and said, "Did you execute a coup in my absence?"

Seamus nearly toppled onto the floor. "I thought you were in D.C."

"Private jets fly both ways." She retrieved the two suitcases, left them parked against a wall, and plopped down onto a chair in front of the desk. "I figured I'd check email and see if Morgan left me any messages. I guess I can put this away." She holstered the gun. "How was *your* day? Mine sucked. Did I ever tell you how much I hate cover-your-ass politics? I figured the worst that happens is I get stuck on desk duty and can't accomplish shit. Wrong again. *My* boss wants to suspend me. *His* boss wants to can me, and *that* guy's boss makes me sign and date my resignation letter and then offers me a just-between-the-two-of-us deal to keep me investigating the militia. They got another think coming if they believe that charade will protect their asses. You hear what I'm saying?"

"What I hear is a coiled spring wound so tight it'll soon sprong. Start from the beginning because I don't know what any of that meant."

"Never mind. Not your problem. It means I found a way to keep working on my undercover assignments." She mimed adjusting a hat on her head. "Shifting gears, I'm putting on my CEO hat. Don't you dare laugh. Give me the ten-thousand-foot view. Who you trust and who might be responsible for all this?" She pointed past him to the pizza box on the credenza behind him. "Any left?"

Seamus handed her a napkin and a cold slice of plain cheese pizza. "Gabriella strikes me as smart, and a straight shooter with finances. Besides being the CFO, she's doing much of what a chief operating officer would do. She was on track to step into Robert's CEO role in five years. With—"

Around a mouthful of food with no taste she said, "So she's pissed that Robert named me the interim CEO?"

"The opposite. She wants no part of a family feud. Now, you want ten-thousand feet, or should I muck in the weeds?"

Ashley stuffed in the last of the pizza and mimed zipping shut her mouth.

Seamus gave her an eye-roll like he didn't think she could do it. "Summarizing, I'll be shocked if she's been leaking material. Not Gerald Nakourma, the corporate counsel, either. I did your bidding and determined which cab company he called. Different outfit from the one that abducted you. I talked to the driver the intended firm sent for you, a nice guy from Somalia. He still seemed upset about how this big white dude scared him off. Matches what the lobby guard told you. Anyway, Gerald's probably terrific at dotting Is and crossing Ts, but he's a belt and suspenders kind of guy. Again, short story. He has lots to lose if Pendergast Holdings doesn't prosper or has to sell."

"You're saying zero chance?"

Seamus put on a big frowny face and mirrored her zipped lips. Got her smiling. "Come on, you know better than that. Given the right circumstances, you can buy anyone. I don't see him taking that kind of risk. Whereas your half-brothers . . ." He squared the papers on his desk and drained the water glass. Typical Seamus stall tactics. She waved him on.

"They are pieces of work. Robert planned to fire one. One is developing illegal or at least immoral pesticides. The third is extremely competent, unless you think stealing on a grand scale is a problem."

Ashley pinched the bridge of her nose. "Screw looking at my emails. I need a drink before you tell me who's who. If you help with my luggage, we can walk to your hotel, where I'm also staying. The last time I caught a cab from here did not go well. I'd like to have my hands free." She patted her jacket above her secreted pistol.

THIRTY-EIGHT

Monday, May 4, Evening CDT

SHE AND SEAMUS HANDED THE signed exit form to the security guard. He responded to her good night with a jaunty salute and released the exterior door. Seamus maneuvered her two suitcases onto the sidewalk. She wanted an unobstructed view and told Seamus to walk ahead, which had the bonus that she could avoid small talk or discussing business and concentrate on keeping them safe.

Seamus refused the hotel doorman's offer to help with the bags. She caught up with him before he got to the front desk. "Let's get a drink first." He veered toward the bar and grill next to the lobby and led her to a two-person table far away from the crowd of millennials yucking it up, a bevy of craft beers in front of them. He tucked her suitcases and his briefcase under an adjacent table.

A server dragged herself to stand before them. "What can I get y'all?" She used a pencil to push a stray lock of hair behind her ear.

Ashley ordered a Manhattan; Seamus a house Cabernet and a medium-rare Shroom Burger featuring four kinds of mushrooms and two cheeses. "Lettuce, pickles, onions, brown mustard, no tomatoes. A side of sweet potato fries."

"Sorry I ate your last disgusting piece of pizza. I didn't realize you were still hungry. When did you start eating pickles and onions?"

"It's for you. The way you scarfed that slice, I know you didn't have dinner. Skipped lunch, too? You're not twenty anymore. Your brain needs food to deal with stress."

"Yes, Mom."

As the server delivered their drinks and water, Seamus asked her, "How did a nice southern girl like you end up in Minneapolis?"

A smile crept onto her face. "A full-ride scholarship a thousand miles away from my parents. I'm finishing a double major at the university this spring. Electrical Engineering combined with Computer Engineering. What brings you two into town?"

"Family," Ashley said at the same time Seamus said, "Business."

Seamus laughed. "Family business. That's no slouch of a double major. And you're working this job, too?"

"I usually work weekends, but I'm trying to squirrel away some money to pay for a move to wherever I end up finding a job. Let me check how your order's coming."

"Cheers," Ashley raised her cocktail and clinked glasses with Seamus's wine. "I see you're still chatting up the servers."

"A little kindness never hurt anyone, and I've found that it's the so-called 'little people' who—"

"Can make your life miserable or easy. Speaking of miserable, give me the scoop on the brothers. Start with Junior."

"I guess I've used that line before. But it pays off. To that point, Morgan's taken a real shine to you." Seamus indulged in a long sip of wine. "Junior isn't the brightest of the three, but he knows his shit. He runs Pendergast Holdings' most profitable business sector. Thoroughly understands it and consistently hits his targets. Too consistently. Gabriella says she brought up the issue with Robert. I'll give you hundred-to-one odds Junior's skimming big time."

The Manhattan went straight to Ashley's head. Seamus was right, she needed food. "But he's worth millions."

"He'd be worth considerably more millions if Robert were dead. As would his brothers. And if they force the company's sale, they get their hands on the money much sooner. Do you know who gets Pendergast Holdings' profits?"

"Anton Hack told me each brother owns fifteen percent of the stock. Robert owns—"

"Those are voting shares. Each voting share contains only one-tenth of a dividend share. Meaning, your brothers each receive one and a half percent of declared dividend. The dividend is peanuts because Robert, who owns all the other dividend shares, reinvests most of the profits in the business. Last year each brother's dividend was only thirty-five thousand. Your brothers make decent money, but they aren't super rich."

"I get that each of the three benefits on Robert's death. But something triggered this now. Was Robert planning on firing Junior? Otherwise, why wouldn't Junior just keep doing what he's been doing?"

"Firing Junior and shining a light on his misdeeds reflects poorly on

Pendergast Holdings. Robert's plan is genius and allows him to give Junior a temporary pass. The FTC, Federal Trade Commission, will object to the merger Robert wants on antitrust grounds. Robert can circumvent that by spinning off much of Junior's division into a separate company, removing the antitrust issues. They'd take it public and leave Junior in charge. Junior'd either mend his ways or deal with the consequences of public accounting reviews. Two birds, one stone. Post-merger, Pendergast Holdings is stronger, and Junior is no longer papa's problem."

"Making Junior strongly motivated to keep the status quo."

"Or force the company to sell, which is why he might leak information to the competitors. According to both Gabriella and Gerald, Robert planned to fire Bradlee. Neither would say why. His financial performance has been mediocre, but I don't think that was it."

"He's boinking the staff," Ashley said. "Or so says Morgan. And Garrett?"

"She'd likely know." Seamus swirled the wine before taking a sip. "My bet is Garrett is the smartest of the three. I may be wrong about the pesticides becoming a problem. The new products he's bringing to market later this year will be highly profitable. But if I read the environmental studies correctly, they suggest selling the product may expose Pendergast Holdings to crippling lawsuits. I'm not a chemist, but I can't understand why EPA is allowing them. I suppose with this administration, anything that has the potential to produce a job or make a buck is good. The other possibility is the company is bribing someone at the EPA. Even if the products are legal, they're immoral. They're the equivalent of cigarettes for the environment." He shook his head. "I'm letting my politics show."

Screw waiting for food. She downed the rest of her Manhattan. "Is there reason to think Robert would agree with you? What motivation could Garrett have to leak information?"

"Here comes the food," Seamus gestured past Ashley's shoulder. "You should ask for her resume."

"Why would I do that?"

"CEOs should be on the lookout for talent. I like her work ethic, and I'll bet she's smart. And it costs you nothing."

Ashley considered the CEO reference a low blow. He knew she hated this entire enterprise. "I'm glad someone's having a marvelous time with this whole thing."

The waitress delivered the burger to Seamus. He passed it to Ashley, who cut it in half and wafted in the steaming vapors of beef and melted cheese, topped with the tang of bread and butter pickles. She took a bite and heard herself mm-mming like a contented cat lapping milk fresh from the cow.

Seamus said to the server, "Sometimes I know her mind better than she does."

"Another Manhattan? Cabernet?"

Ashley wanted a second drink, but tomorrow morning would go better without a hangover. "Thanks, no. You can bring us the check."

The server placed the bill between them. Seamus said, "Are you looking to stay in the area?"

"If I could, but I'm more interested in the right job. I've had offers, but none of them thrill me."

"Shoot me a copy of your resume. I can show it to some people. Nothing might come of it, but you never know." He handed her his card.

She thanked Seamus, using the correct "Shay-mus" pronunciation. Tucking his card into her pocket, she left with a bounce to her step.

Ashley focused on the food, embarrassed to look at her dinner companion. She'd succumbed to her pity-party, ignored his suggestion, and all it had cost Seamus was a few seconds of time and a business card to make the server's day better. Would she ever learn?

He pushed the bill to her side of the table. "Yours, I believe."

She frowned. "Hey, Mr. Moneybags, I thought you were buying me a birthday drink. Besides, you ordered the burger, not me."

"And who scarfed that burger down? Seriously, you've got a ton to learn about being a bigwig. We talked business, meaning it's on the company's tab. Good corporate policy requires the boss to pick up the check rather than approve the expense report of the underling. And you be da boss."

"You're getting a lot of satisfaction reminding me. Maybe I should cut your pay in half."

"One drink and now she's a comedian." He was shaking his head, but at least she had him smiling. "Seriously, corporations developed most rules for solid reasons. If you're not sure how to do something, ask Morgan. She'll protect your ass."

"Fine. Fine. I'll ask. Does your room have double beds, or did you spend the extra bucks for a king-size?" She enjoyed catching Seamus off guard, watching him wondering where she was going with this.

His eyes crinkled in amusement. "First you cut my zero pay in half, and now you're worried my exorbitant expenses are hurting your bottom line?"

"No, I'm sharing your room, and I want to know if we're sleeping separately or together."

She burst out laughing at his scarlet face. Maybe the Manhattan had loosened her up. Regardless, the look on his face was priceless.

Thirty-Nine

ASHLEY WOKE UP FEELING REFRESHED. She rolled over to check on Seamus. His side of the bed was empty, the sheets cool. The clock read seconds before six. Why did the bum leave to run without her? They were supposed to be training buds. Well, she could get in a little yoga, a practice she tried to maintain along with her early morning run. If she had enough time, she might take another bubble bath. The one last night had relaxed her right to sleep in the tub. Seamus had to wake her up. At the memory of what happened after that, an internal glow warmed her. Maybe if he got back early . . .

She shucked her nightshirt, folded, and stored it in a drawer. Rooting around in the two suitcases she had packed with clothing from her Lincolnia apartment after meeting with Deputy Director Ambrose, she found a sports bra, running shorts, and mat. Placing the mat to face the windows, she flowed through the positions of the salute to the sun. The flow wasn't smooth enough. As she repeated the routine, her muscles released the tension they'd held. She progressed to more advanced poses, holding the strength positions until her muscles quivered to near exhaustion. While in an arm stand, legs held parallel to the floor, an unfamiliar ringtone sounded. Seamus's?

She popped up, realized it was her new burner phone, and recognized Tabitha's number. She answered with, "You okay?"

"A ransom note. Stuck on an arrow. My God, it could have killed a guard. He was standing—what should we do?"

Ashley used her FBI command voice. "Tabitha, is anyone hurt?"

"No, but it almost hit—"

"Take a deep breath. Easy in. And out. In and out. Again. Those were great. Okay, make sure nobody touches anything more than they already have. Got it?"

"The guard knew that. It asks for forty million and not to call the police. You told me to contact you if—"

"You've done great, Tabitha. Stay inside. I'm coming."

Tuesday, May 5, Morning CDT

MET ONLY BY THE SMELL of fresh-brewed coffee, Ashley entered Robert's solarium unmolested. Where were the guards? Returning to her no-caffeine resolution, a good inhale would have to suffice. In the kitchen, Tabitha, sporting bed-head hair, sat at the table, her hands cupped around a steaming mug. She had cinched a velour robe tight over pink plaid jammies. Bunny slippers covered her feet. Ashley wouldn't be caught dead wearing that outfit. Tabitha's vacant eyes suggested she should drink the brew, not use it as a handwarmer.

Over Tabitha's, "Wow, you look way different," Ashley barked at the two female guards, sipping coffees, chatting by the sink. "What the hell are we paying you for. I just waltzed in through unlocked doors with no challenges. And why isn't one of you guarding the note?"

"It and the arrow are in the parlor," the taller one said. "We're the day shift, and we observed your approach on the monitor." She pointed at the four monitors sitting on the kitchen counter. "Tabitha identified you."

Her face grew warm. So much for her disguise. Tired and slipping, she had failed to spot the cameras. "I'm such an asshole sometimes. I didn't realize they already installed the extra security. Night shift still around?"

"Out front dealing with a reporter."

Media exposure, something else she didn't need, but the price she paid for having Seamus leak information yesterday. "Be right back."

She paused at the open front door to gauge the situation. The guards, halfway between the house and the street, blocked the reporter, their go-away gestures accomplishing little. The reporter was videotaping his confrontation using a hand-held recorder. She activated her cellphone's voice-recording app and yelled from the porch, "Turn off all your recording devices and I'll talk. If you do not, I'll have you arrested for trespass. You have ten seconds to decide."

She didn't have a leg to stand on for the trespass charge, but he might not realize that. The silent guards remained in place, legs wide, arms prepared for action. She counted down from ten. Through four, the reporter, a young, lanky dork with an upper Midwest accent, argued for freedom of the press. At three, he shut up. At one, he said, "Fine." Hitting zero, Ashley spun around. He squawked, "I turned it off. I turned it off."

Once the guards confirmed he had, she walked to meet him. "Let me see your cellphone." She held out her hand.

"Why?"

"Because they make excellent recording devices."

He sheepishly pulled a phone from a side pocket and exited an app. "Can I take notes?"

"In a minute." To the guards she said. "I'll handle it from here. I know your shift ends soon, but I'd like to talk. Can you stick around? I'll approve time and a half."

They jumped at the extra pay, and Ashley reminded herself that playing with house money didn't mean she should throw it away. Otherwise, she was on the greased skid of entitled spending. To the reporter, she said, "Let's move your van from in front of the house. It could alert your competitors, and neither of us wants that. I'm Ashley Pendergast Prescott, and I appreciate your flexibility." His name was Harlan. She gave him her best flirty smile and touched his arm in the way that flattered most men. Given her recent luck, the guy was gay.

"It's true?" Harlan stopped.

She continued walking, forcing him to tag along. "Harlan, many things are true. What particular truth did you want verified?"

"Someone kidnapped the billionaire Robert Pendergast for a huge ransom."

How the hell did he hear about the ransom? She decided to string it out to learn more. "I don't know how much he's worth. How—"

"But the ransom was forty million?"

Why would the kidnappers notify the press? They reached his van, and Ashley moved to open the passenger door. Harlan blocked her way. "I'm not sure I can have someone ride with me. Company policy."

She slid passed him, opened the door, and got in. "Drive around the corner." She pointed. "I won't tell, and you'll have me all to yourself."

In less than a minute, Harlan had them parked against the curb far enough from Mississippi River Road that no one driving by could easily see them.

"Look, Harlan. I'm willing to give you some exclusive intel. Call it from a source close to the family but no mention of my name. You type it up and get it to me, and if it's accurate, I'll sign a statement to convince your editor that it's legit. But it's a trade. I need to know what you know and how you learned it. I don't care *who* your source is, just *how* you got it. Deal?" She offered her hand and gave him a dazzling smile.

A worried expression wrinkled his smooth-shaved face. "I think I have to talk to someone to make that kind of deal."

She yanked the door open. "Fine. One of your competitors will. And remember, we see you on the grounds, it's trespassing."

"Deal. Is it true that you haven't talked to your father in a decade, and that you've taken charge of Pendergast Holdings?"

"Don't waste our time, Harlan. You already know I'm his daughter. You didn't blink at hearing my name or ask whether to spell Prescott with one 't' or two. Nobody has taken over the business. The board of directors, of which I am not a member, has responsibility for the company. Now you talk or I'm gone."

"We got a message on our tips hotline. When did—"

"Not your turn. What precisely did the message say?"

"That Mr. Pendergast's kidnappers demanded a forty-million-dollar ransom. That's it. I swear."

"They say how the demand was made, verbal or written?"

"Written. That's all I know. Is it true?"

She touched the back of his hand, widened her smile. "Now's the time to take good notes." She waited for his go ahead. "Robert Pendergast, Senior has been missing for seventy-eight plus hours. Here's what no one knows, Harlan. The ransom note arrived attached to an arrow shot into his front door."

"Whoa."

"Harlan," she tapped his forearm twice, "ask yourself this: Why would kidnappers tell a news station about their demand? They always say not to call the cops, right?"

"I hadn't thought of that. Why do you think?"

"Oh gosh, I wouldn't know, but I'll bet folks at your station will have some ideas." *And I'd love to hear them because it makes no fucking sense to me.* "If I want to contact you if I learn anything else, do you have a business card?" Not that she planned to use it, but she wouldn't mind if he got the idea they were buddies.

His eyes lit up, and he scrambled to extract a card from his pocket. He used his pen to circle his cell phone number and email. "How will I get a hold of you?"

"I'll be traveling. Messenger your article to my attention at Pendergast Holdings' office in Minneapolis. I'm looking forward to it. And if I learn anything useful, I have your contact info." She patted her pocket and winked.

Tuesday, May 5, Morning CDT

SHE DEBRIEFED THE FOUR GUARDS and Tabitha in the kitchen and learned the arrow with note had arrived soon after six. They hadn't called the local police because Tabitha insisted they wait until Ashley arrived since she was FBI.

"Look, guys," Ashley said, "I don't want to be the typical FBI asshole who stomps on everyone's toes. St. Paul has a missing-persons file on Robert. Your guys can evaluate the note and decide to involve the FBI or not. Okay?"

The four guards visibly relaxed.

"And I want to up the security, so your firm not only guards Tabitha wherever she is twenty-four seven but also the house whenever she's out."

They would make that happen and the four guards adjourned to the living room to divvy up tasks, leaving Ashley alone with Tabitha.

"You okay?" Ashley asked.

"Worried sick for Robert. Otherwise, okay. What are your plans?"

Tabitha's voice sounded strong. Ashley decided the young woman had gotten over the initial shock. "I'm gonna take a big stick and whack a bunch of hornets' nests at Pendergast Holdings and see what swarms out. Oh, and DNA test kits for you and me should arrive today. I'll stop by this evening, and we'll do the swab thing to learn if we're sisters or what. Unless you don't want to discover you're related to an asshole?"

"Better that than be on your wrong side."

"Don't kid yourself. I'm worse with family, which my stepbrothers will soon attest."

Forty

Tuesday, May 5, Morning CDT

WALKING ACROSS THE PLUSH CARPET to Robert's office, Ashley's neck tingled, sensing everyone's eyes on her. Morgan greeted her with a smile, a cup of scalding water, a selection of caffeine-free teas, and a stack of pink messages. "You look, um, different."

"My CEO disguise." She thanked Morgan for the teas, chose a chamomile, and asked her to triage the messages into urgent, ignore, in between. "No one gets in here unless I invite them, okay?"

"You got it, boss."

The simple act of sitting behind Robert's desk brought back her crabby mood. Once she learned where and why Robert had disappeared and who had provided him Niki's address and cellphone number, she was done with this place. Her mantra for this interim-CEO gig was fake it until you make it.

Before she could fake it, she had to master her emotions—or at least fake mastering them. She closed her eyes and inhaled the earthy aroma of the tea—it gave off a smoky dried-grass scent. She took a sip, a little sweet for her preference, but better than grassy. Closing her eyes again, she visualized Glacier Park. Cool, serene, calm. She took a deep breath—

A knock at the door. Morgan stood in the doorway, apparently waiting for permission to enter.

Ashley waved her in. "My bad. What I said about no one getting in doesn't apply to you. Except if I'm talking to someone behind a closed door, you have carte blanche. Sit, please. What have we got?"

Morgan sat like she was at a piano: straight spine and nothing touching the chair back; her hands folded on her lap. Poised or extremely nervous.

"You've had three calls from the press," Morgan said. "All want you to comment on Mr. Pendergast's kidnapping for ransom. I rated those urgent, although not critical. I got one of them to tell me that the information came from an anonymous tip posted on their website."

Morgan did not ask if it was true. Very impressive . . . unless she already knew. "I want Cece to handle the company's 'no comment' response. Schedule her first."

"Sounds like a plan. Nothing else urgent. Gabriella would like a few minutes sometime this morning if you can fit her in. She wouldn't tell me the subject. Robert had a ten o'clock scheduled with her today."

"Go with ten since it's already on her schedule. And, if possible—by which I mean if they are breathing—I want to talk with each of my brothers before Gabriella. Fifteen minutes each should do it. Will you set those up?"

Morgan flipped three more messages from her in between pile.

"All three wanted meetings?"

"Yes, and none said what for, other than they were critical, urgent, or vital, depending on the brother."

Interesting that she put them in the non-critical.

"I have one that I can't evaluate. Is Gex a first or last name? He claims you know him. Says he has information for you. Again, wouldn't share." She handed Ashley a message with Gex's cell number. "The rest are from people within the organization who want to tell you how important they are. That's not what they said, but . . ."

Ashley repressed a smile. She could like this girl. "Thanks. Keep those at your desk for now. If you deem a phone call urgent, tell me. Otherwise, put everyone off. Once you arrange meetings with my brothers, please track down Seamus McCree and tell him I want him there for Junior and Garrett. That's all I have."

Morgan was halfway to the door before Ashley remembered to say, "Thank you, Morgan. I appreciate your insight."

Before Ashley could call Gex, Morgan stuck her head into the office. "Cece is here."

Ashley said to send her in. "I don't need you to take notes for this one."

Without waiting for instruction, Cece headed straight for the rightmost chair, sat, and crossed her legs. Ashley informed her that media claimed they'd received anonymous messages suggesting Robert's kidnappers left a ransom note.

"We don't know anything about Robert," Ashley said, "and the company is not aware of any ransom requests." *Was this how Malachi parsed the truth?* "What should our approach be?"

Cece explained it didn't matter whether they knew of an actual demand, her response would remain the same. Corporate policy was to neither confirm nor deny any kidnapping or ransom or anything relating to individual employees. Period. End of story. Next question.

Ashley handed Cece the three messages. "Excellent. Please take care of these. I'll have Morgan forward you any more we receive."

"Will do." Cece's response was perky. She uncrossed her legs, preparing to stand.

Ashley held up a restraining finger. "One last question. Are you fucking Bradlee?"

Forty-One

Tuesday, May 5, 0900 CDT

MORGAN USHERED IN JUNIOR, WITH Seamus trailing. Junior's expression seemed controlled, watchful. Behind him Seamus shrugged, motioning with his hands that he had no clue why she had him here. Junior, empty-handed, sprawled in the right chair. Seamus, carrying a legal pad with half the pages folded over the back, sat on the other.

Junior spoke before Seamus had settled into his chair. "I appreciate your responding so quickly. There are several items you should be aware—"

"That's not why you're here," Ashley said. "I'm told you're skimming money from the company." She held up a hand. "Don't bother denying it, anyone in your position would. I wanted you to hear me direct Seamus to engage a top-notch firm to address accounting controls, contract negotiations, expense reimbursement policies, and any other way top executives steal from subsidiaries they control."

Junior's face flushed to the hue of a bruised plum. His neck corded with fury. His hands grew white from gripping the arms of his chair. "You have no clue what you're saying."

Ashley gave him her sweetest smile. "You're right. I don't. But my friend Seamus consulted on financial-crime investigations for decades. If you're clean, I'll apologize for wasting company money. If not, every scrap of evidence goes to the prosecutors. Was there something else you wanted?"

Junior burst from the chair, knocking it to the floor. "Here's the thing, little sister." He hissed the word *sister*. "You persist with these personal attacks, and I will make you pay with everything you hold dear. You like working undercover? How'll that work with your picture plastered across the tabloids? I'll sue your ass and shove you in such a deep hole the sky will look like a pinprick. And then I'll burn the ladder. Mark my words." The walls shook from his slamming the door.

Seamus said, "That went well."

Ashley had no clue if he meant it or not. Whatever. It was done, and Seamus understood his marching orders. Tea had worked through her system, and she took the opportunity to use Robert's private facilities. Morgan offered her more tea. "Done for the day or I'll be peeing every fifteen minutes."

"Robert dictates meeting notes . . ."

"We're good for now." Ashley caught a flash of disappointment cross Morgan's face. Well, hell, she'd be curious too, seeing Cece leave her office sniffling into a tissue and Junior departing with the fury of a stampeding elephant.

From down the hall she spotted Garrett and Seamus chatting as they headed her way. "Good news, Morgan. I want you to document this one. Let's see how fast your shorthand is."

"Yes, ma'am."

Under her breath, allowing only Morgan to hear, Ashley said, "I love a woman who likes what she's doing."

Garrett chose the same chair Junior and Cece had picked, but unlike Junior, he brought a pad of paper. She'd have to remember to ask Seamus if there was some power significance to right chair versus left.

"Hey sis, you settling in okay? I can't imagine how difficult this is for you."

He sounded sympathetic, but the real message might be how over her head he knew she was. Time to fake it. "I can use everyone's help, that's for sure. I understand you're running the most dynamic part of Pendergast Holdings." She noted his face said he was skeptical. "And have some intriguing new products coming online. Robert left a few notes for me. Seamus tells me Robert asked you to study the environmental impact of the new pesticide?" She let her voice rise Valley Girl style to a question mark, suggesting uncertainty.

Garrett slid a glance to Seamus and back to her. "Dad is totally up to speed on that."

"For sure," Ashley soothed, "but I'm not. Growing up in Montana, I've seen what happens when pesticides end up in the wrong place. Huge lawsuits. All that crap. I want assurance that won't happen to us. There must be studies and . . . what else should there be, Seamus?"

"I'm more of a finance guy and chemicals are not my area of expertise. I wouldn't know what studies to look for, but I'm sure Garrett knows what information Robert wanted before he'd approve the product. Plus, I suspect the run-rate projections include contingency evaluations and stuff like secondary effects on company costs of existing product insurance. I think what Ashley is saying is that as interim CEO, she wants to make sure we have completed the due diligence before approving production. Do you have that all documented in one place?"

Ashley's mind glazed at "run-rate projection," but Garrett seemed to follow Seamus and that was what counted. Garrett rubbed his face. His hand partially covered his mouth. *Planning to lie?* "Not consolidated, no. I can ask my troops to gather that for you. It may take some time and pull people away from other important things."

Ashley gave a sympathetic nod. "I don't want anyone to go to a lot of extra work. But I feel like a pesticide is something that could bite us in the future. Is two days long enough to have someone gather everything you have, and for you to tell me if there's anything missing?"

Garrett paused before answering. "Sure, we can shoot for Wednesday late afternoon. Where do we stand on the merger proposal?"

"I've asked Gabriella and Seamus to make a recommendation to me this afternoon." *Had she or had she only thought about doing it?* "We'll schedule a board meeting for you all to decide. I'll vote Robert's shares with the majority."

Garrett showed himself out.

"Did you get all that, Morgan?" She had. "Good. Add an addendum to state I want Seamus to find an expert in pesticides to work with him to evaluate the material Garrett provides."

Seamus said, "I don't even know where to start."

"You're a bright boy. You'll figure it out. Me? I'd contact whoever did the expert testimony for the folks who sued the asses off the chemical companies."

"Did anyone ever tell you that you delegate well?"

"One of my mother's nicknames for me was Little Miss Bossy Pants. That should not go into the notes, Streak."

Tuesday, May 5, 0930 CDT

MORGAN ESCORTED BRADLEE INTO THE office and, following Ashley's earlier instructions, slipped to the conference room table and sat. Ashley bet Bradlee would take the right-hand chair. She should have been playing Powerball.

"Whatever you told Junior sure made him angry."

"I said that if he was cooking the books, I'd see his ass in jail."

Bradlee threw his hands up and shot a nervous glance in Morgan's direction. "Wow, how to make friends and influence people. I can tell you I'm not cooking my books, not even padding my expense reports."

She jotted a note to have Seamus look at Bradlee's expense reports. Cece's too. "That's not why you're here. You can resign today or I'm firing you for screwing the help."

Given his volatile nature, she expected an explosion.

His smile never faltered. His voice didn't rise. "I don't think so. First, you've violated my employee rights. We have HR procedures to follow and this," his arm performed a slow sweep of the office, "isn't close. Second, I have an employment contract that contains an arbitration clause. Third, you have no proof." He rose and pointed at her, his hand forming a gun and pulling the trigger. "You're clueless about business. Let me put this in softball terms you'll understand. It's the bottom of the ninth with the bases loaded. The count is three balls and no strikes. You just missed the coach's signal to take a pitch and instead hit into a triple play. Single-handedly you lost the game. You have zero understanding how much your blunder will cost you. My advice? Find a lawyer."

Ashley sucked on her tongue, pulling in her cheeks to generate moisture in her desert-dry mouth. Last night Seamus had warned her to check with Morgan on company policies, and she'd spent all morning doing what was right without regard for rules. She shot a glance at Morgan, who was studying her notes. What was done was done.

"Before you and your high horse walk out, read this." She pushed across the desk a photocopy of the statement Cece had made detailing their affair. "She has photographs. I haven't seen them, but I believe her."

Ashley watched his eyes flicking right, left, right, skimming the detailed accusations. She expected him to deflate. If anything, he grew taller, and his eyes flickered in amusement. "No witness, is there? Wouldn't surprise me if she doesn't sue you for coercing this statement and threatening to fire her if she didn't sign. You are in deep shit and short shoes. Was there anything else you wanted to discuss?"

Tuesday, May 5, 0945 CDT

Malachi presented himself to Morgan in response to Ashley's call to the head of Human Resources requesting they send up whoever handled sexual harassment issues. "Good morning, Morgan. Any idea what the boss wants?"

"She'll tell you. How was your trip to D.C.?"

"Complicated."

Morgan gave the door two solid taps and opened it wide. "Malachi's here from HR. Do you need this documented?"

Ashley sat behind Robert's desk looking defeated: tired eyes, slumped shoulders, hands folded. Her features changed from worried to surprised.

"Right, you told me you worked in HR. Yes, Morgan, I want you here." She added a please after a brief delay. "And shut the door."

Malachi hoped to lighten the mood. "You thought all I did was fly on planes and deliver messages? Robert would never have that." He motioned to the chair on the right for Morgan, who waited for a nod from Ashley to sit. He settled into the other chair. "Sexual harassment, I understand. Has someone been bothering you, Morgan?"

Morgan demurred. Ashley eased the typed sheet across the desk to him. He read Cece's confession, reached the end, saw Cece had signed and dated it. "No witnesses?"

"I fucked up big time. Morgan, please read a verbatim of my disastrous meeting with Bradlee."

Morgan complied. It was worse than he expected. To buy thinking time, he pushed his reading glasses up and rubbed his eyes until they hurt. "I wish you'd talked to me first, Ashley. Morgan, can you fetch Cece and bring her here? Let's see what we can salvage." Morgan waited for Ashley's head bob before she left.

"*Can* we salvage it?"

He hated to be the one to squelch her hopeful tone, but truth was truth. "Our policies protect the accuser, the accused, and the company. This," he held up Cece's signed statement, "fails on all accounts. I know your heart was in the right place and this kind of confession works for police work. We have different standards. We take every accusation seriously and investigate it. Depending on what we find, we might counsel the individual involved, give that person a reprimand, sometimes terminate their employment. Without an independent witness, this document is worthless. Worse than worthless. Let's hope Morgan finds her. If she does, I'll interview Cece alone. She has her own privacy rights."

Ashley hit her skull with both hands. "Oh, fuck me."

"I could consider that sexual harassment."

Her faced bloomed red with anger. "That's not . . ." Her face cleared. "Oh, I see. You're yanking my chain. I'm glad you think this is funny."

She didn't get it. Malachi ironed the creases from his forehead with a rigid hand. "Sexual harassment is an abuse of power. I despise all abuse of power. But the only way to stop it is to have leadership that cares and follows the rules."

Morgan stepped into the room. "Cece's not in the building. Bradlee's gone too."

Forty-Two

Tuesday, May 5, 1000 CDT

GABRIELLA LINZ ARRIVED WITH MORGAN at Ashley's office door at ten on the dot. Inviting them in, Ashley explained Morgan was documenting her conversations to allow Robert to know what had transpired in his absence.

Gabriella said, "Makes sense. In this case, however, I must insist that we meet privately."

Ashley didn't sense any threat in the words, rather a simple statement that Gabriella did not want Morgan to hear whatever she planned to say. Morgan was already backing from the room. "Thank you, Morgan." Ashley waved Gabriella to the chairs in front of the desk. She chose the same chair everyone else had. "You have my attention."

"Robert asked me to work with our investment bankers to develop a contingency plan to take the company public in case we couldn't pull off this acquisition. That would allow his sons to sell their shares and prepare for an orderly leadership succession."

"The entire company, not just Junior's division?"

"I see Seamus has briefed you. Robert and I want to complete this merger. He worried that if the brothers knew of the contingency plan to go public, one or more of them might prefer that and work to undermine the acquisition. My understanding is only Robert, the investment bankers, me, and now you, know of that possibility."

Which explained why she didn't want Morgan in the room. "Why tell me? Why not wait for Robert's return?"

"Because Robert obviously trusts you, and he and I planned to sneak to New York this Friday to meet the bankers."

Ashley pulled the corners of her eyes tight to fight the pain building behind them. "Don't cancel. I still have hopes Robert will show up. Any other bombshells? If not, I need you to apply your steady hand on the ship, which I have spent the morning trying to capsize."

Gabriella's eyebrows raised and lowered, but she said nothing.

"In the last two hours, I've accused Junior of skimming profits, and said if I proved it, I'd see him in jail. I ordered Garrett to prepare a detailed risk analysis of the pesticide the EPA recently approved. And to complete my trifecta, I accused Bradlee of sexual harassment and asked for his resignation, totally screwing up the correct protocols."

"Interesting."

"That's it? Interesting?"

Gabriella crossed her legs. "Have you asked yourself why Robert thrust you into this situation? I have. You're what we in the business call a 'change agent.' People like you have the potential to take companies to the next level of growth and opportunity. Or destroy them. In less than two days at Pendergast Holdings you detonated a tactical nuclear warhead. *That* is interesting. While your tactics may be blunt, your instincts are on target. Junior *is* stealing. Bradlee's a ticking time bomb. If Garrett is hiding something about the pesticide launch, now is the time to learn what."

Gabriella tapped herself on the chest several times. "I am not a change agent, but I am supremely qualified at what I do. You rock the boat. I'll shift ballast to keep it stable. I pray you'll succeed or fail quickly so we can recover. You want my advice?"

Ashley did.

"Press forward on all three of your fronts. And hire a lawyer. Right or wrong, at least one of them will sue you."

Tuesday, May 5, Late morning CDT

ASHLEY STARED AT THE CEILING, considering her next move. She had sicced Seamus on Junior's stealing and Garrett's pesticide and had no expertise to add. Investigating Bradlee *was* in her wheelhouse. She called Morgan into the room and pointed her to the seat. "Cece wasn't Bradlee's first company paramour, right?"

"Paramour is painting it with too nice a brush. I doubt there's any love, illicit or otherwise, involved. I know of three others for sure. There may be more before my time."

"Any still working for the company? No, never mind, that's not the important question. Do you think any of them would go on record? We can guarantee there will be no repercussions." Ashley thrust her hand making a stop sign. "That's inaccurate. We can only guarantee it won't affect her job if she still works for us, but not what it would do for her personal or professional life if word leaked. Don't mind me. I'm talking until I think of something to say. How do you know the other three?"

"May I use Robert's computer for a sec?"

They switched seats and, with a clicking of fingernails on keys, Morgan entered a password, scrolled to a file folder, typed in a long password, opened a folder titled PI Reports. "You should read these."

The phone on the desk rang. Morgan picked up the handset and punched the flashing light. "Pendergast Holdings." She listened. "She's in a meeting. May I take a message?" Morgan covered the mouthpiece and whispered, "It's Mr. Gex again. He says it's urgent that I break into your meeting."

"Get his number and tell him I'll call him right back."

Morgan jotted down the digits Ashley recognized as Gex's office number.

She dismissed Morgan with her thanks. Once alone, she pulled her assortment of phones from her knapsack where they had remained electronically cloaked. Her personal phone showed five missed calls this morning from Gex, no messages. Tiny had left a message between Gex's fourth and fifth calls. "I'm home and bored. The highlight of my day has been watching a nature program about flooding on the Mississippi."

Mississippi: their code word for "I'm in trouble, come get me." Was Tiny telling her he needed her help or was he warning her?

She gambled and called him, who cut off her question about how he was feeling. "Someone forgot I'm on administrative leave from the PFF task force and copied me on an alert message. Agents spotted PFF's Sergeant Oliver outside Niki's apartment building. I don't know what you're up to, and I don't want to know, but I figured you should be aware he's acting hinky."

He clicked off before she could even thank him. Her Niki UC phone displayed one message from the sergeant. "We hope you'll be available Wednesday night. Let me know."

"We hope" was not a standard summons, weekday nights were rare, and Oliver was hanging around where he shouldn't be. Was this in response to her message directed to the Colonel asking whether he wanted her to do work with the Chinese arms dealer? Or something else?

Here she was playing CEO for the day, mucking that up to a fare-thee-well, and no closer to learning which weasel Robert had used to get Niki's cellphone number and address.

She signed into the TOR browser with Robert's computer and checked Niki's email. Niki's cover job translating documents written in Mandarin had several rush assignments they hoped she could accept. She replied with a quick, Sorry Swamped. The Colonel had sent a message last night saying he wanted to discuss how she should do business with the Chinese arms merchant. He'd have Sergeant Oliver contact her.

Question answered. She could catch a commercial flight to D.C. tomorrow to make the meeting. That left twenty-four hours to deal with her brothers. Time to act like the trained investigator she was, pin Bradlee's wings to a specimen board with incontrovertible evidence, and eject him from Pendergast Holdings.

As an afterthought she checked the burner phone for which only Tabitha had the number. One message. Left thirty minutes ago. Whispered. "Ashley, this is Tabitha? Your sister? Maybe? I'm not supposed to know, but I overheard the FBI agents here because of the arrow and note and everything talking about you? They just learned you're wanted for murder in Washington and suspect you may have faked your own kidnapping? And maybe you've been covering up your responsibility for Robert's kidnapping? I know that's total B.S. But they're coordinating with local police to arrest you. Oh, they're calling for me. Gotta go."

So much for Ambrose having my back.

Morgan tapped and stuck her head in. "Reception called. Two St. Paul police officers are here to see you."

Ashley donned a smile. "Great. Show them in when they get here."

Morgan closed the door. Ashley dumped the phones into her knapsack and sped to the bathroom. Inside, she remembered her laptop and the portfolio Robert had left for her were still on the desk. And the open computer files Morgan wanted her to read. Hearing voices outside the office she dared not risk retrieving them. Locking the door behind her, she escaped into the stairway heading to the street.

There, she hailed a taxi, directed it to the Pendergast hanger at the municipal airport. She'd somehow order a crew—another CEO fake-it-until-you-make-it moment. Using her personal cell, she called Gex's office. "I'm sorry you missed him," the admin said in an excited breath. "He's tied up with the director through lunch and most of the afternoon."

What the hell is Gex doing *that long* with the director of the FBI?

Forty-Three

MALACHI ENTERED HIS OFFICE FOLLOWING a lunch hour spent sweating at the gym and found Cece pacing the room. "You're aware our incompetent interim CEO coerced me into making a false statement? She threatened to fire me if I didn't sign my name to that pack of lies she created. It's a perversion of the #MeToo movement."

Malachi closed the office door, took his time settling in at his desk chair, and motioned for her to sit. She released a theatrical sigh but complied.

In a marginally softer voice, she continued. "I don't know what that woman has against Bradlee, but it's wrong to accuse an innocent man. And it's not right to threaten me. If Robert were here, that would never have happened. You tell the board that if that woman is still here tomorrow, I will sue her, the company, the individual board members—most of them, anyway—and anyone involved in besmirching my reputation and threatening my livelihood." She crossed her arms over her chest and jutted out her chin.

He stifled his reaction to applaud her performance, concentrating instead on shuffling papers on his desk to give himself time to unpack her accusations. She assumed he'd seen her statement. Had Bradlee seen him visit Robert's office and told her? No doubt Bradlee's hand controlled this production, making it critical that Malachi avoid missteps. He found a blank pad under some memos. "Do you wish to file a formal complaint? We'll get your statement typed up, and you can sign it in front of witnesses."

He read uncertainty in the narrowing of her eyes. Why wasn't she eager for that result?

"I want all copies of that thing she made me sign destroyed. If she apologizes in writing and if she quits Pendergast, I won't sue. Otherwise—"

His desk phone rang, interrupting her rant. He ignored the call, holding his hands out to her in supplication, "I understand how upsetting this is for you. Here's what I suggest: We document your allegations with a signed statement in front of witnesses. That allows us to follow policy and formally investigate your complaint. It's kept confidential. You'll have the—"

"I know you're a straight shooter, Malachi. The Board trusts you. You must see how much damage she's doing. I'm not signing anything until I talk with my lawyer. And I expect the company to reimburse me for that expense. If she's not gone. I'm suing for beaucoup bucks. You tell 'em."

She stormed out without waiting for his response. So much for the positive buzz from his lunchtime workout. He could not keep this information to himself. In theory, he should tell his boss, but he was a poker buddy with Bradlee. Better to consider it a legal issue and bring it to Gerald Nakourma. He'd write up his notes before—

His assistant burst in. "That was the third phone call you missed from the jetport." She moved papers on his desk, searching for something. "I left you a detailed message. Right on the center of your desk before I went to lunch. What did you do with it?"

Malachi raised his hands in surrender. "Probably buried. What's the problem?"

"I'll get the copy." She hustled to her desk and returned with the duplicate dated fifty minutes earlier. Ashley Prescott was demanding the plane fly her to the Shenandoah Valley Regional Airport, the one they had used to spirit her from D.C.

Someone had to save her from herself, and Robert had elected him. He deserved a raise. "Approve the flight but hold it until I get there."

"What shall I tell your afternoon appointments?" she called to his back. "Will you be in tomorrow?"

"Darned if I know."

Tuesday, May 5, 1400 CDT

LAUREN, THE SAME FLIGHT ATTENDANT, greeted Ashley with a smile and led her onto the plane. "Sorry for the interminable wait, Miss Prescott. This your daily commute?"

"Geez, I hope not. I'll need to mainline beta blockers. Are you like the pilots and have maximum hours you can be in the air?"

"Nope, and anything over forty hours is double time. Since I'm booked the rest of my week, this flight is a real bonus. You don't look that nervous."

"Good drugs. I haven't eaten in forever. Do you have snacks?"

"I'll see what we have. You have time before we take off. We're waiting for one more passenger, and the pilots still have to perform their inspection."

To lessen the chances of accidentally seeing Lake Michigan, Ashley buckled herself into a seat facing backwards. Lauren offered her a choice of beef filet, Cornish game hen, sole, or pizza.

"Pizza sounds great."

Lauren brought a white cloth embroidered with the Pendergast Holdings logo: pH, stylized like the chemical symbol, done up in University of Minnesota colors with a maroon p and gold H. She placed on the table real silver, Limoges china, and a goblet that rang a pure bell tone when Ashley tapped it with a knife. "Seriously? For pizza? I can eat it with my hands."

Lauren snorted a laugh. "You pay for all this. Do whatever you want. I can't afford to have Malachi report me for violating our service standards."

"Malachi?"

"He should be here soon. Everyone knows M and M are the boss's eyes and ears."

Ashley was clueless what that meant. She was faking it and not making it. "M and M?"

From behind her Malachi said, "She means Morgan and me." He reached past Ashley and gave Lauren a fake punch. "You're not supposed to gossip to the boss lady."

"Truth isn't gossip. Let me check on your pizza."

What the hell is he doing here? Lauren departed, and a question occurred to Ashley. "Robert's basically frugal. This jet is huge. How can he justify its expense? What does he use it for?"

"It's a money-maker. The company rents it to others when it's not in use. Your unscheduled trip worked because they'll drop us off before picking up a dozen people in Orlando who want to leave Disney early because it's supposed to rain the rest of the week."

She rolled her eyes. "Really?"

"God's honest truth." He held up his hand in the Boy Scout's oath. "Which reminds me. You should consider the tax bite from these personal flights."

Since he didn't react the first time, she made a production of rolling her eyes. "Yeah, right. Give it a break, Malachi."

"I'm not kidding. We charge ten grand an hour. Our internal cost is closer to six thousand. The company picks up that cost but credits it to you as income. Don't you remember how all those Trump cabinet officials got in trouble for personal use of government airplanes? Same thing."

She did the math in her head. The taxes on the trips she'd already made were equal to four months of her salary. *Holy Mother of God.*

"The good news," Malachi continued without seeming to notice her silence, "is that they don't charge for their time on the ground."

Lauren interrupted, serving a steaming mini-pizza, fresh salad, and presented a bottle of Chianti, "Wine?"

"Leave the bottle," Ashley said.

Tuesday, May 5, Mid-afternoon EDT

TWELVE THOUSAND DOLLARS INTO ASHLEY'S twenty-five-thousand-dollar flight, a sharp bang sounded, and the Gulfstream shuddered like a right cross had nailed it. An oxygen mask bobbed in front of her, pushed sideways by a rush of freezing air.

The pizza in her stomach threatened to come up. Even with the beta blocker, her heart tried to punch through her chest. Ashley grabbed the mask and slipped it on. Sucked in. Got nothing. Feeling lightheaded, she released her lap belt to change seats. Malachi, mask in place, reached across the table and yanked once on the line to her mask. She breathed a lungful of blessed air. Malachi motioned for her to put on headphones.

She slipped them over her head and heard the pilot speaking, ". . . descend to five thousand feet. Request clearance to land at the nearest airport." Ashley grew lightheaded again, realized she was hyperventilating, and forced herself to breathe only after counting to ten. Planes can fly without cabin pressure. This wasn't her nightmare. Heck, they didn't even need both engines.

She checked the engines. Seemed fine. Her gaze drifted to Lake Michigan far below. Her stomach clenched, and she screwed her eyes shut.

The pilot, in a calm Chuck Yeager voice, continued talking with traffic control until they signed off. "Folks," Chuck Yeager said, "We're not sure what happened. The cabin depressurized, and a light says the external baggage door is open. Air traffic control has cleared us to five thousand feet. The closest airport is on the Michigan side of the lake. Once we maintain a stable level, you'll see my co-pilot checking the damage. I know this is unsettling, but rest assured this aircraft is safe and there's—"

A muffled bang occurred from deep within the plane. Ashley listened hard for another sound and forgot to breathe.

"Sorry. Be back to you in a few moments," the still calm pilot said.

Nothing changed for a minute, and Ashley forced her eyes open, took a breath. Malachi's apparent calm matched the pilot's voice. Beyond Malachi's shoulder, Lake Michigan was much closer than it had been. She looked away. The plane flew smoothly. No turbulence. Other than the hiss of air, it was quiet. She looked out the closest window. The starboard engine was dead. Knowing the answer, but praying she was wrong, she checked the other side. Both dead! Her throat choked shut. A million-pound gorilla squeezed her chest while nailing her head twice a second with a ball-peen hammer.

Malachi shook her shoulder. He motioned for her to take off her mask and raise one ear of the headphones.

"We're low enough to breathe normally. Relax. These Gulfstreams glide for miles."

"Sorry for the interruption, folks," the implacable pilot's voice came through her headphones. "A fuel pump sensor triggered the safety systems to stop both engines. We're checking to see if we have a leak or if we can override the shutoff. Our revised flight plan will take us to the Southwest Regional Airport in Benton Harbor, Michigan. We'll be busy up here, but we'll keep you informed."

She scanned through the windows, right and left, front and rear. No land. Anywhere. Everywhere, whitecaps blew off the waves.

Forty-Four

Tuesday, May 5, Late afternoon EDT

"OKAY FOLKS," THE PILOT SAID. "I have good news and bad news." Niki had no patience for that line. Get the ugly shit out and deal with it. "We've been in touch with the St. Joseph Coast Guard Station. They have a chopper in the air to rescue us. The bad news is we'll be making a water landing this afternoon. Lauren will assist you in donning a life jacket. It is important that you do not inflate your jacket until you exit the airplane. I repeat, do not inflate your life jacket until you exit the airplane. Otherwise, you may become trapped inside."

Niki grabbed the barf bag and emptied her stomach. Spat the last of the burning vomit into the bag and rolled the top of the sack, sealing the stench. She was going to die. Not from the crash. Not from hypothermia. Oh no, she'd survive those. Then she'd drown. Her lung sacs bursting from attempting to breathe like a fish. Blood filling her lungs.

Malachi shook her shoulder, pinching the muscles. "Snap out of it." He wore an orange life vest and had a six-inch knife in a sheath strapped to his leg. He was a damn SEAL and could swim to shore. Could Lauren swim? The pilots? Was it a requirement for flight crews who traveled over water?

Malachi touched her face. "Give me your full attention." He pointed two fingers at her eyes and then at his. "Slow your breath. You're hyperventilating." He helped her put on a life vest, pulled the straps tight.

The thing wouldn't hold a duck above the water. "This is useless."

"Inflated, it can float an elephant. Here's what will happen. The plane lands on the water parallel to the waves. The air in the cabin keeps the plane floating. That gives us plenty of time to help Lauren launch the raft, which we have positioned near the door. We exit onto a wing. You'll pull this string to inflate your life vest. Everyone gets into the raft and the Coast Guard rescues us. It's a thirteen-person raft and there are only five of us. We'll be fine."

"That's easy for you to say." She knew she was breathing too fast again and forced a slow breath. "You were a fucking SEAL. Remember? I. Can't. Swim."

"Ashley." He grabbed her arms and brought her so close to him she could kiss him, except she had vomit mouth, and she pulled back. "You don't have to swim. The PFD keeps you afloat, and you told me you're a water-treading champ. You're doing fine with your breathing. Stay in control and everything will be okay."

Lauren's voice came through the headphones. "We're in our final glide. The pilot is air sailing with level wings, nose is up and into the wind, still dropping speed."

Niki made the mistake of glancing out the window. BIG WAVES she could almost touch. Her breath caught in her throat. No way this little plane could land without breaking into a million pieces. And with that thought, she became calm. A smile curled on her face. The impact would kill her before she could drown.

Malachi said, "Even if you don't believe in God, now's a good time to pray. He'll hear you." He offered her his hand and closed his eyes.

At least she'd die with human contact. She shut her eyes and worked to bring up her mental picture of Glacier. Couldn't. Like a moth drawn to the flame that would kill it, her eyes opened and she stared at the approaching water. She had one hand on her seat belt buckle, ready for a quick release.

Malachi squeezed her hand. "You'll be fine. Just remem—"

The plane wrenched left and an arc of water plumed from the wingtip as the wave grabbed hold. The force ripped her hand from Malachi's and released her seatbelt. She grabbed at anything that might stop her from bouncing around the cabin like a free ball in a pinball machine.

Tuesday, May 5, Late afternoon EDT

ASHLEY CAME TO, BLURRY VISION failing to focus on the curved white surface of the shadowed cave where she found herself. Her heart was jackhammering through her chest. She was breathing but not getting enough air. Water fucking everywhere, pushing her from side to side as the plane rolled in the waves. And cold. She tried pushing against the water to stop her movement and succeeded only in spinning around. Spreading her fingers wide, she pressed against the white above and stopped her spin, allowing her double vision to resolve.

Oh my God, she was still in the plane! *Do not inflate the vest in the airplane.* One simple direction, and she had fucked it up. She forced her legs down, hit something solid, bobbed, and swallowed a mouthful of cold water. From a remembered t-shirt motto came the message, "Unsalted and shark free." *The Great Lakes.* What the hell was her mind doing?

Sealing out thoughts of drowning.

Using her fingers as suction cups, she rotated, spotted Lauren slumped in her seat and Malachi pushing the compressed life raft out an exit window. She screamed his name.

In a voice as calm as the pilot's had been before they crashed, he told her to walk to him. She tried to stand, but the inflated life vest made that difficult, and the plane's rocking each time a wave struck it made it impossible. Nothing came out when she called his name. She pulled the PFD down to breathe better through chattering teeth. Didn't change anything. But she'd live if she just held on. He'd save Lauren, and he'd save her, and she'd find whoever had sabotaged the plane and hold his head in a toilet and flush until—No. She would not do that to her worst enemy.

Malachi released an unresponsive Lauren from her seat and dragged her to the open exit window. Was the flight attendant alive? Ashley couldn't bring in enough air to question Malachi as he wrestled Lauren out the window. *Hyperventilating again.* She grabbed a submerged tabletop with one hand to steady herself against the increasing strength of the rocking waves. With her other hand, she pinched her nose and covered her mouth. She closed her eyes and counted toward fifteen, when she'd take her next breath. At seven, the airplane rolled, breaking her grip, and plunging her under the water, inflated life vest and all.

An eternity later, she surfaced. After spitting water and hacking up mucus, she could breathe again. Spinning, she discovered Malachi had deserted her. Then she realized the windows were now on the ceiling. But not the open exit window, only a closed one.

The one Malachi had opened was underwater, and focusing on where it should be, she sensed movement.

Letting the vest float her, she used chairs and tables to pull herself to the spot Malachi had been. She raked her extended hand through the roiling water, touched his shoulder with her fingertips, then banged her knuckles on something metallic. Following its edges, she found Malachi and realized the metal was a seat that pinned him underwater.

She anchored a leg around a table and, keeping her face away from the frigid water, yanked on the seat with both hands. It moved but did not dislodge. Changing tactics, she plunged her head into the water and grabbed lower on the seat frame. Twisting against whatever was securing it, she pulled it off Malachi, and his eyes, nose, and mouth rose above the water.

She hugged his head. "Thank God you're alive." She released him and pointed above to the exit window now on the ceiling. "We've got to open it and get out of here."

"You might be able to do that," he said. "My only way out is by going underwater, and we need to stay together."

What the fuck was he talking about? "Stand up. I'll support you and you can easily reach it. We can get up onto the table's edge and pull ourselves out."

"Listen carefully." His eyes pinched shut. "I have a busted arm and my legs don't work. I may have broken my back when the plane rolled. I can't reach that window overhead, but I can use my one good arm to pull myself through the submerged exit window."

An icy hand squeezed Ashley's throat, cutting off her air.

"Give me a little time to get out, then remove your PFD, take a big breath, and drop to the floor. The window's right there, just pull yourself through. Air in your lungs will pop you right to the surface. The raft has everything we need, including survival blankets, so we don't develop hypothermia. Lauren and I will be waiting for you. The pilots didn't make it."

He let go of the table and slapped her face. He stifled a moan and said, "Snap out of it, Ashley. You. Must. Trust. Me. You will not drown on my watch. Do you understand? You owe me that. You owe Lauren that."

The blow surprised her. She sucked in a big breath. He was right. She did owe him, and Lauren, and the pilots, and whoever did this.

"You know what to do?"

She nodded. Knowing what to do and doing it were two different things.

"Good. See you on the outside." He let go and dropped into the water.

Several seconds later, he reemerged. "Too much buoyancy to fight against. Use the knife on my right hip and puncture one bladder of my PFD."

Ashely followed his flank down to his hip, found the sheath, and loosened the knife. That process steadied her nerves. She pressed the tip of the knife to the PFD and pushed.

"Stab it," he commanded. "We're out of time."

She waited for the apex of the fuselage's roll and stabbed his PFD. With a whoosh, the bladder deflated, and Malachi disappeared under the water.

She'd been a gymnast before she gave it up for softball. Even with cold, shivering legs, she could scramble onto the sideways table, open an exit window, and pull herself out. The life vest would keep her afloat. But what if she landed on the side of the plane opposite Malachi and the life raft? She could float forever, but with only one arm, paralyzed legs, and half a PFD, Malachi needed her help to get himself and Lauren onto the raft.

She couldn't abandon them. Besides, she couldn't die. She had too much to do. Right?

Her trembling fingers released the PFD. She took several deep breaths, dropped to the floor, found the opening, and pulled herself partway through. Pressing her knees to her chest, she worked one foot through the opening and used it to leverage the rest of herself through.

FORTY-FIVE

AIR IN ASHLEY'S LUNGS BROUGHT her to the lake's surface. To stay afloat, she kicked her feet and lashed at the water with her hands. Something latched onto her arm—a monster lamprey. She shook it off, and the struggle spun her around. She spotted the life raft. Empty and distant. And disappearing behind a massive wave coming her way to drive her to a watery grave. If the eel that clamped onto her again and was pulling her backward didn't down her first.

Malachi yelled in her ear, "Stop fighting me." He spun her around, and she realized they were floating next to the fuselage. He shouted over the waves lashing the plane, "When the plane rolled, the tether to the raft broke. It's designed so a sinking plane won't pull the raft down with it. Help me take off my PFD. It will keep you floating so you can get the raft."

Ashley's brain kicked in. The raft was not even a hundred feet away. Did he forget he was a SEAL? Even with no legs and only one arm, he could surely swim that far. He was talking stupidly, suffering from shock. "I'll hang onto the plane. You swim and get the raft and bring it to me."

"Ashley, the plane's gonna sink. Get away from it now or it will take you down. You take my PFD. I can do without it. Help me get it off."

"I told you, I can float forever. *You* need to swim to the raft before you get tired." To get him to stop worrying about her and start worrying about getting himself to that raft, she had to show him she didn't need his help. She curled her legs up, pressed her feet against the plane's side, and sucked in all the air her lungs would take. At the top of a wave, she pushed away and promptly sank. She kicked off her shoes and grabbed her ankles, making it easier for her inflated lungs to pop her to the surface. Her heart hammered against her ribs. An eternity passed before she bobbed on the surface. She windmilled her arms and remained on top of the water.

A wave lifted her, and she saw the raft in the trough ten feet below. If only it were a dog, she could whistle it in. The wave subsided, and before the next ten-foot wave swallowed her, she sucked in a hurricane of air. But she rose again, flesh and bone flotsam. Her arms prickled with cold and exhaustion; she couldn't keep this up for long.

Over the spatter of white foam blown off the wave crest, she heard Malachi yell, "Circle your arms. Think marathon, not a dash. Gentle, and it helps if you walk your legs in the water."

"I'm good! Just do your SEAL thing and bring me the damn raft."

"I can swim to the raft, but with only one arm, I can't bring it to you. That's why I wanted you to take the vest. With it, you can doggy paddle to the raft."

Well shit. She hadn't thought that through. He wasn't brain dead. He was sacrificing himself to let her live. No fucking way. She was the FBI. *Fidelity. Bravery. Integrity.*

Through the blowing foam, she glimpsed the raft and a floating body. Lauren. How had she forgotten Lauren was out here? Close, but not close. Doggie paddle, he'd said. She risked reaching one hand and pulled at the water. The lake slid through her fingers, and the motion threw her off-balance. *Ducks and otters and the like have webbed feet.*

She leaned farther and swept the lake with a cupped hand. The movement spun her in a slow circle as the wave brought her up and then dragged her down. *Dogs don't use one paw.* She used both hands, lost balance, and dunked her face in the water. Reared up in a panic. *Remember, tread water.* She controlled herself and used both arms again, less jerky, and she convinced herself she was closer to the raft. Tried again. And again. Her shoulders ached; her legs frozen lead, but she was making progress.

A lifetime, maybe two, later, her fingers brushed the rubber side. Two more strokes—or what passed for strokes—brought her close enough to grab the blue line circling the raft. She ignored her shaking arm muscles and searched the water for Lauren. She registered the swell and decline of a wave, and suddenly the raft was on top of her, pressing her down into the accepting water. Her lungs squeezed to extract their final molecules of oxygen and, in what one part of her brain identified as a panic attack and the other part of her brain could not control, her muscles refused to operate. *I will not fucking die.*

Her urge to breathe became her only thought. To combat it, she created a competition. Could she count to ten? *Yes.* Twenty? At eighteen, a wave spit her from under the raft, leaving her holding the blue line. She pulled herself to the raft's side, and she and it rose and fell together. She scanned her surroundings for an orange life jacket. Couldn't see it.

Or the plane. The plane had vanished—taking Malachi with it? She experienced an urge to let go of the rope, push the raft away, and embrace the inevitable. The only reason she was alive was to suffer more.

I will not fucking die. She shoved the negative longing for an easy death into a minuscule ball, spat into the water, and shouted at the waves, "You'll have to do better than that, if you want to kill me." She pulled on the raft's top, intending to climb in. Her legs curled under it, prying her hands off, and allowing the craft to skitter away. She fought the waves slamming her sideways and doggy-paddled to it. From twenty years ago came the recollection of how she learned to mount the top bar of the uneven parallel bars. Coach had her bounce on the lower bar, building momentum, and in one explosive push, use her core muscles to lever herself onto the bar.

She started bouncing and, with a cry worthy of a shot-putter, heaved herself up and over its side, tumbling onto the raft's floor, entangling herself with wide straps coming from the opposite side. She crawled along the straps and looked over the side. Grab bars and a fabric boarding ladder. If she had only known. What else didn't she know that might kill her? Kneeling at the side the waves were hitting, she spotted Lauren floating nearby and yelled, but got no response. Tried to convince herself that Lauren was breathing. Couldn't. Her stomach erupted with barely enough warning for her to lean and vomit into the lake. She scooped water into her mouth to rinse away the bitter taste of bile.

Checking for a paddle or oar, anything to navigate, Ashley found rope, first aid kit, knife, ration bars, a mirror, and survival blankets. She fought the urge to get warm and secured one end of the rope to a handle on the raft. Chanting, "The rabbit comes out of his hole, around a tree, and back into his hole," she tied it around her waist with a bowline knot.

The notion of going into the water again made her dry heave. *Chickenshit.* Fidelity, Bravery. Integrity. Her FBI. Her motto. Her belief. I can do this. I *will* do this. She wanted to jump off the raft's side to get close to Lauren, but every time she stood, the waves dumped her to the floor. She descended the boarding ladder. Stepping off the last rung into the water triggered a spasm of panic that locked her hands onto the ladder. *A fucking dog can do this.*

Ashley counted to three, pushed the raft away, and dropped into the water. She fought her panic, controlled her arms and legs sufficiently to reach Lauren. Dead. *At least she hadn't drowned.* Ashley looped the rope around Lauren and used the dead woman's life vest to float them both. Reeling in the rope, she pulled herself and Lauren to the raft. This time, she clambered up the ladder and hauled Lauren in.

Lauren no longer needed her life vest. The idea of taking it made Ashley want to retch again. She bargained with herself that she would don it if she had to return to the water. Otherwise, she owed it to Lauren's parents to protect their daughter's body.

Ashley searched for Malachi and the pilots—even though Malachi had told her they hadn't made it—and saw nothing but waves. She checked Lauren's pockets for anything useful. Her slacks held her ID and three hundred dollars. Ashley shoved them into her front pocket for safe keeping. She covered Lauren with a survival blanket, wrapped herself in two of them, and soon felt warmer.

Lauren, Malachi, and the pilots had died in service to her. She curled in on herself, a deep sadness threatening to suck the marrow from her bones. Shock? Grief? Survivor's guilt? Nothing she *felt* would bring them back. She owed it to them to bring down whoever was responsible.

From a distance came the whomp, whomp, whomp of a helicopter. She shed her blankets and flashed the mirror. The helicopter changed course, dropped lower, and hovered several hundred yards away, its blades frothing the lake. Two orange suits, with red sleeves, snorkels, and black fins the size of beaver tails, dropped into the water and raced to her like torpedoes.

She crawled to the boarding ladder to help them aboard. The Coasties ignored her and ascended the raft's side like it was child's play.

Forty-Six

Tuesday, May 5, Evening EDT

ASHLEY LAY IN THE HOSPITAL bed, attached to beeping monitors sporting squiggly green lines and red numbers. She felt like she'd just completed the spin cycle of a washer. Pain everywhere. She channeled the pain into anger. Anger that her decision to take the Pendergast plane had caused innocents to die. Anger at Robert for roping her into his business. Anger that she didn't know who was responsible.

A young Asian woman entered, filling the room with the stink of hand sanitizer. "I'm Doctor Ahuja. How are you feeling, Lauren?"

Right, Lauren's ID had been in her pocket. Hers sat at the bottom of Lake Michigan, along with her phones and everything else in the knapsack. Her instinct told her that she shouldn't yet correct the mistake. "Sore, hungry, grateful to be alive, and ready for you to sign my release." She swung herself into a sitting position and clenched her teeth against the pain.

Dr. Ahuja put a restraining hand on Ashley's shoulder and pressed her down onto the bed. "Relax. We're keeping you overnight for observation."

The last thing Ashley wanted was anyone observing her. "Doc, I can't stand hospitals. They're Club Med for germs. My clothes?"

Dr. Ahuja frowned. "You don't remember?"

She did. To access her wounds, they'd ripped and cut Tabitha's interview clothes. Replacing those was another expense she couldn't afford. And . . . right, she hadn't been alone in the helicopter. "How's Malachi Cluff?"

"Stabilized in intensive care. I can't say more. HIPAA, you know. I'll send the nurse in to get you some food."

Alone again, Ashley felt the temporary rush of good feelings at remembering Malachi had apparently swum out to the raft and passed out, his good hand and arm locked into the blue rope. The PFD had kept him afloat. She deflated remembering Lauren had not been as lucky.

Staying incognito as Lauren meant whoever wanted to kill her would think they had succeeded. That gave her time, but it wasn't fair to Lauren's family. Reprehensible, really. After an internal debate, she compromised: she'd keep that secret until she escaped tonight. Once safe, she'd undo the misinformation.

A nurse came in. The kitchen was closed, but on her next break she would get something from the cafeteria. She checked Ashley's pulse and blood pressure. "I have a ton of paperwork from billing for you. On arrival, you weren't in any shape to give us your health insurance information." She made eye contact with Ashley and grew rigid. "Who are you? You're not Lauren Brock. You have the wrong eye-color."

Contact lenses? Won't work. "I'm swearing you to secrecy." *Not that it has any validity.* "I am an undercover FBI agent. Someone sabotaged the plane to kill me. Therefore, to protect you and everyone who works here, I can't tell you my name. Lauren, the flight attendant, died. I secured her credentials in my pocket to give to her family."

The nurse retreated to the wall, crossed her arms. Defiance personified.

This has to work. "It's critical that I leave. No one here is safe if they discover I'm alive. I'd have walked out already, except I have no clothes. You can verify my story with a phone call. Will you help?"

Wednesday, May 6, Morning EDT

WITH AN ELEVEN-HOUR DRIVE to National Airport behind her, Ashley returned her rental car. In the rental agency's restroom, she peered through puffy eyes at her image in the mirror. She hardly recognized herself peering back, a bruised, battered woman wearing clothes many sizes too large. Her pain had increased from a washing machine spin cycle to a cement truck filled with gravel. She shuttled to the terminal and bought a burner phone from a kiosk. Seamus McCree picked up on the first ring, as he had the night before when he convinced the nurse that Ashley was who she claimed to be and then rented her a car using his credit card and Lauren's driver's license.

She plugged her ear against the pedestrian hubbub and assured him she was doing okay.

He said, "I won't waste your time telling you all the crap I had to go through to correct the misidentification, but it worked. The authorities are withholding names until they notify all next of kin, including Lauren's parents."

"Thank you for that. Did you get all the messages from my accounts?"

"Yes, and I contacted everyone you wanted. On your personal phone, Gex has a dozen telling you to come in. They need to talk to you. A local St. Paul reporter, Harlan Mumbled Last Name, wants you to call to confirm or deny something unspecified. You want his number?"

That's not good. She wrote Harlan's number on the rental receipt using a pen she had swiped from the rental car counter.

"On Niki's phone number," Seamus continued, "a Colonel Pete, says he's found a spotter for you and wants to get the two of you together Thursday evening, as in tomorrow, to test the equipment and teamwork. Union Station, six o'clock. He'll talk with you privately about the other matter when he sees you. I assume you know what all that means?"

She did: Standard PFF procedure was for her to call only if she couldn't make a meeting. Tomorrow at six p.m. someone would meet her at Union Station and escort her to wherever Colonel Pete planned to test her, the spotter, and the rifle. She presumed the other matter was Sam's proposal to interpret for him. "Anything else for Niki?"

"You have an email from a Sergeant Oliver. Says Colonel Pete doesn't need you tonight, but he, the Sergeant, not the Colonel, wants to meet you outside your apartment at eighteen-thirty. Your other phone and email accounts are empty. There's shit happening here you should know about."

Disappointing that Sergeant Oliver was continuing to act weird. "Do a reply to sender and don't strip his message at the bottom. Type in all caps and no punctuation, 'YES SERGEANT.' No signature."

Seamus repeated then executed the instructions. "We have no further demands from the kidnappers. The FBI found Robert's car in long-term parking at the airport. I gather they're checking with airlines to see if he flew somewhere. Sounded to me they think this is a rich guy hoax. I suggested they check cameras to determine who was driving. They told me to mind my own business.

"At last night's board meeting, Gerald Nakourma confirmed you gave me your proxy and if something happens to me, the proxy goes to a friend of mine who's a bank board chair. That should keep me safe. They won't want a banker in here because he'd blow the cover off anything skanky going on. I insisted they appoint Gabriella interim CEO or I would call a board election at which Tabitha, who has been great, and I would file a slate of independent directors. And if they undermined any of the efforts you had put in place, I would do the same thing. They caved. I'm still working on lining up directors. When I do, you or I will call for the election, regardless."

Ashley laughed. "You can be one scary dude. Remind me to never get Seamus McCree's Irish up."

"Over Gabriella's name, we issued the press release Cece and I wrote. There's a bunch of other stuff you don't want to hear now. Oh, and I'm using Morgan to help me."

"You done good. Did you convince Tabitha to leave town?"

"She's as pig-headed as you."

"Well, *there's* the pot calling the kettle black. Make sure she keeps those bodyguards. And thank you, Seamus. I really am sorry for getting you involved in this mess. I don't know when I'll be in touch next.

"Given it's temporary and assuming I live through it, it's kind of fun."

"You're a sick man, Seamus McCree."

"Whatever. Don't hang up, there's more. Tabitha remembered that Robert Senior is a universal donor. That means he's O-negative. She's AB-positive. She can't be his daughter. To understand what's going on, I collected the water glasses each of the brothers used at the board meeting. I added swabs from you and Tabitha and some hair with follicles Tabitha collected from Robert's hairbrush and sent everything to a private lab that's done DNA work for me."

More Pendergast lies. "I love you for being so . . . so Seamus. I don't know what I'd do without you, and if you repeat that to anyone, I will kill you."

Seamus had cleared up the hospital's confusion concerning Lauren but had left them still in the dark about the female survivor's true identity. She crossed her fingers the hospital didn't ask Malachi the right question, because the truth-teller would cough up her name. The longer the killers thought they had succeeded, the safer everyone would be.

Forty-Seven

Wednesday, May 6, Morning EDT

THE CLOTHES AND DISGUISES ASHLEY preferred were at Niki's apartment. Since someone had spotted Oliver near that complex, chances were good Gex had agents staking it out. She had some stuff at the apartment she shared with Liya. It was less likely Gex had that under surveillance, but not impossible. If he had agents inside, she was screwed.

She bought a shawl in an airport gift shop. With the baggy clothes, sneakers she scuffed from pristine white to grungy, shawl covering her head, and stooped walk, she became an older Eastern European woman. Once she left the train and had walked to within four blocks of her Lincolnia place, she looked for signs of surveillance. The FBI loved pretending to be plumbers, electricians, cable installers, because only pros noticed those.

She spiraled in toward home, avoiding a street with a cable installer parked at the curb even though the guy *was* pulling black wire from a spool. Probably okay, but better not to chance it.

On the stoop, she retrieved the spare key from the hidden magnetic box attached to the porch light. She smiled, remembering Liya taking out the garbage or collecting the mail and letting the door close behind. The key had been their solution, and now it let her inside. She disarmed the alarm and petted Liya's two cats as they wound around her feet, purring their greeting. "I missed you too. Let's save the lovey-dovey for later. I need a hot shower."

Liya had stacked Ashley's mail on the side table. On top of assorted fliers and junk was an envelope sent registered from the FBI. She ripped it open and skimmed the three-page official notification from the number two person in the Washington, D.C. office . . . paid leave until the investigation of the incident . . . special hearing scheduled for . . . Her throat tightened. She had officially screwed the pooch; the hearing was yesterday.

She didn't want her shit to rub off on her roommate. Since Liya was between boyfriends and wouldn't have plans for a lunchtime quickie,

Ashley had plenty of time for a long shower before collecting what she needed.

She tossed the notification into a wastebasket and piled the junk mail on top.

Wednesday, May 6, Late morning EDT

ASHLEY STEPPED FROM THE STEAMING bathroom in her altogether. A frowning Liya stood in the hall, holding the FBI notification like it was a dead mouse. "Get dressed. We need to talk. Gex told me yesterday you're AWOL and subject to arrest because you missed your shooter investigation meeting. He asked permission to bug our apartment. I said no way. When my phone notified me someone had disarmed the alarm, I zipped home, planning to rip Gex a new one if he had a team working here. Talk to me, sister."

Liya could have reported her already if she had wanted. If Ashley didn't explain, Liya *would* call.

"Someone's trying to kill me." Ashley related the highlights of the last few days.

Liya sat on the bed and thumbed on her cellphone. "Give me a sec."

Whatever Liya was doing, it was beyond Ashley's control. Ashley willed her hand to stop shaking so she could use the bathroom mirror and cover her facial bruising with makeup. Liya called in to her. "They've released the names of the deceased, including Lauren Brock. Your Malachi is in critical but stable condition, and an unnamed survivor has left the hospital. That's you. Why are you here, not at the Bureau kissing ass and making your excuses?"

Like sisters they were, but still Liya had sworn an oath to the Bureau. "If I let you in on a secret, do you promise on everything you hold dear that you won't tell a soul?"

Liya stared hard at her. "If it's not illegal, then yes. I swear. We've been best friends since the academy, Ash. If it's illegal, don't say word one. The best I can do is to turn my back while you leave. I'll report you after I come home tonight and find the discarded clothes in the trash."

That was a generous offer, and warmth for her friend welled in her heart. "Not illegal. Here's what only two other people know." She told Liya the secret, and they strategized how Niki could stop the militia.

FORTY-EIGHT

Wednesday, May 6, 1815 EDT

DISGUISED AS AN OLD LADY surrounded by shopping bags and enjoying a double-chocolate frozen yogurt, Ashley sat on a bench several blocks from her scheduled meeting place with Sergeant Oliver and waited for him to pass. She had mentally switched into Niki mode while she had watched everything through half-lidded eyes, relaxing in a warm microclimate created by sun reflecting off the storefront windows. She spotted him a block away. He was early and dressed casually with a camera on a strap hanging from his shoulder. He sauntered by; his glance skimming her and lingering on a sweet young thing with shorts the size of a tissue.

Rick soon reported from the bus stop opposite Niki's apartment that Oliver, camera at the ready, had taken a position that gave him a good angle to capture pictures of her leaving the building.

She rushed finishing her snack and gave herself brain freeze. Stooping like an aged washerwoman, she tottered up the street. Oliver seemed oblivious to his surroundings, focusing on the front entrance of her apartment.

She plodded in front of him and received an annoyed look, but no recognition. She spun to face him. "You spying on me, Sergeant?"

Oliver's jaw unhinged. He fumbled his camera but held on. "Corporal Niki? What the fuck?"

"Meeting you at the appointed time. I know we've gotten crosswise, and I feel real bad about that. It's not my fault I can shoot. I learned young and don't consume caffeine. I drink beer, though. Let's grab a couple brews and talk things over. See if I can make it up to you."

Surprise on his face changed to suspicion. She had to get him to act before he considered the full ramifications of her offer. Knowing beer had caused much of his added gut, she said, "Come on, Sarge. One beer won't kill you. You drink beer, don't you?" She laid a tentative hand on his arm, bringing her body close enough so she could confirm he was carrying his gun. "I'll even buy the first round. Here's the thing: Shooting targets is one thing, but I've never killed anyone. I need your expertise on that."

He waved toward her building. "You got beer in your apartment?"

"My local bar's down the street." She pulled a roll of bills from a pocket. "People were generous today. It's my treat."

"You panhandle?"

"When work's slow. Good disguise, huh?" She tugged his arm. "Help me out here, Sarge."

He tried to cover his sly smile with a cough and a throat clear. "One beer. Maybe two since you're buying."

Wednesday, May 6, Early evening EDT

AT THE BAR, NIKI ALLOWED Oliver to hold the door for her. She abandoned the old lady's stoop and strode into the establishment, spotted Liya. Her roommate looked like any professional office worker, her head bopping as though her earbuds were pumping music with a steady beat. Niki selected a seat facing the front door at a two-up halfway into the joint and several tables away from Liya. Oliver settled with his back to the entrance. Perfect.

They placed orders and, while the server went to fill them, she excused herself to "use the facilities." On the way, she jostled Liya's table, got a double blink of acknowledgment. Niki did her business and prepared herself for the action.

On Niki's return, Liya blocked her path. "Hey. I gave you ten bucks because you said you hadn't eaten all day. Now I see you wasting it on booze. Gimme my money back."

"Out of my way, bitch."

"Not until you give me back my ten bucks." Liya placed her hands on her hips, widened her stance.

Niki stared past Liya to the entrance. *Come on, come on. Where are you guys?* "You can't prove nothin'. Step aside before I lay you out like last week's sausage." She shoved Liya enough to make her take a step to regain her balance. Two burly D.C. cops strode through the front door and one remained at the threshold. Niki assumed the fourth guarded the rear door.

"Hey," an officer said in a voice that pulled everyone's attention from the altercation to himself. "Everybody stay where you are. Take it easy. You two, step away from each other and let me see your hands."

Niki and Liya complied. Although Liya should have already broadcast

Oliver's description through her concealed microphone, Niki wanted to make sure they focused on the correct guy. She pointed. "I'm with him, and I have a concealed carry. Right ankle."

Liya yelled, "She stole my money."

The cops had moved to stand behind Oliver, talking past him to the women. "Keep your hands up and get down on your knees. Lean forward and place your hands in front of you. Good. Now, lie all the way down. Easy does it."

She and Liya followed his orders. Liya remaining in her role, yakking about wanting the money Niki had accepted on false pretenses.

Niki's position allowed her to see the other two cops now standing behind Oliver, replacing the two original officers who moved in to "handle" Niki and Liya. While one covered them, the other cuffed and patted them down, securing Niki's weapon from its ankle holster. Liya was not carrying. One cop escorted Liya to an empty table to "take her statement."

The officer with Niki sat her in the chair and asked for her concealed carry license. "My boyfriend's got it." She motioned with her head toward Oliver.

On seeing their attention shift to him, Oliver's face changed from teenager rooting on a cafeteria food fight to parole violator carrying an illegal pistol the cops would soon find

Wednesday, May 6, Early evening EDT

NIKI WATCHED OFFICERS DUCK OLIVER into the rear of a patrol car before her cop placed her in a separate vehicle that smelled vaguely of vomit and Lysol. "Leave before they do," Niki told the driver. "The target and everyone in the bar must see you transport me from the scene. Can you drop me at my apartment? It's only a few blocks. I'll feel better with these bracelets off."

"No can do. My orders are to hold you until some FBI guy shows."

Like a pricked balloon, Niki's toughness deflated in a whoosh to become Ashley's worry. Liya and Rick had coordinated with the local police to conduct the sting operation Ashley had designed to take Sergeant Oliver off the street and give her free rein with her PFF undercover work. But she'd gambled and lost. One of them—she'd bet Rick—had squealed to the bosses. The Bureau would skewer PFF's little fish, declare victory, and let whoever ran the militia escape along with the Chinese arms dealer and the weapons. She'd be walking the streets looking for a job.

She didn't have to wait long for Deputy Director Ambrose to open the other rear door and slip inside. He flashed the driver his ID. "Make this look good, officer. Take off with lights and a whoop or two of your siren."

"Where to, sir?"

Ashley expected Ambrose to say the Hoover building, instead he said, "Find a coffee shop."

Once there, Ambrose slipped the driver ten bucks through the grill. "Go get yourself something and walk the block. With the back doors locked, we can't leave until you release us. Five minutes will do it."

The officer accepted the money and left at a quick pace. Ambrose removed a black box the size of a lighter from his pocket. "Know what this is?" He didn't wait for her reply. "It jams all communication devices within fifteen feet. Who knows of our arrangement besides Liya?"

So Liya, not Rick, had betrayed her. Which meant maybe he didn't know about Rick? With Ashley's secreted GPS device and sound transmitter disabled, if something happened to her, no one would know. She licked her dry lips. "The only way she would help me was if I told her the truth. She confirmed it with you?"

"As any agent in good standing should. Our agreement stipulated that only you and I were to know you were working for me. You earned my trust when I asked for your badge and resignation letter and you gave them to me. Apparently, I was wrong. Tell me why I shouldn't drag you to headquarters and produce your resignation."

Her entire career rested on her next few sentences. She couldn't produce enough spit to choke down her parched throat. Her words sounded rough. "I believe protecting our country is our highest duty, hands down, more important than salvaging my FBI career. I'm confused, though, because I followed your order to do 'Whatever is necessary to make sure this assassination does not happen.' Sergeant Oliver had become an unreliable pawn that we removed from the chessboard. That buys me time to finish my work with Patriots for Freedom. The Chinese arms dealer was news to ATF. Shitcan me and we lose him. No one knows where the money is coming from or who the actual leadership is. You'll sacrifice my ability to get that information for what? A few headlines for grabbing a bunch of

Patriots For Freedom's little guys. How about two hundred automatic weapons? Gonna let those loose into the wild? That went real well a few years ago when ATF did that. To do my job, I requested help from my closest friend in the FBI. If that's what you want to hang me on, I'm truly fucked and you will be, too."

"Are you aware the director himself intervened and terminated the undercover aspect of the PFF task force?"

Why did she bother wasting her breath?

"Ashley."

Her head snapped up at his sharp tone.

In a thick drawl he asked, "What would you have me do since the director has spoken?"

She gave him a searching look. His question was honey to catch the ant. Fuck it, Ambrose couldn't screw her more than he already planned to. "You could decide protecting our country is *your* highest priority, too."

Forty-Nine

Thursday, May 7, Morning EDT

COLONEL PETE WATCHED SERGEANT OLIVER arrive at the plexiglass and drop into the seat. Showing his experience, he waited for the jail guard to uncuff him before lifting the handset. Colonel Pete had spent much of the time between Oliver's panicked call last night and this morning's conference uncovering the lies Oliver had told PFF. One thing had become clear: PFF needed a better vetting process. They should never have recruited Oliver.

Even though the phone reeked of disinfectant, Colonel Pete pulled his sleeve over his hand before lifting the receiver to his ear and plugged his other ear against the hum of the overworked air conditioner.

Oliver said, "When's the bail hearing? What's the plan?"

That depends on what you tell me in the next few minutes. Using his kindly parent voice, he asked, "Have you told them anything?"

"Course not. Only first-timers and dumb fucks talk to the cops without a lawyer."

"As your counsel, I said you would not answer questions or provide a statement." Putting edge into his voice, he continued. "Problem is, when you told us about that misunderstanding in Chicago, you neglected to mention you violated parole. Illinois wants you. Forget bail. You can get a lawyer to fight extradition, but you'll never win."

Oliver's smile faded. He rubbed his neck with his free hand and rolled his shoulders. Nervous tells. Reality was sinking in. Colonel Pete wanted to make sure the jerk knew exactly what he was facing.

"What made you go into a bar with a piece? A stolen piece, according to the charges. And you compound it by not telling the cops you're carrying. You got more charges against you than Custer had arrows in him. Same effect."

"What do you mean?"

"Hyperbole. Custer died. You should get out in twenty years, give or take."

Oliver rose from the chair, arms waving like he was fighting a swarm of bees. "Twenty years? That's crazy. I bought that gun legit. You can negotiate that to ninety days and court costs. What did they charge Corporal Niki's ass with?"

"Maybe a fine for not having her concealed carry license on her."

"Not for disturbing the peace? If it wasn't for her, I wouldn't be here. Do you know she's—"

Time for the angry superior officer tone. "Zip it, Sergeant. We'll take care of Corporal Niki. You focus on yourself. Don't get any stupid ideas about us setting up a jailbreak. That would bring unwanted attention to us. You will serve time, but we have friends to help while you're inside no matter where they take you. Some people in your situation might consider trading information for a lighter sentence. Believe this, Sergeant Oliver: if you snitch, your twenty years will become a much shorter life sentence. Do you understand?"

Oliver went gray. He grabbed the chair like it was a lifeline. "Why are you threatening me? That traitorous bitch is the one you should worry about. Do you know she's meeting with an ATF agent? I saw them together. I was gathering more evidence to show you."

Colonel Pete's eyes became snake slits. "Keep talking."

Thursday, May 7, Mid-afternoon EDT

Colonel Pete had paced a path inside the barn by the time her black Lexus LC 500 Inspiration arrived. He opened the door for the lady.

"Give me a kiss," she said. "This better be good. I'm missing the third act of *La traviata*,"

He air-kissed her cheek, keeping his arms close to his sides, not wanting her to smell his nervous sweat. "Sources tell me Sergeant Oliver spent two hours with a pair of FBI agents. Two hours is a long time of saying nothing. He lied to us on joining. He's a liability."

"Then take care of it."

"He says he was gathering evidence to prove Corporal Niki is an undercover ATF agent. Claims he saw her talking to a guy at the zoo and followed him to ATF headquarters. Supposedly, he has pictures of the agent. Cops have the camera. I'm to meet the corporal tomorrow to prepare to kickoff Operation Big Wigs."

"You believe him?"

"He blames the girl for his problems. Probably attempting to get even. But it's clear our vetting process has holes."

"Tell me your plan."

She approved it without change, got into her car, and rolled down the window. "Well, Peter, in the next thirty-six hours I expect you to tell me at least one person died."

FIFTY

Thursday, May 7, Late Afternoon EDT

ASHLEY, DRESSED AS AND THINKING like Niki, added another layer of makeup to cover bruises and the lack of sleep from her aches and worrying about meeting Colonel Pete. Not sure she could keep any food down, she had spent the last several hours at Niki's apartment, calming her nerves with a long soaking bath, remaining in the tub until the water became intolerably cold. She looked and felt like a bruised raisin. A worried, bruised raisin, which one more layer of makeup might hide.

She'd soon know who'd meet her at Union Station, whether Gex would intervene, and how Colonel Pete reacted to Sergeant Oliver's arrest, none of which she could control.

Her dice and coin flip had her leave by a side door. On her way to the Metro, she spent an hour executing her tricks to reveal any watchers. Clear.

She arrived at Union Station a few minutes before six, purchased a bottled water, and made a circuit of the food court. Senses heightened. Burnt coffee here, a lingering whiff of body odor there. Fragments of conversation overheard. Argument on the edge of nasty. Two people greeting each other and going their own way. A lady with a stroller but no kid. Farther on, a father, bent low, helping his daughter with her first steps. Aw. On her second pass, the tables remained empty of anyone she recognized. Niki sat at the table Oliver had last used and browsed an abandoned newspaper.

Over the top of the paper, she spotted the girl who babysat her cell phone whenever she was with Oliver. The girl passed by the table twice, giving no sign she noticed.

Maybe the youngster didn't know how to make contact. Niki got up and followed her, getting close enough to say softly, "You're looking for Corporal Niki, right?"

Her contact spun to face her, a picture of surprise, mouth moving, speechless.

What did she expect to happen? "Where's Sergeant Oliver?"

"They didn't tell me. Give me your cellphone."

Picturing it resting with the plane deep in Lake Michigan, Niki involuntarily shuddered. "They arrested us and released me. I waited for him, but they kept him. Made me a little paranoid. Like if he talked, they could maybe track my phone? Smart woman that I am, I left it home."

The girl's face hardened. Had Niki pushed her concerned act too far? Time to gamble. "Look, I realize you have to make sure it's safe. Let's slip into the ladies' room. I'll strip and you can do a full-body search. Come on." Niki strode two steps and stopped because the girl didn't follow. "What? You afraid I'm seducing you? Time's wasting. The Colonel's waiting."

That got the girl moving. No way would this kid recognize that the replacement button Liya had sewn in the front of her jeans was transmitting everything they said. Nor would she have a clue that Niki's left rear-pocket zipper camouflaged a GPS transmitter. She'd aced the first test with the girl. Her next interaction carried significantly more risk.

Thursday, May 7, Early evening EDT

NIKI'S ESCORT DROVE AN OLDER Tundra pickup with specialty Maryland plates for the Libertarian Party. Niki asked if she was a party member and if the four-digit number, which she enunciated for her electronic listeners, meant anything special. The Bureau hadn't identified her escort from pictures. Unless the girl had stolen the plates or truck, Niki's transmission would allow them to ID her and where she lived. A small win, but a win.

Maybe the girl wasn't as dumb as Niki credited her. She did not answer, and they drove in silence until they pulled up to the gravel pit gate. "Far as I go. They'll meet you down the road."

"You waiting for me?"

"Nope."

Niki closed the door behind her, and the truck reversed, spun a semicircle, and spat gravel accelerating away. That got her heart pumping.

It was cooler here than in the city. The air swirled in a stiff, changeable wind, blowing dust devils across the open ground. Smelled like rain. Walking the deserted roadway, the hairs on her neck rose. She'd make a fine target for someone practicing a live long-distance kill shot. That put a hitch in her step. To lessen her anxiety, she hummed "Twinkle, Twinkle Little Star." Remembering an agent was, hopefully, listening to her pathetic attempts to carry a tune, she shut up and increased her pace.

A flicker of movement in the largest building drew her attention. Colonel Pete and Sam, the arms dealer, appeared. The Colonel, dressed in civies, carried the sniper rifle. Sam had chosen night ops clothing, black everything except no head-covering or face paint. A tendril of doubt burrowed into her consciousness. She had no physical cover, no one to rescue her if anything went wrong, no one even to mourn her if she died. She was fucking crazy to be doing this. Of course she was. That's what made her exceptional. She shoved the negativity under her foot and crushed it into the gravel with her next step.

At the appropriate distance from the men, she stiffened to attention, executed a salute. "Sir."

"At ease, soldier. Your driver tells me you have taken certain precautions since Sergeant Oliver's arrest. Why were you meeting him last night?"

"I don't know, sir. He said it was urgent. He didn't see me walking up the street, and that gave me a chance to observe him taking pictures of my apartment building. I wanted to know what was going on, but I was leery to be alone with him. I suggested we grab a beer at a local bar where there'd be lots of people."

"What did you talk about?"

"We didn't. It was FUBAR. Some crazy woman accused me of stealing her money or something. I never got straight what she was saying. A bunch of cops were there. Next thing I know, I'm in a cruiser, behind the grill, 'cause I didn't have my concealed carry license with me."

Colonel Pete had Gex's trick for concealing his thoughts, making it easy for her to show surprise with his curveball. "Sergeant Oliver's lawyer claims he saw you meet an ATF agent. He thinks you're a snitch."

She hooted so loud a crow flying past changed its path. "Sir, if I was, I'd have to be fucking crazy—excuse the language, sir. Crazy to come here alone. I'm here because I believe in our cause." She tilted her head, like an idea had just occurred to her. "How would Sergeant Oliver know what an ATF agent looks like? Was he wearing a jacket with letters on it?"

"What do you understand our mission to be, Corporal?"

"To take control of the country away from the rich and their quisling politicians and judges who rig the system to grow richer while keeping their jackboots on the necks of everyday citizens of these United States. Sir." She stiffened into a marine-worthy attention.

"At ease, Corporal. Sergeant Oliver violated a parole he neglected to reveal on his application. His incarceration puts us at risk. After today, we'll abandon this facility and anyplace else he's been. Let's concentrate on *your* important future with our cause." He displayed the rifle. "Sam agreed to spot for you. In return, I agreed that you may interpret for him on another deal he's working. That suitable to you?"

Niki allowed herself to beam with excitement. "Yes, Sir!"

Colonel Pete had her set targets at various distances. She returned from that task to find Sam had already dialed in the windage adjustments to the sniper rifle. He was clearly in charge of this part of the day, experimenting with distances and locations to test her response to a variety of wind directions. He ignored Colonel Pete and spoke Mandarin, sharing his thought processes to make accurate adjustments, and coaching her to wait to take her shot until conditions were stable. With each round she became more confident. Until she missed one because she continued her trigger pull during a wind gust.

She slid a sideways glance at where the Colonel had been standing. Not there. He had left them alone.

"Many have the skill to shoot accurately," Sam said. "Few have the required patience. Better to not take a bad shot and let the target think he is safe than take a bad shot because it's the only one you have. Miss and you alert the target and make him wary."

That was a perspective she hadn't considered. Target shooting was a timed event. Assassination was not. "I don't get it," Niki asked while waiting for the gusting wind to stabilize, "why are you doing this?"

"Fear and instability sell weapons. Look at your country. Every time a Democrat wins your presidency, guns and ammunition fly off the shelves. If Patriots for Freedom follows their plan, your bullet will be the first of many to generate tremendous fear and great instability. I have many weapons to sell. Enlisting you to interpret is an unexpected bonus."

"You know the target?"

"We're losing light. Let us remain in the present and make a good last kill shot."

She thrust aside her desire to determine who the intended victim was and became one with the bullet. The gun recoiled into her shoulder. She and the bullet ripped the heart from the silhouette target's chest.

FIFTY-ONE

COLONEL PETE WAS RELIEVED WHEN Sam reported in his British English that Corporal Niki was ready. Sam's assessment of her fitness level and Niki's ready agreement to be his guest for the night meant she'd live for now; Sergeant Oliver might already be dead. Niki and Sam both complied with his request to don hoods for the trip to his country place. He chose roads with gentle curves to make it impossible for them to determine the direction they were heading and introduced several unnecessary loops to further add to their confusion. False trails complete, he asked Niki to tell him what she was feeling.

The cloth muffled her answer. "Anxious would cover it."

"Oh?"

"I've never shot anyone, and I'm concerned how I'll react. I don't know what our plan is, and that worries me."

Rational enough, time to reassure her. "This isn't a suicide mission."

"That's not what I meant. I'm a visual person. I like to picture how things work, to see it happen in my head, feel its success. Knowing Sam's skill at calibrating wind and distance, today I pictured the bullet's path from my gun to the target's heart. It gave me confidence. I'll be able to apply that to the actual person tomorrow, unless a subconscious part of my mind takes charge and worries about what happens after."

Olympic athletes used the visualization technique to prepare for success, so what she said made sense. Which didn't mean he should disclose more than he intended. "Let's say our initial goal is to cause mass consternation in the country. Which person would be the most effective target?"

He appreciated this soldier's willingness to think before she answered. Forty-five seconds passed.

"I hate to say this, sir, but no single death will do it. We've had four presidents assassinated, and others, like Reagan, shot but survived. The country knows how to deal with that. Frankly, nobody in the Senate or House matters a hill of beans. They're like shark's teeth. Knock out one and another grows in its place. Supreme Court justice? Has there ever been a successful attempt? Would that upset the entire country? Nah. So, not a politician. At least not ours. Killing someone like the North Korean president on U.S. soil would make a lot of normal folks worry they'd respond with nukes."

PFF could have used her in the high council strategy sessions. "That is an interesting observation. Go on."

"I suppose after all the chants of 'Lock her up,' killing Clinton would stir up lots of folks who would think she got what she deserved. And others would believe Trump's rhetoric was responsible. But I can't see it changing anything. The people in power are still in power. Even if an election swings from one party to the other, nothing fundamental changes. To quote you, both parties serve the same masters. And we've had famous people killed before and nothing happened. Look at John Lennon. And it can't be something random, like the 2002 D.C. sniper attacks. We have mass murders and school shootings weekly and its ho hum, lower the flag to half-mast for three days, bury the dead, carry on."

Precisely the points they had considered. "What if there were an assassination a day? What type of victims would force the government to react?"

Her response was immediate. "In that case, anyone could work, provided the public understood they were deliberate, not random acts."

She'd lost the thread; he redirected her thinking. "What runs the country?"

"Ah, I see. Money. You kill the rich."

Smart girl. "Better, the *adult children* of the rich and powerful. Make sure everyone knows it's because dear old daddy is worth a hundred billion or voted to provide rich-people tax-breaks or created judicial rulings that benefit the billionaires. Members of the oligarchy don't hoard money for their own use. How can you spend five or ten or a hundred billion on yourself? They use it to project power through their children and their foundations."

With measured words, she said, "That could work."

"Now imagine," the Colonel said, "that in addition to individual assassinations, PFF raids family compounds and harvests the adult children. All accompanied by a well-publicized manifesto, pumping Elton John's 'Burn Down the Mission' into the airwaves. The masses will awaken, and the rich'll force the government to declare martial law."

"Won't that cement the military-industrial complex in place?"

"At first. People willingly trade individual freedoms for security. Until they find they have neither security nor freedom, then they revolt. Individualists founded the United States. Colonists came here to get away from the heel of oppressive governments and economic apartheid. They rebelled against the king and the landed gentry. Our individual freedoms still drive most new immigrants to come here. Even those slaves we dragged here preferred destitute freedom over the plantation tradeoff of bondage for security. In the U.S., if generals use martial law to impose the old order, their own soldiers will gun them down. It'll be bloody anarchy for a while. But with PFF leadership, ordinary people will soon again be able to exercise their God-given individual freedoms. We'll retake the country from, as you say, 'the rich and their quisling politicians and judges.' Tomorrow starts the new second Battle of Lexington. Your shot will be the one heard round the world. But people won't realize it until much later."

He hadn't meant to enter speech mode, but she deserved to know something of the bigger picture. "After we reach the safe house, I'll show you the details of tomorrow's plan."

Thursday, May 7, Evening EDT

NIKI HADN'T WORRIED ABOUT TRYING to figure out where they were going; the zipper GPS tracker on her jeans would let the Bureau follow her. She removed her blindfold to discover they had arrived at a well-maintained farmstead composed of a fieldstone house, large barn with rustic hex sign under the peak, silo with a metal roof shining in the moonlight, all surrounded by freshly planted fields smelling faintly of fertilizer. The shifting breeze tickled her skin, and the creak of a majestic eagle weather vein, green with the patina of oxidized copper, rotated to point east. Before she could learn anything more than that the place was on the north side of an arrow-straight road, Colonel Pete ushered them into the house.

He had Niki and Sam change into Vietnamese-style pajamas and removed their clothes to who knew where. The three of them sat on stools at a kitchen bar eating tomato soup and grilled cheese sandwiches. "The target," the colonel said, "is a former president's adult child. You will have no problem recognizing the individual."

Niki ran through the possibilities: the Obama girls—barely adults, the Bush twins, Clinton's daughter. She had no clue what Reagan's kids looked like or any of the earlier ones. Except Bush forty-three was a president's son. She might not recognize George Herbert Walker Bush's other kids, but she'd know him. "Is there Secret Service protection?"

"That ends at age sixteen," Colonel Pete said. "It's a charity event. We've reserved a hotel room that faces the venue's entrance. It's seven hundred thirty-six point seven meters from the room's balcony to the door. You've been nailing targets much farther away than that. Tonight's weather front blasts through and leaves clear skies and a light breeze of three to five miles an hour."

"Vertical height?" Sam asked and Niki translated.

"The balcony floor is thirty-three meters above the ground."

"The distance to target is horizontal line or hypotenuse?" Niki asked.

Niki detected a hint of exasperation in his, "It hardly makes a difference."

"Three-quarters of a meter." Sam told Niki not to translate and instead ask about the post-assassination plan.

His quick answer meant either he was a math savant, or he already knew the answer. She was beginning to wonder whose operation this actually was. Not that she expected a post-assassination escape because there wouldn't be an assassination. But she needed to follow the script and ask.

"You'll break down the rifle and store it in its case. The nearest staircase exits to the rear parking lot. A car and driver will be there."

She cycled back to gaps in the plan that she needed to understand. "How do we get keys to the room?"

"The front desk."

Alarm bells went off. "Whose name is this room under?"

"No one real. One of our members is on the desk from ten to six in the morning. I will deliver you. After your mission, you'll return here to debrief, change to civies, and be on your way. We'll whisk you away from the immediate area before police respond. Should police control any part of the planned exit route, our driver knows the area and can navigate around anything."

Sam said, "Colonel, I prefer to use my hotel to gather my strength and transact other business not related to you. I assume this will not be a problem."

Niki translated and was relieved that the colonel immediately acquiesced to Sam's request. That provided her an alternative escape route. "Where are security cameras inside the hotel? Do external cameras cover the entire parking lot or only the entrances? Which streets have police cameras? Any red light monitors?"

The Colonel linked his fingers behind his head and leaned back. "Why did you even think to ask these questions, Corporal?"

Fear squeezed Niki's chest. *Do not show expertise.* She scooped in a spoonful of soup. Comfort food, indeed. "TV shows and news. And I read a lot. Doing this repeatedly means not getting arrested. Get caught and they kill us or label us crazies. No panic from that. The military uses facial recognition to target people for their drone attacks. Cops will have access to the technology for investigating a high-profile assassination. One decent picture and we're screwed."

"Relax." The colonel gave her a smile she didn't trust. "I'll pull up a secure browser and show you everything."

Using mapping software, Colonel Pete illustrated the cones of coverage for each surveillance camera. PFF's proposed escape route was dark once they exited the hotel lot. The parking entrance caused a choke point where a pair of cameras captured the driver and license plate of every vehicle entering or exiting. "There's no attendant. Before I deliver you, our man will manually rotate them to point at the ground."

Cameras covered the main entrance of the hotel. "Face away and no one can identify you. The clerk will run a loop through the front desk monitor to prevent that camera from recording you checking in. Their elevators have eyes, but the stairwells do not."

The level of expertise demonstrated by PFF's intelligence suggested to Niki they had deeper pockets and broader assets than the FBI task force had thought. Still, there were issues. "A lot can go wrong during registration. Why not get the keys in advance?"

"Our asset works only Thursday through Saturday nights. He assures me he can feed last week's recording through to cover your arrival."

Not reassuring. Unless every speck of dust were the same in the background, FBI techs would discover the ruse. And if the clerk messed up, it guaranteed her picture would grace the nation's screens. To save his ass, Ambrose would disavow their agreement, and she'd be screwed. She must find a better way in, concoct a plan to *not* assassinate the target without

Sam knowing that was her intention, and stay free and alive afterward. Piece of cake. Not.

"Costume party." The words were out of her mouth before she knew she would say them. "We can wear masks and the cameras are no longer a problem. Where can we get costumes this evening?"

Fifty-Two

NIKI DIDN'T CALL THE COLONEL on his first lie, a change in plan that had him drop them off near another downtown hotel to catch a cab to the chosen hotel instead of taking them there himself. She dressed as a geisha, kimono long enough to cover her ankle holster and boots, a fan hid the portion of her face makeup wasn't already disguising, gloves covered her hands. Sam's pirate costume included leather gloves, an eye patch, full mustache and beard, and a fake sword hanging from a wide swashbuckling belt. He carried the sniper suitcase and a blue duffel that held clothes. The clock behind the clerk read 3:37.

Niki did not recognize the hotel clerk, a late twenties male with a neatly trimmed mullet and fingernails gnawed to the quick.

"I love your outfits. Reservation?"

Without speaking, Niki showed him a piece of paper on which she'd printed the name of the person renting the room. The clerk moved to his computer and tapped its keys. Niki palmed the clerk's cellphone from the counter, its screen showing a first-person shooter game, and stuck it in her pocket.

The clerk slipped a room card into a small folder. "Your room number is inside. Elevators are on the left." He tapped a note he'd laid on the counter:

Good you have costumes. Security company fixed the cameras. Take the far stairs not the elevator.

Niki nodded her understanding and led Sam past the elevators to the stairway. They exited at the top and found room 715 opposite the stairs. Niki tapped a keycard against the sensing device. The lock clicked open.

She held the door open for Sam and followed him in, laying the keycard and its holder next to the television. Through the balcony door, Niki spotted a well-lit museum across parking lots and lawn. She grabbed the blue bag from the bed where Sam had placed it. "I'm changing clothes." In the bathroom, she discovered the Colonel had replaced her clothes with running shorts, a tee shirt, sweatshirt, and a beanie for her head. Not exactly inconspicuous and what the hell would she do with her ankle rig? Had he picked these clothes to make sure she'd have to leave unarmed? She wondered if the GPS in her cargo pants zipper still claimed she was at the farm.

She changed and pulled up a browser on the clerk's smart phone. To her query of the special events at the museum, she learned Laura Bush would speak at ten o'clock, marking the opening of an exhibit on the changing roles of Afghan women in the last thirty years, with an emphasis on their current challenges.

Unless the colonel had lied again, one or both of Laura's daughters must be joining her. Actually, the colonel *had* lied. Under Obama, Congress had passed a law to extend lifetime Secret Service protection to all former First Ladies. Maybe Colonel Pete didn't know that? His words and PFF's planning no longer seemed reliable.

What did Sam know? His taciturn nature made it difficult for her to tell whether he was feeling uncomfortable. She had scant time before he would wonder what she was doing in the bathroom. Opening the phone's messenger app, she sent Liya instructions to cancel Bush's appearance, then gave her their room number. She deleted the message and her browsing history and reopened the clerk's shooter game. She slipped on thin cotton gloves and wiped them across the screen, hopefully smudging her prints, then flushed the toilet.

While she ran water in the sink, she examined Sam's clothes. The Colonel had returned his, which were off-the-rack wash and wear fabrics you could get in any department store. No hidden pockets, seams, anything extraordinary. Someone had removed the tags with a sharp blade.

She shoved her costume into the bag and left Sam's clothes folded on the toilet seat. Domestic Niki—now that was a laugh.

She shut off the water, extinguished the room light to prevent being backlit while on the balcony, and stepped from the bathroom. "All yours." Outside, she stayed close to the building to avoid anyone spotting the rifle barrel as she scoped the museum's well-lit entrance. No obstructions.

What was Colonel Pete's plan if things went sideways? If she didn't pull the trigger, was Sam to kill her? Kill her regardless? How long had Sam and Colonel Pete known each other? What exactly was their relationship?

Behind her, she heard the click of the bathroom door closing.

She went into the dark room and waited for Sam to move to sense where he was. Every nerve tingled. She stepped toward the bed and bumped into him. Before she could react, he ripped the rifle from her hands and put her in a chokehold.

They will not take me alive. Choose your time. You'll only have one chance.

"What did you use the phone for?"

She didn't think he'd seen her take it. "To learn who the target is." She told him what she had discovered. "Did you know?"

She felt him slide the phone from her pocket. He pushed her onto the bed. Not yet time.

"Please stay there," he said from some distance away.

For an older man, he sure moved with catlike quiet. In the phone's glow, she saw Sam now stood next to the bathroom, the rifle leaning against the wall behind him. He held a nasty blade in his right hand and worked the phone with his left. She had missed the weapon and searched for the blade's origin. The bottom portion of the telescope was missing. Sam had transformed it into the knife. His tripod, his weapon, his advantage.

"Are your orders to kill me?"

His head snapped up. She refused to look away from his penetrating glare.

"*The Art of War* teaches us to rely not on the likelihood of the enemy's not coming, but on our own readiness to receive him; not on the chance of his not attacking, but on the fact that we have made our position unassailable. I carry this knife in defense until I understand my position. I find American women intriguing, especially a corporal who acts like a general. What do you think will happen when the clerk finds his phone missing?"

"He's already decided not to call us or come up here and demand it. He won't tell anyone he screwed up and allowed us—me—to grab it. We can drop it off on our departure. He can pick it up the next time he's in."

"The mission has us leave by the stairs to the parking lot."

"That escape plan sucked. I have a better one." She held her body steady, unwilling to give off any sense of fear. "I am confused, and it would comfort me to know why you accepted this role."

Sam cocked his head, looking curious. "When on a tiger's back, it is difficult to dismount."

"That says everything and nothing. What happens with the arms sale if you are not there tomorrow to complete the transaction?

Sam's silence lasted more than a minute. She pressed her point. "Generals order soldiers on suicide missions for the greater good. Ben Franklin, one of the U.S. founders, had a saying, 'Three may keep a secret if two of them are dead.' Colonel Pete, you, and I make three."

"You think he plans to kill us."

"You didn't answer my question about the arms sale."

"If you distrust the colonel, why are you here?"

She could deliver *this* speech with passion. "In 2008, the rich and powerful of this country drove our economy into the shitter. Millions lost their jobs, their homes, their life savings. All because government is beholden to the rich. No big bankers went to jail for what they did. Exactly zero politicians. No one at the Fed committed suicide for missing all the signs. Oh sure, a few unlucky schmos got nailed for tax fraud, and a bunch of little suckers got caught doing what the rich told them to do. Today, the rich have an even larger chunk of the national pie.

"I want a government that is of, by, and for the people. All the people, not just rich ones or smart lawyers and accountants who can find loopholes for their masters. I believe in that. That's what Patriots For Freedom believes. Taking this shot advances the chances of forcing governmental change. I will take it, but I won't give up my life for it. Life is precious, and I'm still in love with it."

At the time Colonel Pete had first suggested the idea of killing rich kids she had noted the irony that, given the Daughters Trust, they could consider her one of those very people. Sam's silence suggested he was evaluating her words. Niki suspected that even while he cogitated, he was aware of everything, including the slight odor from her perspiration. She got off the bed and waited on balanced feet.

"You think too much to be a good soldier. This is both an American strength and weakness. How did you plan to leave?"

"We pull a fire alarm in the hall. Elevators don't work after the alarm. It forces everyone to use the stairs. We join the confusion of panicked guests and maids, use the front entrance, and walk down the street."

"Leave the rifle?"

"We take only the bag with our clothes and most of our DNA." She smiled. "You can sell them another rifle."

That seemed to satisfy him, and they spent the next many minutes in watchful silence.

"Come." Sam grabbed her arm and guided her to the patio door. "Do you see the reflection?" He pointed. "We are not alone."

Following his directions, she peered through the scope, not seeing anything at first. With a sudden shift in perception, like she'd experienced when a black vase on a white background transformed into the shape of two white heads in profile, she saw the shadow of a person holding a long-barreled rifle. Following the darkness toward the still-low sun, she found the individual partially obscured by a rooftop garden.

"Would your colonel assign two teams?"

Or a Jack Ruby to her Lee Harvey Oswald? "Belt and suspenders." She had to explain the expression to him. The more she watched the shadow, the more it puzzled her. The gun never pointed at her or the museum. She suggested to Sam that it might be Secret Service creating a perimeter.

"We would do the same in my country."

"My movements on the balcony to prepare for the shot will draw his attention."

Sam scraped open the sliding door and rearranged the balcony furniture. The marksman swiveled in their direction. Niki stepped back even though she was sure he couldn't see into the darkened room.

Sam returned and spoke close to her ear, "The furniture now provides you more cover in the shade. When the sun reaches the far side of the balcony, I will distract them by performing Tai Chi. The wind and distance are what we expected. Your previous calibration will be perfect. This will work. I am sure of it."

Fifty-Three

Friday, May 8, 0830 EDT

NIKI SLIPPED INTO PLACE ON the balcony an hour and a half before the museum event was to start. The Bushes might arrive just in time for the ribbon cutting and Laura's remarks, or they might come early to enjoy a private preview before the official event. Sam, dressed only in boxer shorts, performed a slow series of Tai Chi movements, taking frequent breaks, either resting in a chair, or going inside to replenish water and use the bathroom.

Remaining stationary, Niki watched the watcher. Sam's movement attracted his attention for a while until the watcher stopped scanning in their direction. Well done, Sam. She performed her own closer inspection of her Chinese associate. His body was lean and hard. A jagged appendectomy scar told of field surgery to save his life. A through and through bullet wound had a more recent story, leaving a neat circle of scar tissue in the front of his thigh, and a ragged pucker of still-pinkish tissue covering the exit wound. He'd been twice lucky.

The first limo arrived at oh-nine-thirty carrying what Niki fondly thought of as blue-haired ladies. Hair permed into tight curls, stubby heels, skirts below the knees. Good lord, they wore gloves. A fashion statement, surely, because the temperatures were already in the high sixties. Museum staff escorted the women through a passage marked by ropes connecting stanchions running from the street to a door at the far right of the entrance.

Think like a sniper, except one who has to miss and make it look good. She could miss low and hit the car. Did bullets ricochet from an armored car? Probably, and with the way things had been going recently, she'd kill a baby in a stroller.

She followed the guests up the path, scanning for a tree big enough to plant a round in. Nothing plausible. And it must be credible to fool Sam. He'd kill her for sure if he decided she had missed intentionally.

Nothing right or left of the walkway to the entrance would work. A ceramic pot containing an unidentifiable-to-her shrub had potential. Dirt would capture a bullet. But if the plant was fake, stones might fill the pot, and she'd have the same ricochet problem.

Great. Two terrible choices: a round into an armored vehicle or the pot. Picking might depend on exactly where the limo parked. Her stomach threatened to crawl up her throat. She felt certain needing to miss well made her more nervous than if she had to kill, say, a kidnapper standing next to the victim.

Soon each change in the traffic light delivered one or two limos, Bentleys, or other luxury cars. Valets helped the mostly women from the vehicles and whisked away the private cars. No one, other than the staff who helped those who wobbled, was younger than sixty. That changed with a black Lexus LC 500 Inspiration. Its driver, a middle-aged woman, rippled with energy. Those legs knew exercise. The next limo pulled up and Niki flipped her focus onto the new arrival, who turned out to be another senior citizen.

Sunlight was edging closer to her position, bringing increased temperatures. Sweat stuck her shirt to her back. Without changing position, she flexed muscles to prevent cramps.

"Four limos coming," Sam whispered. "Could be them."

"Let me know if you determine which limo they're in. My first chance is right after they get out of the car." *And I'll put the round into the limo.*

Four limos stopped. Each driver walked around his vehicle to open the passenger door facing the museum. A man with a full head of gray hair, dark navy suit, exited the third car.

She followed him in the rifle's scope, her quickened heartbeat echoing in her ear. He ducked to help a woman from the car. Could this be President Bush, and the fucking bureaucracy hadn't stopped them from coming? A tweak of rage shot through her system. She automatically counteracted it by visualizing sunrise in Glacier.

She refocused on the man, willing him to show his face.

"Is that Bush?" Sam spoke from the other side of the furniture, where he could retreat once she made the shot. Or kill her.

"Don't know." She placed her finger on the trigger. He'd expect that.

Something clawed at her brain to give her a message. Focusing drove it away. She ground her teeth. Could she swivel and shoot Sam? He wasn't threatening her. Killing him violated both her professional and personal ethics. Even if he *was* threatening, the risk of a bystander casualty was high for a no-look shot. Sadly, the diversion didn't shake loose her brain's message.

In super-slow motion, the gray head emerged from the limo. Through the scope she observed his perfect hair part followed by an ear, a sideburn cut close. She slid her finger from the trigger. "No Secret Service agents." Her quiet Mandarin words deadened the electricity on the balcony.

"Yes. He would have them." He moved away and flowed into another Tai Chi pose.

"Time?" she asked.

"Two minutes left. They might arrive late to avoid others."

Maybe. Her stomach's ease suggested the authorities had received and delivered her message. During the next five minutes, two additional groups arrived and entered the museum. Ten minutes after the hour, several young men disassembled the ropes hanging from the stanchions.

Niki said, "Either they aren't coming or arrived somewhere we couldn't see."

"Keep watching, I will dress."

Niki had no alternative than to remain in her vulnerable position and look through her scope as he passed behind her. She held her breath and strained to hear what was happening in the room. Seconds crawled to minutes.

Friday, May 8, Morning EDT

COLONEL PETE HATED THE WAITING part of any operation when nothing he could do would change the outcome. Sitting in his study with its sweeping view of rows upon rows of corn freshly sprouted, he sipped his fresh-squeezed orange juice and reread the Washington Post's article discussing the long plan China was implementing in Africa to dominate that continent. *Let them have it.*

A cellphone tinkled a polite request that he answer. He swept the screen open and put the phone to his ear. "They announced Mrs. Bush has come down with a stomach bug, and she and her daughter won't be coming. Think someone tipped them off?"

Or you did it yourself to test me and the systems I devised. "Only seven of us knew."

"Well, it wasn't either of us."

"I'll take care of it." He disconnected. He hadn't been comfortable using

Sam. Time to feel comfortable. He used speed dial, the connecting buzz interrupted by a strong male voice, "No action here."

"Deal's off. Bring them to me. Preferably alive, but either way, I want to see them."

Friday, May 8, 1015 EDT

"LET US RETREAT."

Relief washed over Niki at Sam's words. She crawled backwards into the hotel room, keeping a low profile in case the sniper was still watching. Sam closed the door and pulled the drapes. He broke down the rifle and packed it into its bag while she pulled a beanie over her hair and zipped her ankle holster with gun into the clothes bag.

She grabbed the ice bucket and several tissues. "Remember," she said, "if we have to speak, English only." Using tissues, she opened the door and flicked the security latch to block its closing. That allowed Sam to open it with his foot instead of his bare hands. She found the fire alarm on the wall opposite the elevators. No one watching, she pulled the alarm and slipped into the alcove containing the icemaker.

The piercing whoop-whoop-whoop masked the rattle of ice cubes dropping into the bucket. She jogged down the corridor with a full bucket in hand. A woman appeared in a nearby doorway. Niki asked, "Did you see a guy running past? He yelled fire, pulled the alarm, and ran that way." She pointed toward the far end of the hallway.

"Uh-uh."

"Better safe than sorry," Niki said. "Let's go." Niki held the room door with her foot to allow the woman to grab her purse. While the woman's back was turned, Niki tucked the ice bucket inside and stuffed the tissues into her shorts' pocket.

Before reaching the stairway, they passed two maids cleaning a room. Niki asked them in Spanish if this happened frequently. Their "no" convinced them to leave their stuff, and the four entered the stairwell together. By the time they descended two floors, enough people had joined the retreat to separate Niki from the others. Good. If questioned, most guests and workers wouldn't have any idea who had come from which floor. She trusted Sam would soon pass the reception desk and drop off the phone she had swiped.

At the second-floor landing, the stream of people split around a woman with a walker. *Shit. Shit. Shit.* The law of unintended consequences. Niki squatted next to the woman. "Is anyone with you, ma'am?"

"My husband went for a newspaper. I don't know where he is."

Niki grabbed the arm of a paunchy middle-aged guy passing by. "Sir. Please help us here and take this woman's walker down."

"No fucking way, lady." He continued down the stairs.

Niki's vision blurred. She wanted to catch the bastard and break his leg.

"Let the asshole go," the old woman said. "If you'll give me your arm, I think I can do it."

"But your walker?"

"Won't do me any good if I die."

Niki wished she could assure the lady that death was unlikely, provided they didn't trip.

One last set of footsteps pounded down the stairs above them. A huge guy rounded the landing, tats covering his arms and neck, at least the part she could see through his long dreadlocks.

Niki moved to block his way. "Hey, can you lend a hand?"

His six-five towered over them from the step above. In a Brooklyn accent, he asked, "What may I do to help?"

May? "I need to carry this woman down the stairs. If you can take her walker?"

White teeth shone in his wide grin. "Not to diss your strength, lady, but I think we should reverse roles." He joined them on the landing and bent down to the woman's level. "Madam, may I have the pleasure of carrying you to safety?" Without waiting for a reply, he scooped her up. "See you at the bottom."

The exit delivered them to the edge of the parking lot. Niki rubbed her hands over the places she had touched the walker to blur any fingerprints before delivering it to the older lady, now in animated conversation with her rescuer. "Thanks," Niki said to the giant, who had acted as an unwitting shield.

She spotted the escape Kia parked in a far corner of the lot. Two things were wrong. The trunk was not open to accept their gear, and instead of a single driver, two guys were talking. One she recognized from the militia; the other looked like a feral cat.

Two fire engines raced into the parking lot. Under cover of their distraction, she slipped around the far corner of the building and walked away, forcing herself to slow to a pace that would not attract attention.

"Hey, Niki," came a voice from behind her. "Nice legs."

Fifty-Four

Friday, May 8, 1020 EDT

NIKI SLOWED HER STEPS, LETTING Rick the Prick catch up. She scanned ahead, looking for pinch points where the FBI could control her if they planned to take her in forcibly. Wide open. They must expect her to go willingly.

Speaking only loud enough for her to hear him over the background cacophony of sirens and honking cars, he said, "Sergeant Oliver was making a squeal deal, and they slit his throat. Dead. That was me on the roof. We think two guys were waiting for you at the hotel. Liya and I agree you should bail."

Was a slit throat what the Colonel had planned for her? "I saw. They getting picked up?"

"Can't until you're safe. Otherwise, we tip them off. We got the desk clerk on a speeding rap with drugs in his car. Won't hold up, but he's off the street for now. Liya has your Chinese guy under surveillance."

"Last I heard, the gun sale is still on. We're going together."

"That's crazy risk. Everyone wants you to walk away."

Wanting her to walk away meant they weren't forcing her to quit. She looked at the falsely bearded Rick. "By sticking with Sam, we can hopefully locate and stop the arms sale. Am I the only one worried about those weapons?"

"I see I can't convince you. Take this." He slipped her a cheap-looking watch. "Next time, speak English if you want us to understand. Google Translate struggles with both your dialects."

She stopped, but Rick kept walking. Over his shoulder, he said, "Love the shorts and combat boots. Great look."

Rooted in place, she watched him turn onto the next street, away from the direction she'd take to meet Sam. What the hell? A wishy-washy preference for her to stand down; Rick with an excellent disguise and covering her from a sniper position; Liya following Sam. This was not Gex's style; he'd have her locked in a Bureau car heading to a debriefing.

No way Liya and Rick could do this on their own. Ambrose had to be running this op.

Friday, May 8, 1025 EDT

NIKI PASSED LIYA NINE BLOCKS later, not acknowledging her roommate, who stopped to check a window display. Two more blocks and Niki reached Sam. "Shall I join you at your hotel?" she asked in English to inform her listeners that she had made contact.

"I would not want it any other way."

His smile seemed genuine, but his words could contain a threat. Testing his intentions, she said, "We can grab brunch, coordinate tonight's plans, and I'll go to my apartment, change clothes, maybe get a little shut-eye."

"No, Corporal Niki. We stay together."

Niki caught one additional glimpse of Liya during their walk to Sam's hotel. At the door to his room, without knowing whether the watch was transmitting her voice through the walls, Niki spoke the room number out loud, as though she were memorizing it. Inside, Sam pulled closed the curtains and ordered room service, giving her listeners one more chance to catch the room number. Switching to Mandarin, he instructed her to place her order. "Have you heard about devices that can record conversations using vibrations from a window or a water glass?"

Niki feigned ignorance of a technology she understood well. Sam described various electronic eavesdropping techniques until room service arrived. One whiff of the food and saliva flooded Niki's mouth. Sam picked at his meal. Niki ate like a jackal, not sure whether stress caused her hunger, or it was simply because she'd missed breakfast. She placed the food trays in the hall to prevent room service staff from interrupting them and asked Sam how he expected the sale to take place. He was forthcoming with details, which was great if her watch transmitted through curtains and glass, and her listeners found someone to translate Mandarin. Given Rick's warning, that seemed unlikely.

In case they could hear and translate, she asked, "How are we getting there?"

"Hotel has cabs, even at two in the morning."

"True, but we're heading to a sketchy area of the city. The cabbie may refuse to travel to a warehouse that time of night. And if he does agree, he'll remember us. Better we get there while it's still light and wait. If we cab to my place, I can ditch this ridiculous outfit. Bring the blue bag with us so I can rearm myself with my ankle rig. There are a bunch of places near there that we can grab takeout dinner and then catch a taxi to the warehouse."

"Chinese?" He waggled his eyebrows.

Friday, May 8, Early afternoon EDT

NIKI GAVE THE DRIVER THE address to her apartment. That would alert her followers to the first part of her plan. To be consistent and not stoke Sam's suspicions during the next cab ride when details mattered, she chatted up the driver and noted landmarks they passed. At her building, Sam insisted on accompanying her into the apartment. She enjoyed a quick shower, put on fresh clothes, and strapped on her ankle holster. Unlike Rick, who had snooped while she showered, she found Sam sitting on the couch exactly where she'd left him. She grabbed a couple of energy bars from the kitchen and stuck them in the same pocket she stored her concealed carry license.

They walked to a Thai place where they purchased takeout and caught another cab that brought them to an address Sam provided. If this were Niki's weapons sale, she would give the driver an address close enough they could walk to the warehouse, but not close enough that the cabbie could tie them to a specific area.

Her tour-guide routine worked great at keeping her listeners informed of the route until they hit the warehouse district. Niki's tactic changed to wondering aloud what people kept in Federmeyer Brothers Storage and what caused someone to have three blue doors and one red one. She was resorting to describing graffiti before they arrived at Adams Dental Supplies. Parked next door was an excavator and Niki pulled the two together into a joke about root canals, which she had to explain to the both of them while Sam paid the fare.

She and Sam didn't move until the cab was out of sight, then he led her back in the direction they had come. "Good idea," she said, "giving him the wrong address and going too far. How far from here?"

"The food won't go cold."

Sam's comment sounded like he meant it as a conversation ender. Once they arrived, maybe she could provide a more precise location. The universe owed her some good luck, right?

Fifty-Five

Saturday, May 9, Very early morning EDT

FIFTEEN MINUTES BEFORE PFF PERSONNEL were scheduled to arrive to buy the weapons, Niki made her ploy to get outside. "Once the Colonel gets here, he'll expect me to report to him. I should wait where he can see me."

"My man will join you."

That killed her plan to report what she had observed of the warehouse to whoever was listening to her watch. She stifled an inner groan. One of the three armed guards donned optical night gear and led her through a side door into an alley. Staying close to the building, he brought her to the front entrance.

Clouds had gathered while she was inside, and it smelled like rain. Even for a quarter past two in the morning, it was creepy quiet. Too quiet to provide verbal information to her backup with the guard within earshot.

Colonel Pete's red pickup and a Penske rental truck arrived at 0230 hours. Had they been waiting around the block until the appointed time? Colonel Pete and the truck driver both got out. Either vehicle could hide many additional passengers.

She tugged the long-sleeved shirt to cover her new watch and stepped into the light, making sure her hands were visible as she walked. "Colonel, did I assume correctly you want me here to translate?"

The driver of the truck, the feral cat from the hotel parking lot, covered her with a machine pistol.

"Sam bring you?" To his companion, he said, "Search her."

Niki stopped and held her arms out straight. "Yes sir. Pistol in my ankle holder. When Mrs. Bush didn't show, I figured I should be your eyes and ears." The man gave her pistol to the colonel, who slipped it into his pocket, then continued his pat down, finding and returning one energy bar, one wrapper, and her concealed carry license.

"The daughter was your target. How did you know?"

"We checked the museum's website. Sam is inside with at least three armed men. One has an assault rifle trained on us now."

"Undoubtedly. Why didn't you use the car in the hotel lot?"

"Sam doesn't fully trust you, sir. He feared a trap. We grabbed a bite in his hotel room, stopped by my apartment for me to change, and we've been here for eight hours. It's just the three of us, sir?"

"Tell me, corporal, what did you observe at the museum?"

She described everything, including spotting a sniper on a distant building and their method of escape. "I wondered if you had two teams targeting the same individual."

"Not my style. The hotel clerk has not reported in. Do you know what happened to him?"

"I thought his shift ended. You can ask Sam. We split up. He passed the reception area, and I used a stairwell."

"Explain why you triggered the fire alarm."

The more questions he asked, the more acid churned in Niki's stomach, a bitter taste creeping into her mouth. *Answer as a subordinate would.* "I figured we should try not to be recognized leaving the hotel. With a mass evacuation, nothing would highlight our departure to the cops checking video recordings."

"But there was no shooting."

"She didn't show. We still thought it was a good exit plan."

"What did you learn from Sam?"

"He practices Tai Chi and is light and quiet on his feet. He's fond of weird sayings, like, once you're on a tiger, it's hard to get off. Sam spotted the other sniper and got paranoid on me, suggesting the sniper might be there to eliminate us once we—after the event. The fact that he even thought of that shocked me. He made it clear he wouldn't use your driver. I worried Sam might kill me. I was pretty nervous, sir. Maybe I still am. Seems I'm running at the mouth."

"It's wise to take precautions. Two days ago, I stationed a squad in this area to cover our exit. They've been lying low, making sure we have no surprises. I expect Sam has men hidden in the dark corners of this building in case we try to steal the weapons. It takes time to build trust. Even the best actors eventually slip up and reveal their true selves. Don't you agree?"

Was Colonel Pete saying he was on to her? She glanced toward Feral Cat. He was picking his teeth with a curved knife that glinted in the streetlight. Her knees turned to jelly. She locked them in place, pressing her toes into the ground. Either the Feds had heard everything or they hadn't. Her only damn choice was to be brazen. "I've always been a little too gullible, sir, so I'm not sure if that's true for everyone."

He cocked his head. "What's the setup inside?"

"I don't know, sir. I entered through a door on that side." She pointed. "They kept me in a nearby office."

The colonel's eagle-eyes seemed to pierce her. "Alright, let's do this." He returned her pistol and led her to the warehouse, where he pressed a red button next to the human-sized door.

"Where is money?" A heavily accented guard asked.

"We'll transfer the money once we see the weapons."

Niki translated.

From further inside came Sam's voice in Mandarin, "Allow them in. We'll show them we are dealing fair. Are there only two of them?"

"And me," Niki said.

Colonel Pete told the driver, "Stay with the truck. Remain vigilant. Corporal, with me."

Their footsteps echoed in the cavernous space. Dim lights marked the passage to stacks of wooden boxes that looked like the one she had seen at the quarry. She peered into the unlit corners of the warehouse but couldn't tell what the darkness hid.

Sam offered them a crowbar. "Open however many you like. Check all two hundred rifles if you want. You know our reputation. We are honest merchants."

Colonel Pete counted rifle and ammo boxes. He inspected four rifle boxes. Unlike the box at the quarry closed with short tacks, these required him to pry off the tops. The nails protested with long creaks that sent a shiver down Niki's spine. Satisfied, he composed a text message and showed it to Niki before sending it. Niki informed Sam the text said to "transfer the money."

Sam swiped his finger on a tablet, waking it up. The screen cast a bluish light showing rows of shelves filled with plumbing parts. This, Niki figured, was the moment for duplicity. If the Colonel wasn't acting in good faith, he would try to seize the weapons. And if Sam was dishonest, the danger would occur once he confirmed the money had transferred.

She kept alert for trouble while her brain spun with possibilities. Had the Feds had enough time to organize a Stingray to emulate a cell tower and capture all the transmissions? Could the FBI geeks follow funds through whatever offshore accounts and cryptocurrency they were using?

The tablet chimed, bringing her back to the warehouse.

Sam typed with two fingers—a password?—studied the display. "Let's do it," he said in English and gave a thumbs up. The loading dock door rose. Colonel Pete motioned for the truck to back up for loading.

"Help pack, corporal."

Niki kept herself positioned to get a jump on Feral Cat in the event of a federal raid. They transferred all the boxes into the rental truck, and he closed the truck's rolling door with a clang that sounded like a rifle shot. "Shit," she exclaimed. "That scared the crap out of me."

His shaking head and slitted eyes expressed his disdain. She would not turn her back on that guy. Behind her, the loading dock door creaked shut. Colonel Pete joined them. "Corporal, you drive my truck. I'll ride shotgun."

Niki's nerves jacked one notch tighter. She had never seen him allow anyone to drive his truck.

FIFTY-SIX

"FOLLOW HIM." THE COLONEL POINTED at the Ryder rental. "You still want to work with Sam?"

Niki put the pickup in gear and pulled behind the rental. "If it's useful to you, sir. And doesn't interfere with my militia assignments."

"Keep your eyes and ears open. Let me know if he contacts you. I want you to report directly to me, not to anyone else, even if they say otherwise. Is that understood? Something's happening. Tactically, we should shorten lines of communication. Because of your exemplary work here, I'll be sending your name along for promotion to sergeant."

"I'm honored, sir. I won't let you down." At the first intersection, the rental truck, with the two hundred automatic weapons and hundreds of thousands of rounds of ammunition, turned left.

The Colonel pointed straight ahead. "That way."

"The Ryder truck's gone left on its own? We're solo going forward?" She hoped someone was bright enough to realize she had given them directions.

"Less suspicious than a caravan at oh-dark-thirty. Same reason our perimeter defense will remain in position and stagger their departure starting at sunrise."

"Is this all because of Sergeant Oliver's arrest?"

"Caution saves lives."

That was a curious response that didn't answer her question. Niki varied her speed between two and four miles above the limit. Two minutes later, a car's lights came on a block behind them and pulled into the road. Random, or good guys forming a trap?

Colonel Pete stared into the side-view mirror and thumbed off the safety on the machine pistol lying in his lap.

Niki said, "I see him." She also spotted a bread truck two blocks ahead and suspected she heard a chopper in the distance. Passing through the next intersection, she peripherally caught movement in both directions. The trap was closing. "How many in that magazine?" she asked to let them know she had an armed passenger.

The colonel concentrated on the side-view mirror. The suspicious vehicle maintained its distance. Niki heard Colonel Pete exhale and realized she, too, was holding her breath.

A burst of light from the sky caught them. At the colonel's command to "Go," she floored the accelerator and moved ahead of the spotlight.

The bread truck swung into the street, and the driver bailed. Two cars backed from parking spots to complete the barricade. The car behind them engaged its dash flashers and bright lights and the helicopter spotlight found them again. Cops with rifles rose from behind the roadblock. They had chosen the location well. Her mind raced: how could she stay undercover and stay alive?

Over the whine of the engine, Colonel Pete yelled, "Stop, but give me time to empty my gun and store it under the seat." He ejected his clip and opened the glove box.

How long did she have before they started firing? She jerked her foot off the accelerator, pulled far to the right, and engaged in a J turn, a maneuver she'd practiced at the academy, but never in a truck. She yanked on the hand brake and spun the wheel left. With the stench of burned rubber filling the vehicle, the rear end skidded to a halt with them facing in the opposite direction. The spotlight flew past them.

Niki removed her ankle holster, tucked it and the gun under the passenger seat, and placed both hands on her head. Colonel Pete did the same. "Helluva maneuver, corporal. Remember, no one talks and the worst they got you for is speeding and reckless driving."

The rearview mirror showed armed men in tactical uniforms approaching. Whatever happened, at least she had prevented a bloodbath.

At their command, she smoothly exited the truck, showing them her empty hands. They shoved her to the ground, pulled her arms behind her, and cuffed her wrists. A cop's knee dropped hard on her back, his other pressed her neck, pinning her face to the cracked sidewalk. Hands searched her, finding nothing. "What's your name?"

Gex would want her to end this and reveal her identity. And Ambrose? "I am Corporal Niki, serial number one, two, three, four, five, six. The Geneva Convention does not require me to provide you with any additional information."

From a few blocks away came a burst of automatic fire followed by a ten-second rumble of heavy gunfire. The pressure on her neck increased. "That shit don't fly around here. What is your name, asshole?"

Colonel Pete calmly provided an in-town address and told the officers his registration and insurance were in the glove box. As the guy leaned more weight on her, she flashed to George Floyd. Was that how she'd end? Someone lifted her cuffed hands, pulling her shoulders and making her yelp at the pain. She wanted to scream that she was FBI, and he was under arrest for violating her civil rights. Not that she could ever prove it: Unlike the Minneapolis or D.C. police, Feds never wore body cams.

"Help," Niki screamed. "He's raping me."

They dropped her hands and got off her neck. She worked her jaw around. Sore but not broken. From behind her came a growled, "Get up."

Without help, a normal person can't easily get up from lying on their stomach, hands cuffed behind them. Niki's pre-teen gymnast experience had taught her flexibility and strength moves others didn't have—moves she chose not to display. They'd think she was escaping and whip her legs from under her. More voices were heading her way. She'd wait them out.

"I said, get up." A steel-toed boot struck her ribs.

Through gritted teeth she muttered, "Fuck you, Nazi pig."

"What did you say? I'll show—"

"Enough, man," a second voice said. "Do that again, I'll arrest *you*. That the woman?"

"She was resisting."

"Right. FBI. I have an arrest warrant for her. We'll take it from here."

FIFTY-SEVEN

A FEMALE EMT STRAPPED NIKI to a gurney and the FBI guy cleared a path to a waiting ambulance. Niki remained silent until she was inside the transport with the two of them. "What the—"

Liya, posing as an EMT, clapped a hand over Niki's mouth. Rick ripped the watch from her wrist and chucked it outside. He closed the doors and pounded on the roof. The ambulance rumbled forward.

Liya removed her hand. "Watches have ears. Girlfriend, you look like shit. Ambrose instructed us to engineer your escape before you arrived at the same jail where they killed Sergeant Oliver. You and I are switching places. We gotta be quick and trade clothes."

Niki admitted to her confusion.

Rick released the gurney straps and unlocked the handcuffs, talking all the while. "You missed your shooting review board. Sergeant Oliver died in jail. Gex had no problem convincing the director to bring the operation to a close. But he pulled Gex off the wrap-up and Ambrose assigned himself. Gex is royally pissed and wants you nailed to a cross. Your no-show at the board gave him an excuse to haul your ass in. Lot of people want to help him, but Ambrose isn't one of them. He and the three of us—" He circled his hand to include the three of them. "—are the only ones that know we're extracting you."

Liya had stripped to her underwear and was waving for Niki to trade clothes. With Niki's mind reeling at the implications of what they were doing, she yelled at Rick. "At least be decent and turn around."

"Not on your life, I must watch my prisoner very carefully."

Niki sighed. "Fuck you, Rick."

"If only you meant it." He shielded his head with his hands as if she planned to slug him. "Joking. Or trying." He covered his eyes. "You have any idea what Ambrose is up to?"

Niki stripped. "Why the charade? Why not drop me at the curb?"

Liya said, "EMT driver's not in on this. Your passport, five hundred bucks, your emergency credit card, and a copy of your medical insurance card are in the front pocket of these pants. The cash is enough for a one-way ticket to St. Paul. Don't use that credit card unless you have to. Go dark. Learn what's going on with your family. Let Rick and me take care of this end."

Niki's stomach clenched at mention of flying. Deciding she'd do anything, including hopping a freight train, before she'd take an airplane allowed her to hold it together. She pulled Liya's pants high on her waist, shoved the shirt sleeves up to bunch at her elbows. It would have to suffice. "You learn anything about the kidnappers at the diner?"

Rick said, "Not much. They were two of a dozen guys from the same SEALs unit who formed a security firm doing a lot of protection work here and abroad. We've caught rumors of black ops, but nothing firm."

Niki slipped on Liya's loafers and felt like a clown with the gigantic clodhoppers. "Maybe double socking will help. Rick, give me your socks."

The ambulance made a quick right and slowed down. Rick strapped Liya's legs to the gurney, and Niki belted down Liya's chest and covered her with a blanket.

"You and me, Niki." Rick gave her shoulder a friendly pat. "Let's get this perp into ER. STET."

Niki felt herself flow into her new role, Niki EMT. "It's STAT, you jerk."

Saturday, May 9, Morning EDT

WITH MASS TRANSIT SPOTTY ON a Saturday morning, it had taken Ashley two hours to reach her Lincolnia apartment. She changed into her own clothes, wrote Liya an apologetic note, stole her keys and car, and was on the road by six-thirty. GPS said seventeen hours' drive time to Minneapolis. She'd gain an hour with the time change, and driving ten miles an hour over the speed limit would save another two. She'd have to stop for gas. With luck, she'd get there by nine that night.

The tires' hum on the interstate provided background white noise to accompany Ashley's thinking. Gex had prevailed and, other than testifying at trials, her PFF undercover assignment was toast. Probably her career. Saving her career had seemed so important just a few days ago. Now, with the weapons no longer a problem, she just wanted to exact justice on whoever had leaked the information to Robert that had ultimately torpedoed her job.

The FBI would find Robert or not, and they'd either solve her attempted kidnapping and the plane sabotage or not. Ambrose would screw her and Liya and Rick or not. Not a damned thing she could do about any of that. She locked those worries into a mental steamer trunk and sat on its lid.

Focus on what you *can* do.

Regardless who had brought down the plane and killed the three crew, the leaker bore responsibility, and she was the only one who seemed to care. Or was she? She'd thought the same about the weapons, but Ambrose, Liya, and even Rick had proved her wrong. Still, her number one priority was to discover and punish the asshole who gave Niki's cellphone number to Robert. Number two was to extricate herself and Seamus from the Pendergast Holdings tar pits without screwing up the outstanding work Seamus had done. Third, have her sisters' conversation with Tabitha. Well, third in her priority; it might happen first. That was fine, provided she didn't let it interfere with the first two.

She visualized herself unlocking the steamer trunk, tucking in all concerns about what she'd do after the FBI fired her, slamming the lid, and double-locking it this time.

As she passed each mile marker, she verbalized her objective. "Focus on the leaker." That felt good.

At the first pit stop, she picked up energy drinks and a burner phone. Back on the road, she called Seamus. He picked up, and after assuring him she was fine, she told him she was driving to his hotel and needed to keep a low profile.

"Why come here where somebody wants to kill you? That's nuts. Go stay at my camp in the U.P. No one will find you there."

"Because the answers I need are in Minnesota."

"You realize if you come here, you risk screwing up everything I've put in place, right? You show up, and you're back to being the interim CEO, destroying my efforts to install Gabriella Linz. All the—"

"We'll make sure that no one knows I'm there until we concoct a way around that. That's what lawyers are for, right? I'll get to your hotel around nine. After I get a good night's sleep, we can make a plan to handle Pendergast Holdings and return you to normal life."

At his sigh, she pictured him tilting his head and peering over the top of his glasses toward the ceiling.

"You're a pig-headed fool and should listen to reason," he said. "Your idea doesn't work on several levels. First, I'm staying at Robert's house. It saves the company money, and after the arrow incident, Tabitha was nervous about being there at night by herself, even with the guards. She's home this weekend with her mother. Your suitcases are in the closet of the bedroom I'm staying in."

"Fine, I'll meet you there."

He released another sigh. "Look, I don't have time to talk. I've got meetings all frigging day. It started with breakfast, where Gabriella filled me in on her Friday meeting with the New York investment bankers. Later this afternoon, Garrett will tell Gabriella and me everything he's learned about bribes to EPA regulators and various foreign officials. Right now, I'm late meeting Gerald Nakourma to brief outside counsel on Bradlee's expected wrongful discharge suit against us and Junior's challenge of Robert Pendergast's proxy."

Which were both totally on her. She apologized, and Seamus cut her off.

"Whatever. It's where we are. FBI agents have been pestering Tabitha and me. They claim they have no leads on Robert, and they want to discuss the kidnapping and the plane sabotage with you. I really don't think it's a good idea for you to come here."

At mention of the plane, her stomach somersaulted, and her face turned hot with embarrassment. What kind of person was she? She had not given Malachi a thought since she returned to D.C. "How is Malachi?"

"Okay, considering. A blow to the spine caused temporary paralysis. His arm's casted and in a sling for the collarbone, but he'll fully recover. He got back yesterday, although for security reasons—are you listening?—Morgan is the only one besides me who knows he's around. Oh, and Tabitha, who overheard me talking."

"Give me his number. I'll call him."

"Fine. Be that way. I'll have Morgan call you on this number. Do everyone a favor. When you hit Chicago, head north. Go to my place. I'm serious."

And he was gone.

In all the years she had known him and all the trauma they had shared, she had never heard him sound so stressed. Her fault, which doubled her resolve to discover who gave Robert her contact information and make him pay in spades.

For the next twenty miles, while waiting for Morgan to call, she changed her mantra to *focus on what you can do. Find the leaker.*

She answered her phone, expecting Morgan, and was surprised to hear Tabitha bubbling on nonstop about being so glad Ashley had escaped serious injury. It would have been terrible to find out she had a sister and then lose her like that. She snapped her finger.

Ashley broke in. "So we are sisters?"

"Yes. No. Sort of. It's complicated."

Ashley smacked her forehead with her palm. "Nothing about the Pendergasts is ever simple. First, tell me how you got this number."

"I heard about the accident and thought you were dead. I was devastated. And then I learned you *were* alive, and I made Seamus promise to tell me as soon as he heard from you. He had Morgan call me, and now I'm talking to you, and I think I'm going to cry."

Ashley would have preferred this conversation to be face-to-face, not while she was driving eighty miles an hour. Morgan was obviously not going to give her Malachi's number—probably violated some corporate policy. To learn anything while she was driving, she'd have to start with Tabitha. Still, she reminded herself to make sure this was what Tabitha wanted. "You sure you want to talk about this over the phone?"

"That's why I called. We're half sisters."

Remembering what Seamus had told her about Robert's blood type, of course they couldn't be full sisters. But that meant her mother had lied to her. Someone had knocked her up. Who? "Do you know who your father is?"

"No! That's the thing. When I did that genetics module in middle school, my parents told me my biological father was a sperm donor. Now that we share the same father, I was hoping you could tell me."

Ashley passed a car like it was standing still and glanced at the speedometer: ninety! She braked and pulled into the right lane. "Wait. We have the same father and he's not Robert? How is that possible?" Everything she thought she knew about her family was wrong. Everything. "Have you talked with your mother?" Once she slowed to seven miles over the limit, matching those around her, she engaged the cruise control.

Tabitha sniffled. "I feel like it's a taboo subject. There's more. Did you know Seamus got DNA from Robert's three sons? You won't believe this. Garrett has the same father as us!"

"He what? They must have screwed up the tests."

"Seamus swears by this lab. Garrett, Junior, and Bradlee have the same mother. The other two share a father, but he's not Robert either. No one is Robert's biological child."

Ashley pictured a genealogical tree with lines connecting generations, making it look like a rat's nest. "Who knows besides you?"

"Garrett heard me tell Seamus. It was like I'd poleaxed him. Once he picked himself off the floor, he said now he understood why he had liked you better than his brothers. He said he was delighted to have another half-sister and looks forward to getting to know me better. Even if it's all lies, he's a sweet guy."

"Do Junior and Bradlee know?"

"I didn't tell them. Garrett might have."

Or being older, they might have already known.

"Maybe when you get back, you and Garrett and I can spend some time together?" Tabitha's voice rose in a question mark, hinting at insecurity?

Did she not believe Garrett or was she worried about what I'm thinking? Her assurances to Tabitha would be more convincing in person. "Absolutely. We can talk more when we're together. Speaking of talking, I want to call Malachi and find out how he's doing. Do you have his number?

FIFTY-EIGHT

Saturday, May 9, Afternoon CDT

MALACHI HAD BEEN RESTING WHEN Ashley left a message on his phone. He wanted to know how she was but didn't want to be on the receiving end of her pity or remorse or whatever she was hiding under her tough-guy exterior. Curiosity and guilt at not calling her back won several hours later.

They queried each other about their injuries. He minimized the extent of his and figured she probably did the same. After the how-are-yous and the health lies wound down, he was prepared to end the call. Before he could, she changed the topic.

"Tabitha gave me the DNA results." She elaborated on what those results showed, then asked, "Did you know? Yes or no."

He provided a hesitant yes, wondering where this turn of the conversation was heading. She didn't make him wait.

"Okay, Malachi, time for the truth. I'm still five hours from Minneapolis, so I have plenty of time. Spill everything you know that was going on with Robert. Remember, one hundred percent truth. Start with this whole sperm donor business."

He considered hanging up. But she was his boss, and he liked his job. He needed a more diplomatic solution than simply pressing the end call button. And didn't she deserve to know? Unlike the other material he held for Ashley that Robert wanted him to give to her after his death, Robert had not sworn Malachi to secrecy about the details of her birth. He cleared his throat, which had gone dry.

"Robert and his wife wanted a family," he said. "He'd caught mumps in college and was one of the rare cases where it caused sterility. He found a sperm donor. I don't know who, but he used the same one for Junior and Bradlee. With two boys, he wanted a girl and thought a different donor might work better."

"That explains Garrett. Then came me."

It wasn't as simple as that, but she only needed an overview. "His wife refused to have any more children. He divorced her, married your mother, and got his daughter. For reasons he did not share, that marriage ended within months of your birth. That left him with a daughter, but not one he could raise. He tried again with a different woman. Tabitha was the successful result."

"Yes, but he didn't get to raise her, either. If Robert's reason for another child was to experience a daughter in his home, what happened?"

Malachi debated with himself: Tabitha should learn that answer first, but it showed a side of Robert that Ashley did not know. It might soften her view of him. "Babies and hormones are funny things. Robert hired Tabitha's mother to be a surrogate. But while she was pregnant, she fell in love and soon married. She asked to cancel the contract. Her husband begged Robert to let them have the child. Robert could have insisted on following the contract, but he realized the greater good was to allow Tabitha to remain with them. He even forgave them the money he'd already paid."

Ashley muttered, "That doesn't sound like the Robert Pendergast I know."

Responding to Ashley's statement edged into moral ambiguity. She had developed a warped picture of Robert. That was unfair, and he wanted her to understand Robert's larger truth. Yet if Robert were still alive, Malachi had no right to play truth-teller. Even assuming one person could know another's truth. He temporized and disliked himself for it. "He kept eyes on Tabitha but did not interfere with her growing up. After your mother died and you rejected Robert's entreaties to join the business, he created a trust for you. He figured he was responsible for Tabitha's existence and included her."

Malachi waited to see how Ashley responded to this new information. Would she stay focused on the current family crises or shift her interest to her mother and Robert? Even if Robert was dead, he was reluctant to address that topic.

Ashley broke the silence. "Thank you, Malachi. You've given me a lot to think about. I'm sure Tabitha and I will have more questions, especially after she talks with her mom. Can we switch gears? Someone wanted— make that wants—me dead. As we both experienced, they don't care about collateral damage. Is that why you're keeping your return to the Twin Cities quiet?"

He smiled at her assumption. "I'm not interested in being hounded by the press or other busybodies. I'm concentrating on recovering so I can get back to work."

"Are you just saying that because I currently control your employer?"

That was the first bit of levity he had heard from her. "One hundred percent truth."

"Good to know. Robert started this mess when he sent you to get me. He—"

"We don't know that." Although, Malachi had to admit it seemed that way.

"I suppose you're right. What was his plan?"

Malachi looked at his fingernails for a long moment. A part of him wanted to join her in speculation, to talk through alternatives. But if he did, he risked accidentally providing false information. "I don't know."

Over the line came a long sigh. "Not good enough, Malachi. A man doesn't disclose details of his infertility without sharing a lot of other stuff. If Robert's alive, he deserves your help to rescue him. If he's dead, doesn't he deserve your help in finding his killer? Let me rephrase the question. What do *you think* Robert's plan was?"

"Robert would not have me speculate about his plans."

"Bullshit, Malachi. We both killed people in D.C. to prevent my kidnapping. Someone killed three crew members flying the company plane, hoping to get me. Robert has been gone for eight days. Don't hide behind your professed loyalty to a man and a plan that didn't work. Stand on your own two feet and live with the results. Did Robert plan his own disappearance?"

Her vehement accusation stunned him. Was he using his vow to not bear false witness to avoid taking responsibility? He rose and paced his kitchen, the idea hammering his chest, making it hard to breathe. He leaned against the refrigerator. "Robert's sons were not meeting his expectations. He respected you because he could not bend you to his will. He also thought well of Tabitha, but he hadn't yet tested her mettle."

Again a sigh from Ashley. "Judge, instruct the witness to answer the question."

He wanted quiet to think things through, but Ashley wouldn't allow him to retreat. Nor, in honesty, did he want to. "His family's succession at Pendergast Holdings concerned him, and he decided to test you all by being unavailable. He wanted to evaluate whether any of you would forge an alliance, work together. Or would everybody grab however much of the pie they could? For any of that to happen, you had to be here, and Tabitha had to learn she was also part of the family."

He caught his reflection in the kitchen window. He looked like boiled sausage, gray, furrows cleaving his face. "Robert had learned that Junior was cheating the business. He'd already told Bradlee that he wouldn't cover for him again if he had another dalliance with an employee. Garrett was a nice enough kid but doesn't have the killer instincts to be a leader, and Robert worried his sexual orientation would leave him open to pressure. Tabitha was young and immersed in her research. You had spurned his advances to join the company. He wanted to force your hand to participate in the firm's management while he applied concentrated pressure to the officers of Pendergast Holdings, LLC. Discover who crumbled to coal dust and who hardened into a diamond. His words, not mine. I said it was a terrible idea. That if none of the sons could run the enterprise, he should sell it or hire talent. He was sure that once you tasted the power, you wouldn't want to let it go. Facts didn't hold a candle to his hurricane of belief."

"And he sent his messenger to fetch me like a dirty sock."

The scorn in her words revealed she saw him as a tame dog, lapping up Robert's, "Good boy." He wanted to yell and scream that she had it all wrong. He had never sought Robert's approval—but he'd like hers.

A long breath settled him and he continued. "Robert planned to stay at his girlfriend's family camp near the Boundary Waters up past Ely. I stocked it with a month's worth of supplies. I was to provide him with updates on the company, and he could return at the quote-unquote right moment. He never arrived."

Ashley snorted disgust. "Maybe he and the girlfriend had another plan."

He pushed off the refrigerator and paced circles around the table to burn off the tension he felt constricting his chest. "Possible. Robert loves contingency plans. Because the three guys at Ike's Diner knew who you were, at first I thought Robert had sent a second crew. But when they mentioned millions of dollars . . ."

His knees buckled at the memory of pulling the trigger and seeing the man die by his hand. He slumped into his chair at the table. "Definitely not Robert. But they knew you were worth millions."

In the background, an engine revved up and the road noises grew louder, then softer again. "How many people," she asked, "know of those policies?"

"One night in his office, Robert mentioned that if you stayed, he'd have to increase your policy from ten to forty million. But to answer your question, those covered know and probably a lot of the finance folks."

"Who else knew of Robert's original plan?"

"He said no one besides me and his girlfriend, and he claimed he told her only that he wanted to be by himself for a while, not why. He wasn't always forthcoming. Possibly Morgan?"

Ashley said, "Maybe, but I doubt it. If you knew Robert didn't plan to talk with me, what was the plan once I got here?"

"That's not right. He *did* plan to talk with you before he left, after which I was to give him status reports. I've tried contacting him." The despair gripped him again. "Nothing."

"You've got to tell all this to the FBI."

"I did. While I was in the hospital. I believe they confirmed everything with the girlfriend. They're the ones who reported no one had been to the cabin after I stocked it."

"Really?" Her surprise sounded genuine. "It would have been nice if they'd told me. Well, not my investigation. One last question: Do you know who gave Robert my undercover phone number?"

Finally, a question that caused him no moral anguish. "I do not."

"Thank you, Malachi. I know that wasn't easy for you. I have Morgan's number, just not with me. Can you give it to me?"

Since she already had the number, it was only a timing question. So, even though it might technically violate company policies, he figured he could give it to her.

"Thanks. Heal quickly, Malachi. When I see you in person, I have a favor I want to ask."

A favor? And why, given everything she had just asked, did it need to be in person?

Fifty-Nine

Saturday, May 9, 2100 CDT

Ashley pulled into Robert's driveway, having made better time than she expected. The outdoor lighting installed in her absence popped on, removing any deep shadows from the back yard. She parked in the garage—no reason to have Liya's stolen car out where everyone could see it. She removed everything from the car and approached the house. The lights were great, but she didn't see any security cars, and no one hustled from the house to verify her identity. She guessed Seamus had pinched pennies and canceled the guards because Tabitha had gone to her mother's.

It worried her for a moment that in implementing the security upgrades, they might have changed the door code, but they hadn't. The kitchen air carried an overlay of burnt toast, of which she saw no evidence. She called for Seamus. No response and the dead air spoke to the house being empty all day. He wasn't much of a cook. With Tabitha gone, she'd bet he was still working or having a late dinner out.

That thought caused her stomach to grumble. Power drinks had gotten her here, but she really should eat something real. She had a half hour before she needed to leave to meet Morgan at Pendergast's offices. The refrigerator offered nothing quick. She wanted a shower more than food, and before that, she wanted a gun from Robert's safe.

She unlatched the cellar door and flipped the switch. Light trickled past the door's edges. The bottom door hinge emitted a horror-movie squeak that brought her shoulders up to her ears. She forced them down. Was she the only one bothered by the squeak, or was it nerves?

From the remaining weapons, she chose a snub-nosed .38, loaded it, and shoved it and a box of ammo into her jacket pocket. With the safe already open, she decided it was stupid not to take a few minutes to find out what else Robert had kept with the portfolio he had created for her.

She removed everything from the safe, storing the stuff in piles on the floor, hoping for a big red arrow pointing to "Robert's deepest secrets." What a disappointment. The other portfolios in the interior safe contained coloring books and sticker magazines she had played with the summer she stayed with Robert. Why he had kept them was a mystery. She put everything back in its place and spun the lock.

Ten minutes for a quick shower, change of clothes, and out the door.

Saturday, May 9, 2200 CDT

WHILE ASHLEY WAITED AT THE guard's desk in the lobby for Morgan to arrive and let her into the office, she rifled through the sign in/out sheet confirming no Pendergast employees were on site. Seamus had been the last to leave, fifteen minutes before she arrived. Ships passing in the night.

Morgan loped from the parking garage elevators, asking for forgiveness for being a few minutes late.

"No apologies necessary. I'm thankful you came."

"Sorry it's so late. I force my parents to leave the house every Saturday to have dinner and a movie. It's hard on them caring for my sister. She has Down's and can't stay alone." Morgan paused to sign in. "It's our special sisters' time. What do you need unlocked?"

What she wouldn't give for a normal, functional family. "That's extraordinary of you to give up your Saturdays for your family. I—"

"Don't canonize me. I'm not giving up anything. I never bother hitting the clubs until after midnight."

Morgan was full of it, but Ashley chose not to argue.

Morgan let them in the door on the executive floor, flicked on the lights, and they made a beeline for Robert's office. She unlocked the door and led Ashley inside. "I put away that big folder and computer you left on the desk. I didn't think you wanted them lying around for prying eyes."

Listen and learn. "Prying eyes?"

"Oh yeah, if it's visible, Junior thinks it's fair game. Cece too, and Bradlee seems to have caught her habit. A few others, but they have less access and less opportunity." She rotated the safe's dial, pulled open the door, and handed the portfolio and laptop to Ashley. "What else can I get for you?"

"Did you know he was contacting me? Wanted me here?"

"Friday, he jotted a note that he had authorized Malachi to use the plane to get you. Malachi confirmed it Saturday morning. Let me unlock the cabinets for you. When you're done, push the buttons in to lock them, okay? Anything you want my help with, or should I skedaddle? I know you don't want me to let on that you're back. Is that because you're planning to surprise them at Monday's big board meeting?"

"That wouldn't exactly be giving Seamus and Gabriella the space they need."

"I guess I thought you might be there since Monday is what my parents would call a 'Come to Jesus' meeting."

Ashley arched an eyebrow, prompting Morgan to provide details.

"It's Seamus's plan," Morgan said. "He's something else, isn't he? Where did you meet him?"

Ashley shivered. A decade later and she still reacted the same way every time she recalled the winter night Seamus had found her during a blizzard, naked and freezing to death. That had happened during her first undercover assignment. "A long time ago, in a galaxy far, far away. Seamus's plan?"

"He's forcing the brothers to resign from the board and bringing in outside directors unless Robert shows by Tuesday morning. He's gathered evidence of a ton of shenanigans to add to the material Robert already had. I know because he hands me pages and pages of chicken scratch, and I type them up and shred his notes. He's a challenge, but deciphering illegible handwriting is my superpower. He never lets those files out of his sight. Takes them home every night."

"Do the brothers suspect anything?"

"I doubt it. It's not on the agenda. Seamus had me type up resignation letters for the three of them and Cece. You want to see them?"

She did. If Robert didn't surface, Seamus dismisses the three brothers from the organization. If Robert materialized, they were his problems to take care of. Genius.

Morgan, perhaps thinking Ashley was hesitating rather than thinking, said, "I can leave my computer on. They're stored in Robert's password-protected folder. Let me give you the password."

"Great. That will be helpful. You've gone beyond anything I could expect. I do appreciate it."

Morgan looked a little disappointed. Ashley supposed she would be too if they traded positions. Robert's secrets were here somewhere, and his password might be the abracadabra she'd been missing.

SIXTY

Saturday, May 9, 2215 CDT

BECAUSE ROBERT HAD BEEN STREWING breadcrumbs for her to follow, Ashley's first task after seeing Morgan out was to review the remaining contents of the portfolio he'd provided. If that didn't answer her questions, and she doubted it would, she'd look for physical clues in his office and tackle Robert's password-protected computer if all else failed. She spread the contents of the portfolio across Robert's desk. It had been a hell of a week since she had retrieved the material from the gun safe. No way Robert could have anticipated the trauma it had triggered. She flipped past the cover memo and a copy of the Daughters Trust document to the pages she had not reviewed and discovered what Seamus would call a business SWOT analysis of his five children. Hers was on top.

She skimmed the Strengths and Weaknesses. They reminded her of her performance reviews: strong on intelligence, perseverance, adaptability, leadership, independent action; areas for improvement emphasized she was "not a team player & has trust issues."

She skipped the Opportunities section once she realized it was an analysis of how she could be valuable to Pendergast Holdings. The Threats component was dead on. The analysis warned that she would ruthlessly attack any legal or moral issues she discovered, regardless of who it affected or the financial impact on the firm.

Robert had penned a note at the bottom: May 3rd - gave Malachi contact info. Ordered him to bring her ASAP. Authorized plane.

Hoping to find information related to how Robert had obtained Niki's undercover information, she flipped the sheet over and found only a bunch of circles he'd scratched to get ink flowing in the pen. The bitter taste of disappointment filled her mouth.

Checking the other SWOT analyses, she confirmed Robert had known Junior skimmed money, Bradlee was involved with Cece, and Garrett's being gay might open him to blackmail or arrest in certain foreign countries. Tabitha had an IQ north of 150, was highly empathetic. Her weaknesses included self-doubt, being too selfless, always putting others first.

All Ashley had learned was that each of them was screwed up in their own special way, and she and Tabitha were opposites in many regards. She swept the papers into the file, noticed it was eleven o'clock already. She should check in with Seamus before he went to bed and confirm he did not want her at that Monday board meeting.

Her call clicked into voicemail. She left a quick message telling him where she was and that she'd be back before morning. She knew the alarm code, so please arm the damn thing.

"Okay, Robert, where's your secret stash?"

She found no false bottoms in the desk drawers. Using a mop handle she took from a storage closet, she poked up the acoustical tiles. Not even a dust bunny. She riffled the contents of the file cabinets: not discovering anything that wasn't what it purported to be. She didn't have the week necessary to examine each page.

What the hell made her think she'd find anything if Morgan didn't know of a smoking gun? She slumped in Robert's desk chair and rocked it, letting the motion calm her. She hadn't tried the trick of rubbing pencil lead across the indentations on a note pad to bring up what was last written. Talk about desperate.

She pulled drawers open, looking for a scratch pad and came up with an unopened "From the desk of Robert Pendergast, Sr." cube of 250 sheets glued together at the top. She dumped the drawers and didn't find a partial cube. Or a calendar. Didn't every executive keep a calendar? She supposed they were electronic these days. She called Morgan.

"Oh sure, it's electronic, but Robert had me also maintain a paper one. Every morning, I bring it in, and we confirm his schedule. At night he leaves it at my desk with his notes added. It's in my bottom right drawer if you want to see it. There's a key to my desk taped onto the bottom of Robert's desk lamp underneath the green felt that peels back. We chose that as a safe place after he threw the original away along with a bunch of junk he had accumulated in the drawer."

Ashley tipped the brass lamp, peeled back the felt and found the key and also spotted a gob of putty. "Got it, thanks, Morgan. Have a good time at the club."

A giggle came down the line. "That's the plan."

She pried off the putty and with it came a transmitter with a miniature battery and an antenna running up the lamp stem. All the "W" questions tumbled over each other—who, what, when, why, and where was the receiver located?

Her first thought was Robert had bugged his own office, but a thorough search did not turn up any recording device. If not him, who? She found no bugs at Morgan's desk, but she uncovered the same transmitter in the offices of Gabrielle Linz, all three brothers, and the room reserved for the auditors that Seamus had used. Gerald Nakourma's office was clear. With no sign of a recorder anywhere, had she prematurely crossed off the corporate attorney and remaining board member?

And whoever had planted the transmitters also had access to Morgan's key. Time to look for that written calendar, which was what had triggered her discovery of the transmitters.

She found the ledger-sized calendar with two pages per day where Morgan said it would be. Robert frequently made notes, and she spotted Niki's number and address written on the margin for a week ago Wednesday. Above it was a ten-digit number. A phone number she had dialed hundreds of times.

SIXTY-ONE

Sunday, May 10, 0030 CDT

ASHLEY PARKED ROBERT'S MERCEDES IN his garage and remembered to bring in a spray can of oil to fix the squeaky basement door. She punched in the security code. When it didn't beep, she noticed the door was cracked open. The security system was off. She shook her head and sighed. Seamus could be scatterbrained—the absent-minded financial genius. Nothing she could do but find the humor in it.

She shut the door and set the portfolio from Robert on the kitchen table, next to a corked bottle of Cabernet Sauvignon that hadn't been there before. The drainer contained a plate and silverware. Sniffing the air, she guessed Seamus had picked up a salmon dinner on the way home.

She drenched the basement door hinges with the penetrating oil, pulled up on the handle and worked the door back and forth until it opened silently. After easing the door shut, she engaged the latch, and froze. *Had it been latched before she fussed with the oil?*

No brain function left; it was time for bed. She flicked off the kitchen light, proceeded to the parlor to douse that light, and stopped at the entrance, her training commanding that she appraise the scene.

On the floor to the right of a chair, a yellow legal pad with a ballpoint pen clipped to it rested on a pile of thick folders. Seamus had been working there. A half-glass of wine sat on a coaster next to his cellphone, which was plugged into the wall. Thrifty Seamus would never leave half-drunk wine. He'd drink it, pour it back in the bottle, or cover the glass with plastic wrap. An open book, spine up, lay in the chair. Once in his presence, she'd left a book open like that overnight, and Seamus had nearly torn her head off.

She yelled his name and raced to the bedroom he was using. A still-made, empty bed greeted her. She pulled her gun, checked bathrooms and Robert's study. No sign of him. Remembering the cellar door, she flicked on the basement light and searched. No Seamus.

"God damn you, Seamus McCree. I told you to keep a guard for this place."

Venting done, she verified the front door and all the windows were locked. Seamus must have left through the back door, but why? She kicked herself for not telling Malachi to install a system that recorded the security cameras.

She engaged all the exterior lights and scoured the grounds for any sign of a disturbance. Her gut already knew what her mind was coming to accept. Someone had taken Seamus.

A light was on in the old lady's house across the alley. Had the busybody seen something? Screw that it was after midnight, she had to find out.

The woman greeted her at the door with, "You must think I don't do anything but watch that house all day and night."

Ashley hoped that was exactly the case, especially since the voyeur was wide awake and dressed. Offering her best semi-ashamed smile, she said, "I apologize for disturbing you so late at night. If I hadn't seen your light on . . ."

"Oh fiddlesticks, I'm a night owl. Don't expect me to function before noon. Except Sundays, I rarely get up before ten."

Ashley's mother had been like that. "I'm more of a morning person, myself. Did you see anything tonight?" Remembering it was after midnight she clarified. "Well, yesterday."

"As a matter of fact. Come upstairs where I have my notes."

Ashley followed her up a narrow staircase to the window with a view of the alley and part of Robert's parking area. It amused her to find a pair of ten-powered binoculars and a note pad on the table. The woman flipped back a page in the pad.

"The security people first showed up at a quarter after two—"

"I was more interested in anything after ten tonight." Ashley read a flash of disappointment cross the old lady's face.

She flipped forward in her notepad. "Ten-thirty-three the man who has been staying at the house and is much older than Tabitha left. I do hope she hasn't taken up with an older man. That rarely ends well for the woman. Not my business, I suppose."

Ashley blushed, recalling her own experiences with that particular older man. "That's my friend Seamus. You saw him leave?"

"Oh yes." She flipped a page in her notepad and referred to her notes. "Is he okay?"

Ashley wanted to choke the old gal, but this was probably the highlight of her week. She prodded, "He left . . . ?"

"I thought maybe he wasn't feeling well. Those two bodyguards helped him into their SUV twenty-four minutes after his arrival. I might have missed that, but seeing the SUV drive up earlier made me curious, you know? Being different and all."

Ashley had missed something. "Different how?"

The woman licked her finger and pushed away one more page. "You left in Robert's Mercedes. They arrived twenty-five minutes later. How do you like it? I prefer driving stick myself and something a little smaller like that Prius with the Virginia plates you drove. Anyway, that's the first time those security guys parked in the garage. The afternoon when they checked inside the house, they parked like they always had. Course they were only there for fifteen minutes and that was the afternoon, so you're not interested in that. This time, they parked in the garage, and I didn't see them again until after Seamus had gone inside. They brought him from the house—hauled him, more like. His head slumped on his chest, his toes sort of bounced on the ground."

"Tell me about the two people."

"Man and a woman. Your friend is what, six-two. This guy was taller and twice as broad. The female was . . ." She stared at the ceiling before finding the word she was looking for. ". . . dumpy. Now I think of it, they helped Seamus into the garage. The woman drove the SUV. It was big and black. Well, dark, anyway. Coulda been blue or even green. The guy closed the garage door and got in the back. That's it. Can I get you some water? You look sick yourself. And if you don't mind my asking, what happened to your eyes?"

Sunday, May 10, 0115 CDT

Malachi woke to a racing heart, heard the phone ring again, and checked the clock. A quarter past one on Sunday morning. To his cautious hello, he heard Ashley say, "I'm at Robert's. I think someone kidnapped Seamus."

"You sure he isn't getting laid?" Realizing what he had blurted to someone possibly involved with Seamus, blood rushed to his face. Way to go, genius. "I'm sorry—"

She talked over his attempted apology, told him what she knew and what she guessed. "There's a Board meeting scheduled for Monday. Can I shove that forward to this morning, even though it's a Sunday?"

"Official board meetings require advanced written notice. You could call an advisory meeting. What are you thinking, and why haven't you called the police?"

"Because they won't do anything tonight other than waste my time." She presented her idea and asked if it would work.

He couldn't fault the logic; the problem was getting the brothers into the office. "What if you call them at, say, oh seven hundred? Tell them you're here and plan to take control. You're calling a board meeting in one hour to make it official. If they want their objections recorded, they have to be there. They know the rules don't allow you to do that. One may even tell you that. They don't know *you know* you can't do that. If you retort with 'Yeah, watch me.' or however you would normally respond, they'll show up if for no other reason than to rub your nose in another mistake. Setting the meeting for oh-eight-hundred allows Bradlee to still get to his church service and Junior to keep his late-morning golf date. Garrett won't—" *Drat. That won't work.* "There's a problem. They know you don't have the votes by yourself. You require one brother to vote with you. Junior, for sure, will call your bluff."

Ashley chuckled. "On that, I'm a step ahead. I talked with Tabitha and confirmed Seamus had canceled the guards while she was at her mother's house. Her votes give me a majority. Let's not drag her in from her Mom's since we can't *actually* vote on anything. I can get away with telling them she's coming. Same with Gabriella, right?"

It was scary how quickly she came up with this stuff. If she ever learned what she was doing, she'd be one hell of a manipulator. "Before you call the brothers, tell Gabriella your plan. That way she can support it. At least one brother will try to pry helpful information from her. She might even want to be there. The other thing to keep in mind is the brothers all have contracts, you can't just willy-nilly fire them."

"I'm sure there's a firing-for-good-cause provision. Remember, the whole thing is to get Seamus back. Firing can wait. If I'm gathering all the miscreants together, should I ask Cece to join us? Tell her we might require a company announcement, which is the truth if anyone resigns."

"You must handle Cece through normal HR processes. If you don't, she'll sue you and the company and you'll probably lose. You want me there?"

"You're on medical leave. I have plans for you, but first you have to recover." Without a goodbye or anything, she disconnected.

What he wouldn't pay to be a fly on that wall. That woman was born to boss. And again, what was this mysterious plan she had for him?

Sixty-Two

Sunday, May 10, Morning CDT

ASHLEY WAITED UNTIL ALL THREE brothers arrived before she joined them in the boardroom. She had called Gabriella, Junior, Bradlee, and Garrett in that order starting an hour and a quarter before she planned to begin the meeting. She read their reactions as shock, surprise, fury, and amusement. It was a good thing she'd followed Malachi's suggestions and gotten Gabriella on board because Junior *had* called to pick her brain about the impromptu Sunday board meeting. He had also contacted Tabitha, who had the presence of mind to tell him she supported Ashley a thousand percent before she made a panicked call to Ashley to find out if she had screwed something up.

Bradlee was the last to arrive, and Ashley followed him in, carrying copies of the files Seamus had produced. She remained standing and announced Gabriella and Tabitha were not coming. The brothers would listen to her, or she would arrest them and deliver them to the FBI.

"I am aware this cannot be an official board meeting. That comes tomorrow. Here it is, plain and simple. Robert is still missing. Last night someone kidnapped Seamus. I think one of you is responsible or knows who is." Into the resulting cacophony she yelled, "Shut the fuck up, sit down, and listen to what I have to say."

They settled.

"Either Seamus is in this office by ten-hundred hours—ten o'clock—or I release the information in these files to the police and the press. I don't care which of you it is, or if it's all of you together. My only objective is to have Seamus returned safe and healthy. If he's here within two hours, no one will press kidnapping charges. As Pendergast Holdings' directors, you each have a responsibility to know what's in every file."

She started with Junior and shared evidence that he had siphoned hundreds of thousands of dollars each year through kickbacks he received from suppliers who padded their invoices to cover the "leakage." Some of it was in the U.S., but much was from their international operations. "You even formed a separate company that rents warehouse space at bargain-basement rates from a Pendergast Holding's division under your control. It then sublets the space at market rates and you pocket the difference. Maybe if you make full restitution, you'll only do ten years. Otherwise, you're in prison for a long, long time."

By the time she finished, Junior's face had drained from cardinal red to pasty white. She pointed to Bradlee, who seemed shocked by Junior's misdeeds but now glared at her. "You'll find signed affidavits from four women about your affairs with employees. You forced two to quit, the other two settled their suits against you. The company has released them from the nondisclosure agreements they signed. Compared to Junior, you taking the women on business trips to sales conventions is small potatoes. Unlike Junior, you preyed on other people."

"Bullshit. It was all consensual."

"Have you missed the #MeToo movement, Bradlee?" Her voice rose with the anger of millions of abused women. "The media will rip you apart. Your wife may divorce you. Your children will hate you. You may find no one wants to hire you. That's the rage of women fucked over by men." She dropped his file in front of him with a dramatic gesture of disgust. "You sure can pick 'em. Cece's been seriously padding her expense reports."

If she looked at the peckerwood a second longer, she might lose it and choke the bastard. To Garrett, she said, "I don't care a bit that you're gay. Why you've stayed in the closet is a mystery to me. But bribing government officials? Seamus has a ledger sheet showing payments to foreign governments and to domestic individuals, up to and including the chairperson of the House Committee on Agriculture."

She doubted Junior and Bradlee heard anything past her declaration of Garrett's sexual orientation. Garrett's expression was sad, like his team had lost the seventh game of the world series. She handed him his file.

"Remember, all I want is to see Seamus walk in here. If he's not here in two hours, I will distribute copies of your files to wherever will do you the most damage."

Garrett raised his hand like he was in high school. She gestured for him to speak. "Why aren't you worried about Dad?"

Thank you, Garrett. She had hoped one of them would ask that obvious question. "Because I suspect he's already dead. Last night, someone snatched Seamus from Robert's house. They didn't kill him there, giving me hope he's still alive. I'd rejoice if Robert showed up. He could take charge, and I could wash my hands of this entire mess. I have nothing more to say. Do you?"

Bradlee left his file on the table and stormed out. She hoped he was hurrying to arrange Seamus's release. She suspected he wanted to get to church and pray it would all go away. He probably thought he was bulletproof against the accusations. He wasn't, and she felt sorry for his family, who would bear the scars for life.

Garrett said, "Junior, I'd like a private conversation with Ashley. You mind?"

Junior's color had remained pasty, but his expression had changed from fury to hatred. Ashley surmised she had shaken him with how much Seamus and the auditors had uncovered. What she didn't sense was even a titch of fear. Junior tucked his file under his arm and left, leaving the door open.

Garrett, she couldn't read. All those years of hiding his sexual orientation had taught him to mask his emotions. "What is it, Garrett?"

"Good theater, sis. To prove it's not me, I'm staying here until ten. Do you have access to Seamus's notes, or did they vanish with him? I ask because, if you have them, they'll show that he and I were working together at uncovering who in our organization was making the illegal payments, and how they were hiding them. Believe me or not, I didn't know. Being gay is not the issue you think. Dad's response was to forbid me from traveling to countries with draconian laws. Mother was the reason I kept it under wraps. In her illness, she'd think it was her fault. You saw my brothers' reactions. Clueless. I got used to hiding. It was easier than coming out. Several years ago, someone attempted to extort money from Dad with a bunch of lousy pictures a PI took. I said he shouldn't pay a cent. I was who I was. Being out will be a relief. Anyway, find Seamus's workpapers. He wrote them on that yellow legal pad he used. Maybe Morgan typed something up?"

The hurt in his eyes tore at her, but even if everything he'd said was true, she'd do it again to show the other two brothers she was serious. "What happens if it all becomes public?"

"I have no legal issues. I didn't make the bribes or know of them. The company will pay huge fines. Because I should have known, I'll quit if I'm not canned first. There's other stuff I'd rather do. Junior may have to quit, too, but I'd bet the firm sweeps his misdeeds under the rug. No one wants to admit their accounting policies are that inadequate. Even if you inform the authorities, Junior's lawyers will negotiate a settlement that provides for a fine and a brief stay in a white-collar jail."

He ran a hand through his hair. "Bradlee has no clue. He might slit his wrists before this is done. His wife is not the forgive and forget kind. She'll take him for whatever she can get. Once Bradlee's no longer her meal ticket, Cece will show her true colors and dump him. Probably sue him, too. But then again, voters might make him president."

"What you're saying is I once again failed to understand how companies work and my big play has no teeth."

He shrugged. "I guess we'll see in the next ninety minutes. I'll be in my office." Like Bradlee, he didn't take his file with him.

She waited until he was opening the door before she said, "Someone bugged all the executive offices. In your office, they taped one to the wire holding up that photo of the fox in mid-pounce. Did you take those?"

"Photography is my dream job. You put the bug there?"

It saddened her that he could even ask that question. "No. Any other thoughts who did?"

"Corporate espionage?" He shook his head. "Might have even been Dad. He obviously didn't trust us, and he might have bugged his own office to listen to what went on when he wasn't there. How about Morgan? She'd be the perfect spy—everyone trusts her."

To avoid the listening devices, Ashley used the internal stairs to Malachi's office, picked up a phone at one of the nearby cubicles, and called Morgan, who had apparently just gotten home. She claimed no knowledge of Robert bugging any offices.

Her next call was to Malachi. He answered with a tentative hello. She informed him Seamus was still missing. "Are you allowed to perform company business while you're on sick leave or whatever you call it? I don't want to break another corporate rule, like when the government shuts down, and we get furloughed—"

"Nothing like that, which is why I offered to be with you. In fact, I've found something interesting about Cece and—"

"Hold that thought. I'd like to run something by Pendergast Holdings' Head Conscience Guru."

"Chief Conscience Officer." He chuckled. "Guru sounds a little vain, but I could live with it. Something bothering your conscience?"

"If Seamus does not show up, am I right to distribute that information to the police? To the press?"

"That's not how it works. *I* ask clarifying questions. You thank me for my time. And *you* decide how to proceed. Here are some things for you to consider: Would you do the same thing if Morgan or I had disappeared instead of Seamus? Would you give them the material if there had been no missing persons? What if they agreed to resign? Or if Seamus was the culprit and Junior uncovered the evidence? You see what I'm getting at?"

"My motivation. Revenge or Justice. Revenge is not a good idea. Justice is."

"Your words, not mine. Also, consider if it's an all-or-nothing situation. Does one course of action apply equally to all three sets of behaviors?"

She rubbed her temples. "You're making my brain hurt."

"Good. Then I'm doing my job."

Sixty-Three

WITH MALACHI'S QUESTIONS ABOUT WHETHER she was acting as judge, jury, and executioner roiling her brain, Ashley returned to Robert's office. Nine o'clock and no news of Seamus. Or Robert. She had until tomorrow's official board meeting to decide how to handle her brothers.

Garrett seemed the easiest. She'd bring in experienced investigators, determine who had done what and, once she learned the details, plan her actions. She set aside Garrett's file.

Garrett's assessment that the company might prefer not bringing criminal charges against Junior notwithstanding, she'd leave that decision to the new board of directors. She'd give Junior a chance to resign. If he didn't, she'd work with legal counsel to can his ass. That was nonnegotiable.

She tossed his file on top of Garrett's and added Bradlee's to the stack because Pendergast Holdings would not countenance sexual predation on her watch.

Cece's file stared at her. Why had Seamus been interested in her? Ashley flipped past the stuff she had already looked at regarding expense account irregularities and found Cece's credit report. Before Ashley had gone undercover, she had locked hers down. With all the data breaches, she was glad she had.

Huh. Cece wasn't an abbreviation of Cecelia or any of its variations, Ashley's guess. Cynthia Clarice Kraznik had a 750+ credit rating. Credit cards paid in full most months. Yellow highlighter drew her attention to three mortgages. Two related to the purchase of her first house and buying its larger replacement. A year ago, the agency reported a third mortgage relating to a business.

She retrieved her laptop and checked the street view on Google Maps of the first address: a cozy bungalow, 1,600 square feet. The second house was a big step up to a two-story house, minimum 3,000 square feet on a decent-sized lot. The newest mortgage was an auto salvage place. She didn't see Cece as a grease-under-the-nails gal.

Seamus had printed Ramsey County tax records from the internet, listing Cynthia C. and Crandall P. Kraznik as owners of that property. Ashley could swear someone—Morgan?—said Cece was single. Her ex? In penciled chicken scratch, she deciphered two circled phrases: *source of funds?* and *money laundering?* Well, the money aspect of things would attract Seamus.

She pulled up the street-level version of Google Maps captured by Google's video car—or whatever they called them—showing the junkyard. Wait, hadn't Malachi said he had found interesting information regarding Cece?

She rang him up and asked what his Cece news was.

"I was talking to some former SEALS buddies to get a list of who served with the two guys we . . . met . . . at the diner." He swallowed hard. "One name that popped up was Kraznik. Might not mean anything, but it seemed like an uncommon name."

"First name Crandall?"

"Hold on. Let me check."

Scanning the computer screen of the junkyard while she waited, she locked onto an Xcel utility truck looking worse for wear parked at the edge of the junkyard. Robert's nosy neighbor had seen a similar truck the night she had last seen him. She searched the internet for images of Crandall and found the taxi driver who had kidnapped her!

The nosy neighbor's description popped into her mind: A dumpy woman and a guy taller than Seamus and much wider. Cece and Crandall. She dug her fingernails into the palms of her hands. If she had looked at these files last night . . .

Woulda, coulda, shoulda gets you nothing. Google Maps claimed it was a fifteen-minute drive. She needed transportation and Malachi was an hour away. She raced from the office, leaving the phone connection with him open.

Sunday, May 10, Morning CDT

GARRETT TOSSED ASHLEY THE KEYS to his Tesla without asking questions. She stopped at Robert's garage to pick up a bolt cutter and navigated to the auto salvage place using the car's GPS. She entered Niki Undercover mode, becoming hyper alert, pistol in hand, letting every sense feed her reptilian brain.

A cobweb covered the top left corner of the locked door labeled "Office - Parts." She followed the building's side, ducking below the two windows, to a wire-mesh vehicle gate. She spotted the rear of the Xcel truck—moved since Google had last been by.

Tire tracks across the parking lot suggested considerable traffic between the gate and massive sliding doors, perhaps leading to where they stripped cars of their parts? The place had minimal security: no razor wire, no motion-sensor lights, no sign indicating dogs patrolled the yard. Is there no reason to protect dead cars? Or maybe she wasn't spotting miniature electronic surveillance, like the bugs in the Pendergast offices.

She shoved the gun into the back of her waistband and, lugging the bolt cutter with her, climbed the fence and shimmied down the other side. The rattle of the fence would alert any living thing to her presence, but all was quiet. She approached the rusted Xcel truck whose fully inflated tires had decent tread. Every other nearby vehicle sported worn tires or sat on blocks.

She squatted to look for evidence of recent use. A rectangle of disturbed ground hid any sign or smell of dripping oil.

The pressure of a ticking clock told her to get moving.

One loud snip of the bolt cutter removed the padlock guarding the doors. *Add breaking and entering to my list of crimes.* She rolled the door open enough to slip inside, flicked on the overhead lights, and closed the door. A well-trod path across the floor led past racks of bins filled with truck parts to an open wooden door that provided entrance to a dim hallway.

She cleared an office on the left containing two scarred wooden desks: one clean, the other littered with paperwork. Photos of dead deer and gloating hunters adorned the near wall. In one, Crandall knelt holding a compound bow. *The ransom note?* An enlarged photograph hanging between the two windows drew her attention. Three rows of uniformed SEALS stared forward. She found Crandall second row left. Next to him was the guy Malachi had shot in the diner. In front of them was the individual she'd killed. Link confirmed.

Her nerves screamed danger. She dropped the bolt cutters, pulled her weapon, spun and crouched. Nothing.

The door on the right opened to a homey studio apartment with kitchenette, dishes in a drainer, dry to the touch. Keurig coffee maker. Someone liked Dark Magic coffee. A woman had decorated, too much frill for a guy. Selfie of Cece and Bradlee at a Twins game sat on a bureau. Sex toys on the nightstand. The bathroom with shower stocked with products for both sexes. Under the bed, a 17-inch laptop. Room cleared. Mental note: take the computer when she left.

She moved to a metal door in the middle on the left side of the hall. Shiny hinges indicated well-oiled use. A key poked from the lock, but a two-by-six wedged against a stopper prevented the door from opening. Bingo.

Keeping her body positioned to watch behind her, she removed the beam, fumbled the lock open. Using the door as a shield in case someone inside had a gun or charged her, she hauled the heavy door open with her foot.

The light from the hall illuminated only six feet of a room that felt cavernous.

She sensed more than heard a movement and assumed a shooting position, training her weapon into the void. "Come out with your hands up."

Sixty-Four

Sunday, May 10, Morning CDT

"**That won't be necessary,**" **Cece** spoke from behind her. "Drop your gun. You couldn't leave it alone, could you? You're a clever little bitch, I'll give you that. Noticing the Xcel truck on Google's street view."

Shit, she'd talked to Malachi, and to herself, while she was in Robert's office. "How long have you had the offices bugged? Make good money selling information to your competitors?" Niki listened for any hint that Cece was not alone and slowly brought her arms to waist level. "You're the brains and your brother and his friends are the—"

Niki dropped like a rag doll, doing a half-twist in the air like the gymnast she had been thirty years ago. A shotgun blast roared, pellets ricocheting off the metal door. She fired two shots, finding her target. Her knees hit first, and she fired a second double tap before smacking her face onto the floor.

Through tears, she observed Cece's expression change from determined to stunned. The shotgun tumbled from her hands. Four red poppies blossomed on her chest. Like a puppet with cut strings, Cece folded, never uttering a sound.

Niki rose, kicked the shotgun into a corner, and positioned herself next to Cece, her back to the wall. "You in there. Crawl to me. I want to see empty hands sliding along the floor."

Keeping her eyes and gun focused on the doorway, she checked Cece's pulse with her other hand. The butterfly twitching in Cece's neck faded to nothingness, and her bladder released, filling the air with the stench of urine.

"It's Seamus. I'm coming out. Hands first."

One bloody hand appeared from the dark. A second stretched past the first.

Niki assumed a kneeling shooter's position. Someone could use Seamus for a shield. She recognized his bloodied nose and red-soaked shirt. "Thank God you're alive, Seamus. I'd have killed you if you died on me. Anyone else in there? Do you need a hospital?"

"Nah. I got one punch in and bam, I was out cold. I came to in there." Seamus pointed behind him. "That room has the same urine stink as she does, and I found a silver pocketknife." He pulled it from his pocket. "Initials RP. I'm afraid Robert died in there." His eyes widened. "How bad are you hit?"

Truth was, her back stung like a swarm of bees had attacked her. She had no time for the pain and shoved it away. "You may be right, which means we've got multiple crime scenes here. To minimize the contamination, please sit right there."

Seamus lowered himself to the floor and scooched until he rested against the wall. "Do you know what's going on?"

"Some. Maybe. Not exactly. Listen carefully. My name is Ann Smith. If anyone asks who I am, tell them I told you my name is Ann Smith. Got it?"

"Why?"

"Just do it, Seamus. Listen and don't talk." She slid Cece's phone from the dead woman's pocket and dialed a memorized Washington, D.C. number. Deputy Director Ambrose answered, and she described what had happened. "I suspect Robert Pendergast died here, and they buried him underneath a utility truck. The Robert Pendergast kidnapping is still an open FBI case. If you make some things happen, I think we can make the FBI look like heroes." She told Ambrose her plan.

Ambrose put her on a short hold. "A local FBI team will arrive within an hour. They'll notify local authorities once they secure the scene. Sit tight." He disconnected.

She wasn't proud of her decision, but you'd never lose money betting that bigwigs want to protect their fat asses. "Seamus, I don't know how this will play out. Do not act surprised by anything. When they question you, tell the truth, including my name. Who am I?"

"She said her name is Ann Smith."

"I'd give you a great big smooch, but I couldn't explain your blood on my lips. Stay there while I check something before the police arrive."

She grabbed the laptop from the bedroom and opened its lid. Desktop folders confirmed what she suspected: R-Office; R-cell; J-Office; J-cell, B-Office; B-cell and so on. She opened the M-cell folder, clicked on a file dated the day this whole mess started, and heard Malachi begging Robert to call him before he met Ashley at Ike's Diner.

Cece knew every damned thing Robert, the brothers, Gabrielle, and Malachi had been doing. Lord, what was her game plan? The lab would sift through this stuff. She closed the laptop's lid and slid it under the bed.

She yelled to be heard, "Seamus, you remember the name and number of that reporter?"

You had to love the man and his numbers. He had no guess for the guy's name, but he remembered the ten digits. The name came to her as she dialed. "Harlan, this is Ashley Pendergast Prescott. I know I never got back to you. I'll explain, but right now I have a story you desperately want. There's one little catch."

Sunday, May 10, 1100 CDT

WHATEVER AMBROSE TOLD THE LOCAL FBI office worked. The first four agents arrived within thirty minutes of Ashley's call to him. Two secured the scene. One transported Seamus to the nearest emergency room. The fourth brought her to a private doctor, who removed eight shotgun pellets, patched her wounds, and provided scrips with the name left blank for antibiotics and souped-up painkillers. Dismissing her thanks as unnecessary, he left with an admonition to use the antibiotics.

The agent ushered her to a bathroom where a makeup artist joined them. His makeup kit was bigger than he was. She checked the finished product in the mirror. Staring back was a late-middle-aged Irish woman, fair skin, slightly sunburned, freckled nose. A person who colored her hair an unnatural red to hide the gray and wore some kind of fruity fragrance. Putty filled in her cheeks and added wrinkles to her neck. She idly inquired if facial recognition software could identify her.

"Not without x-rays," the makeup artist said. "I'm leaving you some touch-up supplies. I don't know how long you plan to stay in character."

She thanked him and followed the agent to his car. "Anything new from the scene?"

"I'm not at liberty to say."

"Are they at least looking for a body beneath that Xcel truck? The family has a right to know."

He gave her a sideways glance. "Sniffer dogs confirmed human remains. They're digging."

"Assuming I'm right and it's Robert Pendergast, Senior, I suggest having

Bradlee, the middle son, make the identification before you interview him. At a minimum, he was romantically involved with the dead owner of the junkyard, and it might shake him up enough to get the truth from the lying cocksucker."

The agent snorted. "Tell me how you really feel." He wiped the smile from his face. "To prevent you from further contaminating the scene, we're taking you to our local headquarters. We've agreed with St. Paul to share interview duties. They assigned a detective with whom we have a good relationship. We said you are an undercover agent who wormed her way close enough to the subject to guess the location where they held the kidnap victims. Because you're undercover, the official report will not include your name. Unfortunately, Seamus McCree already spilled the beans that you're Ann Smith, which may show up in private interview notes. You know those don't always stay private."

She silently thanked Seamus for following the script.

"We've said you're in trouble for entering the unlocked warehouse without backup. Ms. Kraznik got the jump on you, wounded you, and you killed her in self-defense. You'll be subject to our shooting incident review. The detective comes from a family of blue. You'll have no issues with the shooting."

"It *was* justified."

"No doubt. Anyway, take him through what happened. Afterwards, I'll take you wherever you want. But." He removed one hand from the steering wheel and without looking at her wagged a finger. "Deputy Director Ambrose said to tell you that if you know what's good for you, you'll be in his D.C. office at ten tomorrow. Sharp."

Sixty-Five

Sunday, May 10, 1345 CDT

ASHLEY HAD THE AGENT DROP her at the corner of the alley leading to the rear of Robert's house. Seamus responded to the doorbell and peered through the glass at her. "How can I help you?"

"It's me."

He fumbled at the lock and opened the door. "I didn't recognize you. You look like you belong in South Boston." The alarm beeped. "Let me shut this before we summon the cops. You okay?"

"Nothing a hug won't solve. You?"

He folded her into his arms and held her tight. "No concussion and nothing broken." He led her into the kitchen, shutting off the alarm on the way.

"You already drink your glass of wine? I could use one myself. And something to eat. Where's Tabitha?"

"I asked her to stay with her mother, and I had Malachi authorize the security guards to maintain a watch around-the-clock. I—"

"Good. Have Malachi order the same for you. Until we know who all is involved, no one is safe." He rolled his eyes. She had no time or patience for an argument. "I'm not taking no, Seamus. I want you to pull the trigger on terminating Junior and Bradlee tomorrow and get that independent board in place. Am I correct, you're giving Garrett a pass for now? Good. I'd love to be there, but I have a command performance before Deputy Director Ambrose at ten tomorrow morning. That's a seventeen-hour drive, and—"

Someplace in the echo chamber of her skull, she heard her appalling words. She grabbed him around the waist and pulled into him, hard. "Oh, Seamus. I am so sorry. I haven't thanked you for what you've done or apologized for nearly getting you killed. It's all me, me, me. With this red hair I look and sound like Lewis Carroll's Queen of Hearts. 'Off with his head! Off with his head!' I'm becoming the fucking Pendergast Robert wanted me to be, and I can't stand it. Cut off my head, Seamus, and stick it on a pike."

He had the audacity to laugh at her. "Wow. A little stressed are we, your majesty? First, you need to eat. We both know you don't want my cooking. I'll order pizza. We'll create a to-do list and prioritize who does what." He shuffled the two of them toward the phone. "I love Lewis Carroll. The real logic and the faulty logic in his books. I never knew you were a fan."

"Disney. Twenty-sixteen. I watched it undercover. I don't deserve you."

"And your point is?"

She pushed away from him and slugged his arm. Her knuckles stung only a little. It probably wouldn't leave a bruise.

"Good you got that out of your system," he said. "Because you're going to hate the next two things I'm going to tell you. First, I'm ordering food, and you will stay and enjoy it."

Ashley did a mental calculation. Going east she lost an hour, but she'd proved she could cut off two hours from Google's estimate. If she left at three, she'd have enough time to return Liya's car, shower, change, and still make Ambrose's ten o'clock summons. Seamus brought her into Robert's home office, found a fresh legal pad and sat behind the desk. She paced until he pointed to a chair and said, "Sit. I don't want to get slugged again."

She complied, dread turning her core to ice.

"How much sleep have you had in the last two days? Even if you don't kill yourself or anyone else driving to D.C., you'll be in no shape to face a deputy director of the FBI. You need food and a full night's rest. That means taking a private jet to D.C. tomorrow morning."

She launched from the chair, every muscle of her body chilly and tingling. Cramming her fists into her pockets, as much to control the shaking as to assure she didn't punch out Seamus's lights, she couldn't speak; couldn't think; was even having difficulty breathing. She collapsed back onto the seat and lowered her head between her knees, watched her sweat drip onto the carpet.

Seamus said nothing as she fought to control her panic attack. She'd never experienced one, but this had all the signs the Academy had taught them to recognize when dealing with the public.

When she lifted her head, planning to tell him to fuck himself, he said, "Ask yourself this one question. Would you have reacted like that if you were rested, hydrated, and had eaten properly?"

She stared at the bastard, wondering what she had ever seen in him.

"You're so tired, you can't even cuss. Flying is the horse you have to get back up on. You know this. No one is going to know you're on a plane except you, me, and whatever company I call. You'll be fine. The crew will be fine. Do you realize that you're nodding yes?"

Everything he said was true, which made her body's betrayal that much worse. "I can't afford that, Seamus. I'm already in the hole by I don't know how many thousands. And unless I turn things around tomorrow, I'm unemployed."

"I know some good bankruptcy lawyers."

In a flash of lightning, everything she had been experiencing turned to blinding anger, and she truly saw red. She had to leave before she killed him. She pressed her hands on her knees, stood, and saw the twinkle in his eyes. The bastard was pulling her leg, her reaction proving his point. She gave him a wan smile and sat down. "Funny man."

"Pendergast Holdings must have a D.C. lobbyist or twenty. Morgan will get you an afternoon appointment with one, making it a legitimate business trip."

"Who'll see me with no notice? I don't know anything about lobbying."

"I'll have Morgan tell them their account is up for review. Ask them to defend their fees. Take notes, even if you don't understand half of what they're saying. It helps if you write illegibly."

He offered a crooked grin, which she mirrored. *Fake it until you make it.*

Seamus left a message with a local jet charter firm to call him back, then called Malachi and related her demand that Malachi engage bodyguards to cover him and took it upon himself to order additional guards to accompany her to the private jet. He left a detailed message on Morgan's work phone, asking her to schedule the lobbyist meeting for tomorrow afternoon. One page now covered with notes, he folded that over the back. "Next?"

Her stomach still ached, but that could be hunger. Her breathing was normal. She wasn't shaking. She was okay now. Tomorrow before she got on the plane might be a different story. "Let's talk terminations."

He gave a nod of approval. "I've been working with Gerald Nakourma to draw up termination papers for Junior and Bradlee. It's not like firing the guy who mows your lawn. I think we can be ready by late tomorrow, but I can't promise it. Either way, there's nothing you can do at this point. Garrett and I have been working together to uncover who's making illegal bribes. He's good people and wants to do the right thing. He should stay. Next?"

"I'll call Harlan and give him the interview I promised." She glanced at the wall clock. "Past the deadline to get it into tomorrow's news cycle. Damn."

"Have him hold it until we fire the brothers. It might have more impact that way."

"Lemonade from lemons. Okay, I'll convince him to hold off. 'Til he hears from you?"

He wrote more gibberish on the pad. "Will do. You know, you've kind of pissed me off."

"Because I almost got you killed or because I slugged you?"

"Hell no. Those I can forgive. The bitch is you saved my life. That's two for you and only one for me. I hate being in debt."

That broke her up. Stress poured off her in great guffaws of laughter. She caught her breath and said, "You are one sick dude, and I love you for it. Far be it from me to remind you that I got you into this. How can I ever repay you?"

"You'll think of something."

Sixty-Six

Monday, May 11, 1001 EDT

NIKI, AS ASHLEY THOUGHT OF herself for this assignment, arrived in full Irish Mom disguise and waited until a minute past ten to enter Deputy Director Ambrose's office.

Ambrose greeted her with, "You're late. If I didn't know who was on my calendar, I wouldn't have recognized you. I appreciate your discretion." He motioned her to a guest chair, taking the other one, they sat side-by-side looking at the portraits on his credenza. "I'm afraid I have bad news."

She continued staring at the portraits. What a bastard to make her jump through hoops just to fire her. She would not make it easy on him.

"You were right. They found Robert Pendergast buried under the utility truck. One of his sons identified him this morning. I'm sorry for the loss of your father."

With the unexpected words, a weight of uncertainty lifted from her shoulders. She'd been sure Robert was dead. Perhaps later she would experience grief. Following her mother's death it had slipped through cracks in her armor at times she least expected it. Right now, she felt relief that Ambrose wasn't getting rid of her. "Thank you for letting me know, sir. What else can you tell me about the investigation?"

"Sorry, can't. I have another piece of unfortunate news."

Oh shit, here it comes. She tightened her stomach against the blow.

"The guy driving the weapons truck died at the scene, and no one was at the warehouse by the time we arrived. We've dropped charges against Colonel Pete. He carried a registered gun. You were driving, not him. Given your current legal issues, the brass has determined they don't want to risk putting you on the stand to testify that he paid for the weapons."

"That's bullshit."

He lifted his brows at her outburst. "Weren't you the one who thought the arrests were premature?"

She squinted one eye. "And this is the way you're making that happen?"

"You give me too much credit. Not my decision. I know you've set your heart on being an undercover FBI agent. And you might have been our best, but you've broken rules, not followed procedures. A lot of people at the Bureau want you dismissed."

At "might have been" an intense pain blossomed in her chest. She couldn't believe he had shot her. She looked; he hadn't.

He offered her a warm smile. "But without your work, the risks you accepted, the rules you broke, the procedures you ignored, we would never have confiscated those weapons. Ignoring our rules and procedures also solved the Minneapolis kidnapping cases."

Her heart fluttered with possibility. Was he saying she'd have another chance?

"It's also what got you shot. Yet, your decision to contact me changed what could have been a PR disaster into a roaring success. The Bureau has received positive press across the country starting with the piece you gave to that guy Harlan. *The Washington Post* even carried the story despite being unable to verify Ann Smith ever worked for the FBI."

He handed her a copy of the Washington paper with a column in the business section circled in red. The pain in her stomach felt like a burning ulcer. Her mouth didn't have enough spit to wet an atomic particle. For each example of her not following the rules, he had recognized how her actions had saved the day. Where was this going? Was this the way Southern gentlemen worked, stretching stories like they drawled words? She hooked the corners of her mouth into the ghost of a smile, sucked on her cheeks to moisten her mouth, and waited.

"The shooting review panel for the D.C. diner incident has cleared your actions. From all reports, so will Minneapolis."

Alleluia!

"But I can't reinstate you."

She stared at his mouth, which continued to form words she didn't hear. On the flight into D.C., she had concluded this was the only result the rule-bound FBI could reach. And yet, as each beat of her heart sounded the death knell of her wishes, she had still believed fate would save her.

This was her pattern. Until the moment of her mother's last breath, she had believed a miracle would spare her. Her immediate reaction had been to cover her despair with a false calm, handling all the post-death details: writing an obit, arranging a funeral and burial, settling the estate. She needed calm right now. "And Gex?"

Ambrose cocked his head.

"He's the bastard who gave Robert Pendergast my undercover phone number."

"Correct. Gex retires at the end of the month. The director is looking for someone else to take charge of the training at Quantico."

"You knew?"

"I take the integrity of the Bureau seriously."

How long have you known and not told me? "Does Gex know you know? Is that why he is retiring?"

"Gex knows that the director knows. What are you really asking?"

Malachi's questioning her motives sprang to mind. What *did* she want, revenge or justice? A slipped word to her roommate or Tiny or Rick about Gex's actions, and the rumor would sweep the Bureau, ruining his sterling reputation. Sweet revenge, but at what cost to the Bureau's image, which she had worked tirelessly to uphold? Any momentary pleasure would leave a bitter hole in her psyche. Justice meant assuring Gex could no longer hold a position in the FBI. "It's proper that he can't damage anyone else's career like he did mine."

Ambrose offered her another one of those warm smiles and a single nod. "Yes, well, he's not *solely* responsible for damaging your career. But let us not dwell on the past. You are incredibly talented, and productive far ahead of anyone else. And frustratingly non-bureaucratic. Wearing your disguise today is a perfect example. Every other agent would dress in their sharpest blue suit for this meeting. Probably wear an American flag on their lapel. You are unique and I have a unique proffer I'd like you to consider."

"A proffer?" She heard herself echo his words. Into the growing silence disturbed only by a ticking clock, she said, "Please tell me what you have in mind."

"Assistant Director of National Intelligence Park and I share a concern that nearly two decades after nine-eleven, our intelligence operations have again become bureaucratic, slow to respond, territorial. Consider all the bureaucratic hoops the Bureau goes through before it authorizes an undercover assignment. We must move faster. The ADNI and I would like you to work for us, report only to us, on assignments with national importance. Between us we can provide whatever support you require."

He held up a cautioning hand. "But I want to make this clear: you cannot remain an FBI agent. You will become a code name only. A ghost. We'll compensate you well. Weeks or months might go by between assignments. But when you *are* active, it might be all-encompassing. The ADNI insists that if you get married or enter a long-term relationship, our agreement will end. His reasoning is that either you'll refuse an assignment at a critical time, or the pressure of having a life partner might inhibit an all-out effort."

She sprang to her feet and found herself in her Wonder Woman pose. "Respectfully, sir, that is total bullshit. We don't tell our soldiers they have to quit because they get married. How is this any different? ADNI Park can—" She stopped herself before she said, "shove that restriction up his fucking ass." She continued, "That's intolerable."

"Fire down, Prescott. I said you'd refuse that condition. I also said I'd hire you myself if necessary. You've called his bluff, and he'll fold. He and I agree you should have two case officers. I think your roommate, Agent Aaliya Zylstra is perfect. She's proved her loyalty to you and to the Bureau. What's more natural than for you to remain in your common apartment? With no change in her duties, she could be an information conduit. ADNI Park has someone in mind for the second person."

She interpreted his leaning back to signal he wanted her response. She sat, folded her hands in her lap. If this was a genuine offer, it made sense Ambrose and Park wanted plausible deniability. But they could be tossing her a bone, a ruse to ensure she did not make a stink about her termination. They'd pay her a few months off the books, sufficient to incriminate her in some way she wasn't sophisticated enough to anticipate, and then threaten to expose her if she didn't go away quietly.

How badly did they want her? She watched his eyes for telltale micro expressions. "I understand each of you wants someone under your control. The longer I stay Liya's roommate, the more she's tainted by my quote-unquote, resignation. I don't know ADNI Park or his people. I feel it's safer for everyone if we use two people no one in the FBI or Intelligence hierarchies would suspect. Can one be Rick Kaska?"

For the first time, she witnessed his eyes giving away his surprise. "I thought you two had friction. You called him 'Rick-spelled-with-a-silent-P.' Was I misinformed?"

No reason to relate what she had discovered about Rick. "I may have been more the prick than he. Is that a yes?"

"If he agrees, I can make that happen." He picked up his phone and told his assistant to summon Agent Richard Kaska and release Agent Zylstra.

He was totally self-assured, already having summoned Liya. Little did he know. "Good," she said. "The second person is Seamus McCree."

His face wrinkled into a frown pulling into pursed lips. "The kidnapped man you rescued? Impossible. We can only use people with top secret clearance, already vetted in our operating procedures."

"Listen to yourself, sir. You're asking me to go off the books. To take risks no FBI agent could take because we won't let them. Sorry, I keep thinking of the Bureau as we. *You* won't allow. And you're still harping about your operating procedures? Thank you for the proffer, sir, but I don't see how this can work." *Face the facts, Niki. You're history. One last gambit.* "Maybe I should talk with ADNI Park."

His eyes showed she'd surprised him a second time. "No, wait. Explain why you want Seamus McCree."

She folded her hands and rested them on her knee. "He is the one person in the world I trust one hundred percent. No reservations. Not that he's perfect. Far from it. He'll protect me, but not my ego. When *he* thinks I *should* hear something, I listen even if I won't listen to anyone else. And he can be a good sounding board for me."

"It sounds to me like you're in love with him."

"I know I can trust him. I believe you can, too."

Ambrose's smile did not falter. Niki did not interrupt the silence, which lasted at least a minute. "Once again, I must remind myself that you think differently from other people. That's why we need you, and why we should trust your judgment. I'll have to meet your Seamus McCree. Make sure he knows your requirements. Do it in—"

A tentative tap at the door interrupted him. Upon Ambrose's command to enter, Rick Kaska walked in wearing a white shirt, red tie, and blue suit with an American flag on his lapel. Niki burst into laughter.

SIXTY-SEVEN

NIKI LEFT RICK TO DISCUSS his future with Ambrose and exited the Hoover building for what might be the last time. She hadn't had time to process everything that had happened, but for the next few hours she had to revert to Ashley Prescott and focus on Pendergast Holdings business. That meant retrieving a message from Morgan on Ashley's phone telling her when, where, and which lobbyist to meet. She dialed her voicemail and heard the automated voice, "Your mailbox is full. You have twenty messages."

She had hoped Seamus might have news about firing Junior and Bradlee, and she thought Tabitha might call. Including Morgan, that made four. What the hell happened?

The Minneapolis lead FBI agent on the kidnappings wanted her to set a time for the shooting review panel to interview her. To protect her identity, they would use audio only and employ voice-altering equipment to prevent the review board from knowing what she sounded like. That was quick.

Two: Morgan provided the lobbyist information.

Three: Harlan sputtered an incoherent apology and hung up.

Four: Bradlee left a profanity-laden message, threatening her with all manner of violence. His termination must have happened faster than Seamus had led her to expect. One problem resolved, anyway.

The next six messages were hang-ups from Bradlee's phone. Ten of twenty down, and Niki was feeling less anxious about the filled mailbox. Especially if the remaining ten were Bradlee hanging up.

Eleven: Robert's personal attorney, Anton Hack, wanting to discuss, "Additional responsibilities on account of the passing of Robert Pendergast, Senior." Terrific, what new land mines had Robert laid for her?

Twelve: Harlan again. "I know I promised no word until I heard from your friend Seamus. No way I could have expected the editor's response. I need to explain. Call me."

Niki rubbed her eyes, watching the kaleidoscope patterns change while she teased out the meaning of Harlan's message. Truth was truth, but her plan had been for whoever fired Bradlee to provide him the same documentation she had provided Harlan to prepare Bradlee for the shit storm coming his way. Harlan's editor had done something unexpected with the inside story of Robert Pendergast's kidnapping featuring Cece Kraznik and her married lover, Bradlee Pendergast. What?

Eight remaining.

Thirteen: Seamus informing her neither Junior nor Bradlee had come into the office. He and Gerald Nakourma, the corporation attorney, were creating certified documents to secure their terminations. They would deliver them to their homes. Meaning Bradlee hadn't known about his termination before his calls to her.

Fourteen: Another profanity-littered message from Bradlee. This one with a kernel of information: "She took our kids and drained our bank account. And it's *all your fault.*"

Fifteen: A dial tone from an unknown number.

Sixteen: The Minneapolis FBI agent again. Pushy, wasn't he? "Thought you should know that early this morning, Junior, his wife, and children flew to Mexico City with connecting flights to Cape Verde." She recalled from the recesses of her mind that Cape Verde, officially the Republic of Cabo Verde, had no extradition treaty with the United States. Damn her again. Junior had escaped because she had made clear the charges against him during her impromptu board meeting with the brothers on Sunday.

Four messages left. What additional disasters awaited her? Oh wait, only four because the mailbox filled. Maybe Junior had the right idea to ghost.

Seventeen: Malachi, having heard that Robert was dead, wanted to know how Ashley was doing.

Eighteen: Seamus, "I hope your day is going better than mine. Garrett gave me his resignation today. I tore it up and said I need his help to lock down the bribery details. Plus, I piled on a huge guilt trip about leaving you in the lurch. He agreed to keep working if we truly needed him. We do. Act nice when you see him. He may not have been best friends with his father, but he's suffered a significant loss."

Nineteen: Rick, "I got summoned to Ambrose's office. Any clue why?" She wondered what he would do now that he knew. If nothing else, she had gotten a good laugh seeing him dressed exactly as Ambrose had suggested was appropriate for meeting with a deputy director.

Twenty: Bradlee yelled, "Live with this, bitch." A hiss meant the connection remained open. At fifteen seconds of nothing, she considered hanging up. Sometimes the receiving phone didn't realize the other party had disconnected, and this was—

Over the line came what sounded like wood scraping against a solid object followed by a sharp crash. The hiss returned, continuing until her three-minute message limit expired.

Sixty-Eight

Monday, May 11, Afternoon EDT

ASHLEY FAKED HER WAY THROUGH the late lunch meeting with the head of the lobbying firm that earned more than two million dollars a year from Pendergast Holdings. The only thing she knew for sure was the food was excellent and the guy acted petrified he would lose the account. Whatever. That hour of boredom had saved her thousands in taxes, and that, as Seamus would say, was a hell of an hourly rate.

At her apartment, she penned a note to Liya explaining that she had arranged for a car-transport firm to return Liya's car two days hence. Because Ashley was *persona non grata* at the FBI, she planned to move from their apartment. She'd pay rent through June. With no further need for the Irish woman disguise, she showered and put on fresh clothes. Considered checking phone messages again, decided it was depressing, and spent the time playing with the cats until she left to catch her charter to St. Paul.

The cats weren't ready to stop playing and followed her to the door, weaving around her feet, impeding her progress. "I promise, guys. I'll be back." She didn't mention it might be to pack her stuff.

She shared the charter flight with three execs from a company headquartered in Minneapolis. They left her to her thoughts, which bounced between remembering the airplane crash and wondering about Bradlee. If she survived to St. Paul, she'd stop by his house, confront him on phone behavior, and convince him that threatening her was a losing proposition.

She dismissed the Uber driver at Bradlee's home, a tidy Tudor four blocks and a million dollars away from Robert's house, figuring the walk to Robert's would cleanse her from the expected unpleasant interaction. Bradlee's car sat cold in the driveway. Good, he was home. Dusk was fast approaching, but she didn't see any lights on inside. And he didn't answer the doorbell.

Typical bully. Yell and scream and curse on the phone but not have the balls to confront her in person. She lifted the brass door knocker and beat a resounding tattoo. From behind the house came the sound of a whimpering dog. She followed the sidewalk around the garage, through a gate, and into the backyard. A brindled Plott Hound had tangled his line with bushes near the stoop.

"Ah, baby, let's get you free." She offered her hand for the dog to sniff. He wagged his tail and gave her a lick. She checked his rabies tag. "Thanks, Max. Now let me get you untangled." She used his collar to unweave the knot he'd created. Once she had him free, he loped to his water bowl on the teak deck and lapped it dry.

"How long have you been out here, Max?" The dog came to her and bumped her hand. She scratched him behind the ears, and he leaned into her. When she stopped scratching, he trotted onto the deck, sat before the door, and offered a polite woof.

Ashley sucked in a lungful of air, getting ready to confront Bradlee with one more abuse to lay at his feet. The dog gave a second woof and looked at her as if to say, "Why don't you let me in?"

She opened the storm door, intending to knock on the wooden interior door. The dog rushed past her and pushed the unlatched door open, dragging his line inside. She stomped on the cable, halting his progress halfway into the kitchen. "Hold up, big boy. Let's get you unhitched. Bradlee, it's Ashley. I've come for you to yell at me."

She unclipped the cable from the dog's collar and tossed the line outside. Nose to the ground, tail straight down, the hound ran to a closed door and whimpered. Ten-foot ceilings made the room feel huge. A plate, fork, and coffee mug sat in the drainer. A tumbler, partially filled with the discolored remains of a drink, sat next to a bottle of scotch on an oval table in the breakfast nook. The dog's whining grew more insistent. Drawing near, Ashley noticed a crack of light showing under the door. She yelled Bradlee's name. No response.

Cop instinct kicked in. She grabbed a dishtowel from the side of the refrigerator to avoid leaving fingerprints, pushed the dog aside, and opened the door enough to slip through.

From the fifth step down to the basement, she saw a wooden chair lying on its side with a cellphone next to it. She would later tell the police that was the moment she realized the scraping sound she had heard on the last message from Bradlee was a chair dragging across a cement floor.

Her next step revealed Bradlee hanging from a rope.

Sixty-Nine

Monday, May 11, 2100 EDT

COLONEL PETE FOLLOWED THE EMAILED directions into Virginia horse country west of Washington. For more than a mile, he had seen nothing but silent fields bounded by white-board fences. At the designated GPS coordinates, he parked on the right side of a dirt road, turned off his engine, and killed the lights. The machine pistol felt comfortably heavy in his lap. If he was going down, he'd take someone with him.

As his eyes grew accustomed to the darkness, he sensed under the heavy roiling clouds the pattern of a distant row of trees. A rumble of thunder sounded from far away and scattered raindrops pattered on his windshield. The woman was late. How long should he wait before deciding the sole purpose for this trip was to get him away from his country place?

A series of branched lightning lit the western sky and backlit a sedan creeping toward him with its lights off. It nearly reached him before he recognized her black Lexus LC 500 Inspiration. She pulled tight to his truck, preventing both of them from opening their doors.

He angled his machine pistol to point through the car's window to the driver's head. Her windows zipped down, and she motioned for him to lower his. Interesting that she gave him a position looking down on her. He didn't see anyone else in the car. She rested both hands on the door frame.

No weapons. He breathed a sigh of relief and pressed his power window button.

"Peter," she said once he lowered his window. "Why did they drop the charges before your bail hearing this morning?"

"My lawyer didn't know. He presumed they had no witness to connect me to the weapons. That means Corporal Niki kept her mouth shut. She handled herself well. I informed her I was putting her in for sergeant. What's her status?"

"Unknown. They brought her to a different jail. Did the Chinese arms dealer set you up?"

"Our eyes in the area saw nothing. Besides, why would he give us the weapons?

"My exact thought. And you didn't tell Sergeant Oliver. He couldn't have given up the information?"

"Absolutely not."

"I believe you. You do understand we'll have to decommission your unit, right? We'll monitor the situation and if nothing happens, we can integrate the best people into another unit."

Which was one reason they functioned with many independent cells. It made sense, even though it was disappointing. "You want me to destroy the records?"

She scratched an eyebrow. "I suppose we'll have to. Thanks for being so understanding. It's a setback, for sure, but I know we will prevail."

Her car powered ahead, leaving his pistol pointed at the paddock across the way. He'd considered himself one of the best people, but the last few days had not gone according to plan.

He reached for the ignition key and stopped at a sharp rap on his passenger window. The business end of a rifle pointed at his head.

SEVENTY

MAX'S COLD NOSE INSISTED ASHLEY get up and attend to the dog's morning routine. Ashley had been bone-tired by the time she had finished with the cops and walked with Max to Robert's house. After giving the dog a bowl of water, she had flopped onto the bed fully clothed and fallen asleep to the dog's heavy breathing from the foot of her bed.

She walked the dog around the block, realized she had not brought any food for him from Bradlee's house, now a crime scene she could not enter. The internet informed her to give the beast two or three cups of quality food spread between two to three meals a day. Max placed himself between her and the door and moaned. She understood that meant he wanted to come along. She let him sit in the passenger seat, head sticking out the window, while she drove to the grocery store.

Back at Robert's, she gave Max one of several varieties of dry dog food she had purchased. Max scarfed down her offering, burped and farted, and curled at Ashley's feet while she dealt with yesterday's calls. Tabitha planned to stay at her mother's and go to classes from there. Her shoulders relaxed knowing she wasn't facing another sister talk that day.

Seamus requested her to stay away from Pendergast Holdings' office until tomorrow. He and Gabrielle had their plates full. Another reprieve, and to make sure she could leave early, she arranged to meet the Minneapolis FBI shooting review board Wednesday afternoon.

Harlan confirmed what she had suspected. To punch up the second story she had given him, his editor tried to confront Junior and Bradlee with the accusations. Junior had a brisk no comment. The guy called Bradlee's home. He wasn't there, and he had shocked Chloe, Bradlee's wife, with the accusation. Ashley agreed it was unfortunate, but she assured Harlan that she didn't blame him. Unsaid was that she blamed herself.

That left only dealing with Malachi, who said he'd be right over.

Tuesday, May 12, Afternoon CDT

MALACHI WAS EAGER FOR HIS week of exile from work to end. He despised enforced rest. Seeing Ashley for the first time in three days, he realized how drawn she looked. The sharp edges of her jaw could slice cheese.

Uncertain what to say about the deaths of Robert, Cece, and Bradlee, he followed her into the parlor and settled uncomfortably on a chair. He tried a general question on the status of the investigation.

"Cece had bugged all the executive offices and most of your phones— including your cellphone. She knew everyone's plans, which put her in a great position to leak information to competitors. I have no clue whether she seduced Bradlee, or he targeted her. She knew Robert was going to make Bradlee give her up or lose his job. My guess is she kidnapped Robert for revenge money. His autopsy indicated he suffered a heart attack. After his death, she decided I was the next best thing."

The piece clicked for Malachi. "And Cece saw the note from my admin telling me you were using the Pendergast plane to fly east."

"Our rotten luck was that her brother, Crandall, is a demolitions expert and rigged the plane. My sources at the Bureau say they tracked Crandall and the third guy at the diner to some Middle East war zone where they're raking in big bucks while avoiding extradition. The firm the SEALS created claims the four of them went rogue. They'll have the Bureau up their ass, but you can bet nothing will come of it." She raised and lowered her hands in resignation. "You said you had something for me? Then I have something else for you."

Malachi removed a folded scrap of paper from his wallet. "It's a password to an online storage vault. Robert scanned all the letters between him and your mother and wanted you to have them. I believe there's also other information pertaining to you."

She was skilled at not showing her feelings, he'd give her that. She ran her hands up and down Max's back. "Did you read them?"

"I did not. The labels suggest they start before you were born and end with your mother's death."

She unfolded the paper, glanced at the password and website, and shoved it into her shirt pocket. "You should know, I plan to recommend to Gabriella that she eliminate the position of Chief Conscience Officer."

The hole that opened in his chest surprised him. He didn't realize how attached he had become to his insider's position. He would pray on the sin of pride. "You didn't like the questions I asked?"

"That's not it. It sends the wrong message. Doing the proper thing isn't a privilege for the top officers. It should be an expectation for everyone at Pendergast Holdings. If you are interested in the job, I plan to suggest to Gabriella that she promotes you to head of worldwide sales. I want Pendergast Holdings to provide the best solutions for customers. If we don't have them, we'll create them or steer the customer to a competitor to solve their need. The one detail I didn't like with you telling the guy not to buy Pendergast's expensive product is you waited until he asked the right question. Our sales agents should ask questions to be sure whether our product or service is best for every client."

"That means changing the entire compensation structure from commission-based to performance-based, and—"

"Malachi, if I've learned one thing through this entire mess, it's that I don't have the business knowledge to tell anyone *how* to accomplish a task. I'm telling you what I want done and asking if you'll do it. Assuming Gabriella agrees."

"Let me consider it. I heard you use 'we' and 'our.' Does that mean you plan to stay involved?"

She cleared her throat, looked like she was swallowing a frog. "Temporarily." She licked her lips, pressed her hands on her thighs, her fingers white with tension. "But on my terms. Switching gears—do you like the way I did that?—after we're both recovered, will you teach me to swim?"

SEVENTY-ONE

THREE DAYS AFTER SHE DISCOVERED Bradlee's suicide and his note blaming her for ruining his life, Ashley, with Bradlee's Plott hound, Max, glued to her side, ushered Anton Hack, Garrett, and Tabitha into Robert's study. Seeing Seamus reading in the living room, she asked if any of them objected to his joining them to read Robert's will.

It made sense for Hack to sit at Robert's desk. The other four arranged their chairs in a semicircle, Garrett taking the left-most chair. Tabitha came next. Ashley, with Max curled on her feet, sat between Tabitha and Seamus, who held down the right flank. She said to Garrett, "Oldest gets the power seat."

He asked what that was supposed to mean.

"You're the oldest of the family and sat on the far left. Every time someone came into Robert's office at work, that's the seat they took. Didn't take me long to realize that was the power position. I grant I'm not business savvy, but I'm good at reading people. I even used that during my meeting with the FBI."

"Well," Garrett said. "It's an interesting theory. The real reason everyone wanted that seat was because when Dad got agitated, he waved his arms around and knocked over his coffee mug. If you were in the other seat, you got soaked."

Ashley rolled her eyes. "I am so lame sometimes." She caught Seamus smothering a laugh. She deserved it. "Okay, one other thing before we start. Garrett, while I still have majority power, I'm telling the company to purchase some of your nature photographs to replace that god-awful fox-hunting theme in the board room. Make them signed originals and charge what's fair. I'm sure they'll be an excellent investment."

Garret said, "You probably don't realize there's a fine arts committee that has to approve—"

"Unfuckingbelievable. A committee approved those?"

"No, Dad did. That's why we got him to institute a committee."

Her first reaction was that if the committee didn't agree with her, she'd appoint a new committee. She closed her eyes as a wave of dizziness washed over her. Only two days ago she had promised herself to not be like Robert, to use her voting power only when critical to do what was right, and at the first test she had almost failed. She needed to stay vigilant against power's seductive force.

"After, you can tell me how I ask them to consider my suggestion." She apologized to Hack for the digression.

Hack distributed a memorandum with the key points of Robert's estate plan. "Ashley, in addition to your portion of the Daughters Trust, Robert left you his collection of guns."

Despite not wanting anything from Robert, the gift made sense. She was the one who appreciated the fine workmanship of those weapons.

Hack droned on: "Tabitha, besides the other half of the Daughters Trust, you also receive this house and its belongings. That includes the cars. Nothing has a lien or mortgage."

Tabitha heeled away tears. "The thing I'm most sorry about is I can never ask him why he chose my mother, and why he allowed my parents to keep me. Do I have to stay in the house?"

"Robert left no restrictions regarding your bequest."

Ashley gave Tabitha a thumbs up. Mostly to cheer her up, but because she, too, wished to resurrect Robert and ask him a gazillion questions.

Hack continued. "Robert's estate establishes a one-million-dollar trust for each of his grandchildren. The trustee, a local bank, can tap it to pay for education. At twenty-seven the child receives the remainder. The estate provides direct gifts of twenty-five million dollars for each of his children who Pendergast Holdings employed at the time of his death."

"Meaning," Ashley said, "Junior, Bradlee, Garrett."

Seamus leaned forward. "Have they determined when Robert died? Depending on the timing, Ashley might have been Pendergast's interim CEO."

"Doesn't matter, Seamus. I'm not taking twenty-five million on some technicality. Moving right along." She flicked her fingers at Hack to emphasize her desire to move off this topic.

Hack smoothed his lips with his fingers. "It is an excellent point, Seamus. We'll see what the medical examiner's final report states." Apparently noticing she was close to erupting, he added, "Ashley, even if you qualify, you can legally refuse. Garrett, your distribution will take two or three months."

Hack shuffled papers, a delaying tactic if she'd ever seen one. *Oh man, what now?*

"Because Bradlee's suicide occurred within thirty days of Robert's death, it's equivalent to Bradlee predeceasing Robert and voids that bequest."

Garrett said, "No *per stirpes* provision?"

Hack shook his head. "It does not devolve to Bradlee's heirs. That twenty-five million becomes part of the remaining estate. In addition, to receive the bequest, another provision requires any recipient to be physically present in Minnesota for at least one full day within one year of the official notification of death. Junior's clock begins ticking today, and until he returns or the year is up, I'll hold that twenty-five million in escrow. After a year, it reverts to the remaining estate."

Ashley's mood lightened. Junior's graft didn't come close to twenty-five million. Served the thieving bastard right.

Hack continued. "There are a few smaller philanthropic bequests. Everything else becomes the capital of the Pendergast Foundation. Robert appointed Ashley to be the foundation's initial chairperson. Furthermore, he designated you, and only you, to determine the foundation's purpose. You may consult Robert's other beneficiaries, but the decision is yours."

"That's crazy!" Ashley felt mildly embarrassed by her outburst, but it was God's truth.

Hack put down his papers and looked at her over his half-glasses. "The facts speak otherwise. He obviously had faith in you, and from what I have seen, it's justified."

Ashley's mouth tasted of ashes. "Justified? If it weren't for me, Bradlee would be alive. Maybe Robert, too. And thousands of employees wouldn't be worrying if they'll still have jobs, because who knows what holes the loose cannon—meaning me—will blow into Pendergast Holdings next. Everything I've touched—"

"Bullroar," Garrett said. "Pendergast Holdings was rotting from the inside. Dad was so obsessed with his family legacy that he refused to deal with Junior's theft. He threatened Bradlee but paid whatever was necessary to hush things up. He might have known about or even arranged the bribery in my division. Without your arrival we would have released a product that—well, thank God, we saved the environment from massive potential damage."

Ashley couldn't take any more of this shit. "That was all Seamus, not me. All I did was nearly get him killed. Same with Malachi. Three crew members did die. And Bradlee." She blinked away tears. And patted Max's raised head. "I'm a fucking scorpion, not Pendergast Holdings' savior. I only agreed to temporarily stay involved because y'all told me it was the best way to assure our employees could keep their jobs secure. This new crap with the foundation—" She threw up her hands.

Tabitha reached over and gave her arm a squeeze. "It's overwhelming for me, too."

Seamus grabbed her wrists and lowered her arms into her lap, kept his hand on top of hers. "I think you are focusing on the wrong things. The recent events *are* traumatizing, and you have a burden you did not seek and do not want. I know that look. You're still angry at Robert and want to lash out."

He swept his arm to include Garrett, Tabitha, and Anton Hack. "In your position, we'd be angry too. None of us blames you for anything, so hear me out. Accepting this burden," he air-quoted, "provides you new opportunities to make a difference. You've dedicated your life to protecting your country and bringing justice to those who need it. With this foundation, Robert has given you a shit ton of money to support whatever causes you choose."

She didn't need an all-wise Seamus lecture, right now. "Yeah, but—"

"But nothing. You can hire people to run the foundation. Your challenge is to determine which of the many ways of protecting the U.S. and bringing justice you want to support. That's scary, for sure. But not nearly as scary as the undercover work you do."

She read their faces. Tabitha's showed concern. This had to be as stressful for her as it was for Ashley. Garrett wore the same interested expression she had seen the day she appeared wearing her Dolly Parton wig and burst into the Pendergast Holdings boardroom. Hack demonstrated professional thoughtfulness. Even as Seamus challenged her, she felt only warmth and affection. She was still in fight mode, but his calm words had helped bank the fire of her anger.

She faked a similar calmness. "Point taken, Seamus. I'll do what's required with both Pendergast Holdings and this foundation. After that I'm done with it."

Seventy-Two

ASHLEY SAT AT THE DESK in Niki's bedroom in the undercover apartment and triple-checked her list of everything she wanted to accomplish in Washington over the weekend. The list comprised mundane chores around Niki's apartment. Normally, she'd be itching for any excuse to delay this daily-living crap. Today, she looked forward to losing herself in vacuuming, changing the sheets on her bed, laundry. She might even find the iron. Before the day got hot, she'd take a little five-mile run. Tomorrow, she'd reward herself with a slow fifteen miles.

The ringing doorbell interrupted her lacing her trainers. Six-fifteen in the morning was too early for anything good. She checked her video camera feeds on her phone. Standing in the hall was Rick Kaska in cowboy boots, holding up a pair of sneakers by their tied laces.

Did the guy not know how phones worked? A lot had happened in the two weeks since she'd finished her morning run and found the prick pounding on her door. She smacked herself on the hand. She was being unfair. Yes, he was somewhat immature, but he'd stuck by her and had agreed to be her contact with Ambrose. Was he here because of that?

She opened the door and ushered him in.

"No one saw me. I came in the back."

She made a hurry-up motion with her hand. "Something happening with PFF? Colonel Pete?"

"Nothing recent. The farmhouse and barn he brought you to burned to the ground early Tuesday morning. Someone searched and thoroughly trashed his in-town house. No sign of the colonel. No activity on his phones, credit cards, bank accounts. Gex is mouthing off to his buddies that he was right that they should have brought everyone in. But Ambrose overruled him. He agrees with you that the important thing is to learn who runs PFF. We're tracking the middle-level people in PFF you identified. None has steered us to their leaders."

No surprise about PFF. They had always been careful. Hopefully after this blew over, she could reinsert herself into the militia and find answers. "Wait. I thought Gex had retired."

"End of the month, so he's still got two weeks."

Had she been foolish to think Gex retiring meant he could no longer negatively affect the FBI—or her? Her cramping stomach told her this was not over between them. She wouldn't start anything. But if he did, she'd finish it. "What's with the sneakers?"

"Did you know my childhood nickname was Dick? I went away to college and changed it to Rick because, you know, I was tired of people making jokes about me being a dick. But I wanted to apologize because I *was* a dick to think I knew better than you how to operate your undercover assignment. I promise I won't do that on this new stuff. But I might have already screwed up because I didn't consult you and I told Ambrose that you needed to carry concealed and arrest people. That's what you do. Yesterday, he called me to his office and gave me these." Rick pulled a badge and identification case from his pocket and handed them to her.

The circular badge proclaimed United States Marshal. It looked real with its five-pointed star and eagle in the middle. Feeling its weight, her body pined for her FBI Special Agent badge. How long would her grieving last? She flipped open the business-card-sized case. It was a fucking joke. She tapped the name on the card: N Iki. With ice in her voice she said, "Care to explain?"

Rick twitched like a kid called to the principal's office. "Well, we couldn't use your real name. I considered Ann Smith, the name you told Seamus—you know, at the junkyard? It's just temporary until you have a cover name for your assignment. I know you think of yourself as 'Niki' or 'Niki Undercover.' But single names don't work. And poof, I got this brilliant idea. Except, looking at it, I feel like that dick from junior high making a fool of himself by giving you the last name of some Japanese volcanic islands in the Tsushima Strait."

"Are these real?"

"The genuine deal. Ambrose promised the database will include a full-fledged Marshal named N Iki by Wednesday."

She pulled him into a hug. Huh, he'd changed his aftershave from that sandalwood to something . . . what, dark and smoky? "Do you call me 'N?' Like 'Q' and 'M' in James Bond? I love it, Rick. N Iki is so screwed up it's perfect. For what it's worth, I never thought of you as a dick." Malachi should appreciate the irony of that truth-telling sentence.

"Thank you." Rick moved past her to the secretary, uncovered the "**OPEN IN EMERGENCY**" envelope, and held it up. "This has been bugging me since I first spotted it. I have a feeling your new assignments will be even more dangerous than your past undercover work. And no, he hasn't said anything to me about what he has planned. If there ever *is* an emergency, will this help me help you?"

Ashley thought about her private talisman. Rick was trying his damnedest to bridge their gap; she owed him something in return. "No, but go ahead. Open it."

He tore off the side of the envelope and slipped out the 3x5 card on which she had written, *If you had time to open the envelope, it's not an emergency!*

His eyes scanned the card, He flipped it over to the blank back, flipped it to the front, and scanned it again. "It's ironic, right? That's why you said 'no.' In a true emergency, you just act. If you or I have time to open the envelope, it must not be an emergency. In that case, no matter how dire or life-threatening the situation, we have time to consider our response."

"It's all that, but every time I see it, it reminds me how important planning and preparation are to preventing emergencies. Like you creating the N Iki badge and credentials. In a perfect world, I'd never use them because we'll have ample time to create the right cover for my next assignments."

He laughed. "Seems to me the world is getting less perfect every day."

"Exactly." She gave him a fist bump and bent down to tie her trainers. "My bet is I'll be posing as N Iki sooner than we expect. While you put on your sneakers, I'll use my die and coin to determine which way we'll leave for our run."

"Really? For a jog in the park?"

"Absolutely. The bad guys are out there, Rick. Some day, they're going to find me. When they do, I want to spot them before it becomes an emergency."

I hope you enjoyed reading this story. To help me reach other readers, I would appreciate your posting a short review of *Niki Undercover* on your favorite retailer or review website.

Author's Note

To me, life comprises a series of befores and afters—breaks in the space-time continuum that mark events so major there is no going back. Being born is our first. Dying our last. Parents mark their first child's birth as life-changing. Those are individual experiences. Sometimes, a national or global experience creates a similar effect for a large group of people. Bombing Pearl Harbor may be one. I think COVID-19 is another. We are different people, a different nation, a different world pre- and post-COVID.

I began writing this story before COVID-19 existed in humans. My stories include implied real-time dates—my characters age at the same rate I do. (I'm sure I feel the aging process more than they do, though.) Sometimes my stories reference an event or two that took place during the story. Although never stated in the novel, Niki Undercover occurs in 2020, smack dab in the middle of the COVID shutdowns in the United States. I ignored the disease and its repercussions in Niki Undercover.

I made that decision because incorporating COVID into this novel would distract from the story I wanted to tell. Including COVID meant spending oodles of pages dealing with people masking or not, reacting to others who made different choices, reflecting on how the deaths affected characters, etc., etc. While important questions, they aren't the ones this story explores. That is my confession. Make of it what you will.

Niki has been clamoring to tell her story since she first appeared in *Cabin Fever.* Didn't I want to know, she'd ask, how one, driven by her vision of patriotism, could make a difference in the world? Turns out, I did.

My interest in paramilitary organizations in the United States stems from my fascination with U.S. history. They predate the American Revolution. During the war for American independence, irregular paramilitary groups supported both the British establishment and the "Patriots." The actions of these organizations were devastating to those who lived beyond the control of either the British or American armies.

In the 1840s, paramilitary groups fomented the war that created Texas as a country independent from Mexico. In the 1850s, armed militias fought viciously on both sides of the slavery issue (Kansas, bloody Kansas). After the American Civil War, arguably the most famous paramilitary organization was the Ku Klux Clan, which was reinvigorated during the 1920s, and again in the 1950s.

In 2024, the Southern Poverty Law Center (SPLC) identified 52 paramilitary organizations based in the United States. It did not identify Patriots for Freedom (PFF) because (1) it is my fictional creation, and (2) their philosophy does not include white supremacy or religious extremism. PFF does not promote itself on social media or through demonstrations and marches. Their members would not have participated in the events on January 6, 2001. Its leadership's agenda is much more frightening—but we can only see its seeds in *Niki Undercover*.

Lots of people helped improve this novel. My beta readers offered suggestions and asked questions that allowed me to make the story tighter and stronger. ARC readers spotted typos, allowing me to correct them. I especially want to thank my writer friends who challenged me when I thought I was done. They were right, and the story is better for it.

Jan Rubens is always my first, last, and best reader. Any mistakes that remain are mine, and I take full responsibility for them. But I hate mistakes, so if you find a typo or layout error, please let me know so I can correct it for future editions.

My email is jmj@jamesmjackson.com. I love hearing from readers and try to respond to all my email.

James M. Jackson
Amasa, Michigan

James M. Jackson authors the Seamus McCree and Niki Undercover Thriller series.

Jim has also published an acclaimed book on contract bridge, *One Trick at a Time: How to start winning at bridge.*

He calls the deep woods of Michigan's Upper Peninsula home. You can find out more about Jim or sign up for his Readers Group newsletter at his website, https://jamesmjackson.com.

www.ingramcontent.com/pod-product-compliance
Lightning Source LLC
Chambersburg PA
CBHW071234190726
48292CB00007B/2282